The Making of London

£3

CW00435411

Also by SEBASTIAN GROES:

IAN McEWAN: Contemporary Critical Perspectives

JULIAN BARNES: Contemporary Critical Perspectives (with Peter Childs)

KAZUO ISHIGURO: Contemporary Critical Perspectives (with Sean Matthews)

KAZUO ISHIGURO: New Critical Visions of the Novel (with Barry Lewis)

The Making of London

London in Contemporary Literature

Sebastian Groes
with photographs by Sarah Baxter

© Sebastian Groes 2011
Photographs © Sarah Baxter 2011

All rights reserved. No reproduction, copy or transmission of this publication
may be made without written permission.

No portion of this publication may be reproduced, copied or transmitted
save with written permission or in accordance with the provisions of the
Copyright, Designs and Patents Act 1988, or under the terms of any licence
permitting limited copying issued by the Copyright Licensing Agency,
Saffron House, 6–10 Kirby Street, London EC1N 8TS.

Any person who does any unauthorized act in relation to this publication
may be liable to criminal prosecution and civil claims for damages.

The author has asserted his right to be identified as the author of this work
in accordance with the Copyright, Designs and Patents Act 1988.

First published 2011 by
PALGRAVE MACMILLAN

Palgrave Macmillan in the UK is an imprint of Macmillan Publishers Limited,
registered in England, company number 785998, of Houndmills, Basingstoke,
Hampshire RG21 6XS.

Palgrave Macmillan in the US is a division of St Martin's Press LLC,
175 Fifth Avenue, New York, NY 10010.

Palgrave Macmillan is the global academic imprint of the above companies
and has companies and representatives throughout the world.

Palgrave® and Macmillan® are registered trademarks in the United States,
the United Kingdom, Europe and other countries.

ISBN 978–0–230–23478–9   hardback
ISBN 978–0–230–34836–3   paperback

This book is printed on paper suitable for recycling and made from fully
managed and sustained forest sources. Logging, pulping and manufacturing
processes are expected to conform to the environmental regulations of the
country of origin.

A catalogue record for this book is available from the British Library.

A catalog record for this book is available from the Library of Congress.

10   9   8   7   6   5   4   3   2   1
20 19 18 17 16 15 14 13 12 11

Printed and bound in Great Britain by
CPI Antony Rowe, Chippenham and Eastbourne

This book is for my father, who took me there first

Contents

List of Illustrations

Illuminations (I)

Textures (*between pages 142 and 143*)

Illuminations (II)

All photographs were taken February–September 2010.

Acknowledgements

London lives many lives, and the following people have guided me through their versions. Victor Sage supervised, with brilliance and passion, and the necessary patience, the PhD thesis that has, finally, resulted in this book; I cannot thank him enough. Sean Matthews's continuous generosity and enduring faith in me has been a constant inspiration; he also proved a valuable friend in times of need. The AHRC funded this study, for which I am very grateful. Rod Mengham and Mark Currie are thanked for their careful examination of my work. In a way all this started with Richard Todd, whose 'Fictions and Fantasies of London' module I took at the Free University, Amsterdam, in 1998.

I want to thank Iain Sinclair for inviting me on the *Downriver* and *Hackney, That Rose-Red Empire* walks, and was glad to show him my other great love, Amsterdam. Nicoline van Harskamp guided me expertly through her city of guards and counter-surveillance. Sarah Baxter provided access to an altogether different city of the imagination, glimpsed here in these pages.

Echoes of ideas presented here appeared in different guises elsewhere. These publications include *City Visions: The Work of Iain Sinclair*, ed. Jenny Bavidge and Robert Bond (Newcastle: Cambridge Scholars Press, 2007); *J. G. Ballard: Contemporary Critical Perspectives*, ed. Jeannette Baxter (London and New York: Continuum, 2009); *Ian McEwan: Contemporary Critical Perspectives*, ed. Sebastian Groes (London and New York: Continuum, 2009); *American, British and Canadian Studies*, Volume 8, June 2007; the *Literary London Journal*, June/July 2004; *Pretext: This Little World*, Autumn 2005; *The London Magazine*, June/July, 2004. I wish to thank the publishers and editors for their permission to reprint this material.

Many thanks are also due to my friend Douglas Cowie, my life-support system in times of crisis. Other people who I should thank are, in no particular order, Jeannette Baxter; Alistair Cormack; Sam 'Ghost Signs' Roberts; Barry Lewis; David James; Ian Haywood and Vic Hebblewhite for taking us up the Barbican's Cromwell Tower; Peter Barry; Christian Nold; Jon Cook; Peter Childs; Clive Scott; Pat Waugh; Phil Tew; Matt Taunton; Esther Leslie; Doris Teske; Phil Tew; Lawrence Phillips; Alex Murray; and Christoph Bode. I would also like to thank Tim Jarvis for his help with the preparation of this book.

I would like to thank my family for their continued support and understanding. I want to thank my wife, José Lapré, in particular for her patience and support along the journey.

Dank jullie wel.

SG

N8, March 2010

List of Abbreviations

BA	Hanif Kureishi, *The Black Album*
BL	Monica Ali, *Brick Lane*
BS	Hanif Kureishi, *The Buddha of Suburbia*
C	Maureen Duffy, *Capital*
Cr	J. G. Ballard, *Crash*
CT	Ian McEwan, *The Child in Time*
D	Iain Sinclair, *Downriver*
DD	Peter Ackroyd, *The House of Doctor Dee*
DI	Mikhail Bakhtin, *The Dialogic Imagination*
DW	J. G. Ballard, *The Drowned World*
GFL	Peter Ackroyd, *The Great Fire of London*
H	Peter Ackroyd, *Hawksmoor*
I	Martin Amis, *The Information*
Kc	J. G. Ballard, *Kingdome Come*
KC	Michael Moorcock, *King of the City*
L	Maureen Duffy, *Londoners*
LB	Peter Ackroyd, *London: The Biography*
LF	Martin Amis, *London Fields*
LH	Iain Sinclair, *Lud Heat*
LO	Iain Sinclair, *London Orbital*
LOFT	Iain Sinclair, *Lights Out for the Territory*
M	Martin Amis, *Money*
ML	Michael Moorcock, *Mother London*
MP	J. G. Ballard, *Millennium People*
NC	Angela Carter, *Nights at the Circus*
OP	Martin Amis, *Other People*
PEL	Michael de Certeau, *The Practice of Everyday Life*
PP	Peter Ackroyd, *The Plato Papers*

PS	Henri Lefebvre, *The Production of Space*
S	Ian McEwan, *Saturday*
So	Ian McEwan, *Solar*
SV	Salman Rushdie, *The Satanic Verses*
THIW	Maureen Duffy, *That's How It Was*
WC	Angela Carter, *Wise Children*
WCST	Iain Sinclair, *White Chappell, Scarlet Tracings*
WT	Zadie Smith, *White Teeth*
YD	Martin Amis, *Yellow Dog*

Introduction: From 'ellowen deeowen' to 'Babylondon': London is a Language

Masters of London

One particularly insightful way of understanding London is to study the lives the city is given by writers who make and remake it in their imagination. London is not only the fruitful setting, subject matter and producer of fictions, but its myths and fictions are implicated in shaping our understanding of the city. Therefore the material structure of rationally calculable and quantifiable objects, actions and people takes no priority over that imagined city; its literature generates its own peculiar knowledge. This book favours this approach over the safer narratives offered by historians, economists, sociologists and anthropologists. In a world in which 'reality' is 'ruled by fictions of every kind – mass-merchandising, advertising, politics conducted as a branch of advertising, the pre-empting of any original response to experience by the television screen', we need to understand the fictional component to our lives.[1] The literary imagination and the study of fictional narratives therefore have a special contribution to make in assessing the workings of the personal life and the private imagination in relationship to the life of the nation, and beyond.

More so than any other city, London is covered by a thick crust of poetry, urban legends, historical narratives and literary fictions, and mythologies, from Oliver Twist and Jack the Ripper to Sherlock Homes and Peter Pan. Cities such as Paris and Venice, more recently joined by the myth-making machinery of Los Angeles's Hollywood and Mumbai's Bollywood, have a similar fictional shimmer to them, but London's long and dense history make it, more than any other city, a fiction. The various traditions of London literature make it particularly suitable to trace the changes that we, and the city as a measure of ourselves,

1

have undergone. Since the mid-seventies, when Britain recovered from post-imperial socio-economic decline and cultural confusion, London has become the focus of a ferocious imaginative energy. A body of exceptional work has emerged by writers who have unconditionally committed their writing lives to the capital city.

The *Making* in the title points to the constructed and artificial nature of the city; the metropolis is a place that embodies and literalises *process*. Rather than a place that *is* – Amsterdam and Paris spring to mind – London is a living metropolis, a healthy city that is laboured on constantly; it is the ultimate city of *Becoming*. The title celebrates the city's recent transformation but is also critical of the mind-boggling changes it has undergone at the hands of national and global business, local and national government, city planners, architects and urban developers. Unlike rationalised Rome, the divine order of Amsterdam or Hausmannised Paris, London's 'figure ground' (the layout of its streets) is characterised by a 'medieval, messy and organic' London feel that can be explained by the city's history of government.[2] Michael Hebbert states that 'As the city of London stayed within its walls, Westminster matured into a city in its own right. The two cities formed a compound nucleus around which metropolitan London grew in a polycentric, dispersed fashion, without unifying municipal government. Plurality of governance explains irregularity of topography.'[3] Sue Brownhill, a board member of the London Docklands Development Corporation, calls Canary Wharf a '"happy accident" rather than a result of deliberate planning'.[4] This sounds optimistic and liberal, perhaps, but this kind of discourse has too often been an excuse for the *laissez-faire* attitudes which are the cause of the city's changing character, and the continuous restructuring of an entire society, which has led to an increasingly divided world of haves and have-nots, while London even threatens 'to become [...] a Third World city'.[5] And the physical place we can touch, the London of brick, stone and iron is becoming an invisible city, designed digitally and disappearing in an enchanting mirage of cold-gleaming steel and glass.

Throughout history the city acts as a memory map containing traces of power which are inscribed into its material formation. The geographical and architectural codification of power in the cityscape constitutes a discourse that has been read, analysed and responded to by London writers, who are particularly adept at this. This new London is the result of projects that emerged under the governments of Margaret Thatcher, John Major and New Labour's Tony Blair and Gordon Brown. We can read this narrative by flicking back and forth between Canary Wharf and the Imperial Wharf; from the County Hall turned tourist attraction to Lord Foster's City Hall; from the Congestion Charge sign stamped in New Labour red onto the city and Boris Johnson's Tory blue Super Cycle Highways; from the Olympic Development sites at Stratford and Hackney Wick to the redevelopment of King's Cross; from César Pelli's One Canada Square to Lord Foster's Gherkin; from the Millennium Dome to the Thames Estuary; and from the Bluewater and Westfield mega shopping malls. Tower blocks, the motorway, gentrification and gated communities have reshaped the way we live. Added to this is a simulacral London, from the Globe and Dickensworld to the Sherlock Holmes Museum and Jack the Ripper tours, and films such as *Notting Hill* (1999) – fictions which contribute to shaping a modern glossy London myth that conveniently ignores a very real underworld of exploitation and hardship. Some call this urban redevelopment, and others, including Prince Charles, a continuation of the Blitz, in which case the making of London is also its unmaking, a question which is addressed in the conclusion.

This is not a book about town planning, but these remarks stress that there is a very real connection between London's materiality and the actual topic of this book, the contemporary London novel. The '*London*' in the title we tend to think of as the 'purely real, purely representable' London.[6] No such thing exists. Patrick Hamilton's *Twenty Thousand Streets under the Sky* (1935) have become more than fifty thousand streets, motorways, squares, cul-de-sacs, mews and parks, to which we can add marinas, sprawling business parks and golf courses. The sheer material bulk of modern London makes the city unknowable and incomprehensible, except perhaps for Black Cab drivers who have passed the All-London Knowledge. Even that brilliant ordering system of the mess we find on the ground (and cunning propagandist of roads), the *A-Z*, has to give up at London's own mini-Manhattan, Canary Wharf, with its multi-layered streets, piazzas and walkways. Fifty years after Phyllis Pearshall invented the *A-Z*, London went three-dimensional, or, in the case of much new architecture, such as The Gherkin, virtual. London can never be reduced to an abstract theory or to hyper-reality, as Julian Wolfreys would have it: the weight of its history, its Old World heritage and its unending materiality are too much *there*, too much present.[7] London is a place that is laboured on, constantly, and that constitutes an acute social and political dimension. In Peter Ackroyd's words: 'London is a labyrinth, half of stone, half of flesh. It cannot be conceived in its entirety, but experienced only as a wilderness of alleys and passages, in which even the most experienced citizen may lose the way; it is curious, too, that this labyrinth is in a continual state of change and expansion' (*LB* 2)[8] Ackroyd evokes a question about 'the human element', as the rapidity of growth and changes of this often unfathomable maze appears to threaten the sense that we have the means to restore the city to a human scale.

If we cannot comprehend the city around us directly, we should turn to the artistic representations that present to us a dialogue that exists between the material city and those who imaginatively transfigure it in their art. In his visionary circumnavigation of the King's Cross area, *Vale Royal* (1995), Aidan Andrew Dun's narrator notes that 'In wide arcs of wandering through the city / I saw to either side of what is seen / and noticed treasures where it was thought there were none.'[9] Art and literature particularly allow us to see behind the surface of material things and events because they transfigure the lives of the city and its inhabitants by means of their idiosyncratic, creative imagination. Martin Amis puts it well when he states that 'I have to push it [London] through my psyche and transform it. So it isn't, in the end, London anymore. It's London in the patterning of my cerebellum [...] what I feel I'm here for is to write about this city and what it's like to be alive in it now.'[10] The private reimagination of the totalising structure is another way to reclaim the human scale of the city.

It is this process of transfiguration which the narrator of J. M. Coetzee's fictional autobiography *Youth* (2002), a South African émigré living and working temporarily in London, fails to achieve:

> He does not as yet know England well enough to do England in prose. He is not even sure he can do the parts of London he is familiar with, the London of crowds trudging to work, of cold and rain, of bedsitters with curtainless windows and forty-watt bulbs. If he were to try what would come out would be no different, he suspects, from the London of any other bachelor clerk. He may have his own vision of London, but there is nothing unique to that vision. If it has a certain intensity, that is only because it is narrow, and it is narrow because it is ignorant of everything outside itself. He has not mastered London. If there is any mastering going on, it is London mastering him.[11]

Unlike Coetzee's narrator, the texts studied here, each in their own way, 'master' London. Maureen Duffy, Michael Moorcock, J. G. Ballard, Angela Carter, Iain Sinclair, Peter Ackroyd, Salman Rushdie, Martin Amis, Ian McEwan, Hanif Kureishi, Will Self, Zadie Smith and Monica Ali give us different experiences and visions of London. We need these masters of London: they shout back at the infinite labyrinth, 'half of stone, half of flesh of stone'; they offer alternative narratives, and in the process master the city on our behalf by making sense of the madness, the endless materiality and innumerable people that would otherwise destroy us. Their work also forms a public space, a Speaker's Corner of the imagination, where the voices of the citizenry, often unheard or falling on deaf ears, may be restored.

London, modernity and mythical vision

The ultimate master of modern London is T. S. Eliot. Coetzee notes that '[t]his man had targeted London as the metropolis of the English-speaking world, and with a diffidence concealing ruthless singleness of purpose had made himself into the deliberately magisterial voice of that metropolis.'[12] It is perhaps no coincidence that the most famous poem of and about modernity, Eliot's *The Waste Land* (1922), is also a London poem, which famously declares the phantasmagoric metropolis an 'Unreal City'.[13] Modernity is embodied by London, a city that is a wandering maze of endless possibilities, a site in between dream and idea, and provides us with a spiritual landscape profoundly intertwined with the modern experience and consciousness.

The impact of *The Waste Land* (1922) on twentieth-century literature and our understanding of the city is extraordinary, and the work serves as a central point of reference for many of the writers whose work is discussed here. Within the poem, the proliferation and plurality of voices optically fragments our perception of the metropolis, recreating the world around us as a multiperspectival concept rather than a phenomenological percept, 'a heap of broken images'.[14] Conventional categories and hierarchies, such as class and gender, were all challenged by their subjection to imagined transgression. Anti-linear and fragmented, *The Waste Land* offers a city that enacts surrealist techniques of defamiliarisation upon perception and consciousness. It captures the violence and velocity of modernity – with new machines introducing radical changes and new ideas in an emerging capitalist democracy, but the poem also shows the traumatic impact of the First World War upon the collective consciousness, raising the possibility a Western civilisation in decline. Eliot also recoded London in terms of previous capitals of grand civilisations, in particular Roman, and thus European culture.

The father of the modern novel, James Joyce, was obsessed by *The Waste Land*, and he also saw London as exemplary of soulless, mechanical modernity, where the absence of community had dehumanising effects. In a letter to Frank Budgen, Joyce wrote: 'London isn't a city. It is a wilderness of bricks and mortar and the law of wilderness prevails. All Londoners say, "I keep to myself." The malicious friendly sort of town can't exist with seven million people in it.'[15] Joyce's work is paradigmatic of modernism because it placed the aesthetic mind with its creative ordering mechanisms within the modern city. Yet his writing of Dublin, in *Ulysses* (1922) in particular, never went beyond a consciousness facing the perils of the industrial, wholly commercialised realm whereas London-based modernist writers' literature, from Joseph Conrad and Ezra Pound to Virginia Woolf and Ford Maddox Ford, grappled with the metropolis as the centre of an Empire with a global totalitarian force at the height of its power.

Joyce's textual city is, first and foremost, a city produced by formal characteristics: the exploration and parody of genre and literary tradition, including the mocking of the London voice of Charles Dickens, allowed Joyce to find the idiosyncratic narration that would restore a sense of the personal, human scale. What Eliot and Joyce also injected back into this mechanised existence was mythical vision, the ability to see within the trivialities of everyday life patterns that transcend its apparent banality. Joyce's Dublin and Eliot's London are palimpsest cities whereby the mythological is superimposed onto the minutiae of quotidian lives, so that the universal and eternal is made visible just below the surface of experience. The profane, secular city, corrupted by disfiguring forces of commerce and politics, makes way for the sacred cities of classic

Figure 1   Jacob Epstein's Rima, Hyde Park

writers, including Dante's underworld, Rome, Shakespeare's London and Baudelaire's decadent Paris. Simultaneously, Eliot pitted London's voices as an antidote to history and as a form of knowledge which the powers of the state and commerce are less easily able to commodify and exploit. London is such a fruitful territory for mythographers because it is a city thick with myth, some wholly its own, others universal and eternal. Turn the corner and you will stumble over a story or a statue the significance of which goes back hundreds if not thousands of years. Maureen Duffy's *Capital* (1975) opens with the words: 'He couldn't help it if the bones poked through the pavement under his feet ...'[16] These myths include the neglected London Stone; Queen Boudica, whose revolt against occupying Roman forces led to the burning down of Londinium; the fabulous Bartholomew Fair's spectacles with its fairies and giants on display; the Great Fire of 1666; Jack the Ripper; the jungle girl Rima – fictional heroine of W. H. Hudson's *Green Mansions* (1904), who can be found, carved out of stone, in Hyde Park; and the famed Blitz spirit, which could be felt again after the terrorist attacks on 7 July 2005.

Classical myths also knit London together. The City of London is guarded by dragons and griffins; on Holborn viaduct we find four bronze goddesses (Commerce; Agriculture; Science; and Fine Art). And, if you find yourself on Piccadilly Circus and look up, you will see, in this centre of synaptic overload, a statue of Cupid, lonely and ignored in the rush of everyday life. Yet Eros is still loose on London's streets, even in the twenty-first century. One important point about the presence of these ancient myths is that within our hyper-rational, sped up, shrunken world a proto-modern way of understanding the world around us still persists. Another is that myth is a fundamentally democratic mode: its origins lie in oral communication, and its narratives and knowledge belong to the voices of the people and not the official powers' writings of law. And London's voices are an object of critical focus within this study because living speech resists easy commodification, and because they allow us to travel back into the past.

The strength and density of these mythologies can be explained in part because historically, London has no certain origins or a clear beginning. Aside from a few paragraphs in Caesar and Tacitus, there is hardly any written evidence of London's existence during the Celtic period.[17] Before archaeological excavations in the early nineteenth century established London as a Roman new town, the absence of a written history left much room for mythological speculation about the city's origins. Geoffrey of Monmouth proposed that London was founded by Aeneas's great-grandson Brutus, who built a new Troy on the Thames, and derived

Figure 2   King Lud, St Dunstan-in-the-West, Fleet Street

its name from the mythical King Lud, who can still be found, tucked away in an alcove in the churchyard of St Dunstan-in-the-West, with his two sons.[18] This tradition was continued with Lagamon's *Brut* (1155), which speculates on Brutus as the founding father of London. Edmund Spenser's writing in the 1590s served as a model for John Milton's *The History of Britain* (1670), which also records the story of Brutus and his *Troia nova*. Milton states that 'oft-times relations heretofore accounted fabulous have been after found to contain in them many foot-steps, and reliques of something true.'[19] As Peter Ackroyd notes in his London biography, even today London Stone is an ancient if forgotten object representing 'the power and authority of the city', which functions as a tangible reminder of London's mythical origins (*LB* 19).

The absence of a clear beginning allows the literary imagination to supplement fact with myths and fictions. In 'Lost London Writers' (1999), Michael Moorcock notes that there are two particular strands of London writing:

> Dickens was the greatest writer to turn London into a creature, but he had many imitators and rivals [...] they contributed to the idea of the Thames as a stinking, murky Styx, its surrounding slums the city corrupted, fascinating heart [...] Some [...] tried to paint an accurate

picture of London through fact and fiction ... they created an authentic myth, more potent than fact.

The myth becomes derisory when sentimentalised by Hollywood, but easily survives assault. In that invented city Holmes and the Ripper, Jekyll and Hyde, struggle forever in a foggy Whitechapel never bombed or redeveloped and the whole stew of English class, repression and neurosis, achieves a universal symbolism.

Almost buried under that heavy myth lies the equally authentic city in Steele, Smollett, Fielding, Gay and Thackeray. It is a domestic city, a vulgar city, a cruelly snobbish and comically arrogant, a busy, greedy, good-humoured and democratic city. A jolly jeering fishwife rather than a leering whore.[20]

Moorcock's model can help pinpoint the various changes that London in literature has undergone over the past three decades, but we should also treat it with caution. Most writings are a mixture of the two strands, whereby one competes with the other. In some writers, such as Maureen Duffy and Michael Moorcock, London's founding mythologies seem to prevail while in others, such as Ian McEwan and Zadie Smith, the factual seems to dominate only to give way to pockets of mythological significance buried beneath the surface of the text.

What the fictions of contemporary London writers share is that they all capture the contemporary by reacting to often rapidly changing politico-economic and socio-cultural contexts. Since the late seventies, artists, poets and writers have, in many cases furiously and violently, responded to the Thatcherite rhetoric about free market capitalism and individualism, and to New Labour's continued rationalisation of people's private and public lives by means of targets, which has resulted in a control society in which the citizen is subjected to a process of perpetual monitoring and scrutiny. Starting in the mid-seventies, this period can be called 'Long Thatcherism', and it is characterised by a belief in free market principles (which were encouraged in health services), the privatisation of public services (telephones, gas, water), the cultivation of nationalistic iconography (from Thatcher's during the Falkland crisis in 1982 to Blair's Cool Britannia in the late 1990s), and an often blind devotion to private enterprise and financial services. Politicians were addicted to spin doctors who carefully managed information and who conducted politics as if it was a form of Public Relations, resulting in the triumph of style over substance.

In response, contemporary London writers have raised numerous important questions, for instance, about who owns public space and whether London, as a capital city that after a protracted period of economic downturn resurfaced as one of three nodes in the global economy, is still representative of Britain. They criticise the wholesale commodification of just about everything and ask fundamental questions about the state of Western democracy. The post-9/11 climate of anxiety saw renewed and intensified religious tensions, while the protests by British citizens against the Iraq war were ignored. Recently, civil liberties have come under threat by a proliferation of modes of surveillance, from forests of CCTV cameras to the Oyster Card. These are just a few issues at stake in contemporary London, yet the coherence and intensity of the creative response has resulted in the emergence of a corpus of writers who have reappropriated London in their writing. In *Lights Out for the Territory* (1997), Iain Sinclair floats the idea of London writers forming a *body poetic*:

> Writers, wishing to "rescue" dead ground, will have to wrest it from the grip of developers, clerks, clerics, eco freaks, and ward bosses. We are welcome to divide London according to our own antholo-gies: JG Ballard at Shepperton (the reservoirs, airport perimeter roads empty film studios); Michael Moorcock at Notting Hill [...] Angela Carter – south of the river, Battersea to Brixton, where she hands over to the poet Allen Fisher; Eric Mottram at Herne Hill [...] Peter Ackroyd dowsing in Clerkenwell in quest of Dr John Dee; [...] Stewart Home commanding the desert around the northern entrance of the Blackwall Tunnel; [...] King's Cross was up for grabs and Aidan [Dun] was elected. (*LOFT* 145–6)[21]

Sinclair derives this idea from Joyce, who famously stated that in *Ulysses* (1922) he wanted 'to give a picture of Dublin so complete that if the city one day suddenly disappeared from the Earth, it could be reconstructed out of my book'.[22] The point that Sinclair makes is written in the spirit of Joyce's totalitarian project, and what these writers together have cre-ated is an 'anti-body', an alternative mapping of London that reacts to and against current events.

This book is a humble attempt to sew together the textual body parts into the monstrous, multilayered London palimpsest that Sinclair alludes to in *White Chappell, Scarlet Tracings* (1987): 'You will never rebuild the city from these words. You would build a monster.'[23] Acts of phenomenological, intertextual and theoretical mudlarking will hopefully give us a sense of the vocabulary, textures and techniques, obsessions, colours, speeds and atmospheres of contemporary London writing, resulting in a typology and textual topography of London at the end of the twentieth, and beginning of the twenty-first, centuries.

The city-as-body metaphor forms an important measure of change. Ackroyd's *London: The Biography* (2000) argues that:

> the image of London as a human body is striking and singular ... [t]he byways of the city resemble thin veins and parks are like lungs. In the mist and rain of an urban autumn, the shining stones and cobbles of the older thoroughfares look as if they are bleeding [...] It is fleshy and voracious, grown fat upon its appetite for people and for food [...] it consumes and excretes, maintained within a continual state of greed and desire. (*LB* 1)

Ackroyd's use of this metaphor harks back to a long literary tradition. In *Areopagitica* (1644), Milton already proposed the analogy between London and the human body. In *A Journal of the Plague Year* (1722), Daniel Defoe saw a fevered and diseased body, and William Blake's work imagined London as the woman Jerusalem. William Cobbett famously stated London was 'the great wen of all [...] The monster, called, by the silly coxcombs of the press, the "metropolis of the empire".'[24] In his study of the eighteenth-century London novel, *London Transformed* (1978), Max Byrd notes the paradoxical attempt of writers 'to humanise the city, to bring it into terms with the human scale of the imagination':[25] as the rapid growth of the city started to transcend the limits of human understanding, the city was kept under imaginary control by writing it in terms of 'a human body, as human language, as human art'.[26]

This seductive yet deceptive anthropomorphism is a strategy within liberal humanism that deploys metaphors derived from the natural world, a tradition that runs strongly within the English literary imagination. The body metaphor goes back to Aristotle's *Poetics*, which are derived from biological observation of the natural world. In this model the language of realism establishes a linear and teleological model of universal continuity that allows us to trace the changing events in a logical sequence of causal events.[27] Yet Dickens's later work already struggled to justify this kind of organic analogy. Victor Sage notes that 'Dickens is quite obsessed by the sheerly anatomical existence of the body, whether human or animal; and at the same time increasingly resistant to the seductive anthropomorphism of those organic metaphors of growth and development which Foucault thinks of in *The Order of Things* (1966) as the nineteenth-century episteme itself.'[28] Linear and rational models have continuously been mocked and challenged by writers, especially in the twentieth century, when our understanding of the world became partial, subjective and increasingly uncertain and infinitely more complex.

So complex, perhaps, that our attempts at understanding the nature of the modern metropolis is more a desire for an ideal than an acknowledgement of the limitations of our knowledge.

Capitalising London: the postmodern city

This book happily commits an impropriety by violating the etiquette that prescribes we should never talk about money. London is a city whose very being is intertwined with the nation's and the world's economy, and this relationship can be felt in many different ways.[29] If you want to understand London, you need to understand money.

What money and literature share is that they are symbolic values attributed to paper; they are symbolic carriers of signs that have representative power that connects us to other people. There exists a shared development of language, literature, money and the city, and the novel functions as a kind of touchstone where all come together. Therefore the contemporary London novel forms the locus that continues to mediate changes, and which measures them as well.

In *The Order of Things* (1966) Michel Foucault discusses the historical connection between money and language, and he analyses how the evolution of the monetary system transformed money; instead of just an objective instrument that measures wealth and commodities, it became a 'commodity like any other – not an absolute standard for all equivalences, but a commodity whose capacity for exchange, and consequently whose value as a substitute in exchange, are modified according to its abundance or rarity: money too has its price'.[30] Foucault explains how the hegemonic exchanging position of precious metals in the seventeenth century is replaced by an emphasis on the exchanging function itself. The absolute relationship between coinage (its intrinsic value having the two functions of measure and substitution) and commodities is substituted for an arbitrary one where 'money (and even the metal of which it is made) receives its value from its pure function as a sign' so that '[t]hings take on value, then, in relationship to one another' only.[31] In other words, fluctuation in the availability of commodities and speculation thereon make value relative.

A similar shift takes place in our understanding of language as a system of representation. In *The Coiners of Language* (1994), Jean-Joseph Goux uses the analogy between language and money to explore changing notions of realism in the works of novelists such as Gide, Mallarmé and Zola. In literature, gold has traditionally signified solidity and truth, and is therefore equated with the possibility of transparent writing as means of conveying reality objectively and empirically. Just as economists thought that money was a neutral means of exchange, the literary author thought of his activity as the re-creation of reality: 'As long as gold circulates "in person," we are in the realm of realist literature. When gold is replaced by tokens (of dubious convertibility) we enter the domain of nonfigurative experience.'[32] Ferdinand de Saussure's structuralism, which pointed out the arbitrary relationship between signifier (a word) and signified (that which it refers to) determined by the social context, entails, in Rod Mengham's words, another 'descent' of language, which becomes an increasingly unreliable carrier of meaning:

> Indeed, in certain modern literary texts, there is such an unusual stress on the need to release the signifier from its obligation to the signified, to allow the language of the text a much greater freedom to be drawn into structural play, that the linguistic sign starts to be exchanged almost exclusively among themselves, without very much interaction at all with what they are supposed to refer to.[33]

The basis of traditional representation itself is undermined, which also has major implications for our conventional understanding of politics, religion, class, gender, nation and ethnicity as the realisation that the intricacies and contingencies of language itself shape our perception of the world undermines their stability. Language plays a great part in creating our understanding of reality, but this unstable system is not of our own making; we inherit it, and are subjected to its powers and volatility.

In the post-war period, money, the city and language have become even more complex systems dependent upon and determined by a market value created by human needs and desires. With the intellectual leap made in post-structuralism this unmooring of the fixed meaning of and between these three factors becomes even more problematic during late capitalism in the post-war period, when the destruction of their fixed meaning seems to be complete. With the 1973 decoupling of the US dollar from the gold standard there emerged an increasing intangible, ephemeral capitalist system determined by the increasing complexity of financial exchange and speculation, and money going digital, completing Marx's prediction in *The Communist Manifesto* (1848) that 'All fixed, fast-frozen relations, with their train of ancient and venerable prejudices and opinions are swept away, all new-formed ones become antiquated before they can ossify. All that is solid melts into air, all that is holy is profaned, and man is at last compelled to face with sober sense, his real conditions in life, and his relations with his kind.'[34] The representative ability of money is lost, with the disastrous 2008 recession as evidence, and this is why we need literature, which can function as a laboratory where representation can be brought back under control.

Literature's most fundamental tool for making us understand the world around us is through metaphor. Whereas the Romantics and Victorians thought of the city as a monster and a labyrinth, the modernists portrayed it as a dehumanising machine. In postmodernity, the city contributed to the idea that we can no longer know 'reality', but that the contemporary experience is what Amis calls 'this collision or swirl of vying realities'.[35] This is exactly why we need the city, because the representational problems the modern metropolis poses are directly related to our understanding of the contemporary experience. In *City of Words* (1971), Tony Tanner notes:

> But there are certain conventions for establishing the status of referents in the book. When James says London, or Joyce says Dublin, we permit ourselves to draw on our associations from more orthodox geographies. But when Nabokov says America and Zembla and puts them together in the same frame as though belonging to the same dimensions – cohabiting on one place – then our reading of the signs is necessarily more confused, the old associations are unsettled, and normal confidences as to the location of the 'real' are shaken.[36]

The contemporary era, its literature and theory, have become characterised by the destruction of the stability of conventions that allow us to establish the status of the referent. This is exactly where the importance of semiotics – the science of signs – lies, as it combines the changing relationship of the city as measurement of civilisation's expression of itself, and the sign system in which it is captured. As Tanner states: 'The point is not that existence itself is labyrinthine; the suggestion is rather that the labyrinths man builds are his varying attempts to make statements about the *labyrinths* he lives in.'[37]

The key postmodern tropes present the city as text, as narrative, as palimpsest, as a narrated labyrinthine space that can be circumnavigated with the eyes and mind. The act of reading becomes the creation of a space of enunciation where reader and writer may engage in a meaningful dialogue. Italo Calvino's meditation on Venice, *Invisible Cities* (1972), is one of the finest examples: 'Your gaze scans the streets as if they were written pages, the city says everything you must think, makes you repeat her discourse.'[38] Iain Sinclair's work presents us with various ideas about the city as text: in *Lights Out*, he walks the letters VOX ('voice') into the city, and in *Slow Chocolate*

Autopsy (1997) he acts as interpreter for the unedited city-as-narrative. A key figure here is Michel de Certeau, who states that: 'The act of walking is to the urban system what the speech act is to language or to statements uttered.'[39] This idea is informed by urban semiotics, which foregrounds both the city and literature as collections of signs that can be interpreted. Yet this interpretation can *only* take place, as both A. J. Greimas as well as Henri Lefebvre state, if it is inscribed into a very real socio-cultural context. The role of the reader in making sense of the city and the London novel as a cognitive geography is important because it creates a political geography that connects the imagined with the real.[40] For the postmodernists, the city-as-text and text-as-city is important politically because it allows authors to un-write and re-write. Salman Rushdie's *The Satanic Verses* (1988), for instance, approaches London as a text – 'letter by letter, ellowen, deeowen, London',[41] to linguistically unstitch the metropolis and to open up spaces into which the immigrants can inscribe themselves.

Embedded within this book is a visual essay by Sarah Baxter, which is in dialogue with the textual cities. Throughout *The Making of London* we find 'illuminations', which, sometimes comically, sometimes seriously, illustrate key themes that contribute to shaping our understanding of London at the beginning of the twenty-first century: the proliferation of modes of surveillance are countered by an anonymous street artist

Figure 3   Battersea Foreshore

on Brick Lane, the reinvention of a power station as a space central to cultural life, the hundreds of lives within the Trellick Tower displayed as mini-dramas, et cetera. These images expose mystery and the sublime as easily overlooked facets of urban life. In the middle section we encounter London 'textures', a series which invites us to look at the city as a proliferating series of surfaces: the shrapnel-damaged RAF St Clement Danes church on the Strand, the swirling surface of the Thames, the vertiginous view of the city from the thirtieth floor of the Trellick Tower. The emphasis on surfaces uncannily, and erotically, draws attention to the hidden spaces of the city, and the secrets that lie, potentially, behind its façade. Together these photographs expose transcendent moments of beauty and evoke the sublime in places; above all, they present a vision that both captures and shapes the aesthetic unique to London, while completing a texturology of the contemporary city.

This book consists of narrative walks that produce readings of different textual cities. Or one may think of it in the way that David Mitchell, echoing Jonathan Raban's classic London novel *The Soft City* (1974), suggests in *Ghostwritten* (1999):[42]

> As the fine denizens of London Town know, each tube line has a distinct personality and a range of mood swings. The Victoria Line for example, breezy and reliable. The Jubilee Line, the young disappointment of the family, branching out to suburbs, eternally having extensions planned [...] Docklands Light Railway, the nouveau riche neighbour [...] Central, the middle aged cousin. That's about it for the main lines, except for Metropolitan which is too boring to mention, except that it's a nice fuchsia colour and you take it to visit the dying. [...] The Northern Line is black on the map. It's the deepest. It has the most suicides, you're most likely to get mugged on it and its art students are most likely to be future Bond Girls. [...] London is a language. I guess all places are.[43]

Thinking of London as a language is valuable because it moves us beyond the postmodern notion of the city as readable and (re)writable text, which emphasises an idealistic position that is sometimes in danger of obscuring the material struggles of everyday life. And this is also why we need the London novel. Writers are interpreters and translators of the various, often conflicting discourses the city offers – Rushdie calls it 'Babylondon' (*SV* 459) – and they take their city right inside our minds to construct profoundly real, imaginary Londons.

1
'Fabricked out of Literature and Myth': Maureen Duffy's Londons

The sinewy vigour and flexibility of the London demotic

Since the beginning of the 1960s, Maureen Duffy has produced an *oeuvre* consisting of six collections of poetry, seventeen novels, sixteen plays, including three for television and three for radio, and seven works of non-fiction, characterised by a generic eclecticism, aesthetic experimentalism and political progressiveness.[1] Duffy's writing is often polemical: she writes about topics considered uncomfortable by mainstream writers, such as lesbianism, terrorism, the rights of the animal kingdom, the values of the arts and censorship.[2] Her work has the intellectual acuity and clarity of vision to predict and determine the political and literary context, rather than following it. She was one of the first British novelists to come out in her first novel, *That's How It Was* (1962); her Aphra Behn biography, *The Passionate Shepherdess* (1977), anticipated Janet Todd's bestseller by a good twenty years; and her animal rights handbook *Men and Beasts* (1984) remains central to a debate that made it onto the mainstream agenda only in the late 1990s. In many ways similar to Dickens, who established the Guild of Literature and Art, a 'version of a kind of life insurance scheme for writers and artists'[3] that protected them by means of copyright, Duffy co-founded a representative body for writers, the Authors' Licensing and Collecting Society (ALCS) in 1977 and has occupied numerous prestigious positions in the arts in Britain and Europe.

Duffy is also a writer who has unconditionally committed her writing life to the service of London and Londoners; her work can be seen as a series of experimental mappings of alternative, textual models that meditate upon the significance of changes in British identity. The city and its marginalised, oppressed denizens have been a constant presence in, and source of inspiration for, her work, which speaks on behalf of those ignored. Although she has written a London 'triptych' consisting of *Wounds* (1969), *Capital* (1975) and *Londoners: An Elegy* (1983), Duffy has always written London from her early novels *The Microcosm* (1966) and *The Paradox Players* (1967) through to *Occam's Razor* (1993) and *Alchemy* (2004), which juxtaposes a contemporary story about an idealistic, woman lawyer to fifteenth-century London life. Her vision of London is distinct and unmistakably recognisable: her novels explore London's mythical narratives to challenge the 'official' history of London and they foreground fiction to expose the artifice of fixed social categories, and to dismantle mythologies that lead to regressive nationalist senti-ments.[4] As Paul Magrs notes, her writing itself forms 'a conscious echo of the way London [...] contains and compacts endless heterogeneity'.[5] Her London is a city 'fabricked out of literature and myth'.[6]

It is also because of her challenging stylistics and formal 'difficulty' that Duffy's London sits uneasily in the mainstream theoretical frame-works that dominated late twentieth- and early twenty-first-century criticism of London literature. Whereas Peter Ackroyd's pastiches and Salman Rushdie's historical metafiction contributed to shaping the interpretative frameworks of postmodern theoreticians such as Linda Hutcheon and Brian McHale, the eclecticism of Duffy's work proves less easy to pigeonhole. With its origins in Freudian and structuralist thought and with strong ties to her modernist precursors, Duffy's novels perform 'deconstructions' of fixed social categories and perceived boundaries not by renegotiating the dominance of the traditional ideo-logical centre and margins, but by withholding acknowledgement that there exists such a thing as a centre in the first place.

Duffy's semi-autobiographical debut novel, the extraordinary life-writing feat *That's How It Was* suggests that Duffy's genetic and literary roots lie in Ireland, and that James Joyce forms an important influ-ence. The novel is to Duffy what *A Portrait of the Artist as a Young Man* (1914–15) is to Joyce, namely, a *Bildungsroman* analysing the relation-ship between one's personal history and a wider, national history as lived through the life of the capital. It chronicles the narrative of the poor Mahoney family from Dublin now living in the interwar East End, with 'every nation under the sun, with a babel of tongues'.[7] In the absence of the father, the absconded IRA-member Patrick, mother Louey and daughter Paddy survive on stories about Louey's family history and East End myths, which Paddy is distrustful of: 'It was a kind of rite I was performing, an attempt even then to perpetuate times past which always seemed gayer than the present through some-one's rose-coloured spectacles of remembrance' (*THIW* 26). When the

Mahoneys' house is bombed during the Blitz, mother and daughter are evacuated to the fictional village of Wortbridge – the name suggesting both the importance of language ('Wort' is German for 'word') as well as her displaced consciousness ('Wort' also means 'root'), where Paddy becomes aware of her identity as a Londoner when the village children denounce them as 'bloody Londoners': 'I was a Londoner, an East Ender. Deliberately, I wove that conviction into my conscious thought so that it could never leave me. I would always have a place, I would always belong' (*THIW* 42). This conscious fabrication of identity through its dramatisation and performance in narrative is tested and challenged throughout Duffy's writing, and central to this artistry is London as the stage where histories and mythologies are open to (re-)invention and (re-)inscription in the act of fiction-making.

A drowned Atlantis: *Capital* (1975)

Published in the year that Margaret Thatcher became leader of the opposition, *Capital* aptly captures the *Zeitgeist* of the post-imperial socio-economic downturn that was to facilitate the triumphant rise to power of the Iron Lady. The novel depicts the dark social climate by pointing out the rise in the 'suicide rate' (*C* 69) and homelessness, which the novel asks us to read both literally and as a symbolical assessment of the state of the English collective consciousness. The novel cautions against glorified imperial versions of 'history' and nationalistic myths of Englishness, and forms a visionary indictment of the ideological and rhetorical strategies that were to be employed by the regime.

Decline and dislocation are the preoccupations of the novel's protagonist, the amateur archaeologist, trowel-armed Mr Meepers, who is 'in pursuit of the dead' (*C* 25): 'It was the living who passed ghostly around him, through whose curiously incorporeal flesh he moved while the dead pressed and clamoured, their dry cries drowning out the traffic' (*C* 17). At the beginning of the novel, in the sweltering August heat, Meepers has taken on a job as a porter at the fictional Queen's University on the Strand, near Trafalgar Square, in order to pursue his thesis, 'Evidences of urban survival in post-Roman London' (*C* 96). Meepers is a great English eccentric, a humanist of sorts who seeks to prove a continuous resistance (and therefore *presence* in the city) to the imperial fiction of 'history' by seeking to expose the 'official' account of London's decline during the Dark Ages as false. This evidence will establish the city's possible survival during this particular cycle of decline also. After being mugged, Meepers literally loses his ability to identify himself and he becomes homeless. Unable to support himself, he takes up residence in a lodge in Kensington Gardens. Living in the shadow of the Royal Palaces, Meepers reinvents himself as a king of the city's underworld: 'The lodge [...] was almost a palace itself' (*C* 88).

The British crisis is also embodied by Meepers's antagonist, the depressed, middle-class and middle-aged History Lecturer working an extra term at Queen's who strikes us as a version of the foppish, self-deluding palaeontologist Charles Smithson in John Fowles's *The French Lieutenant's Woman* (1969). He wonders, full of self-pity, why his students fail to learn from him: 'Is it a reaction from lost empire, lost world importance that makes them turn up their rather pale faces with glazed eyes that my words fall like rain on bare skin, brushed away or simply left to dry but without any power to penetrate the surface?' (*C* 31–2). This narrator, whose namelessness stresses his identity crisis, is desperately conflicted in his intellectual position: at heart he is a Romantic with a 'passion for the eighteenth century' (*C* 22), but he is also postmodern in his advocating of 'historical relativity' (*C* 21). In sweeping Derridean fashion, nothing exists outside textual traces, and he had dismissed as 'lunatic' (*C* 21) Meepers's thesis on London's history for publication because 'certain periods when historical records cease belong in a sense to pre-history or to some category of ex-history as yet undefined, more properly to archaeology. The Dark Ages, which always seem to me a term that works on several levels in characterizing that untidy period, is less accessible than Egypt or Nefertiti [...] even though comparatively it's so recent' (*C* 21). The intellectually impotent Lecturer's professional failure as a historian is mirrored by failure in his private life: his narrative consists of confessional letters written to his partner, who has left him for America, but they seem more a form of psychological self-help. The Lecturer's crisis is furthered by and projected onto the changing face of London, and he laments the tearing down of an unidentified building by Regency architect John Nash (1752–1835) on the Strand, and the city to him feels like a 'drowned London' (*C* 30): 'The city this morning was a drowned Atlantis under deep waves of mugginess and fumes as if the dew had been drawn up from the pavement not to be burnt off by the sun but hang in a damp ocean shroud over the streets' (*C* 29).

These two strands of this contemporary story are punctuated by a third space consisting of episodic narratives that verbalise London's history, starting with the earliest beginnings and moving through time to the present day. We find a lonely, routed Neanderthal who scavenges for food through London and finds a new family with an abandoned woman and child (*C* 26–9); a prehistoric group of people build a village

Figure 4 Effigy of a Knight, the Temple Church

along the Thames, which they live off (C 42–4); a young boy and an Artor (village leader) make 'a special journey to the great temple' (C 60) where he is chosen to be the new leader, at Heathrow in pantheist, pagan times (C 56–66); and two Celtic warriors (Lludd and Lyrr) are discussing fortifying the walls of their village against attack by Belgians (C 72–4); and so on. It becomes clear that it is Meepers who writes up these imaginary episodes through unconscious extrapolation of narratives associated with his fetishised archaeological objects: a boy throws his dagger into the Thames, 'sent it curvetting over the water in bounding flashes until it stabbed down through the muscled waves' (C 66) and Meepers ponders coins, '[g]old fremisses of c.640 stamped Lunduniu' (C 88). After he falls asleep, Meepers constructs a list of 'Fragments from the Berkynge Chronicle, probably spurious' (C 88). In this sense, the alternative history of London that is constructed out of the remnants of narrative are embedded within the collective unconscious that Meepers represents, and indeed, the angst-ridden unconscious of the nation is threatening to take control over its master completely.

This rhetoric of the unconscious, and the psychological split between Meepers and the Lecturer, alerts us to the Gothic motif of the Double, which Duffy uses to establish a process of 'mystification – the doubts left in the mind of the reader and hero alike as to the boundary-line between hallucination and reality'.[8] Meepers is an archetypal Benjaminian rag-picker, who picks at the scabs of wounded London's history, whilst the Lecturer is the embodiment of the British bourgeoisie who prefer to leave grand narratives intact. In their attitude to modernity they are radically opposed: whereas Meepers thinks of 'those indigestible morsels of things he would never buy, like cars' (C 34), the Lecturer suggests that, in order to alleviate himself from his despondency, 'an outing would do the car good' (C 122–3). Yet essentially they are the same: Meepers is nearly arrested for trespassing in search of a dig and asked if he has 'any I.D.' (C 144) – of which he has many but not the kind the arresting sergeant requires – and the Lecturer too has a 'damaged ego', confessing: 'How I long for some positive assertion of identity' (C 45). Meepers and the Lecturer are Doubles, and the outcast has come to haunt the latter: 'What I began to tell you is that either I've got a touch of the sun or I saw Meepers in the corridor of Queen's [...] I feel if I open one of the doors I might find myself face to face with myself across empty desks and the voice I'd heard from outside turns out to be mine' (C 22). The Lecturer also speaks of the 'dilemma of whether I had invented' (C 45) Meepers, and later tries to reassure himself that 'he's back and I didn't invent him' (C 69). The reader becomes aware that doubt introduces a space of possibility that asks us to be open to Meepers's alternative London history.

Within this complex circuit of revolving narration, reading Meepers as a projection of the Lecturer's unconscious can be justified with the knowledge that the rehabilitation of Meepers's project enables him to cancel out his entrapment in the grand narratives during the imperial period. One such account we find in the Victorian novelist and historian Walter Besant's classic history, *London* (1892), which discredits all arguments for London's uninterrupted existence:

> Most certainly and without doubt this continuity of occupation would have been proved by many signs, tokens and survivals. [The] old streets would have remained in their former positions [...] There is not in the whole of London a single trace of the Roman street, if we except that little bit still called after the name given by the Saxons to a Roman road [...] continuity of occupation is illustrated by tradition. It is impossible for traditions of the past to die out if the people continue. There are traditions of these ancient times among the Welsh, but among the Londoners there are none [...] Everything is clear gone. Not a voice, not a legend, not a story, not a superstition, remains of the stately Augusta. It is entirely vanished, leaving nothing behind but a wall [...] London, I am convinced, *must* – not *may* – but *must* have remained for a time desolate and empty.[9]

For Meepers, the certainty of tone ('must', not 'may') is problematic because it hampers his quest to prove London's continuous occupation, and thus the possibility of the city's survival. Doubt becomes a potent force, a powerful dynamo of the creative imagination.

Making Meepers the anti-hero makes it seem that we are to interpret Duffy's text as endorsing his case. *Capital* is, according to one of Duffy's early critics, Christoph Bode, about '*continuity*, continuity in change, no doubt – and a continuity that is in constant danger of breaking down and therefore has to be preserved and cared for'.[10] As the narrative unfolds, the Lecturer's doubts about his position grow, and he opens up to the metaphysical aspects of his human existence: whereas 'Dead voices radioed to him out of the night' (*C* 212), the Lecturer also becomes increasingly sensitive to the more metaphysical aspects of London's history and more open to London's lost voices: 'I sit here above the city feeling it breathe round me in the dark and the ether even more full of radio chatter than it used to be' (*C* 69). Indeed, as the narrative progresses towards supercession of the dialectic, the

Lecturer takes Meepers into his home, and, after the latter's dissolution, quits the securities of his job for a move to Africa. Duffy's text in fact suggests that 'history' repeats itself in a dramatised form in which master and slave have chosen, or have been allocated, their parts, and she is more interested in the possibilities of this artificial dialectic as a means of unstitching *both* points of view. The shrewdness of Duffy's text presents us with a logic that is just as paradoxical as it is problematic: as a response to national decline Meepers's narrative appears to be merely another form of denial of Britain's crisis as his thesis merely seeks to restore another linear narrative. Meepers's desire for historical continuity is, paradoxically, also driven by a spirit of progress potentially just as regressive and dangerous as imperial history.

This is why Julian Wolfreys's assessment of *Capital* as a postmodern critique of 'an amnesiac present' is an overly sweeping statement: just as IRA members 'clamour to be allowed to destroy ourselves in the name of some mythical freedom' (*L* 207), we have not forgotten history but we remember the wrong narratives and lose mythical vision.[11] Wolfreys also argues that the alternative London histories are 'the narrative staging of structural anachrony, no one moment is privileged, while implicitly every instance of the city's time is immanent with every other'.[12] This paraphrases, however, the intellectual crisis introduced by the Lecturer's historical relativity, which represses the Other through a reductive process of epistemological equalisation that the novel attempts to counter.

Duffy's text reinscribes the underclass Other into London's history through carefully structured, ironic juxtapositions and strategic subversions. Meepers's project undermines, or proposes an alternative model for, the Lecturer's certainty of knowledge, and introduces a potential rejection of the presumed incorrigibility of the Cartesian image of consciousness and the hierarchical ordering of knowledge established by the Enlightenment project, which proposes that we can know the world through rational observation and the collection and interpretation of facts. In the academic's consciousness, this leads to a crisis of the modern self that is projected onto London:

> I suddenly saw the city as a series of anonymous concentric rings that reach further and further from the centre point which is always the I or in childhood me: department, faculty, college, university, city, each increasing the depth of anonymity and isolation, wrapping the gauze layers tighter and tighter until all sound and sensation are padded away. Only the eyes are left free to blink and water as they stare at a world that they can't make meaning of by themselves. (*C* 93)

This geometric model of the self in relationship to the city harks back to Dante's vision of hell as a version of Rome in *Inferno* (1314) – the model that Duffy uses as the blueprint for the structure of *Londoners*. It was Joyce who translated Dante's model into modernity. *A Portrait*'s young Stephen is still submitted to the imperial pedagogy which has its roots in subject-centred analysis that teaches him to conceive his identity according to 'rational' geographical terms:

> *Stephen Dedalus*
> *Class of Elements*
> *Clongowes Wood College*
> *Sallins*
> *County Kildare*
> *Ireland*
> *Europe*
> *The World*
> *The Universe*[13]

In Joyce's novel, the nation initially functions as the most important meaning-giving structure within the citizens' consciousness. *Ulysses* triggers a questioning of history, as his growing awareness of English dominance over historical narratives causes an embrace to the uncertainty of the possible that classical mythologies and repressed periods (such as the Dark Ages) offer. Stephen's subversion lies in his reversal of priority in the relationship between the actual and the possible, so that mastery over the (fictional) world can be recovered by harnessing myth into a framework that recovers meaning *outside* the nation. Joyce's work criticises the pedagogical strategies employed by the state, which also leads to the Lecturer's identity crisis in *Capital*. The collapse of empire manifests itself in a process of economic and cultural marginalisation that triggers a revisioning of past master narratives and a reinscription of alternative, micro-narratives, which is Meepers's project.[14]

Duffy's interest in a mythological understanding of man as an evolution outside historical time is captured in five parts into which the novel is divided – The City of the Dead, New Troy, *Respublica Londiniensis*, Babylon, Cockaigne – which all refer to the various mythological contexts of the Capital. These titles suggest that London's official history and knowledge are subsumed and transcended by unofficial, mythological knowledge, making it seem that the novel offers the reader the choice to either succumb to apocalyptic visions of decline or to redeploy the mythological imagination in order to work against the official models of History. Yet Duffy is also distrustful of mythologies as she explains in her history of England: 'Because our sense of ourselves has been mythically constructed element by element over the centuries and is now seen to be receding further from our present, we are susceptible to even suggestions that seem to threaten its fragile image even further.'[15]

The opening up to alternative possibilities and a reinvention of England after empire is only possible because the protagonists have lost their sense of Englishness: the destruction of ego, as symbolic of imperial power, opens up their vision to alternative versions of history into a linguistic space that connects actuality with possibility through a form of slippage that creates room for imaginative rewritings in which established visions of history may be 'Othered'. For instance, the skull fragment of 'Swanscombe Man' (*C* 25), evidencing the presence of a nomadic tribe of hunters who lived in temporary shelter along the Thames a quarter of a million years ago, 'was probably a woman aged about twenty-five' (*C* 21), who died giving birth.[16] *Capital* criticises the historical tendency to think of time and space in masculine terms, while repressing a female contribution to the shaping of civilisation. The inclusion of the gang-raped prostitute Flower de Luce who starts her own 'business as a bawd' (*C* 143), a cross-dressing King Elizabeth I (*C* 158–60) and lower-class fancy-man who sponges off rich women to achieve a middle-class status (*C* 175–6), makes *Capital* an imaginary collection of anecdotal, incidental micro-narratives, history in 'drag', which corrects official memory by performing gender and class impersonations in fiction.

The novel's complex structure is captured well by Lyndie Brimstone when she notes that *Capital* is 'a five-act drama [...] subdivided into three rotating sections' in which the contemporary narrative about an amateur archaeologist and his 'official' Double, who writes letters to his lover, is interspersed with stories that voice London's history chronologically.[17] At the level of form, then, the novel gives us a complex, and contradictory image of history, with a curious blending of linear, deterministic visions working against the organic model of historical cyclicity that we find in the work of hypercanonic modernists such as Yeats and Joyce, who derived their analysis from the historical work of Giambattista Vico. This image of rotation is important as it implicitly introduces gender into this movement. Whereas male writers are often concerned with a penetrating digging motion that descends into Mother Earth, female writers are seeking liberation to uncover them from the layers of male narratives by digging towards the surface.[18] Rather than indulging in a regressing descent and apocalyptic rhetoric that literally buries its head in the soil, *Capital* is climbing up through time, yielding a fruitful and progressive ascent through history towards the present.

London *avant la lettre*

This image of rotation can also be translated into a circulatory model of money and language. During a lecture on the South Sea Bubble – the South Sea Company's disastrous trade adventures in South America that led to a stock market crash at the beginning of the eighteenth century – Meepers explains how the circulation of money was complicit to this process:

> Coin came to symbolize not only the things but their relationship to each other and then relationships between people through whose hands it passed. Because it is a symbol not a reality money can be inflated or depressed not only by realities like famine or a rich harvest but by illusions, imagination, falls in confidence, alarms, jobbery. (*C* 70)

The result, as one student notes, is as follows: '"That's crazy; that's losing touch with all reality"' (*C* 70). The Lecturer explains 'the whole mad bingo of it' via the image of 'a wheel for perpetual motion' (*C* 71), which is also how *Capital* functions, structurally, but it also forms a comment upon money's importance in shaping the life of the city.

Capital connects the circulation of money to language, discourse and literature as forms of representation which mediate and manipulate 'the real'. The 'historical' sections are deliberate inventions because they are written within the mode of realism. Consider the following passage, in which a Neanderthal roams the place that is, quite literally, London *avant la lettre*:

> Neanderthalensis stood shivering in Whitehall. [...] As he moved up towards Piccadilly he pulled handfuls of black crowberry fruits and stuffed them into his mouth. [...] He must be as sparing with his food as he could. At the corner of Glasshouse Street on the site of the Regent Palace Hotel he paused [...] A few feet below, the sharp handaxes of millennia before lay quietly together on a bed of London clay [...] His slightly bent stance made it easier to lope along than to walk and he was soon at Hyde Park. He climbed the heights of Kensington for a better view. (*C* 26–7)

The story we get here is, strictly speaking, narratologically incorrect: the convergence of this premodern 'Londoner' in as yet uncreated places, whose names were thousands of years from being invented, is temporally untenable; the third-person indirect discourse used to narrate is a contemporary diction. In fact, the very idea that language is used to narrate this episode is 'impossible' in the first place.[19] We cannot know the Neanderthal's experience of consciousness, and a pastiche would render an incoherent jumble of pre-linguistic rubble that misrepresents him.

Duffy's 'translation' is illuminating for a number of reasons. The topographical naming of future London sites is ironical because it exposes how language itself is implicated in the creation of history, a process that is profoundly political. 'Whitehall' is not merely a name for the collective buildings of British government, but, like London Stone, a sign that conveys political power and authority derived from an imperial heritage. By inserting this name into a prehistory where it has no(t yet any) meaning, the name's mythical constellation of significance is defused, making it clear that it is the connection between place and name that creates power. Simultaneously, connoting this lexeme with an illiterate barbarian indicts the institutions that house political power for preferring and promoting particular discourses and the censorship that keeps the ideological centre intact.

As a 'custodian of the dead' (C 117), Meepers brings back the apocryphal narratives of marginalised Londoners throughout history in deliberately 'counterfeit' writing that somehow forms a truthful re-reading of London's history. Meepers works against specific myths by using fiction as a kind of solvent that works against clichés and stereotypes. *Capital* is a humanist novel that advocates the accessibility of the past through an imaginative and counterfactual interpretation of historical (arte)facts. This performance does not take place, as Bode claims, in the form of 'pastiches [that evoke] the past [...] as an *aesthetic* experience'.[20] Meepers is not a ventriloquist's dummy who channels voices from the past into the present in Ackroydian mode, as the third-person narration and the contemporary vocabulary indicate. And unlike Iain Sinclair, Duffy avoids using mystic speech by giving us third-person narratives that aim for an authenticity that Sinclair's fiction denies. Rather than oral communication the reader is given *written* documents as the verbal level is too indirect, too volatile for Meepers, whose desire for London's continuity needs to be made alive through the magical and creative act of writing.

This is an indication of Duffy's trust in writing's capacity to convey knowledge and to evoke epiphanic moments, which offers literature as the space where possible survival is rehearsed. *Capital* shows that literature as an archaeological site of literary excavation is able to contain a palimpsest of history, as this passage demonstrates:

Once again he was stowed in the back of a police car with a claustrophobic presence beside him but now whirled back towards the city walls, along the Roman road that lay vibrating under the modern tarmac skin of the burning tyres, over Llugh's river, by the bowed bridge past the abbey where bony prioresses lisped in provincial French to their lapdogs, through vanished Aldgate and the blizzard ash and flame of a thousand fires long out, by cheapened London Bridge broken down for ever, with the chunk of red Samian invisible in the bag yet warming him like a ruby. (*C* 148)

Capital creates what Richard Lehan calls 'an archaeological realm of layered reality',[21] but what makes Duffy's palimpsest especially interesting is its interest in periods, such as the Dark Ages, which other writers find 'boring', uncomfortable or inaccessible.[22] Duffy brings these forgotten and repressed periods back by injecting these lost narratives into London's fictional bloodstream, and in doing so her novel undercuts versions of history which were soon to be brought back by Thatcher.

Grave new world: *Londoners* (1983)

In *Londoners: An Elegy* (1983) social circumstances and the identity crisis of *Capital* are even worse. England is 'still the sick man of Europe' and its citizens 'are none of us in very good health now' (*L* 12). The crisis is embodied by Al, a freelance writer and an idealistic 'philosopher-in-residence for Earl's Court' (*L* 95) worn down in the service of the city. Al, we surmise, is short for 'Albion' – mythical England – suggesting that he stands for an England coming to term with its diminished status and position on the global map on which it only recently features centrally. Originally, Al is of working-class origins – '"Shit to that," I hear myself gearing automatically into demotic, speaking in my mother tongue' (*L* 68) – but he now finds himself entangled in a middle-class world of publishing under pressure of market forces that impose censorship on his radicalism. His frustration is drowned in various pubs, with the resulting inebriation adding to his apocalyptic mindset.

Al is engaged in a dialogue with his Double, the medieval French poet François Villon (1431–?) whose biography Al is writing. Villon is an archetypal representative of the criminal, rag-picking underclass.

Born in Paris in 1431, educated at the Sorbonne but often an associate of criminals, Villon was charged in 1455 with killing a priest but acquitted on the grounds of self-defence. After stealing from the College of Navarre, he left Paris and wandered for several years. He was imprisoned again, and returned to Paris where he ran into more trouble with the law and had his death sentence commuted to being exiled from Paris after which written traces cease. The phrase from his classic poem, *La lait* (1455(6?), translated as *The Legacy*), 'où sont les neiges d'antan?' – where are yesteryears' snows? – echoes throughout the novel, coming to haunt Great Britain by contextualising the melting away of its glorious, imperial past. Al refers to Villon as his 'master' (*L* e.g. 16, 48, 67); Al addresses Villon in the second person, creating a curious 'you', which has a profoundly unsettling effect upon the reader, who is asked to bridge the gap between the isolated first-person narrator, and the radically different addressee. This is another intimation of Duffy's dialectical play, which affirms that the French poet is a vehicle for identification, and for displacement of the self. The Double signals an inner conflict in which 'the double sets out to steal the identity of the original and degrade him to the status of *his* (shadow's) shadow'.[23]

Al finds himself exiled within his own city, spiritually homeless: 'you get indoors, for that's what it is, home being, as they say, where the heart, that clapped-out, clapped in a barrel organ is' (*L* 9). Al rents a bedsit in a house with expats such as the Germans Wolfgang and Hannelore, the French Léonie and the African Jemal, and he feels that these 'outsiders', some of whom are making a fortune in the City, have invaded and cannibalised 'his' Earl's Court, which was once 'full of commonwealth Aussies and Kiwis, [but] now it's new oil that greases its turning wheels' (*L* 34):

> I've become as much a stranger as Jemal or Wolfgang, more because they don't expect to be at home in my native city. They are the true Londoners, denizens of the cosmopolis. My hometown was danced away around a VJ bonfire while yesterday's snows turned to slush and piddled off down the drain [...] For it's gone. As I lie here with the house like an archaeological site staged above me I know my dad, sharp as he was, would barely recognise this grave new world. Does it matter that we make dreams that only half come true, that are sea-changed in the dreaming and making, so looking back we hardly recognize the country we plotted, and would hate to arrive there, since we're no longer the same people who set out and our dreamland changes as we walk? (*L* 23)

The reader becomes aware of a rhetorical doubleness in Al's narration. We find an elegiac tone which suggests that Al is dispossessed of London, which, genealogically speaking, he owns through his father. The house, originally a symbol of psychological unity, becomes a dystopian image that suggests a fragmented capital where people no longer make their home; London has become a non-place for transients. The play with the title of Aldous Huxley's *Brave New World* (1932) reinforces the dystopian rhetoric.

Yet, embedded within Al's lamentation we find references deriving from his English literary heritage, which is offered to the reader as a way of questioning the surface of Al's elegy. The reference to 'the country we plotted' stresses nationhood as a narrative construct, which subverts regressive emotions and fantasies about a mythical past. If we return to the original context of Huxley's title we find that Miranda's utopian exclamation 'How beauteous mankind is! O brave new world / That has such people in't!' in Shakespeare's *The Tempest* carries tenor. The second reference to Shakespeare's play, Ariel's famous song sung to Ferdinand about his supposedly dead father suffering 'a sea-change / Into something rich and strange', again carries a utopian note that mocks and inverts Al's elegy.[24]

Figure 5 The Theatre, Shoreditch

This analysis fits in with the early post-colonial response to *The Tempest*, such as George Lamming's classic *The Pleasures of Exile* (1960), which plays off the utopian rhetoric against its dystopian counterpart through a double narrative process of reading and counter-reading. The following passage underscores Al's awareness of the irony of the socio-political and cultural changes in the changing demographic of post-imperial London:

> They [immigrants] come and take our jobs and our women or rather our women take them and we give them the jobs the English won't do and the shops that can only pay of a whole extended family, grannies and wetback cousins, arranged spouses and multitudinous winnings, willing small boys work them from ten to ten every day, an eighty-hour week. And they have colonised our imagination and our literature. Perhaps I should write a study: *The Impact of the Indian Sub-Continent on English Literature. Part One: The Conquerors. Part Two: Two-way traffic in Contemporary Writing.* (L 31)

Al starts off with the racist clichés spawned by the tabloid press but his self-awareness forces a U-turn so that the passage becomes dominated by a sense of ironic reversal. This underlines the thought that gender, class and sentiments such as nationalism are dependent upon contingency and primarily performative, and therefore a false enactment of self. Duffy also stresses the fertility of cultural and literary miscegenation that, as the novel's revision of myth suggests, has been part of British history. Shakespeare is, first and foremost, an author representative of a European rather than English tradition, and his work is characterised by openness of dynamic connectivity rather than the narrowness of retrospection. Claire Colebrook aptly notes that 'his works do not offer a unified image of man, or even a unified image of Shakespeare. His texts are more like question marks, with each production or reading raising new questions.'[25] This, again, is the doubt and speculation that Duffy's work so fruitfully exploits.

The colonial repressed have returned to haunt the former imperial centre, making *Londoners* a post-colonial fiction which traces the impact upon the ideological centre. Duffy reminds us that Huxley used *The Tempest* as an intertext for *Brave New World* (1932); and it is thus used ambiguously by Duffy because it points overtly to the dramatisation of his suffering on Al's part. The ambiguity lies also in the fact that Duffy uses Shakespeare not only in a dystopian manner but also in a utopian context. It is not just the repressed colonial Other that has returned, but, as Duffy's use of 'cosmopolis' suggests, representatives from all over the world are present in London, turning the city into a newly emerging internationalist, cosmopolitan world driven by commerce and business, and it is here that Duffy connects with Salman Rushdie's triumphant, optimistic sense of possibility.

Londoners points out, however, that this version of cosmopolitanism is a narrow one, based merely on financial opportunism rather than the one based on collective civic and cultural responsibility which emerged in the work of continental thinkers and writers such as Johann Wolfgang Goethe (1749–1832), who envisaged a World Literature as an imaginative space that opposed the über-rationalised life within modernity, but which also functioned as a means to overcome the unstoppable cultural fragmentation that would take place when making a national literature unrepresentative. We find this alternative cosmopolitan model of Goethe in Al's friend and rival, Goetzle, a Jewish refugee who fled Nazi Germany and established the publishing house Handyside Press, who has gone on to achieve a stellar political career by inventing a new party for post-imperial Britain – he 'might become Prime Minister' (*L* 54), anticipating Ian McEwan's Charles Darke in *The Child in Time* (1987). Al nicknames him 'Guzzle' for his gluttony – he 'is Johnsonian in his girth and by extension in his speech' (*L* 50). Duffy offers Guzzle as an immigrant model that shows at once the nature of the new postmodern world that is emerging in the post-war period whilst also giving us an image of the strategy of adaptation that will ensure the city's survival:

> He is adaptable, a survivor; I am a dodo. My roots are too deep in my childish past, that backward tap root that sucks up the nourishment I write on. Guzzle's are shallow, quick to take over a patch of waste and run in all directions because he has no childhood to betray. That's why the new party will be made from the free floaters who either want to forget or who have never known. I see it as a logical evolution as fewer and fewer have our lost times to remember, and still I can't. (*L* 54)

Al is highly critical of the post-ideological, a-historical Britain of non-committed opportunistic politicians that emerges in the late seventies and early eighties, which creates the vacuum that Thatcher occupies.

Londoners' interest in making connections expresses itself in three distinct forms of literary linkage: intertextuality; iconic figures of literary and cultural history; and literary models that work against a new city whose '[t]opography is the lowest and dimmest circle of this limbo' (*L* 38).

We find the obsessive naming of disappearing, iconic English shops and brands, such as the 'M.G. car' (*L* 40), as the following criticism of globalisation's standardising effects suggests. Al observes street façades with ubiquitous household names of national chains such as Litebite, Jean Machine and Tesco, which 'give us all the fine tunings of infinite capitalist choice' (*L* 225): 'In every minopolis in the land we can buy the same spectrum of breakfast goods and shoes. All the crafts have vanished that made a small difference in our possessions if we were lucky to have any' (*L* 225). This is, again, an ambiguous passage: the process of democratisation has made the material world available to everyone, at the expense of a watered-down identity. In its stead *Londoners* creates an incredibly dense network of intertextual connections and references ranging from Brahms (*L* 14) and Thomas Edison (*L* 14) to Berthold Brecht (*L* 15, 181) and Pier Pasolini (*L* 152).[26] Bode draws our attention to the polyphonic and heteroglossic effect of these sources, and stresses Duffy's representation of 'London as a *literary topos*, a construct of texts, languages, voices, quotations and allusions'.[27]

On another level we find the names of the pubs – a central ordering device in Moorcock's *Mother London* as well – which Al frequents to drown his sorrows and to seek companionship: The Nevern; The Henniker Arms (nicknamed the Knackers and Knickers); and The Fusiliers. Duffy appears to set up a dichotomy between the official world of money and politics and the unofficial, and distinctly local sphere of literature and the pub; as Wolfreys states, '[a]gainst the fact of capitalism and its simultaneous dominance over the city and its imposition of anonymity on its workers is the memory of the City's poets'.[28] Doris Teske introduces a shrewd ambiguity, however:

> Al moves between the different points in the city and in doing so creates a network. These points have fixed functions in the system of the city, they represent the administrative unity of the city [...] but also the cultural and social identity of the metropolis [...] Parallel to the official city, which is made into a system by the exertion of power, stands the public, informal city of pubs, which is permeated by the desire for love, but which, similar to the official city, is subordinate to the reality of the market.[29]

Although '[t]he pub is open to anyone' (*L* 77), the system of pubs does not actually provide an alternative to the official world of London because it is inextricably intertwined with the official economy, which is why Al's local pub, The Nevern, becomes an IRA target. Its visitors are part of a British economy that suppresses the Irish, a continuation of empire. The point of this tension between Wolfreys's idealist and Teske's realist reading is that they occupy two sides of the double rhetoric of *Londoners*. As a freelancer, Al is to a certain degree involved in a capitalist system that enacts a pernicious form of censorship to maintain the socio-political and moral status quo. Yet, this involvement is necessary for the writer's position as not wholly divorced from the public realm. This makes Duffy's work inclusive rather than divisive: 'I once breakfasted with an American editor on his way to the Frankfurt Book Fair where authors are bought and sold' (*L* 35). Thus, although the network of pubs and public spaces is interwoven into the fabric of society, it *cannot* represent an alternative, democratic system outside the official one that is present in the imagination of the people. Indeed, a binary opposition between the arts and money has been relinquished as Al well knows when he considers setting 'a little academic booby-trap by always writing in old money. *Footnote: We have been unable to discover the significance is of what, as we have seen, is a consistent anomaly in this writer's work.* I shall be known as the master of old minting, except that we don't get titles like *maestro* for word-spinning' (*L* 10). This awareness is also present in Al's attitude to Villon: there is an attempt to get Al a radio script, but this involves compromising his (private) personal feelings about the real value of Villon (and the paraphrasing of the c-word (*L* 28)[30]). When Al's story is taken up by the famous film maker Larry Lofts, Al is first asked for 'small' changes, including the change of Villon's Christian name to 'Frank' because 'François's unpronounceable in English' (*L* 181), after which the idea is taken from him without any credit. The narrative's doubleness is resolved by the suggested compromise at the novel's ending, which suggests that in order for Al, and London, to survive, it is adaptation to the new circumstances rather than a regressive stance that will ensure their survival.

We find an even more sustained form of literary exchange in the French connection, which offers another source of cosmopolitanism that potentially counters the narrow cosmopolitanism of late capital: 'Villon is a folk figure, part of European culture. Now we are in the Common Market' (*L* 14), suggesting, perhaps ironically, that England has become less isolated after joining the European Economic Community a decade earlier in 1973. The connection between London and Paris is established by Al, who sees 'the Paris of Joan of Arc and the London of Marie Lloyd as one eternal city' (*L* 15) established through intertextual references. One character, David, asks why the Proustian moustache has come back into fashion: '"It's our search for a lost time," he suggests. "Cheers! Or as the fashionable cant has it: for a cultural identity"' (*L* 43).

The Proustian connection manifests itself in the tone of Al's confessional voice, but the text's attitude to Proust's monumental works of memory actually warns the reader against conservatism and false acts of cultural resurrection. Duffy's text wittily emphasises the problems of writing history, because of its tendency towards male-dominated narration and an enforced amnesia that allows particular narratives to mythologise a nation's past. The importance of the relationship between London and Paris is re-emphasised in the following excerpt, where Parisian mythic *topoi* are constructed through art, culture and narrative:

> Victoria is always that first trip abroad [...], the first escape from England, home and duty. [...] That journey was a true magic first with the pain of the third-class slatted benches all part of the pleasure [...] And then at Paris you stepped out into the Gare du Nord and that palpable smell of coffee, gauloises [sic], garlic that was as exotic as a houri [...] I don't know whether that Paris of the imagination ever really existed or was fabricked out of literature and myth: Abelard, Baudelaire, Les Impressionistes, Jean Gabin, Simone de Beauvoir and *Bless the Bride* and of course you, my master. I knew it was the place to play poet in or painter. (*L* 96–7)

It is the long-standing imaginary offered by Paris and its various cultural associations that is important for Britain's survival. It offers both an exotic Other, but also a profoundly cultured and diverse community, as the inclusive listing suggests. It also pinpoints an important lesson about urban life itself: it is both a place of overwhelming materiality, but also an imaginary stage that presents us with the opportunity to perform and fictionalise our identity.

The Parisian connection also chimes in with Duffy's ongoing dialogue with Joyce. The reference to 'England, home and duty' can be compared to the sailor, W. B. Murphy, who in *Ulysses* quotes the crippled beggar who states: '*For England, home and beauty*.'[31] Duffy's version becomes a rhyming parody of 'duty' and ridicules the narratives of writers who work in service of and sacrifice for a nation that occurs in the imagination. In 'Scylla and Charybdis', the ninth chapter of *Ulysses*, which is set in the library where Stephen discusses Shakespeare's work, Dedalus states that 'Elizabethan London lay as far from Stratford as corrupt Paris lies from virgin Dublin.'[32] This ambiguously emphasises both the geographical distance between the cities, but also the connections between the two capitals. Whereas Joyce saw connections between Mediterranean and Irish culture, Duffy explores how London has come about as a historico-literary palimpsest of transnational textualities. Another French connection lies in the various types of urban walker that the French capital has contributed to our collective cultural history. In Al's network of intertextual references that preconditions his experience of London it is the elegiac mode and the lyrical, splenetic tone of Baudelaire's *The Flowers of Evil* (1857) that plays a clear part. As with Meepers, Al is not quite the Baudelairian *flâneur*, but he appears to act as the rag-picker we find in the work of Walter Benjamin, who based 'his influential surrealist methodology in a range of epistemological and scopic metaphors of which the paradigms are the bourgeois *flâneur* and his vagrant counterpart the rag-picker'.[33] During the journeys, Al points out the phantasmagoric qualities of London that can be used as a means of recoding and reordering the city. Lorries and cars turn into a white water and the city streets become tall cliff façades until Al finds himself opposite a grey and grimy High Anglican church which carries on 'the faith of the Rev. Eliot, Stern Thomas in a cloud of self-conscious incense' (*L* 102). Such hallucinatory mappings enable Al to work against his overly self-aware consciousness, as the jocular reference to Eliot suggests, whilst allowing him to restore a renewed communal self. Thus, Al is a double, cross-cultural construction, whose language is that of the lyrical, splenetic *flâneur* with a desire for a romanticised, semi-pastoral past, whilst being on the brink of becoming a semi-nomadic, literary rag-picker. It is this curious tension which makes him a powerful enactor of counter-surveillance that challenges the power structures invisibly embedded within the city by establishing a cartography of human interconnectedness.

A final literary connection we find in the chapterisation of the novel. *Londoners* takes its ulterior symbolic organisation behind the literal organisation from the thirty-four cantos of Dante's *Inferno*, and Al is a Dante of sorts with Villon in the role of Virgil: 'You take me by the hand and lead me up into the street again' (*L* 25); and 'My guide leaves me' (*L* 27). Like Joyce before her, Duffy takes on a formal restraint that symbolises Joyce's idea of a particular version of history as nightmare from which Stephen is trying to wake up by forging an alternative one. Al has exiled himself from the nightmarish material world into the utopian world of texts in which Albion's destiny can be manipulated and rewritten. Similar to the way that Dante fictionalises corrupt officials and papal cronies such as Boniface, Forese Donati and his brother Corso, with each cosmic ring indicating a degree of evil, Duffy fictionalises corrupt politicians endangering London's social fabric, mass media and publishers refusing cooperation or imposing censorship.

A special rung is reserved for a local mayor who has cunningly orchestrated the destruction of Cartwright Hall 'before the preservation order could be delivered' (*L* 163). When Al is taken to a council meeting by his friend Rick, who is protesting against this move, this corruption is satisfied in the description of the newly erected seat of government, 'council city, the huge red brick and glass complex that's our new monument to civic pride with its courtyard and fountains' (*L* 164) whilst the 'councillor chamber is modelled on a Greek theatre with the mayor presiding from the stage, the actors in the audience and the few spectators barred up high in a harem gallery, impotently mute' (*L* 165). Similarly, the mayor is satirised:

> Her Worship has crinkly permed hair and a jut of bosom broad enough to display the second best mayoral chain. She is the pantomime dame, drag mother, despised by Rick and the Lysistrahod alike, yet I know she will stand in front of the mirror in the mayor's parlour patting nervously at the crimped blue waves, saying, 'Is me hair tidy?' and longing for a piece of bread an honey. (*L* 165)

This description anticipates Iain Sinclair's parody of Thatcher, The Widow, in *Downriver*. The original source here is Juvenal's sixth Satire: 'Tell me, you noble ladies, / Scions of our great statesmen – Lepidus, blind Metellus, Fabius the Guzzler – what gladiator's woman / Ever rigged herself out like this, or sweated at fencing-drill?'[34] The mayor's and Guzzle's punishment for their corruption upon London's citizens is banishment to Duffy's fictional hell, whilst pointing us to the novel's politics of gender and the city.

London is androgynous: all things to all men, and women too

Londoners also demonstrates how changing notions of gender and sexuality reshape the image of the city. Traditionally, London has been conceived of as a (with a now outdated word) 'male-dominated' space; the professional spaces of the metropolis that have been reserved for men – from bankers to bus conductors and publicans to politicians.[35] In ideological terms, London has been the Master-Signifier, representing the white, male, Christian ruling classes. Despite suffrage, two world wars (which tended to reinforce rather than dismantle gender stereotypes) and the feminist 'revolutions' of the 1960s and beyond, the actual perceptions of gender were and are in reality quite slow to change.

In an early poem, 'A Woman's World' (1975), Duffy captures this London aptly when she states that 'London's a world away where husbands act / A mystical ritual of grave affairs'.[36] Al's central characteristic is the absence or uncertainty of gender-specificity. Bode aptly states that 'the whole novel is written in such a way that we can never know Al's gender' and that Al's name tricks the reader into assuming he is a man whose identity has come under erasure, ensuring that 'the text continually exposes and highlights our seemingly [sic] ineradicable tendency to see others in terms of gender instead of seeing them just as human beings'.[37] Yet, our inability to define Al in gendered terms also suggests that *Londoners* posits that, at least for men, the decline of empire is experienced as a form of both emasculation and infantilisation:

> It makes me suddenly wonder what sex London is. Other languages have to sex their capitals because of their own primitive genders but in any case there's no doubt. Paris is female, so's Vienna; Berlin is masculine, Rome feminine. London is androgynous: all things to all men, and women too. We make our choice, make her in the image we need to love or hate. (*L* 88)

This description suggests that Al's symbolic emasculation translates into the potency of doubt that is the creative dynamo behind *Capital* as well, and it anticipates the necessity of a renewed flexibility, an openness of identity that allows for reinvention and reinscription of the Other into the unravelling, or, renegotiated, traditional social fabric.

Duffy's vision of London's androgyny sits within a long tradition in cultural history, but Virginia Woolf's ideas on androgyny in *A Room of One's Own* (1929) are particularly pertinent to Duffy's novel. In chapter six, Woolf speaks of 'a sudden splitting off of consciousness' when a woman walks down Whitehall, a corridor of male power, and she constructs the theory that 'in each of us two powers preside, one male, one female, and in the man's brain' and that the 'normal and comfortable state of being is that when the two live in harmony together'.[38]

Duffy's text suggests that the historical dichotomy in representations of gender (both biological and psychological) is too simple, and her novel sets out to disrupt ideas about both masculinity and femininity by foregrounding a logic that emphasises the performative aspects of gender and urban life. Steve Inwood reminds us that Agricola's establishment of 'civitas' and empire in Roman London occurred through the building of temples, public squares and private mansions, by promotion of the liberal arts and, in particular, by promoting a specific manner of dress, and Agricola knew his civilising ploys had struck root when his Londinium subjects started wearing togas.[39] When Al visits a gay bar he sees a show by a group of transvestites called *The Cockettes*, whose name and performance renders an ambivalent image:

> In the voice of Vera Lynn they proclaim that there'll always be an England. From the back wall where we haven't noticed them leaning until now, they fetch and unfurl union jacks against their dark blue gowns. Then they march and countermarch with them, pomp and circumstance. I look round and see a few lips framing the words.
>
> *'Land of hope and glory, mother of the fee...'* [...]
>
> Does nobody else see any ambivalence in this double parody of Mother England that drags at the emotions and lifts her skirts to show the hairy thighs ... (*L* 190–1)

Here the lexeme 'drag' is exploited by Duffy, with the noun pointing to the actual act of men dressing up, whilst the verb also points to the way in which the act transforms gender by impersonation, while combining it with the nostalgia evoked by Vera Lynn as the nation's Mother for double ideological effect. Angela Carter points out, for instance, that placing the Union Jack in a different context makes Britain's 'national symbol into an abstraction' from where it can be renegotiated: England is defetishised, unmanned, secularised.[40] The Oedipal crisis that underlies Freud's irrational models of human psychology is mocked by Duffy's inclusion of this hybrid image.[41] Duffy's text is destroying the illusory purity of class, gender and nation identities by means of transgressive images.

Yet the persistence of comfortable stereotypes is strong. When Al returns to London on a train after a job interview for a position as writer-in-residence at Churchdown College (*L* 231) outside the city, he notes that London begins to draw round him, running up against the windows just as it did when he was a child coming home for a holiday from evacuation in a lull in the bombing: 'It will always be there, great nurse, grand mother. The tracks cross and run as though they were moving live things and we still' (*L* 232). Although his vision of the city has become less dark and despondent, his return to the city as mother trope shows that he has forgotten the Cockettes' lessons in transgression. Duffy is aware that radical change is not effected by writing. Although conventional forms of language uphold the history of power relations in which men have always a privileged position, this situation will not be changed by only a revolution in language.

It is the bomb attack by the IRA on The Nevern which propels Al into a new career as a teacher of creative writing, outside London. It is only the violence of the explosion which, nearly killing him, awakens him by reviving him from his stupor and spurs his sensory system into reconnecting with the material world and its realities. Stumbling through the ruins of the pub Al thinks: 'I'm not blind am I? [...] Is this how it felt when the gaoler turned the key and let you out? I'm all right. I'm going to be all right' (*L* 240). Al and Albion's regeneration occur through a sensory and ideological liberation that lies in the act of seeing, the remapping of society from which the new communal self can be forged.

This violent ending is tied in with the Blitz mythology established in *That's How It Was*: 'I smell again the unforgettable, unforgotten from childhood mixture of mortar and explosive that clings to the skin and coats the mouth and nasal passages for days' (*L* 240). By evoking the violence of the Blitz, the text creates both the sense that a major shift is taking place within traditional forms of thinking about London, but also that there is a sense of continuity with London's history and traditions. Duffy's work does not deny that the demise of working-class Londoners is a process that is to be left uncommented or unmourned. This shift is certainly traumatic, yet she offers an alternative response to the apocalyptic narratives of Martin Amis and Iain Sinclair. Duffy's writing leaves room for optimism, which opens up the space needed for the new voices to manifest themselves. Liberation and reinvention can be found in people's performativity: whether it is the enactment of the rag-picker who collects an alternative London encyclopaedia, or the artificial enactment of sexuality. Most of all, Duffy's work forms a defence of the necessity of writing and reading London: writing forms representative organs that chronicle the wounds of history, from which important lessons may be drawn. Her own representational forums bring together the many, disparate voices, which create a cartography that is inclusive and open to reinscription: 'The sky's cleared and there are stars. They seem to be laughing, And I'm laughing too' (*L* 240). This realisation gives rise to a cathartic ending that resounds with a laugher that undermines regressive mythologies of loss and which celebrates 'a people conservative yet changeable' (*L* 48).

2
'Of Real Experience Mixed with Myth': Michael Moorcock's Authentic London Myths

My good old London mob

Michael Moorcock's London novels *Mother London* (1988) and *King of the City* (2000)[1] investigate the city's histories and mythologies in order to speculate about the city's past and future, but Moorcock harnesses the form and subject matter of his novel to attack an enemy of apparently limitless power and remorseless ruthlessness in the present: Long Thatcherism. The following description gives us an image of Fleet Street just before the newspapers businesses' 1986 exodus to Wapping:

> There was still frost on Fleet Street's paving flags and the granite, the marble from grander days, the tile and Portland stone all sparkled, rimed as if touched by Ymyr in an ancient lay, and Joseph Kiss reflected on how northern myths had moulded this place making soft news hard and forging a bludgeon, creating cynics of boozy berserkers living as their spiritual ancestors had done by rape and robbery, by violence and dogged heartlessness, pouring daily ashore after a hard pull up some bitter river; but Sunday mornings were by and large free from press. Mr Kiss had longed for the predicted exodus to Wapping or even Southwark though these creatures religiously celebrated habit, mocked all change and feared it, naturally. (*ML* 465)

This passage is similar to Duffy's scene with the Neanderthal roaming prehistoric Whitehall in *Capital* and creates an analogy between London's invasion by the barbaric, pillaging Vikings invading England during the Dark Ages and the primitivism of a right-wing tabloid press promoting values of the Victorian era ('grander days'), which creates dangerous (racist, sexist, class-based) myths by making 'soft news' (gossip, opportunistic journalism) 'hard' (appear as fact), resulting in similar destructive, violent acts. Moorcock subtly embeds an even more sinister layer into the image by pointing out the Nordic mythology which was at the heart of Hitler's conception of fascism, with its belief in Aryan superiority and its drive for ethnic purity. Fleet Street is 'rimed', that is, not only covered in a frost that turns London temporarily into a Scandinavian city, but it is also 'rhymed', as city a site of textual and ideological contestation. We find London temporarily transformed by the imagery and prose of the city's poets, which is pitted against the moral degeneration and cultural decline instigated by Conservative forces, which threaten to turn London, as a symbol of man-made civilisation, into a producer and product of barbarism. This decline is indicated by Moorcock's contrasting of the stillness and sublime beauty of the image with the harshness of the content, suggesting a rupture between lived experience and its manipulation through representation. Whilst the tabloids revert to images and mores of the nineteenth century, Moorcock urges us to embrace change so we can see the present more clearly.

Moorcock's connection of the Victorian age with the present is continued in a short essay, 'Lost London Writers' (1999), which makes a similarly important point, this time stressing the dialogic relationship that exists between writing and society:

> In the last quarter of the nineteenth century, and thanks to the reforming efforts of her writers, London changed. The worst slums were cleared, public health improved and education was made universal. Authors emerged whose literary values were often shared with Wilde, Beerbohm and the *fin de siècle*, but whose work was driven by a more social conscience. They'd taken advantage of idealistic educational ventures like the People's Palace, the Normal School of Science, University College and the Birkbeck Institute, all set up to provide people without means a first-class education.[2]

Moorcock suggests that our ability to understand and transform ourselves and the world is dependent upon the way writers portray the city, and that the imagination has the power to effect real change within existent social relationships and the infrastructure, in the very way we live our lives. It is in this spirit of optimism, and with similar ambitions in mind, that Moorcock, together with numerous other London writers, is engaged in a similar project for contemporary London and Londoners under Long Thatcherism. There is a straightforward reason why this

similar creative outburst under Thatcher and the New Labour governments is necessary: 'Inequalities between London's poorest and richest
boroughs [...] were reminiscent of those identified by Charles Booth
100 years ago.'[3] The economic downturn during the 1980s caused a
social and demographic dislocation that created, in Roy Porter's words,
'a new outcast' caught in 'spirals of deprivation, alienation, despair,
and anti-social activities among a proliferation of a lumpenproletariat'.[4]
Collectively these writers make it their task to speak on behalf of what
Moorcock calls 'My good old London mob. Not lads. Not yobs. Not
bastards. Not a problem. Not the marginalized. Not the insane. Not the
desperate or the hungry, not the envious or the weak, not whingeing
professional victim: just outraged men and women with a strong sense
of how things should be' (*KC* 221).

Mother London, a central London novel that is the main object of focus
in this chapter, and *King of the City* form an inquest into an urban existence in a late twentieth-century Britain in which politicians meddle in
the personal and public lives of the populace in a way that is unprec-
edented. *Mother London* tells a version of London's history since the
outbreak of the Second World War as it is vocalised by three traumatised
protagonists: David Mummery, who is writing an alternative history of
London; the gargantuan gourmandiser Joseph Kiss, a struggling actor and
womaniser; and Mary Gasalee, who has become 'a legend all over North
London' (*ML* 438) after she miraculously escapes from a house bombed
during the Blitz. This visionary trio, called 'The Patients', all suffer from
mental trauma caused by their experiences of the Second World War,
and the novel's complex structure traces the ways in which London's
forgotten and alternative history and voices reverberate still in a city
under siege by Thatcherism. *King of the City* is narrated by the paparazzo
and rock guitarist Dennis Dover, whose post-Diana gonzo narrative
becomes a scathing criticism of the contemporary consumerism and
globalisation that are remaking the world, and London, irrevocably.
King of the City is less successful in its execution than *Mother London*
because the novel falls into some of the trappings of political writing –
for example, its criticisms are verbalised too directly and overtly – yet
it expresses perfectly the exuberance, but also the increasingly artificial
nature of life and culture under New Labour.

In these novels Moorcock deploys his fiction as an imaginative sponge
that constantly plays London's history against its rich and diverse
mythology in an effort to counter the myth-making machineries of the
government, mass media, commerce and organised religion. Just like
Maureen Duffy, Moorcock constructs textual Londons assembled from

the debris of the city's various narratives, and also stages wandering out-casts whose mnemonic mappings of alternative London cartographies are posited against 'official' narratives of London.

Given Moorcock's emphasis on morality it is tempting to rethink his position within the post-war literary canon. Rather than a mar-ginal, prolific writer and editor of science fiction and fantasy work, Moorcock's London novels can be recuperated within Leavisian terms. A staunch defender of the humanist tradition, F. R. Leavis maintained that the finest writers 'are significant in terms of the human awareness they promote; awareness of the possibilities of life'.[5] This is Moorcock's primary aim also: 'A vision is nothing without a moral imperative' (*KC* 228) states Dover, and Moorcock has praised a writer who appears to be far removed from his own novelistic practices, namely Emily Brontë, whose *Wuthering Heights* he admires because '[t]here is a genuine artistic perception in it, genuine understanding of how people relate to one another'.[6] As Iain Sinclair has noted, Moorcock's work has become more acceptably mainstream and has entered 'the official canon'.[7] Yet, the very attempt at finding a single framework with which to categorise and pigeonhole Moorcock's work is a misguided enterprise because his restless texts avail themselves of what one could term a 'nomadism of form', a restless, ever-shifting and paradigm-defying *modus operandi* that defies categorisation, which creates an elusiveness that guards fictional space and prevents his fictional narratives from regressing into myth. In an interview Moorcock states:

> Whatever my qualities as a writer, I am hard to pigeonhole. Critics who see me as 'sampling' different genres don't quite understand that I am not much interested in genres themselves, just what genres can offer me [...] I know I'm a bit of an academic's nightmare. Add to my various literary enthusiasms, my musical career and my career as an editor of a fairly wide variety of publications, and it's no surprise to me to hear that some researchers and writers have actually lost their sanity before they could finish their bibliographies of my stuff, let alone begun their theses.[8]

This chapter is a humble attempt at reading his London work in order to make some connections between the subject matter of Moorcock's novels and the nomadism of form at work within the works to show that this academic's nightmare presents us with London as a complex *bricolage*-city composed out 'of real experience mixed with myth' (*KC* 295).

Authentic myth versus mass media: London and the crisis of representation

The complexity of this relationship between 'the real' and myth is aptly captured by one of *Mother London*'s three protagonists, the 'urban anthropologist' (*ML* 5) David Mummery, who is asked if he is working on a novel. Mummery notes: 'I would tell him I was working on one but knew I had little leaning towards fiction, being too fascinated by the semi-fiction of Londoners' beliefs, by actual miracles such as my own and others close to me' (*ML* 482). Moorcock's London novels are also obsessed with exploring 'the semi-fiction of Londoners' beliefs', which the author, as I noted in the Introduction, calls 'authentic myth, more potent than fact'. Authentic myth evokes literary truth about human relationships situated in a particular physical environment and embedded in a specific historical reality. It represents truth that transcends the opposition between fact and fiction, because it lays bare idiosyncratic and geographically specific knowledge discovered in and produced by the writing of fiction. London's myths are not simply stories or urban legends, but they gain their strength by explaining, unofficially, how the city and its inhabitants have come to exist and survive. Moorcock's short story 'London Blood' (1997) opens as follows:

> There are certain memories that never really reach your brain. They stay in your blood like a dormant virus. Then something triggers them and you don't remember the moment; instead, you relive every detail. It's the reliving, not the original experience, that your brain registers.[9]

Authentic myth is not part of official, 'rational' history writing (indicated by 'brain'), but an unconscious, irrational knowledge that derives its power from effacing the boundary between fact and fiction. The passage also makes an interesting point about the narratological status of these memories: they are never original, but always represented, narrated, mediated. In *The Savage Mind* (1962), Claude Lévi-Strauss reminds us that the function of myth

> is indeed to preserve until the present time the remains of methods of observation and reflection which were [...] precisely adapted to discoveries of a certain type: those which nature authorised from the starting point of a speculative organization and exploitation of the sensible world in sensible terms.[10]

Lévi-Strauss emphasises not the subject matter of myth, but its formal characteristics, its 'methods' – myth is a poetic way of seeing the world, a mode of ordering knowledge by its mediation in stories, which convey truths about a people and nation by narrativising observations and stories. The *speculative* nature of mythologising emphasises that it seeks to achieve fictional knowledge through creative extrapolation of (often oral) narrative in which the outcome is not determined by a desired goal imposed beforehand, and chimes in with Mummery's alternative London history.

Mummery's quest for semi-fiction or authentic myth is, however, captured within a novel – although what kind of novel is less easy to determine – which creates a fictional framework in which the tension between what is real and what is not is couched. This questioning of the nature of authenticity is further undercut by foregrounding the fictional framework in which they are embedded. *Mother London* overtly uses classic narrative framing devices, which are hinted at by references early on in the novel, such as the 'framed newspaper photograph' (*ML* 6) and a gesture such as: 'From behind the glass he [Mummery] watches his Londoners' (*ML* 7). This emphasis on the framed structure has an ambiguous effect, as it both encloses the narrative, emphasising its fictionality whilst legitimising the status of the embedded stories as narratives with a degree of realism. Even this traditional device complicates Moorcock's constant questioning, and attempted answering, of what is 'authentic', and to understand Moorcock's complex novelistic practices, we need to understand how he puts 'authentic myth' into practice.

The novel contain a wide variety of myths, but it centres on the story of Mary Gasalee's impossible, supernatural escape from a house fire-bombed during the Blitz, which is narrated by one of the many nomads that populate the pages of the novel, the gypsy Jocko Baines, who worked as a temporary fire-fighter during the War. Baines tells her:

You just came walking out of that house. There was hardly a brick or stick of it left that wasn't roaring flame. You just came walking out of it, your baby in your arms [...] Your dress was hardly touched, except for that one place where it was on fire like the shape of a boot. It was as if the fire couldn't harm you. It was just like that story in the Bible about Shadrach, Meshach and Abednego, only for the little bit of flame on your back like a fluttering wing, the colour of a rose. (*ML* 438)

The story's primary importance lies in the fact that it keeps Londoners 'going through the rest of the Blitz. The rest of the War, really' (*ML* 432), and the imagination provided by the narrative becomes a tool for survival, and a cure against the fear of death. The title of the novel has a distinct mythico-religious, Catholic resonance: the myth of Mary Gasalee ('Mary Galilee', she functions as the mother of God within the Holy Trinity made up by the three protagonists) substitutes Judaeo-Christian mythology about possible redemption. The Gasalee story thus vocalises the Blitz spirit and forms an allegory of London's own rising from its ashes after the war. The myth's value lies not in its actual occurrence in the novel but in Baines's oral narration to the traumatised subject within the text; the event only exists on the level of representation. There are, as Baines notes, several versions of the Gasalee myth floating about in North London, suggesting that the story derives its strength from being in a state of flux.

Orality and the foregrounding of narratorial unreliability as a potent force rather than an epistemological and cognitive limitation for the reader is a key factor in Moorcock's conception of 'authentic myth'. Baines's ethnic background creates an atmosphere of unreliability, because the gypsy's geographical rootlessness disconnects him from spatial loyalty needed to engender a specific social and moral context. The status of the story is undermined even further because the received perception of Baines's ethnicity formed by the tabloid media connects him with the criminal underworld. However, similar to Duffy's unpacking of social categories as myths, Moorcock unstitches these ethnic clichés in fiction. Baines is aware of the cultural stereotyping of his people: '"We steal chickens, don't we, and start fights. That's what they think. Or they believe we put the evil eye on them." Chuckling, Jocko Baines precisely fills three cups with tea' (*ML* 434). Baines's self-consciousness about this kind of stereotyping imbues his character with knowledge and truth – reinforcing the authenticity of the Gasalee myth, whilst his 'precise' filling of the teacup points to the accuracy of his Gasalee narration: Jocko is a man of measure.

Another key myth explored in the novel is Mummery's discovery of 'the subterraneans' (*ML* 334):

I discovered evidence that London was interlaced with connecting tunnels, home of a forgotten troglodytic race that had gone underground at the time of the Great Fire, whose ranks had been periodically added to by thieves, vagabonds and escaped prisoners, receiving many fresh recruits during the Blitz when so many sought the safety of the tubes. Others had hinted of a London under London in a variety of texts as far back as Chaucer. (*ML* 344)

Figure 6   King X, King's Cross

Despite the 'sparseness of evidence' (*ML* 344), Mummery refuses to give up and descends into tube stations to explore disused branch lines. When Mummery makes contact and leaves a gift behind for the 'aliens', it becomes clear to the reader that a couple of schoolboys are pulling his leg. Nonetheless, the significance of Mummery's delusion resonates on several levels. Taking into account Moorcock's background as a writer of science fiction and fantasy novels, and his work as an editor for the *New Worlds* magazine, the subterraneans are a reference to H. G. Wells's *The Time Machine* (1895), which predicts that the evolution of the modern city will lead to a division of mankind into two species, with the degenerated Morlocks living below the earth's surface. The subterraneans are also a comment on London's criminal underworld, and on a persistent class struggle. In *Subterranean Cities* (2005), David L. Pike notes that the underworld, in a material and not a metaphorical sense, is associated with the feminine rather than masculine power:

> As a physical space, the earth has always been associated with female archetypes in Western myth; the male-controlled realm of the after-life was always a world apart, only metaphorically underground. The close spatial relation to seasonal cycles of birth and death may have

contributed to the connection with the female, but it is a connection that has become ever more arbitrary, while remaining extraordinarily persistent. The equation between activities and persons imagined as subterranean invokes the physical qualities of traditional underground activity and adds to them associations with the feminine that have become a fundamental metaphorical division in modern society – fluid, unruly mobs; diseased and immoral slum dwellers; and at the centre, the figure of the urban prostitute.[11]

More generally, they signify a continuous quest for survival and a battle against regression into barbarism in the heart of civilisation. This underworld race also stands as a metaphor for the counter-culture that Moorcock played a great part in during the 1960s, with its revolutionary urge to subvert conventional narratives and categories.[12] The myth is also a projection of Mummery's desire to write an alternative history of London that would prevent it from being appropriated by 'fact-based', official history written by the government, and nationalistic myths generated by tabloid media.

If we place the Gasalee and subterraneans myths in a historical context, it becomes clear why Moorcock's particular use of these myths is a comment on the dangers of the abuse of power by governments and mass media. In the run-up to the Second World War, Conservative governments argued against the left-wing desire for deep shelters because 'these would be too expensive in labour, materials and money, that they would only protect the small proportion of the population that happened to live near them, and that they would engender a "shelter mentality" which would create a permanent underground population and damage war production'.[13] This Conservative spin turned out to be a fantasy deflated by Londoners' actual stoicism.[14] The Blitz spirit is not myth, as Angus Calder's *The Myth of the Blitz* (1991) claims, but fact. Historian Stephen Inwood states:

> Despite Calder's tendency towards simplification and patriotic exaggeration, most Londoners *did* cope with the Blitz with stoicism and determination, and [...] the 'Myth' was not a myth [...] after all [...] Although [Calder] talks of 'paradigms' being established and claims that 'the basic story' of London's courage under fire was 'scripted' [by Mary Adams, the director of Home Intelligence] for public consumption, he recognizes that some stories, even those upon which patriotic 'myths' are based, are true [...] The tale of popular fortitude in the face of nightly hardships and danger, of 'London can take it'

and 'Cockney cheerfulness', was polished and promoted in films and newspaper articles to win American support, and perhaps to induce people in other cities to live up to London's reputation, but it was not, in its essentials, based on falsehood.[15]

Inwood inverts the idea that the Conservative government and the media created the Blitz spirit, turning reality into myth by the plotting of patriotic sentiment and through repetition. Yet both Calder and Inwood speak of some form of narrativisation ('the basic story' and the 'tale of popular fortitude'), suggesting that a degree of fictionalisation was necessary to forge the Blitz spirit, but also that it was a dramatisation that came from the people themselves, not their elected representatives.

This crisis whereby the authorities create a representational inflation of the objective world also expresses itself in the way London is changing. Moorcock points to, and delivers a scathing criticism of, the emergence of an inauthentic London and the theme parkification of the East End as part of the LDDC's development under Thatcher. In 1980, Mary, Judith and Leon Applefield have drinks in an East End pub, 'The Yours Truly', and they discuss the changing appearance of the East End. They complain about the wine bars in the East End, wondering what happened to 'the costers and the Cockneys' (*ML* 391). David notes that he has not seen the East End in years: '"It's like a theme park!"' (*ML* 391). Mary is unsure what a theme park is, but Judith notes that Katherine Dock '"could be a set from *Oliver*"' (*ML* 391). Leon retorts: '"Disneyland [...] Or rather Dickensland"' (*ML* 391).

The problem identified by Moorcock does not lie in the fact that Dickens and London are artificially staged – for Moorcock imagination starts only when 'the real' is reinvented – but in the false nature of commercial representation.[16] In *King of the City*, Moorcock takes his simulacral London a step further by staging a digitised Tower Bridge that simulates itself by means of 'a bank of screens showing the bridge itself from every possible angle' (*KC* 334). This tourist attraction is created by the tycoon Barbican Begg, who 'had created history in his own way' (*KC* 4), and is under the illusion he is a guard in a panoptical prison. When he demonstrates how the 'magical' Victorian engineering works by raising Tower Bridge, he accidentally topples cars and people into the Thames (*KC* 335). Moorcock warns against the way in which London is increasingly transformed into an artificial cityscape made by heritage fetishists to entertain tourists with polished images of the past. It is Roy Porter who reminds us that 'tourists are vultures'.[17] This process even turns language itself simulacral: when the gullible Mummery is introduced to 'the actual founder of London [...] Brutus the Trojan' (*ML* 349), Brutus tells him that Cockney is the original language of London, perhaps even of the world, and originally from India. Cockney rhyming slang, in contrast, 'was mainly made up for American tourists' (*ML* 350).

Moorcock's criticism of this emerging simulated London adumbrates the work of Raphael Samuel, whose book *Theatres of Memory* (1994) contains similar criticisms of the way in which *representations of representations* of London change under Thatcher. By analysing David Lean's *Great Expectations* (1946) and *Oliver Twist* (1948), and David Lynch's *The Elephant Man* (1980) and Christine Edzard's *Little Dorrit* (1987), Samuel shows how inauthentic models of earlier representations of London's East End appear in 1980s mainstream entertainment. Whereas Lean, 'a practitioner of the Gothic', worked 'in sinister shadows', Edzard's '*Little Dorrit* bathes its characters in colour, with soft focus images when there is romance afoot, and the sombre rendered mellow.'[18] Samuel concludes his piece by identifying an aesthetic collusion of these recent film makers with Thatcherism and its discourse:

> Edzard's *Little Dorrit* might speculatively be explained by the rehabilitation of Victorian values which has been a feature of recent years. In one aspect it reflects that urban pastoral which emerged in the wake of modernization and slum clearances; in another the aestheticization of dying industries. One could note here the representation of the slum as an Arcadia and of machinery as pretty – no longer the monstrous engines of *Hard Times* but, as in the industrial museums, historical monuments. In another aspect the film reproduces the enthusiasms of conservation, in which the past is not a dead weight to be thrown off but a heritage to preserve, and here it seems no accident that Sands films should be located – and the film should be made – in that temple of conservation-led redevelopment, London Docklands.[19]

Samuel is opposed to the artificial conservation of historical sites by heritage thinkers, not because he finds that such sites are not worth preserving, but because their preservation implies the deliberate misrepresentation of historical reality. Such conservationist strategies are dangerous because they are based on some idealised, Arcadian, but delusional idea about the nation's past. In the following dialogue between

Kiss and Dandy, the latter's irony subtly undercuts Kiss's apocalyptic implications of Thatcher's liberal capitalism:

'Those scoundrels from the Thatcher belt, Dandy! Thatching this and Thatching that. It's rural blight, old lad. Arcadian spread. It's hideous! They've no right to throw their weight about in London. Give 'em Westminster as a free zone, but draw the line there. The City saw this coming, you know. We were warned about it a hundred years ago!' Still not wanting to halt his friend's drift Dandy spoke mildly. 'It all sounds a bit like a scenario for an Ealing comedy. *Passport to Pimlico* or *The Napoleon of Notting Hill* ...' (*ML* 378–9)

The phrase 'Arcadian spread' is interesting because it points to the pseudo-pastoral mode of discourse and *modus operandi* of Thatcherism: as a Conservative, Kiss associates Thatcher's policies with ruralism and he points to the pastoral spirit that accompanies the privatisation process sweeping through London. In contrast, Dandy points out that Kiss's misrepresentation of Thatcher's impact on the city lies in a distorted scenario that actually mimics the government's xenophobic wielding of power. This point is driven home by Dandy when he draws the analogy between Kiss's proposition to put a quota on stockbrokers, estate agents and investment counsellors (*ML* 379) and Thatcher's anti-immigration policies. Kiss is aware that London is *always* in a state of transformation, but that it is the radical nature of that change which he despises. *Mother London's* portrayal of the Blitz spirit is, then, not a blunt comparison between the destruction enacted on the city by the Second World War and the damage produced by Thatcherite policies of privatisation and decentralisation, but it certainly makes a more general connection between the various events that have rewritten the material appearance of the city.

The grand, messy flux: Michael Moorcock's nomadism of form

More generally, Moorcock's London 'authentic myths' represent the contemporary city as a site of contestation of different forms of ordering knowledge, ideology and discourses that make and remake London.[20] In order to investigate this crisis in more detail it is necessary to look deeper into the various structures that Moorcock's texts offer. Moorcock's nomadism of form can be demonstrated by framing his London novels within the dense and varied layering of distinct structural devices they contain, such as heterotopia and *bricolage* and Moorcock's interpretation of 'the multiverse', all of which point out the limits of ordering devices which we attempt to impose onto the illimitable city.

Whereas the London of Sinclair, Ackroyd and Duffy is strongly informed by their origins as poets, Moorcock is a popular novelist *pur sang*: like London, his novels are bulky, sprawling like the centuries of accretion and destruction that made the city itself. In Sinclair's words: rather than Julian Barnes's smooth and fat-free novels, Moorcock's London is determined by 'Moorcockian digression, a set of cellulite-heavy parentheses'.[21] In Angela Carter's words, Moorcock's *Mother London* 'is the grand, messy flux itself, in all its heroic vulgarity, its unquenchable optimism, its enthusiasm for the inexhaustible variousness of things'.[22]

The omnivorous and encyclopaedic impetus of *Mother London* requires a resonance of voice which, as Iain Sinclair and Angela Carter have noted, Moorcock's poetics derives from 'the prodigal production of Dickens'.[23] In the sprawl of *Mother London*, and in its episodic structure, we see Moorcock reproducing the rhythms of the city that Dickens's work captures so aptly in his representation of the nineteenth-century city transformed by capitalism, although, as we will see later, he also manipulates his material to make it resemble post-war patterns. Moorcock's Dickensian heritage is also visible in the characterisation of Joseph Kiss, who, in the following excerpt, is described boarding a Route Master: 'Eccentric clothes swirl about his massive person. Advancing into the body of the vehicle he appears to expand to fill up the available space. He plucks off his leather gloves, unbuttons his Crombie, loosens his long scarf' (*ML* 8). Thus, while Kiss's bulk is in accordance with the Dickensian weight of Moorcock's voice, he also resembles Anthony Powell's description of Soho-ite Julian Maclaren-Ross as 'a broken-down dandy, though just what brand of dandyism was not easy to define'.[24] *King of the City* is dominated by Dennis Dover's down-to-earth voice, which Bakhtin would classify as *skaz*, the stylisation 'of the various forms of everyday narration'.[25] Dover's voice is determined by the 'vernacular extraliterary narration'[26] of tabloid speech and Americanisms— 'Believe me, pards, we're living in an age of myths and miracles' (*KC* 1), but the bombast disguises the fact that he is writing his memoirs (*KC* 379), an act that requires sensitive exploration of the remembered self in place and time.

Another good demonstration of Dickens's influence on Moorcock is the description of the secretary of Bernard Bickerton, Joseph Kiss's agent, as 'little Mrs Hobday whom he called The Human Canary; she was all of a flutter in her yellow hair, her familiar suit, trilling at him as gaily as any wild songster [...] She flapped a bright blue arm' (*ML* 61). This description is also a verbal symptom of a similar conceit explored by Carter in the portrayal of her magical bird-woman Fevvers from *Nights at the Circus* (1984), and points to a creative dialogue between various shared interests of the two writers. Both Moorcock and Carter based their respective Music Hall performers (the Scaramanga sisters Cloe and Beth in *Mother London*, and Dora and Nora Chance in *Wise Children* [1991]) on the musical hall performers of the thirties and forties.[27] In *Mother London* it is pantomime which is a stage form central to the city's cultural heritage: Mummery's name is a reference to the panto-actor (the mummer), and during the extremely cold winter of 1947, Kiss, playing a goose in a pantomime act, walks home without undressing and similar weather circumstances years later produce 'white breath as blank speech balloons, as if a cartoonist experienced a sudden failure of creativity' (*ML* 46–7). The problem that Moorcock investigates in *Mother London* is the post-war inability of Londoners to make themselves heard, and Roger Luckhurst's suggestion that in *Mother London* 'redemption for the traumatized city lies in a gaggle of telepaths, psychotically open to the lost voices of metropolitan history' is slightly reductive because the novel's mode of recuperation is a confusing composite of myths and fictions.[28] Yet what should also be noted is that the author recuperates these repressed voices precisely by positing the novelist and his writerly practice as an activity that presents voice *as* space, and that this confusion is a deliberate strategy that prevents authentic myth from regressing into myths.

We should keep in mind Moorcock's experience as a practitioner of genre fiction, and science fiction in particular: he is very well used to exploring and exploiting specific rules of representation with a view to manipulating the reader's expectations. His mixing of the strict rules of genre fiction with the loose baggy monster's form yields an amalgam that shapes the content: whereas the fixed rules of genre fiction form a kind of protection against the trauma and violence of the Second World War, such fixed rules could turn authentic myth into dangerous myths, yet the novel form's flexibility guards against such regression into stereotype. It is this tension between narratological rules and their subversion that gives Moorcock an interesting edge over other, mainstream writers.

Moorcock's novels seem to create a binary opposition between official places of the political and socio-cultural establishment, which enact various forms of repression, against heterotopian sites with a utopian potential, such as the pub and the brothel. In the chapter 'Sherlock Holmes 1981', Joseph Kiss lunches at County Hall with his sister, who at that point plans to stand as a Tory MP (and will have become a government minister in 1985, we find out in the next chapter), and leaves him upset because she asks him 'to act as a man in the street for her party's new advertising film' (*ML* 108). The church, signifier of organised religion, where the funeral of the homosexual Ben French takes place, is portrayed as a space of sexual oppression: '"Hargreaves", still holding back, possibly afraid to reveal his own homosexuality by close proximity to the dead man. Mummery wished he could offer Joe Houghton some gesture of inclusion' (*ML* 125). It is only outside the church cemetery that Houghton dares to sing his homage to this dead lover because it enables him to walk 'slowly towards the distant gates, the picture of renewed self-esteem' (*ML* 126).

Just as in Duffy's *Londoners*, the pub plays a central role, and *Mother London* also reinforces the importance of public space and London voices by using the city's founding mythologies as a structuring device: the twelve episodes of Parts Two and Five, 'High Days' and 'The Angered Spirit', are named after the pub where discussions of the city's post-war transformation by the characters take place. The names in Part Two are derived from London's martyrs who have become important figures in the city's mythology: Queen Boadicea, Thomas à Becket and Captain Jack Cade. The fifth chapter, 'Sherlock Holmes', appears to break this pattern, but the pub's original name is The Northumberland Arms (*ML* 109), after the Northumberland Fusiliers, who sacrificed many men during the Great War. The significance of naming of chapters and pubs after prehistoric, medieval and more contemporary martyrs lies in its identification of an ongoing emancipatory struggle for freedom and democratic values by violence and bloodshed. Chapters four and five are named after Nell Gwynn, the actress and mistress of Charles II, and Princess Diana, respectively. Whereas sixties icon and mistress of Profumo Christine Keeler and Bill Clinton's lover Monica Lewinsky lack a mythical dimension, Gwynn and Diana are truly mythical women, who played an important part of the popular imagination of London, and the nation.[29] Indeed, *King of the City*, written after Diana's death in 1997, continues Moorcock's attempt to explore Diana's importance to the nation's life of the imagination, because the 'twentieth century's most sensationalized car crash had changed everything' (*KC* 3), violently waking the nation from its collective daydream.

By using the pub names as chapter headings, Moorcock's novel stresses the connection between London's public houses and the novel as related public spaces. The chapters function as a public house, collecting the polyvocal chatter of Londoners' everyday stories and myths, which together act out and visualise the alternative representative body of London's unofficial meanings. The network of unofficial, fictional monuments to the city's history forms an alternative space that stands outside the grasp of politics. Simultaneously, they signpost the novel itself as a space where new London martyrs (Mummery, Kiss and Gasalee) are traumatised by and protest against the numerous acts of destruction enacted on London by the Blitz and the post-war governments: the Victorian public house the Queen Boadicea, which had survived German bombardment but was soon to be brought down by concrete banks because the city was redeveloping on land where the rubble of the war was recently cleared.

In his perceptive reading of *Mother London*, Brian Baker states that Moorcock depicts public houses as 'centres of communal life [...] which escape the ordering principles of the state or official culture [and are] the epicentre of a masculine culture of territorial violence'.[30] There are two interconnected problems with Baker's analysis. His representation of Moorcock's pub as divorced from the official world and as 'a masculine culture of territorial violence' goes against the utopian drive that is behind Moorcock's representation of public spaces. The pub, a central part of English life and culture, is described by Kate Fox's *Watching the English* (2004) as follows:

> [A]lthough the pub is very much part of English culture, it also has its own 'social micro-climate'. Like all drinking places, it is in some respects a 'liminal' zone, an equivocal, marginal, borderline state, in which one finds a degree of 'cultural remission' – a structured, temporary relaxation or suspension of normal social controls (also known as 'legitimised deviance' or 'time-out behaviour').[31]

The point that Fox makes is that pubs do not exist wholly outside official society, but their liminality connects official and the unofficial worlds, public and private experiences.

Baker's reading of Moorcock's pubs as utopian sites raises problems because it appears to gloss over the potentially problematic treatment of women in particular, which is related to a second point of criticism. Baker's wholesale acceptance of Moorcock's pubs and brothel as being synonymous with the white, male underworld embodied by the East End gangsters John and Reeny Fox (at first sight a thinly disguised version of the Kray brothers) is a misrepresentation, however. By glossing over the fact that Reeny Fox is a woman, Baker fails to point out Moorcock's deliberate flouting of the East End gangster code, which points to the fact that public houses appear to function as an alternative London because of its *inclusiveness*: when the Princess Diana is 'redecorated to Hollywood Cockney' (*ML* 127) Mummery states that 'Ben [French] loved it' (*ML* 127). The destruction and renovation of public houses creates a network of public spaces that is able to represent all Londoners in the name of a few who fought for these spaces of freedom and democratic values. This is indicated by the name of the Captain Jack Cade (1968) on the City's Cannon Street, 'built on the original site of London Stone which Jack, one of the last working-class heroes to lead a rebel army into London, had struck with his sword, declaring the people masters of the city. The Jack Cade symbolised the high hopes and failed ideals of Patsy's contemporaries' (*ML* 90).

The second representational problem emerges when we look at another potentially utopian space staged by Moorcock as an autonomous zone outside state influence: the brothel. In *Mother London* the brothel is exemplified by the Fox siblings' Earl's Court 'earner' in the chapter 'The Old Bran's Head 1959', and by several other Soho brothels where Kiss comes to quench his lust. It is important that the 'earner' has no name, unlike the pubs: the house is invisible to the outside world; its exterior is not described and its interior is only given away as '[s]carlet as the plush on Reeny Fox's worn-out ottoman' (*ML* 440). It concerns a space that is free-floating, unnamed, and, unlike the pub, truly disconnected from the official political and capitalist system because of its integration into the black economy.[32]

Yet, unlike Moorcock's pubs, the brothel in *Mother London* is represented as a heteropia in the way that Foucault originally intended, not as a place in social reality but as a utopian site that can only exist within the imagination, or in text. Kiss is a London visionary in the tradition of William Blake whose rampant sexual appetite is a form of displaced trauma caused by the violent impact of the Blitz, generating another form of heat. Kiss is plagued by imagined voices of prostitutes who ask him: '*Mr Kiss, can you eat fire?*' (*ML* 441) His sirens continue while Kiss speculates on whether to visit a prostitute on Essex Street, the Water Gate, the little alleys behind Fleet Street or the Thames Embankment, when the voice asks: '*Mr Kiss, Mr Kiss, can you read fire?*' (*ML* 442). This lexical slippage turns the brothel into a textual site performed in the act of Moorcock's writing. This thought is reinforced when Mummery becomes aware of his pleasure in singing bawdy ballads in the brothel. The appreciation of the whorehouse, Mummery decides, has more to do with the power of words than the actual nature of the songs, because people are impressed by the most obvious double-entendres. As he sings on, the approval of his audience, now completely nude, helps him to relax. Mummery wonders how he would ever describe such a scene as this: 'He felt like a Babylonian minstrel' (*ML* 441).

Moorcock emphasises the brothel's textual nature because Mummery is unable to interpret the scene in front of him in conventional terms. Rather than forming a place of women's submission, for Mummery, who experiences the place at the level of language, it is a theatre where gender divisions are actually resolved: 'There came a huge wave of laughter as he reached the chorus. Some of the whores even tried to join in' (*ML* 441). Moorcock's textual brothel thus forms a utopian site where the all-embracing atmosphere of sexual ecstasy stores the subject's fragmentation and thus breaks down gender divisions engrained in society, and introduces ambivalence in social relations. In *Mother London* this is symbolised by the undressing of 'the Guardsman' (*ML* 440), which rather than affirming the heterosexual stereotype renders the image ambivalent. The brothels of Knightsbridge have always had an intimate relationship with the Barracks, which makes this undressing partly a gay convention.

This ambiguity makes any reading of Moorcock's gender politics complex. Indeed, the very title of the novel is problematic, as it introduces a potentially naïve reading of gender in relation to the urban environment. Lawrence Phillips notes:

> While the novel turns to another biological metaphor – London is the 'mother' giving birth and nurturing its people – this is different to conceiving of London as a body in which people are reduced to involuntary functional processes. 'Mother' also evokes a nature symbolism [...] 'mother' London is a symbol of cyclical renewal, of decline and rebirth thereby promising continuity.[33]

In general terms this is true, but the brothel is a space where women's bodies are exploited and violated, often not resulting in 'cyclical renewal' but in male violence and backstreet abortions. It is here that we see the utopian legacy of the sixties in Moorcock's thinking introduce a problem, although, perhaps, as we will see below, he attempts to correct this in the narrative trajectory of Kiss's character.

The problem of Mummery's mental trauma informs the novel's ordering of the city on various levels. At the outset of *Mother London*, the bedroom of Mummery is described as a 'crowded museum of ephemera'

(*ML* 5) containing late Victorian advertisements, Edwardian crested ware, 1920s and 1930s magazines, war memorabilia, posters from the Festival of Britain, toy guardsmen, Dinky delivery vans, miniature aeroplanes: 'his room's surfaces are covered by confused and varied strata, uncatalogued and frequently unremembered' (*ML* 5–6).

The mental map of Mummery given here is an eclectic, even random collection of signs that point to his psychological make-up, but it also signifies more generally a postmodern condition. To understand the complexity of such a condition, it would be useful to frame Moorcock's work in the light of the *bricoleur*. Both *Mother London* and *King of the City* are constructed from the debris of twentieth-century history, at the centre of which lies the destruction and violence of the Second World War. In *The Savage Mind*, Lévi-Strauss states that:

> The characteristic feature of mythical thought is that it expresses itself by means of a heterogeneous repertoire which, even if extensive, is nevertheless limited. It has to use this repertoire, however, whatever the task in hand because it has nothing else at its disposal. Mythical thought is therefore a kind of intellectual 'bricolage' – which explains the relation which can be perceived between the two.[34]

Just as Lévi-Strauss observed that Dickens's *Great Expectations* contained a *bricolage* in the form of Mr Wemmick's suburban castle,[35] Moorcock himself is a *bricoleur* because he is interested in the potential use that can be made of the tools and materials at hand.[36] Lévi-Strauss contrasts the *bricoleur* to the engineer on the basis of the different uses of particular kinds of discourse as a tool for construction of thought. Whereas the engineer employs the language of official and rational logic specially adapted to a specific technical need with a clear goal in mind, the *bricoleur* uses tools and materials at his disposal that are perhaps intended for different goals.[37]

Moorcock's preference for mythical thought and the popular tradition creates another link with the *bricoleur*, as Lévi-Strauss states: 'Now, the characteristic feature of mythical thought, as of "bricolage" on the practical plane, is that it builds up structured sets, not directly with other structured sets but by using the remains of debris of events […] in English, fossilized evidence of the history of an individual or society.'[38] In a footnote, Lévi-Strauss explains that the structured sets – that is, narratives – are generated by means of another structured set: language. This is important because it undercuts and explains the stability and legitimacy of myth by reminding us of Saussure's idea of language as a grid of

Figure 7 St Dunstan-in-the-East, City

indefinite relations with no fixed relation between signifier and signified. The implication is that meaning depends upon a spatio-temporally specific context and thus thwarts the myth-maker's attempt at finding a consistent and stable meaning.

Although Dennis Dover, the narrator of *King of the City*, understands that meaning is dependent on context, he finds that the Holocaust takes up a central, yet unspeakable place in twentieth-century history. It is an event the moral implications of which cannot be relativised. Thus, although both mythical language as well as 'bricolage' obviate the idea of a stable centre, Moorcock's novels posit the Holocaust as a central event within twentieth-century history. The event raises an unquestionably ethical gravitational, undecentrable point of significance which is so overburdening that its consequences and meaning cannot be discussed in language: the protagonists' visionary qualities are the result of the violence and trauma of the Second World War, but also a statement on the post-war condition more generally.

Although in *Mother London* the narratological focus is on the Blitz, which lies at the novel's empty, unspeakable core, the novel is an analogy for the ways in which the post-war subject is traumatised by the events during the Second World War. Baker misreads the complexity of Moorcock's speculations about the relationship between London mythology and its relation to the Second World War, which is partly due to a lack of historical accuracy in his reading of the novel. Baker states that Moorcock 'relocates the mythic epicentre of the Blitz spatially across London. Where the East End, the docks and the warehouses were the target for much of the Blitz, and the myths that grew up around it, the canal-side cottage which harbours UXB is in North Kensington.'[39] However, although it was the East End that was severely hit by the German autumn raids of 1940, a second phase, starting as early as mid-September, 'no longer concentrated on the East End and the docks, but spread its destruction over the rest of London'.[40]

More significantly, Baker does not connect London's wholesale consummation by the inferno to the Holocaust: 'the events are like a stone dropped into the canal, and the ripples of its significance move forwards to the present and back again', he notes, a metaphor that makes it sounds rather gentle, innocent even. Instead, the ripples are that of millions of human bodies being consumed by fire, of the atom bombs on Hiroshima and Nagasaki. In the novel, the cityscape functions not only as the theatre of the Blitz, but London indirectly becomes a map onto which the consequences of the Second World War and Auschwitz are inscribed. The miraculous escape of Gasalee causes her to slip into a coma, which indirectly represents the traumatic guilt of Holocaust survivors: '*Millions of other women died in those yelling fires, died of fright even before the smoke took them. None of us should have died. And that's the outrage'* (*ML* 439). More generally, this passage informs us that all of those living in the post-war era are living in the shadow of, and are traumatised by, the Holocaust. The many references to the inferno and heat of the Blitz are implying a connection to the destruction of Jews, gypsies and gays in the concentration camps. The Holocaust and the unspeakable atrocities that occurred in the German concentration camps during the Second World War are mediated through London's history and its devastating effect superimposed onto the structure of the novel's material, with shockwaves imitated by the temporal arrangement: Part One moves forward in time, Part Two backward, Part Three forward again and Part Five backward. The obliteration of London during the Blitz is a metaphor for civilisation whose very values and sense-making processes are destroyed, and London's rewritings by governments after the war are uncanny reminders of that process. Indeed, Moorcock's work shows that the inability of Western governments to acknowledge their own complicity in such destruction becomes a blind spot of the post-war consciousness. *King of the City* therefore warns us against the dangers of forgetting the Holocaust because it makes us blind to new Holocausts, such as the genocides in Rwanda (*KC* 271–81) and Serbia which are nightmarish repetitions, and a grotesque echolalia of the earlier crimes that foreshadow a 'holocaust waiting to happen' (*KC* 271). The very structure of the novel, as a map of London onto which the heat, violence and trauma of the Second World War are inscribed, destroys causality and the unilinear chain as the basis of a classic mode of rationality that the war obliterates. Lévi-Strauss's *Myth and Meaning* (1978) contains an illuminating question which sheds light on the relationship between the structure of Moorcock's novel and the society it represents:

[W]e have the question: what does a collection [of myths] mean? It could mean two different things. It could mean, for instance, that the coherent order, like a kind of saga, is the primitive condition, and that whenever we find myths as disconnected elements, this is the result of a process of deterioration and disorganization; we can only find scattered elements of what was, earlier, a meaningful whole. Or we could hypothesize that the disconnected state was the archaic one, and that the myths were put together in an order by native wise men and philosophers who do not exist everywhere, but only in some societies of a given type.[41]

The fragmented, anti-linear organised chaos of *Mother London* could either represent the ruins of our post-war society that is in fact more organic than the novel's structure makes it appear, or the disconnected structure is actually an accurate reflection of our experience of the post-war world. In the case of *Mother London*, both strategies are, paradoxically, equally valid at the same time.

Speaking on the structure of *Mother London*, Jeff Gardiner states that Moorcock 'celebrates the modern city, which has become a sentient, conscious character. Moorcock's London becomes more than a single place, but contains a complete realm of mythology – a multiverse.'[42] The term 'multiverse' was coined by scientist Andy Nimmo in 1960, but has been redefined by Moorcock as a

> near-infinite nest of universes, each only marginally different from the next and only widely different when separated by millions of variants, where time is not linear but a field in which all the universes rest, creating the appearance of linearity within their own small sphere; where sometimes groups of universes exist in full knowledge and in full intercourse with others, where 'rogue' universes can take sideways orbits, crashing through the dimensions and creating all kinds of disruptions in the delicate fabric of multiversal space-time.[43]

The multiverse has been explored by Moorcock throughout his novels, particularly the epic fantasy series of the Elric novels and science fiction of the Jerry Cornelius cycle but his literary fiction also makes use of ideas associated with the multiverse,[44] as the long quotation from Mummery's last words in the novel below indicates:

> We move through Time at different rates it seems, only disturbed when another's chronological sensibility conflicts with our own. Choices as subtle and complicated as this are only available in a city like London; they are not found in smaller towns where the units, being less varied, are consequently less flexible. Past and future both comprise London's present and this is one of the city's chief attractions. Theories of Time are mostly simplistic like Dunne's, attempting to give it a circular or linear form, but I believe Time to be a faceted jewel with an infinity of planes and layers impossible to either map or to contain; this image is my own antidote for Death. (*ML* 486)

In Colin Greenland's *Death is No Obstacle* (1992), Moorcock elaborates on this: 'I conceived it as a faceted structure, like a diamond, with a lot of different planes, planes which can be seen through other planes.'[45] In the passage above, Moorcock quotes John William Dunne (an influence on James Joyce) to emphasise that his own concept of time and space is post-Einsteinian rather than based on nineteenth-century models. Victorian excavations forced archaeologists to think of deep time in metaphorical terms, either as a cycle or as an arrow, yet after Einstein temporal concepts become more sophisticated, relative, our knowledge limited, and making room for speculative theories.

Mother London is composed out of different planes, or plateaus. As Colin Greenland puts it: 'Because we're very conscious what we're reading are slices through time, everybody comes with a history attached. Everybody's on their way to and from somewhere, and that generates the space of the city.'[46] However, despite the anti-chronological ordering of the narrative, a linear order is retrievable; in fact much of the novel's strategies draw upon the expectation that the reader will reconstruct the narrative chronology; Moorcock's narrative relies on dramatic irony and play with adumbration. For instance, in 'The Axe and Block 1969' the reader is told that Joseph Kiss had said that he had met Reeny Fox in a brothel but had never really described the circumstances. Once an enthusiast for these places, later Kiss had stopped talking about them (*ML* 423). This connection between Reeny Fox and Kiss is affirmed in the following chapter, 'The Old Bran's Head 1959', when, textually later but narratively earlier, Joseph phones a brothel run by Fox. Despite availing himself of the services, Joseph, already plagued by the daemons of his guilty desires, decides to walk through the city, resulting in a fight with Billy Failing, who abuses and prostitutes his wife. This final chapter of the fourth part shows how Kiss redeems his own sins by becoming a champion of gender relations, human decency and social justice. Thus, whereas Kiss visits a prostitute in the first chapter of the second part, 'Queen Boadicea 1957', he later has a wife (Mary Gasalee), and in 'The World's End 1985' an increasingly mad Kiss spends his time in the company of Dandy or alone in his Brook Market room. This inversion of determination, whereby a narrative event can prefigure the past, points to the Second World War as the destruction of coherence in the experience of the post-war time–space relationship. However, this does not mean that order and meaning are perpetually postponed: the novel form remains a means of ordering, of metaphysical exploration and evaluation of significance. Moorcock's allegiance to nineteenth-century novelistic conventions ensures his novels remain securely moored in a humanist universe, whilst new narrative patterns are imprinting their knowledge onto the shape of the imagined city.

The hub of all our histories

On a banal level, Moorcock's London fiction warns against the implications of post-war bureaucracy and rational planning, but the novel also shows how the violence and trauma of the twentieth century is inscribed into our consciousness, and alters our image of the city. The structure of *Mother London* suggests that because of its remembered myths and fiction London's body is flexible and messy enough to take such transformations, because London's alternative forum of writers is able to insert alternative, creative mappers such as Mummery and Kiss into their geography. By injecting London's mythologies and fiction into the city's representational bloodstream, London escapes from being rationalised by the A-Z, or the drawing boards of architects, planners and developers. While Mummery's underground psychogeography of London is idiosyncratic and at times conspiratorial, Kiss's map is driven by a voracious sexual desire; both are irrational, cognitive explorations of post-war London. *Mother London* thus becomes a re-exploration of the relationship between the rationally ordered, blank-mapped city of technocrats, and the human elements that constitute the life of the city by practising it in their fiction, until the articulation of London's past, present and future regains the city's healthy fabric:

> the rest of London has a tangled, organic feel again, as if the roots have restored themselves. I'll swear some buildings are beginning to regenerate. Levels of aggression have dropped. There's a different buzz, vital and optimistic [...] We'll push open the big grain doors [...] looking out over a city that glitters and vibrates with a new optimism, a positive energy, a will to become, once again, the best and most progressive, the richest and greatest city the world has ever known. The hub of all our histories. Forever glorious. Forever glorious. Forever golden. Forever just. (*KC* 419–21)

3
'A Zoo fit for Psychopaths': J. G. Ballard versus London

A man always out on the periphery: J. G. Ballard and Count Dracula

J. G. Ballard's piece of non-fiction 'Airports' (1997) accurately reflects the author's attitude to London:

> By comparison with London Airport [Heathrow], London itself seems hopelessly antiquated. Its hundreds of miles of gentrified stucco are an aching hangover from the nineteenth century that should have been bulldozed decades ago. London may well be the only world capital [...] that has gone from the nineteenth century to the twenty-first without experiencing all the possibilities and excitements of the twentieth in any meaningful way. Visiting London, I always have the sense of a city devised as an instrument of political control, like the class system that preserves England from the revolution. The labyrinths of districts and boroughs, the endless columned porticos that once guarded the modest terraced cottages of Victorian clerks, together make clear that London is a place where everyone knows his place.[1]

For Ballard, London is an ancient city completely unsuitable for living twentieth- and twenty-first-century lives: messy, congested, squalid, and in various ways badly equipped to cope with the pressures and demands of modern existence. The mass and hypertrophy (gigantism and overgrowth) of the metropolis runs counter to the modern experience determined by speed and mobility, by virtuality and lightness. Ballard's antagonism towards London stems from the idea that the labyrinthine figure ground and architecture of the Victorian city continues to inscribe the consciousness and experience of today's inhabitants with the restrictive values and mores prevalent at the time. Ballard loathes the rigid class system, unashamed quest for personal wealth by the privileged few at the expense of communal and democratic ideals, and the safe, middling artistic culture that aims to satisfy the bland taste of the bourgeoisie.

Ballard's fictional texts give us a deeply pessimistic projection of the city as a repressive machine that has resulted in an imaginative, even counterintuitive vision of London. Whereas many authors attempt to rescue the city by hoarding its histories and mythologies, Ballard's fiction fantasises, in dramatic, often spectacular fashion, about London's destruction. In Ballard's first novel *The Drowned World* (1962) the metropolis is flooded because the polar ice caps have melted. In an apocalyptic story, 'Billennium' (1962), overpopulation demands an increasingly tight and complex organisation of space and time, while in 'Chronopolis' (1960) we see the ruins of the overly ordered world of the past. In the seventies we see a shift away from the city centre to a focus on London's suburbs in an urban disaster trilogy. *Crash* (1973) devises a postmodern mythology set in and around the Heathrow area; in *Concrete Island* (1974) a man is marooned on a piece of no man's land wedged in between motorways; and *High-Rise* (1975) tests out the utopian potential of a tower block community in East London. In the short story 'Theatre of War' (1977) inner London becomes the scene of civil war; in *Running Wild* (1988) children living in the wealthy Pangbourne Village in West London murder their parents; and in *Millennium People* (2003) a group of unruly Londoners blow up the National Film Theatre, the BBC's Broadcasting House and the Tate Modern.

A passage in *High-Rise* (1975) helps us appreciate the significance of Ballard's choice for a life and authorship based in the nowhere-town Shepperton, situated 17 miles to the west of London. At the beginning of the novel, Dr Robert Laing, who has just moved from central London to a hypermodern tower block on the Isle of Dogs, looks at the city from his apartment, observing the following:

> Although the apartment was no higher than the 25th floor, he felt for the first time that he was looking down at the sky, rather than up at it [...] By contrast with the calm and unencumbered geometry of the concert-hall and television studios below him, the ragged skyline of the city resembled the disturbed encephalograph of an unresolved mental crisis.[2]

Ballard juxtaposes the sedated, emotionless aesthetic of postmodern spatiality and the distanced, Godlike perspective it offers to the frenzied

Figure 8   The Trellick Tower, North Kensington

one of the Victorian era, suggesting that the inescapable immersion in the neurotic and unstable life of Londoners is wholly different from life in this vertical city. The passage forms a conscious, if ironic echo of Bram Stoker's early modernist novel *Dracula* (1897). At the beginning of the novel, the London estate agent Jonathan Harker travels from London to Count Dracula's Transylvanian castle to sell him an estate called Carfax, modelled on St Stephen's Church, at Purfleet in East London. During his journey east he has noticed that the precise ordering of time and place has given way to what he considers the chaos of unregulated train schedules and impassable roads in Eastern Europe.[3] When Harker, the embodiment of urbanised Western rationality, nears Dracula's Transylvanian castle he notes:

> We kept on ascending, with occasional periods of quick descent, but in the main always ascending. Suddenly I became conscious of the fact that the driver was in the act of pulling up the horses in the courtyard of a vast ruined castle, from whose tall black windows came no ray of light, and whose broken battlements showed a jagged line against the moonlit sky.[4]

In this passage we are given an impression of the solitary journey up into the mountains, suggesting that the castle provides a Godlike perspective. The image of the castle is metaphorically depicted as a psychological emblem of the menacing East. The 'moonlit sky' and 'jagged line' (echoed by Ballard's 'ragged skyline') suggest psychological instability, reinforced by the absence of light in the castle, a metaphoric darkness. Through this description Count Dracula is characterised as an irrational and insane disseminator of physical corruption, and sexual and mental disease. If we read Stoker's novels as a product of colonialism, we are told to beware the Other; we are warned that Dracula's contagious evil will poison England, and London in particular, from within.

Dracula can also be read as a criticism of colonialism, and an indictment of social and sexual repression in Victorian society. For Franco Moretti, the aristocratic vampire is a metaphor for a monopolist capitalism 'impelled towards continuous growth, an unlimited expansion of his domain' and the symbol of this centrifugal process is an 'ever widening circle'.[5] The blood-sucking vampires are an inversion of the idea that empire is consuming, and sucking dry, both the colonial subjects' bodies through labour and the colonised land itself. In this reading, the Other gets its revenge by reversing the production–consumption cycle in the city that sucks up all the wealth and spoils of empire. Dracula's attempt to build an army of vampires from the heart of empire operates 'a kind of reverse imperialism: the threat that the primitive will colonize the civilized world'.[6] The story turns into a cautionary tale warning against the paradoxical economic doubleness of England's global imperial enterprise, which will reverse the desire for power and consumption.

This colonial, late Victorian connection is affirmed by Iain Sinclair, who notes that 'Ballard was in exile in Shepperton, a returned colonial.'[7] Just as the bloodthirsty Count moves from the East to the capital of the civilised world, Shanghai-born Ballard moved 'back' to London after the Second World War. Just as Dracula settles in Purfleet, at a safe distance to the east of the metropolis, Ballard moves to Shepperton while his protagonists move away from what in the post-war period is no longer the heart of empire. Just as Ballard's texts invert Stoker's paradoxical analysis of Victorian society, he also rewrites previous ideas about what is the ideological centre and what is the periphery. Rather than being an image of Western triumph of rational organisation, London's material structure becomes a symbol of the repressed, unenlightened mind. Ballard's inversion of *Dracula* suggests that technological advancement creates a divorce from 'dark knowledge'[8] which thwarts rational modes of thinking that emerged during the Enlightenment, the belief that the world and the self could be understood through rational interpretation of empirical observation. Contemporary London is a society *after* its wholesale corruption by Dracula's lust for blood, life and money, a city of the Un-dead.

Although the subject matter of Ballard's work is progressive in that it explores and embraces modernity, the colonial legacy also can be located at the level of form. Ballard's work is based on neurotic repetitions in the plotting and naming of characters, which mimics the modern city experience, with its labyrinthine construction, its unending repetition of streets and buildings and the anonymity of its lonely inhabitants. Ballard's repetitions also imitate the monotonous rhythms of the mechanical reproduction part of nineteenth-century capitalist production. Travelling through Ballard's *oeuvre* resembles navigating through London. These obsessive repetitions resonate also in the local texture of Ballard's language; the grammatical construction and stylisation of his sentences are another form of mechanical reproduction, as the following two examples show:

Later, as he sat on his balcony eating the dog, Dr Robert Laing reflected on the unusual events that had taken place within the huge apartment building during the previous three months.

Elaborately wrapped in rice paper, the parcel lay across my lap, emitting the softest breath of rustling fur.[9]

The form of the first example, the opening sentence of *High-Rise*, conveys Laing's reflective and controlled state of mind, as well as the unusual nature of the subject matter. The reader is deliberately forced to stumble over two subordinate clauses before being able to reach the subject, suggesting that the story we are about to read is literally and figuratively 'out there'. The elaborate construction points self-consciously to the artifice and constructedness of Ballard's language, which resembles the 'rationality' we tend to associate with doctors, although this is undercut by the comical, grotesque image of Laing's canine sup; although language still holds up, the civilised intellectual has been reduced to barbarism. The second sentence is a set piece within Ballard's prose-style. It starts with an abbreviated clause that has an elaborating function by commenting on the status of the main clause's subject, here it is modified by the elegant clause with the non-finite verb, establishing a hypotactic relationship between the clauses. Ballard's sentence presents itself as a parcel, carefully (and onomatopoeically) wrapping up its meaning.

What both examples share is their neurotic desire to exert control over form. Martin Amis states that Ballard's 'archaic mannerisms express a morbid fear of the common pronoun. Thus, instead of getting *it, him* or *her*, we get "this harmless mass of water", "this amiable imposter" or "this distraught woman".'[10] Whereas Ballard's repetitions and adjectival proliferation symbolically resemble Victorian planning schemes, his mechanical, anachronistic prose mimics the aesthetic of Victorian architecture. Yet, Ballard's stylisation also suggests the author's, and our own, entrapment in the limits of language, the possibilities of which are socially and culturally curtailed by the ancient power structures it embeds. Although our experience has moved on, the language in which we speak and think lags behind; it lacks the ability to transcend its horizon, thus still resembling a space metaphorically represented by the outdated labyrinth of London.

'A perimeter city': from suburbia to postmetropolitan London

Just like Powers, one of the many scientists that populate his work, Ballard is 'difficult to reach [...] a man always out on the periphery, only at ease working with unfamiliar materials'.[11] He is also mistaken for an author who writes from and about 'suburbia' – a problematic term with its origins in an American context which has become an umbrella term covering manifold ideas – and Ballard's own use of the term has added to that confusion.[12] To understand the complex and changing nature of Ballard's interest in peripheral space in relationship to marginality, it is helpful to situate his interest in urban spaces historically. Lewis Mumford's *The City in History* (1961) traces the emergence of the British suburb in the eighteenth century as a countryside for the civilised. At first an upper-class

> liberation from the sometimes dreary conventions and compulsions of an urban society [...] an effort [...] to have life on one's own terms, even if it meant having it alone: the anarchism of the well-filled purse, the heresy of the private individual's seeking to take over within the limits of the private family the functions of a whole community.[13]

Mumford also argues that in suburbia 'something that had been lost in the city was here coming back in an innocent form – the power to live an imagined life, closer to one's inner grain than what the daily routine imposes'.[14] This seductive idea caused a continuous demographic push outward that has had a big impact upon our understanding of London. In *The Future of London* (1962), Edward Carter pinpoints a crisis in the planning of London due to centrifugal forces:

> The once-upon-a-time London has not only become largely incapable of satisfying modern needs; it has exploded and scattered its homes and the loyalties and emotional attachments of its people into hundreds of square miles of un-urban confusion. [...] In a dangerous and paradoxical way suburbia, rather than 'London itself', has become the breeding-ground of contemporary London sentiment and character: petty-bourgeois and semi-detached.[15]

Whereas 'London itself' was formerly associated with urbane attitudes and inner city squalor, the suburban sprawl has rewritten our idea of what the city means; 'London' has become less and less urbane. This de-urbanisation of the London imagination also means that a certain depreciation and rejection of the values and characteristics that belong to life in the city – heterogeneity and multiplicity, concentration and density, specialisation, tension, drive, progress and change – has taken place.

The suburbia that Ballard describes, however, is not this eighteenth-, nineteenth- or early twentieth-century development of traditional suburbia, of which we still find examples in Julian Barnes's *Metroland* (1980) and Hanif Kureishi's *The Buddha of Suburbia* (1990). Ballard's work explores a spatiality that has developed and mutated under the forces of late capitalism and a sustained Americanisation in the second half of the twentieth century. Ballard's 'suburbia' is the place where the crisis of postmodernity, the endgame of modernity, plays itself out.

Crash describes how the television producer, 'Ballard', is awakened to a new vision of the landscape around Heathrow after he kills someone in a car crash. The narrative proposes a major turn in our consciousness by abandoning the focus from the former hegemony of the city centre as the social and sexual meeting point for people. Now, a new eroticism is found in a triangular zone that runs from the Marylebone flyover along the Westway and Western Avenue (A40), down along the north perimeter of Heathrow to Shepperton, which Ballard emphatically describes not as a suburb of London, but of Heathrow.[16]

This technological landscape is determined by the 'movement' of concrete sculptures generated by the speed of the driver, which triggers what Nick Davis has called 'Ballard's climactic acidic vision',[17] turning the Heathrow area into an illuminated world: 'The glass-curtain walling of the terminal buildings and the multi-storey car-parks behind them belonged to an enchanted domain.'[18] The car crash triggers the realisation of the violent ways in which power structures and technology flow through, and manipulate, the human mind and body. Crashing cars are a metaphorical expression of the sex act that visualises also the crisis of modernity. The dominance of technology forces the human body and mind to become intimately connected to, and confused with, the car and postmodern spaces (motorways, flyovers, multi-storey car parks, tower blocks) because all these forms are governed by the same power structures at work within post-war society:[19]

> Even the smallest movements seemed to be formalized, hands reaching towards me in a series of coded gestures. If one of them had unbuttoned his coarse serge trousers to reveal his genitalia, and pressed his penis into the bloody crotch of my armpit, even this bizarre act would have been acceptable in terms of the stylization of violence and rescue. (*Cr* 23)

The architecture and geography of this landscape emphasise stylisation of the surface and aesthetic rather than content, which draws out a new form of a 'perverse' sexuality: man, car and landscape are no longer organic, closed entities but they become extensions of one another, prosthetics that form an open machine operating sexual connections, without a beginning or end.

Ballard's text warns that the emerging drifts and desires are far from innocent, as Mumford suggested earlier, but rather they are manifestations of desire in which man is no longer central. The novel investigates, but also cautions against, postmodern man's urge 'to strip itself of *all* anthropomorphic and anthropological armouring, all myth and tragedy, and all existentialism, in order to perceive what is nonhuman in man, his will and his forces, his transformation and mutations'.[20] Deleuze and Guattari argue for a direct connection between the homogenisation of space and our consciousness. They describe how 'deterritorialisation' – the unravelling of traditional ordering of space in modernity – is accompanied by the emergence of all kinds of machines that release urges and desires from perverse fixations and familial neurosis: 'Schizoanalysis [...] treats the unconscious as an acentred system [...] as a machine network of finite automata (a rhizome), and thus arrives at an entirely different state of the unconscious.'[21] Rather than thinking of the unconscious as a deep structure or three-dimensional space to be mined by the psychoanalyst, Deleuze's and Guattari's model of *A Thousand Plateaus* (1980) makes this 'spatial' and therefore all on the surface.

This decentralisation of spatiality and consciousness through deterritorialisation also cancels out the traditional centre–periphery dialectic which is still present in the idea of the city–suburb opposition. Although Ballard's work is firstly a criticism of urban living, it develops into a similar questioning of the traditional suburb after its ideals have degenerated: 'Illuminated arrays glowed through the night like the perimeter lights of a colony of prison camps, a new gulag of penal settlements where the forced labour was shopping and spending.'[22] Ballard's version of 'suburbia' therefore seems closely aligned with Edward Soja's verdict on the suburb's regression during postmodernity:

> The sprawling suburb has become a nightmare, a universal megalopolis, a proliferating non-entity [...] What the suburb retains today is largely its original weaknesses: snobbery, segregation, status seeking, political irresponsibility [...] All that is left of the original impulse towards autonomy and initiative is the driving of the private motor car; but this is itself a compulsory and inescapable condition of suburban existence; and clever engineers already threaten to remove the individual control by a system of automation.[23]

Kingdom Come (2006) completes the fascinating trajectory of Ballard's thinking about London's peripheral spaces. In the novel, London is

surrounded and usurped by a new type of metropolis consisting of
suburban motorway towns in London's 'suburban outlands' (*Kc* 4).
The protagonist, Richard Pearson, an unemployed advertising executive with a flat in Chelsea, investigates the death of his father during a
shooting in the Brooklands Metro-Centre shopping mall. When Pearson
drives to Brooklands, a fictional town situated 'between Weybridge and
Woking' (*Kc* 4), he notes the following:

> The traffic into Brooklands had slowed, filling the six-lane highway
> built to draw the population of south-east England towards the
> Metro-Centre. Dominating the landscape round it, the immense alu-
> minium dome housed the largest shopping-mall in Greater London,
> a cathedral of consumerism whose congregations far exceeded those
> of the Christian churches. Its silver roof rose above the surrounding
> office blocks and hotels like the hull of a vast airship. With its visual
> echoes of the Millennium Dome in Greenwich, it fully justified its
> name, lying at the heart of a new metropolis that encircled London,
> a perimeter city that followed the path of the great motorways.
> Consumerism dominated the lives of its people, who looked as if
> they were shopping whatever they were doing. (*Kc* 15)

Kingdom Come transplants spatial developments that have been reshaping our understanding of place since Thatcher and New Labour into a
not-too-distant future. The description of the Metro-Centre is a hybrid
of architecture that already exists. Massive shopping malls such as
Bluewater and Westfield, and the infamous New Labour vanity project,
the Millennium Dome, are projected into a continuous expansion of
the city. This stage also symbolises the endgame of modern urban development that was originally rooted in the idea of the city as an organisational unity, and its fragmentation asks some major questions about
what 'London' actually is in the twenty-first century: 'Power has moved
to the Metro-Centre and the retail parks along the M25' (*Kc* 132)

The type of space that the novel describes is a projection of what
Edward Soja calls the 'postmetropolis' onto an English environment
transformed by late capitalism and cultural globalisation. Soja stresses
an increased regionality that is part of a new urbanism at the beginning
of the twenty-first century, whereby the urban and non-urban become
indistinguishable and increasingly heterogeneous: the city, suburb,
the country, village, inner city, satellite city are traditional categories
that have now become blurred and absorbed into a new form of urban
spatiality, the city-region.

Soja identifies a complex palimpsest of six developments (he calls them 'discourses') that make up the post-metropolitan development: economic restructuring that reshapes the physical environment; globalisation that affects money, work and culture; the simultaneous processes of decentralisation and centralisation of urban space; the fragmentation and polarisation of the city that influences social discourse; the proliferation of security and surveillance that give the urban environment a penitentiary feel; and the city (experience) becoming increasingly virtual or hyperreal due to the influence of hyperspace (from virtual communities to computer-generated artificial worlds) that has changed our understanding of what the urban is exactly.[24] Ballard's text is particularly interested in the effect that this process of fragmentation and, often, polarisation has on the citizen's conception of society and culture.

The dominant consumer culture demands we derive our identity from various forms of shopping; like demigods, we 'create' ourselves from clothing brands and the football teams we support. Ballard notes that the confusion about our allegiances to different identities may lead to a crisis in our self-conception that may trigger violent outbursts to relieve psychological pressure. An external world governed by the principles of the capitalist consumer society and media spectacle impacts negatively upon the subject's inner landscape, and the city's sensory overload inhibits the possibility of seeing and experiencing the world properly. The transgressive powers of perception needed to travel beyond the limited horizon of the city were found in the peripheral zones, but now the commodification of identity makes this impossible: 'All these retail parks are the same. Rootless people drifting about' (*Kc* 66). If we no longer have the ability to identify with the specificity of local place because it has become homogenised, Ballard asks, how can we have a proper sense of ourselves? Ballard's text shows that consumerist identity politics trigger a regression into tribalism and racist violence due to a reawakening of nationalist sentiment and cheap mythology of English racial purity bought into being by the many 'men in St George's shirts' (*Kc* 24).

This critical framing of twenty-first-century London as a postmetropolis, which Soja derives from his analysis of Los Angeles, is confirmed by Ballard's description of his preferred place of residence:

Shepperton, a Thames-side town fifteen miles to the west of London, has improved immensely during the thirty-five years I have lived there. [...] In the late 1960s the twentieth century at last arrived and began to transform the Thames Valley into a pleasing replica of Los Angeles, with all the ambiguous but heady charms of alienation and anonymity. A forest of TV aerials blotted out the poplars and church spires. Multi-storey car parks rose like the megaliths of a future Stonehenge, along with a landscape of dual carriageways and overpasses that eased and cosseted its true heir, the motor car.[25]

A similar analogy between LA and London's margins we get in *Kingdom Come*: the death of Pearson's father 'belonged in Manila or Bogotá or East Los Angeles, rather than in a bosky English suburb' (*Kc* 5). Ballard's comparison between London's periphery and Los Angeles is striking for a variety of reasons. It points out that an American influence upon, or imprinting of, the European landscape occurs, that goes beyond the presence of McDonald's and Starbucks. Ballard suggests that at the very heart of conceiving space – from motorways and high-rise buildings to gated communities and mega shopping malls, an unrelenting Americanisation is taking place in the post-war period.

Due to its film studios, Shepperton, like Hollywood, is also associated with the film industry, and the point that Ballard makes is that much of our contemporary experiences are lived through the dominant cultural and artistic form of the twentieth century: cinema. In Soja's words: 'Involved in almost every aspect of the changing urban imaginary has been the realization that it has become more difficult than ever before to tell the difference between what is *real* and what is *imagined*, what can reliably be identified as fact as opposed to what must clearly be labelled fiction.'[26] Ballard goes even further by suggesting an inversion: 'We live inside an enormous novel. It is now less and less necessary for the writer to invent the fictional content of his novel. The fiction is already there. The writer's task is to invent the reality.'[27] London plays a central role in this process of fictionalisation, because, after Shanghai 'London in the 1960s has been the second [media city], with the same confusions of image and reality, the same overheating.'[28] The level of confusion, or even inversion, can be demonstrated by looking at a passage in Ballard's *The Kindness of Women* (1991), which describes how Steven Spielberg's Hollywood-adaptation of *Empire of the Sun* (1984) convincingly recreates Ballard's own youth in Shanghai near his residence:

> My dream of Shanghai had materialised, like all dreams, in the least expected place, among the imposing houses built around the golf course at Sunningdale, little more than a fifteen-minute drive from Shepperton [...] A genie had sprung from the pages of my novel, and

was busily conjuring the past into life, working with an extravagance more than a match for the original Shanghai [...] The city of memory whose streets I had redrawn within the limits of the printed page had materialised in a fusion of the real and the super-real. Memory had been superseded by a new technology of historical recovery, where past, present, and future could be dismantled and reshuffled at the producer's whim.[29]

The complexity of the spatio-temporal renegotiation of the relationship between the real and the fictional is mind-boggling. The remembered experiences that Ballard writes down in his fictional autobiography are sold to the most famous Hollywood director, who decides to shoot a part of the adaptation, set in Shanghai, near Ballard's home, thousands of miles away, 40 years after the actual events took place. It is as if his formative experiences haunt him across time as well as space, yet an even more important point is that Ballard's own semi-fictional memories of his childhood are retrospectively rewritten, or, if we accept that cinema has to a large extent created our understanding of the twentieth century, are made even more real. London is, then, both a producer of fictions as well as an imaginary construct; the metropolis is the place where films are made and where films are shot, whilst it is also inextricably intertwined with the construction of false perception of the world, as well as of itself.

Another important connection between peripheral London and Los Angeles is Ballard's exploration of social unrest and uprisings in relationship to the built environment. Soja spends a large part of *Postmetropolis* (2000) on the significance of the Rodney King Riots, or the Justice Riots, of 1992, which were fuelled partly by the social division that is inscribed into the minorities' consciousness by the city's spaces. The riots were caused by one of the worst economic recessions that fuelled frustration among the African-American and Latino working poor, but Soja is also aware that it is postmetropolitan space itself that contributed to the violent outburst because the effects of late capitalism and globalisation on spatialisation contribute to social injustice. These events have their roots in spatial segregation, for which Los Angeles is renowned.

Just as *Kingdom Come* translates the aesthetic of the Millennium Dome into the Metro-Centre, the novel also transfigures the Rodney King Riots when on several occasions the racist violence against ethnic minorities spirals out of control: 'Under the cover of a packed programme of sporting events, an exercise in ethnic cleansing was taking place, under the connivance of the local police' (*Kc* 78). The novel points out a gradual return facilitated by the particular identity politics – and the specific production and consumption of space – of the consumer society, which collapses into a mediatised repetition of the persecution of the Other in 1930s Germany, and results in a curious mixture of the King Riots, the Brixton Riots of 1981, the Jonestown Massacre in 1978, and, most importantly, the Holocaust. After David Cruise establishes himself as a self-styled Führer of the white, middle-class consumers, they lock themselves in the Metro-Centre to establish a new republic, and 'a solar cult' (*Kc* 278). The entropic processes of the contemporary consumer culture are merely a curious re-enactment of the irrational consumption of energy during the Holocaust, a re-emergence of fascism in the West via the backdoor, which Michael Moorcock's *Mother London* also warns against. And just as the problems in LA are shaped by two opposing versions of carceral space – the ghettoised poor and the wealthy living in gated communities – the root of this process lies, for Ballard, in a spatial segregation that reinforces a false difference of identity. The ultimate goal for both Soja and Ballard is to pursue 'spatial justice', in which the production of space brings out 'more clearly the potentially powerful yet often obscured spatiality of all aspects of social life' and 'to open up in this spatialized sociality (and historicality) more effective ways to change the world for the better through spatially conscious practices and politics'.[30]

Millennium People: New Labour, new order and gated communities

Ballard's engagement with urban spaces, and the modern city in particular, gives us an acute diagnosis of the state of contemporary Britain, and his final two fictional works form a direct attack on the Thatcher and New Labour governments by creating an explicitly politicised London geography.[31] In *Millennium People* we are plunged headlong into the now deserted gated community 'Chelsea Marina', where a 'small revolution was taking place, so modest and well behaved that almost no one had noticed'.[32] The protagonist, the corporate psychologist David Markham, walks through the estate, now shrouded in an uncanny silence:

> Beyond the gatehouse were the streets of the deserted estate, an apocalyptic vision deprived of its soundtrack. Protest banners sagged from balconies, and I counted a dozen overturned cars and at least two burnt-out houses [...] In front of me lay Chelsea Marina, its streets empty as never before in its twenty-year existence. The entire

population had vanished, leaving a zone of silence like an urban nature reserve. (*MP* 3–5)

Chelsea Marina's inhabitants, led by the charismatic paediatrician and anarchic nihilist Dr Richard Gould, have staged an uprising because of their realisation that they have been misled by key manipulators of a late capitalist system which has started to operate pseudo-fascist tendencies. Markham, who lives in the upmarket area of St John's Wood but joins the Marina's revolt after his ex-wife dies in a bomb attack on Heathrow airport, slowly understands that Gould is using the gated community for more sinister purposes. The aspirational middle-class inhabitants are seduced by Gould into thinking they are rebelling against key cultural institutions which have psychologically manipulated them by bombing a cat show at Olympia, firebombing the bookshop at the British Museum and by blowing up London landmarks such as Broadcasting House on Portland Street, because 'the BBC had played a leading role in brainwashing the middle classes' (*MP* 149).

These attacks on iconic landmarks in a Western capital city are unconscious re-enactments of the attacks on the World Trade Center in New York on 11 September 2001. Like a ringmaster of a global circus of terrorism, Gould uses the post-9/11 climate of anxiety and aggression by acting as a version of Osama bin Laden, whilst the residents of Chelsea Marina become his naïve footsoldiers, fed on his rhetoric of liberation. Not before long, London is taken over by anarchy: 'Protest movements, sane and insane, sensible and absurd, touched almost every aspect of life in London, a vast web of demonstrations that tapped a desire for a more meaningful world' (*MP* 37). Whilst they think they are engaged in an attack on 'The 20th Century' (*Kc* 63), the residents are actually tricked into destroying the very foundations and values of Western civilisation and democracy.

Ballard investigates a new species of Americanised space, namely the penitentiary structure of the gated community. Chelsea Marina is, albeit a middle-class version, a direct reworking of Imperial Wharf, the development project for the wealthy on the north bank of the Thames at the former gas works at Sand's End consisting of retail units, offices, 1,665 new homes, a hotel (named the Conrad), convenience stores, community and medical facilities, restaurants and bars, a mini-harbour called 'Chelsea Harbour' and a public park.

The advance of late capitalism in the post-war period causes the decline of hierarchical structures established under the age of empire, which triggers a wholesale redrawing of the spatial organisation on which it constructed itself. After the deterritorialisation of space, we also see the emergence of new nodes of order emerge, through a counter-process of 'reterritorialisation'. In Claire Colebrook's words: 'Capital arrests its tendency to produce and open flows by quantifying all exchange through the flow of capital.'[33] In Ballard's later texts, such pockets feature in the form of guarded estates and gated communities for the well-off, which emerge first in *Running Wild* (1986), and in the late 1990s is developed into the investigation of gated communities and business parks on the Mediterranean coastline in *Cocaine Nights* (1996) and *Super-Cannes* (2000). By transplanting that space to central London, a very curious renegotiation of what Carter earlier called 'London itself' is taking place in *Millennium People*. Iain Sinclair notes:

> At first gated communities emerged on the periphery of London, but now they are taking over the centre of London as well. There is a sort of inversion going on of the suburbanization that John Betjeman wrote about, where you see the centres become suburban-ized through hideous non-development projects.[34]

Chelsea Marina represents, however, a curious mixture of spaces which are inscribing themselves into contemporary London's fabric, namely a mixture between the Mediterranean, coastal spaces of leisure, the gated community and the simulacral city. Whereas the postmetropolis cre-ates an open, deterritorialised form of spatiality, the gated community breaks up London's traditional mixed use of land and its open, organic figure ground by introducing a self-contained system closed off from the diversity and multiplicity of life in the city, reinforcing the city's machinery of control.

Ballard's transplantation of a leisure resort from the Mediterranean into London makes some interesting points about the ways in which the texture of the city has recently changed. The peculiar atmosphere and aesthetic of south European beach resorts interests Ballard because they introduce a completely different conception of space, which he again related to LA:

> One could regard them collectively as a linear city some 3000 miles long, from Gibraltar to Glyfada beach north of Athens, and some 300 yards deep. The usual hierarchies and conventions are absent; in many ways it couldn't be less European, but it works. It has a unique ambi-ence [...] At present it is Europe's Florida [...] Could it ever become Europe's California? Perhaps, but the peculiar geometry of those iden-tical apartment houses seem to defuse the millenarian spirit.[35]

To understand what the effects of Ballard's spatial grafting are, we should turn to Henri Lefebvre, who has some illuminating things to say about the transformation of the perimeter of the Mediterranean into a leisure-oriented space for industrialised Northern Europe during the late sixties and early seventies:

> as a 'non-work' space [...] this area has acquired a specific role in the division of labour. Economically and socially, architecturally and urbanistically, it has been subjected to a sort of neo-colonization. [...] The quasi-cultist focus of localities based on leisure would thus form a striking contrast to the productive focus of North European cities. The waste and expense, meanwhile, would appear as an end-point of a temporal sequence starting in the workplace, in production-based space, and leading to the consumption of space, sun and sea, and of spontaneous or induced eroticism, in a great 'vacationland festival'. [...] What a travesty such a picture would be, however, enshrining as it does both the illusion of transparency and the illusion of natural-ness. The truth is that all this seemingly non-productive expense is planned with the greatest care: centralized, organized, hierarchized [...] it serves the interests of tour-operators, bankers and entrepre-neurs of places such as Hamburg and London. [...] in the spatial prac-tice of neocapitalism (complete with air transport), representations of space facilitate the manipulation of representational spaces (sun, sea, festival, waste, expense).[36]

Just as Rushdie's *The Satanic Verses* tropicalises London by translating the city into signs and symbols associated with the East, Ballard's recodes London – essentially a space for labour and economic enterprise – into codes (such as the name 'Marina') we associate with vacation, leisure and festivities. One of the points that Ballard's novel makes is that London's current transformation is taking place through 'the manipulation of representational spaces': the Mediterranean's aura of leisure, natural appearance and freedom from the restraints of work is *artificially* created through a great expenditure of labour and rationalisa-tion. Bringing this fictional form of space back to Northern Europe is ironical and confusing as two opposing forms of space clash with one another.

The effect is a double one, with first an outburst of eroticism and vio-lence, but then a retreat into passivity: after their rebellion, the Chelsea Mariners leave for the countryside. David James notes that '*Millennium People* prophesies London's spiral to a sphere of inaction in which the most radically conscientious among its population are ridiculed.

Markham has had to experience for himself how, thanks to its repetitive and recuperative topography, Chelsea had been able to patronize and quell the revolt as a "heroic failure".'[37] The novel's utopian fantasy about the potential transformation through a revolution that actually takes place through a bourgeoisification of social and spatial structures introduced into a traditionally rigidly social structure is unmasked as a manipulation of spatial practices by hegemonic powers, as Iain Sinclair also explores in *London Orbital*.

As I explored in detail elsewhere, one way in which this occurs is by Chelsea Marina mimicking London by copying its original figure ground and street names from the surrounding, expensive Mayfair and Knightsbridge areas, and also the city.[38] Chelsea Marina's figure ground and architecture falsely offer the gated community as an alternative to the official centre whilst being merely a replica. Ballard constructs a fictional geography the spaces of which are inscribed with British colonial history, which functions as a neo-colonial denial of Britain's post-war decline. This linguistic recycling establishes a closed circuit that traps the inhabitants in an endless loop of self-reinforcing signification without reference to 'the real'. Within this late capitalist London, it is only the Thames that retains a degree of authenticity:

> The dealing rooms were a con, and only the river was real. The money was all on tick, a stream, of coded voltages sluicing through the concealed conduits under the foreign exchange floors. Facing them across the river were two more fakes, the replica of Shakespeare's Globe, and an old power station made over into a middle-class disco, Tate Modern. (*MP* 180)

We see a critique of a twenty-first-century simulacral London, which we also find in the work of Michael Moorcock, Salman Rushdie and Iain Sinclair. Ballard's novel aims its criticism partly at the ways in which contemporary rhetorical practices by entrepreneurs, mass media and governments divorce us from our ability to experience the real, which becomes a spectacle readily transformed into a product for our consumption. After the Mariners' attack on the National Film Theatre, images of their terrorist act are circulated by the media almost immediately:

> the late edition of the Sunday newspapers carried vivid colour photographs of the fire at the National Film Theatre. The same inferno glowed from the news-stands in Hammersmith and Knightsbridge. At the traffic lights I stared down from the taxi at the fierce orange

Figure 9 Tate Modern, Bankside

flames, barely grasping that I had been partly responsible for them. At the same time I felt an odd pride in what I had done. [...] We set off for St John's Wood, past the same images of disaster hanging from the kiosks in the Charing Cross Road. Central London was dressed for an apocalyptic day. Arson in the film library clearly touched deep layers of unease, as the unconscious fears projected by a thousand Hollywood films at last emerged into reality. (*MP* 141–2)

Again, Ballard suggests that in the contemporary world a closed circuit of the real and representation has effaced the difference between events taking place in reality and their narration. Ballard's text is ambiguous about Gould's more radical project: *Millennium People* suggests that the necessary sensory perception needed to regain a form of liberated perception requires transgressive acts that make the citizen see the city anew, while such acts are immediately recuperated within the same system it tries to subvert.

Despite this contradiction, Ballard continues to associate the city centre with bourgeois cultural institutions that communicate possibly dangerous messages through their unquestioned iconic status. This becomes clear from the description of another prison of the imagination under attack, namely, the Tate Modern, which opened in 2000:

I strolled through the tourists drawn across the Millennium Bridge, eager to see the damage to this bombastic structure, more bunker than museum, of which Albert Speer would have thoroughly approved.

Like all our friends, Sally and I saw every exhibition held in this massive vault. The building triumphed by a visual sleight of hand, a psychological trick that any fascist dictator would understand. Externally, its deco symmetry made it seem smaller than it was, and the vast dimensions of the turbine hall cowed both eye and brain. The entrance ramp was wide enough to take a parade of tanks. Power, of kilowatt hours or messianic gospel, glowered from the remote walls. This was the art show as Führer spectacle, an early sign, perhaps, that the educated classes were turning to fascism. (*MP* 181)

Ballard's association of the Tate Modern with fascism lies in the dangerous gap between form and content. In an essay on the semiotics of architecture, Umberto Eco states that '*the form of the object must, besides making function possible, denote that function clearly enough to make it practicable as well as desirable,* clearly enough to dispose one to the actions through which it would be fulfilled.'[39] Ballard's analysis of the Tate

Modern points out the triumph of aesthetics over function, as well as its dangers; the architecture takes away agency from the subject (tourists are 'drawn') and exerts an unconscious coercive force on our perception of representation ('cowed both eye and brain').[40]

Millennium People is most overt in its criticism of New Labour's flirtation with 'a ruthless venture capitalism that perpetuates the class system in order to divide the opposition and preserve its own privileges' (*MP* 216). Ballard's already pessimistic vision of London grows even darker as he envisions New Labour's perpetuation of Thatcherite neo-liberal economy and politics with undertones of fascism, implying the collusion of planners, developers and architects such as Sir Norman Foster and Richard Rogers to create a specific pseudo-fascistic texture of the contemporary. The text criticises and mocks New Labour's culture of spin, which increases the gap between rhetoric and reality, as complicit in the promotion of this post-war transformation of contemporary British society and London.

Westminster was about to ignite from within

To illustrate Ballard's attack on New Labour's contribution to a collective failure of perception it is helpful to juxtapose the two protagonists of *Millennium People* to one another. The names 'David Markham' and 'Richard Gould' give important clues to their characters. First, 'Markham' ('mark them') recalls Blake's poem 'London' (1794), in which the narrator wanders through London's streets to 'mark in every face I meet / Marks of weakness, marks of woe'. Blake's narrator is an observer of the city's phenomenological traces, which are transformed into a universal outcry against the suffering of mankind, which may be redeemed through the emancipation of sensory perception offered by the visionary poet. Ballard's protagonist lacks the power of perception to understand Gould's plan, however: This information is important because it signals to the reader that the narrator is unreliable: 'Even I, David Markham, a trained psychologist infiltrated into Chelsea Marina as a police spy – a deception I was the last to discover – failed to see what was going on' (*MP* 3). Markham's limited insight into himself and the world around him, which is reinforced by the fact that his blinding arrogance persists even *after* the events, suggests that the crisis of modernity remains unresolved.

Markham's emblematic name is also close to that of a second intertext, namely Stoker's aforementioned *Dracula*, which is narrated by Harker ('listener'), a similarly naïve narrator who is blinded by his preconceptions and misguided by his limitations. Ballard's text makes connections between the West and the East, suggesting that our attempts to divorce ourselves from the neo-colonial violence inflicted upon others across the world will come to haunt us. Again, the novel makes constant references to 9/11 and other global tensions in which the West is complicit: Gould 'stared through the window at the empty streets and fire-damaged houses with the tired gaze of an overworked doctor trying to carry out his medical work in a wartorn Middle Eastern suburb' (*MP* 12). Just as *Dracula* cautioned against colonisation, Ballard's novel suggests that the disastrous fallout of the uncontrolled spread of capitalism will come to haunt the West.

Several meanings resonate in Gould's name: the precious metal 'gold' contained in his name implies that his perception is heightened, sublime and revelatory, and Gould certainly is able to formulate what Milan Kundera termed 'the *terminal paradoxes* of the Modern Era':[41]

> We tolerate everything, but we know that liberal values are designed to make us passive. We think we believe in God but we're terrified of the mysteries of life and death. We're deeply self-centred but can't cope with the idea of our finite selves. We believe in progress and the power of reason, but are haunted by the darker sides of human nature. We're obsessed with sex, but fear the sexual imagination and have to be protected by huge taboos. We believe in equality but hate the underclass. We fear our bodies and, above all, we fear death. We're an accident of nature, but we think we're at the centre of the universe. (*MP* 139)

His attempt to escape the capitalist paradigms and consumer logic which deny and repress these paradoxes lies in the creation of anarchic, 'meaningless' acts that obviate causality as a conventional way of constructing meaning that sedates the West.

Millennium People contains an emblematic scene where the importance of perception is dramatised. After the attack by Gould's terrorists on the National Film Theatre, Markham flees into a gondola of the London Eye, drawing attention to his fallen vision. Markham fails to recognise Gould, disguised as a waiter, nor the dangers of his perhaps brilliant, but deranged terrorist operations. In the following passage, the text builds towards a sublime, epiphanic revelation:

> As we rose above County Council the fires lit the night air and seemed to burn on the dark waters of the Thames. A huge caldera had opened beside Waterloo Bridge and was devouring the

South Bank Centre. Billows of smoke leaned across the river, and I could see the flames reflected in the distant casements of the Houses of Parliament, as if the entire Palace of Westminster was about to ignite from within. (*MP* 123–4)

This excerpt is a projection of Gould's fantasy of destroying London's political and cultural institutions. We feel the presence of William Blake, and 'London' especially, which connects the power of the church as a religious institution with that of the crown and state oppression of the English people. The iconic tourist attraction also becomes a symbol for the various processes of surveillance that London and its inhabitants at the beginning of the twenty-first century are undergoing, whilst it also suggests an addiction to spectacle that is abused by Gould.

Markham does not pick up on this revelation: 'The first smoke had reached the window of the gondola, laying itself across the curved panes. I began to cough, tasting the acrid vapour that had churned outside the manager's office. I retched onto the rail, and spilled champagne over the floor at my feet' (*MP* 124). The epiphanic moment falls flat: Markham's powers of perception are limited and unable to see that Gould personifies 'evil', appropriating London for his hellish spectacle: 'The flame-lit buildings along the Thames threw their light into his unsettled eyes' (*MP* 125). His restless vision lacks order and is dangerously opportunistic and unpredictable; just like Dracula, Gould is also a 'ghoul' – a malevolent, dark spirit who corrupts people through temptation.

In Gould we not only detect a version of Osama bin Laden, but some of the descriptions are also a veiled reference to the psychological make-up of Tony Blair:

[Gould] had recast himself as a messenger of the truth […] smiling with a kind of shy confidence, a concerned gaze that had nothing of the fanatic about it. He was the caring physician on the ward of the world, encouraging and explaining, always ready to sit beside some anxious patient and set out a complex diagnosis in layman's terms. (*MP* 257)

Another reference to Tony Blair surfaces when Markham asks Gould if he tried on Stephen Dexter's priest's frock: 'The cassock? I was tempted. Let's say I'm in the wrong priesthood' (*MP* 247). Blair also wanted to become a man of the cloth, and his decision to take Britain into Iraq was to be judged by God.[42] This analysis is affirmed by Ballard himself, who states: 'I assume that a large part of Blair's appeal (like Kennedy's) is aesthetic, just as a large part of the Nazi appeal lay in its triumph of the will aesthetic.'[43]

Ballard offers the novel itself as a counter-space where the authority of official figures in power may be questioned and challenged. The Home Secretary, who comes to Chelsea Marina to assess the damage after the revolution, is never described but is merely a two-dimensional emblem filled with power, and he never utters a word when the inhabitants return:

> [T]he Home Secretary visibly lightened, for a moment standing tiptoe. After a glance at the TV camera, he beckoned the motorcyclists aside. Raising his arms, as if on traffic duty, he waved the Volvo forward [...] Smiling cheerfully, the Home Secretary stepped into the rear seat of the limousine. He waved to the returnees, who hooted their horns in reply. (*MP* 281–2)

Ballard shows that political power is transmitted and received through signs and gestures, and he undermines the Home Secretary's 'authority' by passing it off in comedy.

A brave attempt to free America: Conrad, Ballard and 9/11

Millennium People's engagement with contemporary anxieties about terrorism in London after the attacks on America on 11 September 2001 return us to Ballard's reworking of a third important intertext, namely Joseph Conrad's *The Secret Agent* (1907). The text comes at the tale-end of the city's history of anarchic violence in the nineteenth century. We are reminded, for instance, of the Hyde Park Riots in 1855 when, after all Sunday trading in London was abolished, a crowd of 150,000 people gathered in the park and attacked the carriages of the rich. Although Karl Marx's statement that 'yesterday in Hyde Park the revolution began' was over-optimistic, these events did cause great concern.[44] In *Culture and Anarchy* (1896), Matthew Arnold – a cultural critic staged by Ballard as 'Professor Arnold' (*MP* 28, 189) – feared that the Hyde Park Riots of July 1866 threatened to overthrow the principle of authority that was part of his definition of culture.[45] Arnold had a contradictory sense of class, fearing the destabilisation of the class system and the increasing working-class agency over the middle class, while acknowledging that the existing social hierarchies were inadequate for effective government. Although Dominic Head notes that 'the class consciousness that colours Arnold's view no longer applies' to contemporary society, Ballard would argue that London still inscribes its citizens with Victorian hierarchies.[46]

This is also underscored by Ballard's reworking of *The Secret Agent*. Conrad's novel was more directly inspired by a wave of anarchist bomb attacks throughout Europe in the last two decades of the eighteenth century, and by the Greenwich Park bomb attack by French anarchist Martial Bourdin in February 1894 in particular. In Conrad's novel, the retarded Stevie bungles the bombing of the Greenwich Observatory, a symbolic destruction of time that is to upset the stale middle-class consciousness. As the mastermind behind the attack, The Professor, explains:

> A bomb outrage to have any influence on pubic opinion now must go beyond the intention of vengeance of terrorism. It must be purely destructive. [...] You anarchists should make it clear that you are perfectly determined to make a clean sweep of the whole social creation. But how to get that appallingly absurd notion into the heads of the middle classes so that there should be no mistake? [...] By directing your blows at something outside the ordinary passions of humanity is the answer. [...] The attack must have all the shocking senselessness of gratuitous blasphemy. Since bombs are your means of expression, it would really be telling if you could throw a bomb into pure mathematics. [...] Yes [...] the blowing up of the first meridian line is bound to raise a howl of execration.
>   'A difficult business,' Mr Verloc mumbled, feeling that this was the only safe thing to say.[47]

Stevie's accidental blowing up of 'pure mathematics' itself is uncanny because it is unconsciously understood as the destruction of imperial London at the centre of time and space. This act is reworked in Ballard's text, where Gould, as incarnation of The Professor, tells Markham:

> A terrorist bomb not only killed its victims, but forced a violent rift through space and time, and ruptured the logic that held the world together. For a few hours gravity turned traitor, overruling Newton's laws of motion, reversing rivers and toppling skyscrapers, stirring fears long dormant in our minds. (*MP* 182)

As the reference to 'toppling skyscrapers' suggests, there is another reading of the novel, here. Whereas Conrad's text imagined the destruction of London, *Millennium People* indirectly stages the attack on New York in 2001. Bin Laden's attack on the World Trade Center may appear to be subversive because it destroys key symbols of global capitalism, but paradoxically the events subscribe to Western conventions of signification. Essentially, the terrorist act subscribed to and reinforced capitalist values because its spectacular representation by mass media monumentalised, and thus implicitly legitimised and even celebrated, the World Trade Center.

The failed bombing of the Tate Modern bookshop by the 'revolutionary' Joan Chang, who accidentally becomes a suicide bomber, is another sign of the Chelsea Marina residents' folly. Ballard's novel criticises them for the inherent self-defeating contradiction of their logic: their attacks are just another form of spectacle, and thus another form of consumerism. Symbolic destruction is not subversive for Gould because it remains within the realm of conventional signification: 'We're living in a soft-regime prison. The attack on the World Trade Center in 2001 was a brave attempt to free America from the 20th Century. The deaths were tragic, but otherwise it was a meaningless act. And that was its point' (*MP* 139–40). In order to truly upset our perception, seemingly meaningless acts that disrupt rational, causal logic are necessary, which is why Chang's bungling is more memorable and subversive. Markham states: 'Walking past the entrance to the Globe, I listened for an echo of the bomb that had killed Joan Chang, the only meaningful event in the entire landscape' (*MP* 180). Gould's true aim is to establish a mesmerising repetition that sets the consumer society up for an act that is radically and truly different, and beyond conventional signification: 'Chelsea Marina was a place of real promise, when a young paediatrician persuaded the residents to create a unique republic, a city without street signs, laws without penalties, events without significance, a sun without shadows' (*MP* 294).

Conclusion

Ballard's work in general, but his engagement with the city especially, teaches us that if we could recognise that we cannot control the world through rationality, objective interpretation and calculation, we could also come to acknowledge the dark, irrational powers that reside in us, which could help us stop perpetuating trauma and violence on other people that emerge as a part of suppression of the imaginative faculty and feeling. For Ballard, London is a penitentiary space, a container of a history of oppressive memories and structures that must be destroyed in order for human consciousness and the imagination to be liberated. For Ballard, the city's dense packing together of signs leads to psychopathologies which prevent the construction of a New Jerusalem. The impact of an external world governed by the principles of capitalist consumer society and media spectacle impacts negatively upon our landscapes of the mind. The results of this repression and alienation are psychological trauma and neuroses: the city's sensory overstimulation produces a crisis in perception because the spectator's exhaustion produces an inhibiting effect. The transgressive powers of perception needed to travel beyond the limited horizon of words are found in the suburbs, and in the technological landscapes of 'interstitial' spaces, which enable our immersion into new forms of sensory emancipation.

4
'Struck out of Pure Invention': Iain Sinclair and the Problem of London

Approaching Iain Sinclair's London: text and the city

In Iain Sinclair's engagement with London we find a profound and continuously evolving interest in the complex problems that writing the contemporary metropolis presents. The resulting works are 'difficult', intimidating, sometimes inaccessible objects of art. His prose is often in hyperbolic overdrive, full of slippery irony and densely packed with references to obscure sources. Richard Todd states that unlike Peter Ackroyd's writing 'the London of Sinclair's imagination does not attempt linguistic or ventriloquial pastiche: instead its imagery is astonishingly idiosyncratic, its energy charged by the sheer force of Sinclair's imaginative conception of London.'[1] Rod Mengham states that 'for Sinclair the notion of time folding up like a concertina remains at the level of a working hypothesis, a means of conjuring up powerfully unorthodox perspectives on a set of contemporary social phenomena that form the critical focus of an authorial project with strong documentary impulses [...] Sinclair's language is the vehicle of a distinctive personal style, whereas Ackroyd's writing is frequently drawn to the use of pastiche.'[2] The reader of Sinclair's works enters the city through an invocatory exploration of the place's past representations, imaginatively conjured out of the surviving sites:

> Southwark holds its time, with the City, with Whitechapel, with Clerkenwell, holds the memory of what it was: it is possible to walk back into the previous, as an event, still true to this moment. The Marshalsea trace, the narrative mazetrap that Dickens set, takes over, the figures of fiction outliving the ghostly impulses that started them. The past is a fiction that absorbs us. It needs no passport, turn the corner and it is with you. (*WCST* 63)

Sinclair's methodology relies on obsessively using historical texts as well as physical spaces to access the past and represent it: 'The truth can only be remade out of lies. What horror! A life struck out of pure invention' (*WCST* 107).

Sinclair's origins as a poet are highly visible in the level of linguistic ingenuity that shapes his London. Peter Barry describes Sinclair's language as 'curiously phrasal in its effects, consisting of disjunctive, serial hits on successive targets, rather than constituting a flow'.[3] Robert Bond finds that the prose is driven 'on the speed of terse proletarian narratives'.[4] Sinclair's narration also suffers from what Maurice Merleau-Ponty calls 'a condition of association', whereby a polyphonic, fragmentary vocal composite is generated by the trauma of exclusion.[5] In Sinclair's own words: 'I wanted a language such as that invoked by Jack Kerouac in his *Essentials of Spontaneous Prose*: "Not 'selectivity' of expression but following free deviation (association) of mind into limitless blow-of–subject seas of thought"' (*LOFT* 285). Sinclair's citation of Kerouac is a striking example of the contradictions in his work, as the phrase 'seas of thought' is a quotation from William Wordsworth's *The Prelude* (1850), paying homage to Sir Isaac Newton as '[v]oyaging through strange seas of thought, alone'.[6]

Sinclair is sometimes proclaimed a mystic, visionary writer because of his early esoteric explorations of London's ley-lines, 'auditory hallucinations' and obscure mythologies.[7] Andrew Gibson notes that 'it is Sinclair who really pitches for authentic connection with the visionary London tradition'.[8] Brian Baker finds that in the writing 'power, temporal power is transformed [...] into occult forms'.[9] Yet Sinclair's book on John Clare, *Edge of the Orison* (2005), suggests that his obsessions with the occult were misleading:

> I enjoyed my lost years as a book scout [...] Being out on the road, red-eyed, buzzing with caffeine, hammered by monologues, the nervous occultism of fellow dealers, was an excellent preparation: for what? For defacing notebooks, formulating skewed theories, misreading signs. Pre-fictional chaos. I abandoned my attempts to construct pseudo-epics that mingled (without distinction) poetry with prose.[10]

One of his early critics, Simon Perril, notes that 'Sinclair's sense of the human as a focus for the convergence of the twin powers of myth and place is presented in terms that are firmly mediumistic [...] But Sinclair's work refuses to present this idea as a metaphor for the poet's divine right to inspiration. Rather, it is inverted into a study of power and

oppression.'[11] At the heart of Sinclair's work lies an ongoing engagement with the representational problems posed by the writing of a
self that is subject to the collusion of political and capitalist powers.
Sinclair's project is remarkably coherent and, for want of a better word,
rational, and it exploits the occult and schizophrenia as metaphors for
social and cultural diagnosis. Through sheer study, learning and self-
immersion in historical texts, both Ackroyd and Sinclair try to bring
back the materiality of history through esoteric acts of narrative.[12]
Sinclair's work constructs an idiosyncratic, highly personalised mythic
geography of London that recovers an increasingly fragmented city by
mapping its *disjecta membra*.

Sinclair's work has also been shoehorned into frameworks provided
by postmodern theory, which on occasion has led to analyses Sinclair
deems politically correct. Peter Brooker accuses him of failing to procure
a decent opposition to the paradoxes of postmodernity, implying a
charge of racism by reading *Downriver* in terms of 'the matter of white-
ness as the paradoxically transparent mark of an undeclared but hegemonic ethnicity'.[13] Sinclair's work, according to Brooker, is 'governed by a
corporate white male consciousness [and it] colludes in the very norms
of Thatcher's Britain'.[14] Rachel Potter has accused Sinclair of excluding
ethnic minorities and women from his work[15] and Robert Sheppard
states that 'the position of women in his work is problematic' because
they 'are often reflectors of male desire'.[16] Sinclair has responded furiously to such accusations: 'I can only speak for myself. I have no obli-
gation to speak on behalf of other people. That idea is too compulsory,
extremely patronising and politically correct. I never feel that writing
should be judged by what it doesn't do, it should be taken to task for
what it actually does.'[17]

Poststructuralist critics have stressed Sinclair's representation of the
city as a text, which seems understandable when looking at Sinclair's
writing. In *Lud Heat* (1975), Sinclair notes of Hawksmoor's involvement
in the reconstruction of London after the Great Fire of 1666: 'He had the
frenzy, the Coleridge notebook speed, to rewrite the city.'[18] In *London
Orbital* (2002) Sinclair states: 'Through the suburbs at night, the motorway verges by day, we were there; heel-and-toeing it, sucking water
from plastic bottles, trying to find some way to unravel the syntax of
London.'[19] In *Lights Out for the Territory* (1997), Sinclair states 'London
is begging to be rewritten' (*LOFT* 141) and in an interview the author
speaks of 'reading London typography as a series of interconnections
and erased memories'.[20] Indeed, the words 'WANTED: INTERPRETER.
UNEDITED CITY', in Sinclair's collaborative project with Dave McKean,

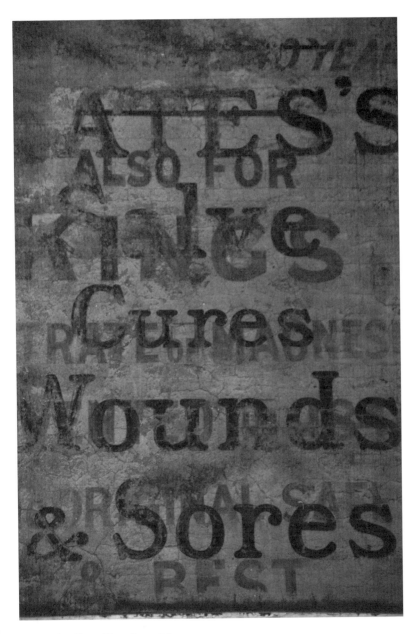

Figure 10 Ghost Sign, Regent Square

Slow Chocolate Autopsy (1997)[21] seem to warrant this approach perhaps most decisively: Sinclair's London is a pure discursive construct, and critics such as Julian Wolfreys and Roger Luckhurst emphasise the 'spectrality' of the writing of Sinclair, the traces that he uses to point out the erasure of a particular London. These readings are certainly helpful because they illuminate Sinclair's obsession with the destruction enacted upon London's fabric by governments, planners and developers.

Yet such overbearing post-structuralist readings can also lead to a disconnection of the material culture that Sinclair's work engages with. Wolfreys asserts that for Sinclair graffiti functions as modalities that 'dissonantly articulate the condition of the city as a textual network, never quite at home with itself'.[22] Sinclair's language games, such as in the cabbalistic repetitions of letters in *Lud Heat*, the reimagining of the Isle of Dogs as the Isle of Doges in *Downriver*, and the walking of the letters 'VOX' into the London cityscape in *Lights Out for the Territory* (1997) do not necessarily make Sinclair's work fit easily into postmodern frameworks. The quality of Sinclair's London cartography lies precisely in his unwillingness to submit to the jargonised vocabulary and categories of accepted postmodern clichés. Simon Perril notes aptly that Sinclair is 'more a modernist magpie than a post-modern prankster'.[23]

The extent to which Sinclair's texts posit London as a topological discourse has been debated. Perril states that Sinclair 'is deeply sceptical of the semiological approach which designates all space as textual; fodder for endless "reading" and interpretation'.[24] Bond hesitates: 'In Sinclair's novel [*Downriver*] local fables are investigated as if they were texts to be decoded – but only partially. We saw that in this novel Sinclair is more interested in the process of decipherment of narratives and traces of the city's history, than in any potential uncovering of fixed facts, or positive act of understanding.'[25] Doris Teske also displays some ambivalence by taking into account Sinclair's former occupation as a book dealer: 'The metropolis is a collection of texts, who speak to book collector Sinclair in their material form. The city is full of bookshops and booksellers flying by, single books move – like the "metaphorai" of De Certeau or Barthes's graffiti – almost independently along unpredictable paths through the urban space.'[26] Sinclair is not a pure deconstructionist who denies an external, non-semiotic reality by his use of the paradox of transparency, i.e. the *evasion* of postmodernist self-conscious author tricks by evoking a documentary fiction, and the simultaneous assertion that fiction is not reducible to documentary fiction. Sinclair's texts are an attempt to become one with the eroding spirit of place to point out how architects, planners, developers and governments destroy 'the non-semiotic dimension of society [...] contained within the subjective, mental, and the discursive'.[27] He also needs to view the city as a system of signs that codifies ideology. Sinclair's city and his own appropriation of literary text produced in and about London, are both made up of collections of signs which can be attributed meaning *only* in a social, and material context.

An epistemophiliac disguise: self and the city

Sinclair's London cannot be approached, however, without analysing his interest in the representational problems that writing the self poses in the process of textualising the city. Sinclair's early prose-poem *Lud Heat* (1975) contains a discussion of Stan Brakhage's work that speculates on the etymology of 'autopsy' in relation to the creation of translucency. In the exordium an 'I' unfolds an alternative map of energies that is superimposed onto contemporary London:[28] '**And I connect the present churches to this mood. Relate them to the four Egyptian protector-goddesses, guardians of canopic jars. I associate them with rites of autopsy on a more than local scale.**'[29] This is not *per se* occult: with the decline of the authority of the contemporary Church, which symbolically expresses itself in a Londonscape where churches are dwarfed by skyscrapers, Sinclair becomes a self-appointed leader who assumes public authority with which to 'rescue' the city from postmodern architecture that conveniently 'forgets', that is, actively represses, history. *Lud Heat* can thus be read as an act of counter-surveillance, constructing an alternative cartography of London that falls outside the power of London's official institutions. Especially during the early part of his 'career', Sinclair's works reject the agreed, purportedly rational discourse of the Enlightenment by exploring and exploiting the occult tradition because '[t]he occult is diametrically opposed to the type of society and ways of thought that were represented by the Establishment culture of the late European industrial revolution.'[30]

The writing self thus emerges as a textual construct, the written self, which is apparently mystical because, as Michael de Certeau writes, it 'is a "siteless site" related to the fragility of social position or the uncertainty of institutional referents'.[31] Denise Riley's *Words of Selves* (2000) provides a similarly apt context to Sinclair's project, noting that the first-person narrator cannot but be artificial and constructed as self-description is always a masquerade and accompanied by a sense of self-trickery in language. '"I" start out as an accidental linguistic perspective,' says Riley, 'yet my contingency is not exactly lonely, for within it lies the realisation that I'm no Crusoe, isolated on a desert island [...]

My proffered self is always something of a dislocated "I" – recalling the protagonist of Beckett's monologue [...] "Mouth".'[32] Riley's emphasis on the fictionality of the linguistically constructed self places the subject back into a social context, which allows us to restore Sinclair's 'mystic' London to intelligibility.

The disembodied, transparent self is a space where the distorting effects of manipulation by political and economic powers are registered and experienced as a form of linguistic estrangement. In *Radon Daughters* (1994) the Sinclair-figure states: 'Writing, the physical act of it, dissolves the ego. Lets the elder voices through. Everything I write, even the act of ventriloquism, is autobiography.'[33] The writing self conflicts, then, with the idea that Sinclair's visionary qualities do manage to create transparency. A difference with Ackroyd's approach is, however, that Sinclair's prophetic qualities are transgressive because codes of the self are mixed up with codes of other literary and cultural signs inscribed in, paradoxically, the absent self.[34] We should therefore also rethink the clear-cut distinction between Sinclair's fiction and non-fiction: the writing self is always linguistically dislocated, a fiction.[35] Whereas in Ackroyd's work the act of ventriloquism equalises the author with its object, Sinclair's texts foreground the narrating subject, while his self-mythologising annihilates the narrating entity in order to let 'the elder voices' through. The narrator and the reader are able to enter London's past fiction by entering a company of past, sometimes unconscious witnesses. Sinclair simultaneously *evades* self-conscious tricks by evoking a documentary fiction, while asserting that fiction is not reducible to documentary fiction. It is the act of witnessing of the narrating subject that gives 'authority' to the unconscious witnesses whose existence and/or writings are acknowledged.

In *Downriver* (1991), the problem of accessing the city through the written self comes to a major crisis, which symbolises the gap that Thatcherite rhetoric creates between lived experience and idealised projections. The commissioners of a piece of screenwriting question the authority and singularity of its self-designated narrator. 'Sinclair' at first tries to defend himself:

> An existential writer that stopped the present writer dead in his tracks. On that single question the whole schmear hangs. '*Who is "I"?*' Answer the riddle or get out of the maze. The slippery self-confessor [...] speaks of 'the Narrator', of 'Sinclair': deflects the thrust of the accusation. The narrator exists only in his narration: outside the tale he is nothing [...] But 'Sinclair' is a tribe [...] It's an epistemophiliac disguise.[36]

Towards the end of *Downriver*, the 'Sinclair' who tries to make a documentary film about the Thames and its repressed stories realises his
attempts have been thwarted by a media executive who is writing the
author out of his own story: 'The jig was up. All patience expended.
Bagman bombarded the innocent pretensions of the text [...] Guilty.
Guilty on all counts. Tumbled. I (I,I,I,I,I,I,I,I,I,I) have been found out.
Deconstructed' (*D* 353). This is a complex passage. First, the repetition
of 'I' affirms Sinclair's modernist interest because it is a direct reference
to Joyce's *Ulysses*. In 'Scylla and Charybdis', Dedalus delivers his lecture
on *Hamlet*, and states: 'I am other I now. [...] But I, entelechy, form of
forms, am I by memory because of everchanging forms. [...] I, I, and
I. I.'[37] The lecture is on Dedalus's theory on Hamlet, but it is simultaneously a profound meditation on the relationship between art, whose
task it is to transform 'potential' into perfection, and the artist, who is
in a perpetual state of flux. Joyce's 'everchanging forms' that the self
takes also alludes indirectly to the modern city as an elusive place of
constant transformation.

Sinclair also mocks the meaning of the word 'deconstructed'
by turning it against itself to suggest that Derrida's project of the
unmasking of the fallacious linguistic underpinnings of social categories and moral strongholds has little power within material reality. Julian Wolfreys's use of 'trace' in his work on Sinclair is limited
because it denies an historical consciousness, or material reality; he
argues that '[t]he city, articulated through text, photography, film,
and installation comes to be revealed as having a "materiality without matter," in the words of Jacques Derrida.'[38] Yet, it is the materialism of the Thatcherite commission that deconstructs any kind of
textual enterprise, not vice versa, because despite the linguistic play
Sinclair's traces remain rooted in a material reality: as a publisher and
book dealer, Sinclair is very much aware of material culture, to which
literature also belongs.

In *Downriver* Sinclair pushes transparency further than in his early
poetry and *White Chappell, Scarlet Tracings*. The 'I' is given narrative
authority through the overlaps created by (linguistic) echoes throughout the text. To understand how these echoes work it is illuminating to
have a look at the first stanzas of Blake's poem 'London' (1794):

> I wander thro' each charter'd street,
> Near where the Thames does flow,
> And mark in every face I meet,
> Marks of weakness, marks of woe.

During his walk the 'I' notes resemblances repeatedly, emphasised by the repetition of words such as 'marks', 'every' and 'cry', and connects the suffering of innocent, ordinary people (chimney sweepers, infants, prostitutes) with that of those cooperating with the religious and political establishment powers and shows a totalising system that creates injustice.[39] Blake's prophetic act, of seeing, hearing and articulating, which is taken up by Sinclair in *Downriver*, exposes the powers that corrupt mankind.[40] In *Downriver*, Sinclair's narrator states that 'Market forces would conspire, in time, to expel him. But that was the nature of the place. The human element was optional' (*D* 96).

Downriver teems with similar echoes and repetitions. In the first tale of the novel, 'He walked amongst the Trial Men', the first-person narrator, 'Sinclair', walks with his sculptor friend Joblard from Tilbury to Tilbury Riverside, where he recounts the history of the sinking of the pleasure boat *Princess Alice* in the Thames. Sinclair's writing shows that it *is* possible that *we* enter the archaeology of past fictions, which lie, metaphorically, in the Thames mud. Yet, in the sixth tale, '*Eisenbahnangst*',[41] the narrator indicates that he had 'grievously misdirected [his] original version of the tragedy of the *Princess Alice*' (*D* 177) and relocates the event upstream, this time entering the Thames's

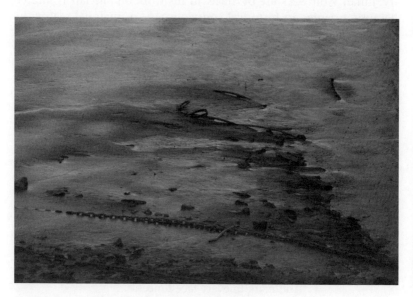

Figure 11   Downriver, Chelsea Embankment

history and relating the ship's sinking as if it is happening right under the reader's eyes:

> 'It was like a spasm, a whirlpool.' The head of the ship lifted out of the water like the jaws of a great shark, passengers slid helplessly down the black shaft: the Thames was 'like a sarcophagus'. A strong tide ran some bodies back down to Rainham and the Ferry Boat Inn. The limbs of the dead ones moving in the wash of the sinking vessel. 'They appeared to be swimming.' [...] I fled: escaping from the accumulated evidence to the scene of the crime. (*D* 177)

Thus, the 'I' manages to enter history by remembering accounts from witnesses and creating narratological equality between their voices and his own into a new version that seamlessly merges the two: the narrator's voice is a solvent that equates accounts of witnesses with his own narrative. Linguistic contagion enhances the epistemological complexity when the 'I' connects this tale to that of Lewis Carroll's Alice, expounding on a speculative theory that Tenniel's illustrations to *Alice in Wonderland* ('an obvious voyeur's trick' (*D* 178)) adumbrated Carroll's unmasking as a child pornographer. Thus, the 'I' like Blake before him makes connections in history that allow the sensitive poet to 'predict' the future: the 'London' in *Downriver* is a speculative projection that aims to correct the present, as Sinclair suggested in response to Angela Carter's distrust of Sinclair's posing as a prophet. Sinclair corrects her assumption that 'he had, as a prophet, zero success rate' because he did not predict Thatcher's resignation in 1990, whilst *Downriver* was published in 1991:

> Prophesy has nothing to do with 'accurately' casting future events, like some speedy weather-man. It has to do with *causing* future events by the power of invocation (or necessary sacrifice). [...] The prophetic element in this text is supposed to make things happen, not to second-guess banal newspaper reality. Mrs Thatcher [...] picked up her cards exactly one year after the typescript was handed in to Nick Austin.[42]

Sinclair deliberately posits this strategy against the way in which Thatcher's rhetoric and historical denial operate by projecting it into a dystopian future to show that the Iron Lady does not hold the sole claim over the shaping of the future.

IT WILL FEEL LIKE VENICE AND WORK LIKE NEW YORK

In *Downriver* Sinclair's Blakean voicing of his narrative self spills over from a lyrical nature into an epic, apocalyptic context. Blake is also an important source for the artistic transfiguration of the Isle of Dogs, one of the main events in the novel. In *Jerusalem*, Blake's narrator states: 'He [Los] came down from Highgate thro' Hackney and Holloway towards London / Till he came to old Stratford & thence to Stepney & the Isle / Of Leuthas Dogs'.[43] 'Sinclair' operates a linguistic response that opposes the radical, irrevocable changes of London under Thatcher. In the novel, the Isle of Dogs has been sold to and colonised by Vatican City, and the text transforms the trivial, banal geography into a comic as well as tragic set of signs when the group of anti-Thatcherite martyrs – a fictional 'Sinclair' and a company of fellow artists – board the satiric 'Vessels of Wrath' to undertake several epic voyages to infiltrate the London they are excluded from:

> The peg of uncircumcised land was known to the outlying squatters of Blackwell and Silvertown as 'The Isle of Doges', and to the cynics of Riverside as 'Vat City'. This deregulated isthmus of Enterprise was a new Venice, slimy with canals, barnacled *palazzi*, pillaged art, lagoons, leper hulks: a Venice overwhelmed by Gotham City, a raked grid of canyons and stuttering aerial railways. A Venice run by secret tribunals of bagmen, too slippery for Vegas; by relic-worshipping hoodlums, the gold-mouthed heads of Colombian cocaine dynasties. (*D* 265)

This passage gives us a coherent set of cultural determinants that reveal the process of Sinclair's representation. The word 'slippery' is an indication that Sinclair transforms materiality linguistically, making use of fierce wordplay to generate a whole imperial landscape of an absolute and closed political city state: 'Venice'. Although Baker finds that in this passage 'power, temporal power is transformed [...] into occult forms', it seems more apt to read this linguistic transformation as a direct reflection on money's transformative, manipulative powers on society.[44] The Thatcherite renegotiation of London in terms of the Italian city state and New York are appealing to Sinclair because they allow him to represent the original Docklands topography and architecture in terms of different sets of signifiers associated with empires, one in decline and another at the height of its power.

There is a specific historical context here that makes it possible to read this passage as a criticism of Thatcherite rhetoric and cunning historical revisionism. The inspiration for Sinclair's verbal parody can be traced back to the marketing campaign that promoted the regeneration of the Isle of Dogs with the phrase: CANARY WHARF. IT WILL FEEL LIKE VENICE AND WORK LIKE NEW YORK.[45] Sinclair appropriates the language of advertising companies, the Thatcher government and planners, architects and developers to point out that their manipulation of language and imagery perverts the London landscape by overcoding it in the equally powerful sets of signs of which Venice and New York are composed. This appropriation has two immediate consequences: Sinclair exposes the abuse of language by marketing companies and the Thatcher government, and, in this process of exposure, the text projects their language into a nightmarish, apocalyptic future by magnifying the consequences. The novel points out an emergent linguistic inflation that is used to deceive the general public into accepting the Docklands project. When Thatcher inaugurated Canary Wharf on 19 November 1989, she boastfully stated that '"The art of politics is the art of making the impossible happen." And that in fact is what we have been doing.'[46]

Sinclair mocks such utopian speeches, and their attempted historical revisionism and rhetorical reimagination of the present, in Chapter 11, 'The Case of the Premature Mourners'. Sinclair reports 'her keynote Marshalsea Speech' (*D* 336) when she reopens the former Marshalsea prison as a dossers' dormitory:

> 'From this day forward,' the Widow began [...] 'let it be known that We are no longer to be considered the prisoners of history. We have forced open the great iron doors of mystification, self-doubt, self-critical inertia. History has been conquered. *Rejoice!* [...] The future is whatever We believe it to be! [...] After We have finished speaking to you today, there will be never again in this noble land be such a thing as a prison [...] A prison is a state of mind. [...] We make you *this* offer: let every man be his own warder, protecting the things he loves best: his *family*, his *home*, his *country*. Then, and only then, will We discover what *true* freedom means. (*D* 336–7)

'Sinclair' satirically exposes the Widow's rhetorical rewriting of 'Britain's perceived identity' (*D* 336) by making visible the gap between speech and lived reality, and by turning it against itself: 'Sinclair' compares the vagrant's imprisonment with the middle-class self-incarceration in Thatcherite values.

The significance of Sinclair's vision of Venetian-cum-Gothamised 'London' can be historicised by contextualising the chapter within a tradition of Venice writing. Tony Tanner's *Venice Desired* (1992) states that Venice is a 'dark' republic because of the nature of its political system, its masquerades and carnival, and its labyrinthine topography and architecture. Tanner notes that

> Venice was effectively a police state with its notorious secret tribunals [...] the fact of its famous masquerades and carnivals [...]; the fact of its labyrinthine little streets and canals and endless bridges; the uncanny silence of its gliding traffic [...] – all these composed an easily available scenario or imaginary topography for writers from afar.[47]

Venice is also a doomed city, adding to its gloomy, yet erotic atmosphere: 'In decay and decline (*particularly* in decay and decline), falling or sinking to ruins and fragments, yet saturated with secretive sexuality – thus emanating or suggesting a heady compound of death and desire – Venice becomes for many writers what it was, in anticipation, for Byron: "the greenest land of my imagination".'[48] We detect a parallel with Sinclair's imagination, which is stoked up by the violence inflicted on cityscape by the Docklands redevelopment. Victor Sage's essay 'Black Venice' (2006) points us to the more ambiguous features of the city:

> When to the labyrinth of architecture is added the exclusiveness and secrecy – the closed system – of the republic, and what Tony Tanner refers to as its reputation as a police state, we get another layer, as it were, of labyrinth. The paradox is of an excessive control residing in the same space as lawlessness [...] Power is always elsewhere, but particularly in Venice.[49]

This paradoxical idea of the city-state as a manifestation of the omnipresence of power and its simultaneous absence is present in *Downriver* as well. Sinclair's Isle of Doges is a revisioning of London as a place that pushes the repressed and marginalised ('squatters') into pockets of poverty, made powerless by their socio-economic imprisonment. Simultaneously, those in power can exert their imagination without restraint because there is hardly any control or accountability, which Sinclair's novel exposes in more imaginative ways.

Sinclair's exposé also shows that behind the rhetoric two radically different orders of mutually exclusive, 'impenetrable' spaces inscribe themselves into the landscape. The remaining East End poor are excluded from their own public space because the hyper-rich Canary Wharf overshadows the mainly low-rise East End, Limehouse in particular. The result is 'interdictory space', a term coined by Oscar Newman in 1972, to denote space that would inhibit crime by creating the physical expression of a social fabric that defends itself.[50] As wealthy corporations or individuals tend to restrict access to spaces for those who can afford a specific space, spatial and architectural schizophrenia arises when two radically different spatial orders coexist in the same area, such as this overshadowing of rundown working-class houses by hyper-real skyscrapers in London Docklands. Other people are excluded from their own territory by spatial prohibition, which is accompanied by a sense of social injustice and a decline in spiritual health.

Venice is associated with carnival and masquerades, and the Isle of Doges is also a performative site turning the novel into a stage for linguistic play and narrative fantasies. Despite Sinclair's dark and tragic incantations, the author's inventiveness generates a liberty whereby the possibility of inversion of value allows for a divine comedy. Images of a Cardinal playing golf at night at the new Isle, or a Stephen Hawking lecture on the origins of the universe to the Vatican are cathartic in their comic impetus, which redeems and forgives, in a Catholic sense, the sins of its perpetrators. The most obvious example of this is the grotesque and hilarious portrayal of Thatcher as a deranged fascist in the eighth chapter, 'Art of the State':

the Widow rose from her stiff pillows – bald as Mussolini – and felt the twitch start in her left eyelid. She ordained the *immediate* extermination of this muscular anarchy, this palace revolt. [The valet] disconnected the 'sleep-learning' gizmo, the tapes that fed the Widow her Japanese humour, taught the finer points of cheating at stud poker, and provided an adequate form forecast to the current camel-racing season. [...] The golden curls were sprung and twisted, lacquered into their proper place. The valet held up the wig for her approval. She made her choice from a cabinet of warriors' teeth, toying between the thew-'em-up-and-spit-out-the-pips version and the infinitely more alarming smile-them-to-death set that the boffins never quite managed to synchronize with her eye-language. The Widow was a praise-fed avatar of the robot-Maria from *Metropolis*; she looked like herself, but too much so. [...] If she ever

appeared in her original skin the underclass would riot and tear her
to pieces. [...] And she also suffered the stinking baths of electrified
Ganges mud [...], the 'hormone replacement' shots. Even now the
lab boys were grinding a fresh consignment of monkey testicles in
the mixer. The eyedrops, powder, the paint: she censored the morning radio bulletins. (*D* 219)

This is satire, thus anything but a subtle attack on Thatcher, and its
directness points us first to a realist reading. The references to the
'"sleep-learning" gizmo', artificial appearance and language remind
us that the Iron Lady was a carefully contrived, fictional construct.
Thatcher had voice coaching to lower her voice an octave, carefully
groomed her image and she used *Zeitgeist*-tapes to keep her in touch
with the contemporary world. The references to fascistic tendencies
are reminiscent of comments of the minor Tory minister Alan Clark
who noted Thatcher's 'personality compulsion, something of the *Führer
Kontakt*'.[51] The set of international references (Italy, India, Germany,
Japan) points to the process of globalisation that was taking flight at the
beginning of the 1980s, and the selling off of Britain.

Beyond the realist reading, the passage's concern with dressing up
and masquerade, the transgression of the boundary between private and
public space, and the attention to the grotesque aspects of the human
body plunge us into the realm of the Bakhtinian carnivalesque. The
Widow's physical deformation is an outward manifestation of her spiritual and ideological corruption that turns her, and her collusive gang of
planners, developers and architects, into monsters.[52] The text de-crowns
and mocks the central figure of authority and power also by invading
the private space of this most public of figures, and in its grotesque representation of the Prime Minister the text expresses a utopian belief in
a future in which fear and authority are vanquished. Julia Kristeva states
that '[c]arnival [...] does not keep to the rigid, that is, moral position of
apocalyptic inspiration; it transgresses it, sets its repressed against it –
the lower things, sexual matters what is blasphemous and to which it
holds while mocking the law'.[53] However, if this novel's comedy itself
is considered a convenient escape valve that temporarily releases the
built up social pressure in order to sustain the hegemonic powers and to
maintain the status quo, the text could be said to somehow work with
the Thatcher regime's rhetoric.

There is a gender problem here as well. Sinclair is not just attacking
the Prime Minister, he is attacking a woman who rejects her femininity
to assert power over the world around her. Sinclair's appropriation and
mocking of Thatcher's body and appearance in his text, as well as the

suggestion of the Widow's taking testosterone shots, are all problematic, leaving the author wide open to charges of misogyny.

The passage is scorchingly funny, however, and knowingly so as it is reworking Jonathan Swift's satirical poems 'The Progress of Beauty' (1719), 'The Lady's Dressing Room' (1732), and 'Beautiful Young Nymph Going To Bed' (1734), which mock female vanity.[54] In 'The Progress of Beauty', the narrator, Strephon, describes the four-hour-long process of the once lovely Celia whose beauty is now on the wane getting ready to go out. Sinclair directly echoes Swift's phrases such as to 'see her from her pillow rise / All reeking in a cloudy steam, / Crack'd lips, foul teeth, and gummy eyes' and make up sculpting the features into 'their proper place'.[55] In 'The Lady's Dressing Room' the same Strephon gives us a survey of Celia's dressing room, describing the tools she uses to keep up her appearance. At the end Strephon discovers that Celia is only a mortal, with a scatological impetus present also in Sinclair's work: 'Repeating in his amorous Fits, / Oh! *Celia, Celia, Celia* shits!'[56] 'Beautiful Young Nymph Going To Bed' describes a prostitute, Corinna, Pride of Drury-Lane coming home after work. She 'Takes off her artificial hair', picks 'out a Crystal Eye' and 'from the Gums / a Set of Teeth completely comes'.[57] When Corinna awakes her body is in ruins and the narrator asks: 'The Nymph, tho' in this mangled Plight, / Must every Morn her limbs unite. / But how shall I describe her Arts / To collect the scattered parts.'[58] This rending of the body in fiction is also part of Sinclair's project, which disperses Thatcher's body, as well as that of London, in fiction.

Although these poems are misogynist and support male authority, Swift's texts are also aware of their problematic nature, which is announced in the problematisation of the relationship between the narrating subject and narrated object. Strephon is called 'the Rogue', suggesting that we should treat this fictional narrator with caution, whilst the satirical mode itself adds another layer of irony: Swift's reference to '*Celia*'s magnifying Glass' is also the mode in which the author writes.[59]

Sinclair is also aware of the dangers of his strategy, and of the potential ethical cost of this for the artist and his art. Sinclair's imaginary rending apart of Thatcher's body finds a curious mirroring in the violence upon the artistic process of *Downriver* and upon the artist itself. Sinclair works in the Orphic tradition of *disjecta membra* whereby the poet's body is torn to pieces by women, and the scattered limbs of the poet form an allegory for the making of poetic traditions. For instance, Sinclair's allusion to 'the Boschian scope' (*D* 260) of his project reminds us of Jacques Lacan's notion of the 'fragmented body' (*corps morcelé*), which he relates to Hieronymus Bosch's paintings of hell as a demonstration that the stable

'I' created from the perception of the body as composed out of scattered limbs is always under threat of disintegration. The poet has a profoundly deep personal investment in his public activity, which amounts to nothing less than a self-sacrifice that might entail his demise.

The passage depicts, then, a wider struggle between Thatcher and the unruly, anarchic body politic through analogy. The passage suggests a destruction of the unitary body as a result of the ways in which the Thatcherite policies destroy the organisational unity of London as a symbol of an increasingly Disunited Kingdom: 'The Widow and her gang had decided that Hackney was bad news and the best option was to get rid of it, chop it into fragments, and choke it in the most offensive heap of civil engineering since the Berlin Wall.'[60] Sinclair's fragmented 'novel' mirrors the ways in which the Thatcherite process of privatisation breaks up London's organic and chaotic 'figure ground', and enacts the same process on Thatcher herself. The passage is not a misogynist passage, but a complex reflection upon the state of democracy.

A paradoxical reading of history: London's *disjecta membra*

Downriver contains another important scene that sheds light on the topographic changes in London's 'body'. Chapter 3, 'Horse Spittle (*The Eros of Maps*)', can be read as a comment on the way in which the globalising capitalist machinery of the City and Canary Wharf subject London to deterritorialisation. The structure of the text, as well as its imagery, suggest that Sinclair writes 'with all the centrifugal desperation of a man who has somewhere lost time and is determined to recover it – whatever the cost' (*D* 134).

This fragmentation can be shown by analysing the manner in which Sinclair constructs his cartography in *Downriver*. Sinclair works in the topographical tradition of Michael Drayton's *Poly-Olbion* (1612), John Mackey's *Journey Through England* (1714), Defoe's *A Journal of the Plague Year* (1722), and Christopher Smart's and Blake's prophetical books. In *Downriver* Sinclair reintroduces the frontispiece to *Poly-Olbion*, which shows Neptune clothed in a dress with the map of England entering the gate of Poly-Olbion, in the form of the fictional nurse/prostitute-stripper Edith Cadiz, who clothes herself in maps:

> Edith's particular was *Laurie & Whittle's New Map of London with its Environs, including the Recent Improvements 1819* [...] she had constructed [...] a costume shaped from this map: part Edward Gordon-Craig, part Maori kite-bird [...] Wearing it, she became an angel of

threat, or a demon of bliss [...] her slightest movement provoked a paradoxical reading of history [...] but she was not sure what it meant. She found herself, suddenly and dangerously, prophetic. (*D* 62–4)

Cadiz's palimpsest-striptease is 'prophetic' because it adumbrates Thatcher's selling off of London's public space and public services. Cadiz's act also suggests that Sinclair opposes Thatcher's one-dimensional historical revisionism by offering a plurality and contradictory readings of London's history, which should be understood as a means of escaping the singularity of Thatcher's vision. A politically correct reading of this passage would read this scene as evidence of Sinclair's misogynistic attitude to women, who are purportedly portrayed as submissive objects for commodification by men, and for male consumption.

However, a more ambiguous reading is possible as well: Cadiz's cartographic striptease alerts us to the idea that Sinclair's is pitting a woman living quotidian reality against the fictional Widow, and that his novel is itself a recovering of history. The novel may therefore be associated with the ambiguous powers of the female subject. The Thames becomes a doubly feminine symbol, with the river not only associated with the womb, but, also as Angela Carter's novel suggests, with female reproductive organs.[61] As it is the Thames which allows the author to move between the past and present, Sinclair's text affirms the necessity of the ambivalent aspects of the female. 'Sinclair' makes clear when walking from Shadwell to Rotherhithe through the Rotherhithe Tunnel:

The tunnel covertly opens a vein between two distinct systems, two descriptions of time. The outfall of the city is bled into the drained marshlands [...] A voice is forged, a bone whisper, that belongs to neither bank. The tunnel is the ghost of something that never had the chance to die. Niches in laboratory light of this shrine lack their votive skulls. Unfocused demands slide over the white tiles, searching for their oracle. (*D* 50–1)

This passage shows Sinclair consciously exploits ambivalence, and that his oracular style is associated with the *pythia* at Delphi, or the hermaphrodite Tiresias from Eliot's *The Waste Land*. In *Subterranean Cities* (2005), David L. Pike notes that the tunnel as a literary space is traditionally associated with the feminine rather than masculine power:

As a physical space, the earth has always been associated with female archetypes in Western myth; the male-controlled realm of the afterlife was always a world apart, only metaphorically underground. The close spatial relation to seasonal cycles of birth and death may have contributed to the connection with the female, but it is a connection that has become ever more arbitrary, while remaining extraordinarily persistent. The equation between activities and persons imagined as subterranean invokes the physical qualities of traditional underground activity and adds to them associations with the feminine that have become a fundamental metaphorical division in modern society – fluid, unruly mobs; diseased and immoral slum dwellers; and at the centre, the figure of the urban prostitute.[62]

Cadiz's striptease is thus both a celebration of women's power, and also a complaint about the treatment of women under Thatcher, as a nurse who has to prostitute herself to make ends meet.

Sinclair associates the megalomaniac project of the London Docklands with an overbearing masculine discourse that distorts perception. It is the absence of women that creates an unbalanced, unhealthy London body: 'Where are the women? [...] Not a female to admire ever since we got on the Island [...] No tribal mothers, vinegar spinsters, no repentant harlots. Not a single one' (*D* 279). Sinclair's analysis of the architecture itself is also ambiguous. Rather than presenting Canary Wharf as a phallocratic celebration of male power – the traditional analysis which we get in, for instance, Lefebvre – Sinclair presents it as a labyrinth that needs to be penetrated and circumnavigated.[63] Sinclair unstitches 'male' power by showing that the phallus is not one sex, but a complex aggregate of confusing impulses. In *Lights Out*, Sinclair offers an ambivalent image: 'Canary Wharf had the vulgarity to climb off the drawing-board. Claes Oldenburg's giant lipsticks were jokes that knew how to behave: they were never intended for the landscape of London' (*LOFT* 227). In an interview, Sinclair compared the Gherkin to 'a gigantic dildo', which again suggests not a phallic symbol of masculinity, but an object signifying female self-empowerment and male impotence. Sinclair's text can therefore be read as an ambivalent criticism of the dominance of named architectural structures that homogenise the diversity of London. It is because of such ambivalence that the politically correct readings of Sinclair's work, such as the ones by Peter Brooker and Rachel Potter, are a misrepresentation of the work, not least because Sinclair's writing submits itself to what Mengham calls the 'violence of spokesmanship, and the violence that is used to prevent others from speaking for themselves'.[64]

London Orbital: city of surveillance and the bourgeoisification of space

As *Downriver* in both form and structure shows, London's geography is radically altered by the deterritorialising powers of late capitalism that undermine the city's unitary principals. The narrative movement is outward, centrifugal, and the novel adumbrates Sinclair's recovering of organisational unity by walking London's orbital motorway, the M25, in *London Orbital*, to find a proliferation of guarded estates and gated communities. The result, *London Orbital*, is an extensive report of Sinclair's walk that mimics and mocks London's increasing appearance as a mental and physical prison. Sinclair's angry and apocalyptic criticism is explicitly aimed at New Labour's perpetuation of the privatisation under Thatcher. The central object of Quixotic fury here is the Millennium Dome, the pre-eminent architectural propaganda of New Labour's political power, 'a tourniquet, sponsored by the Department of Transport and Highways Agency, to choke the living breath from the metropolis' (*LO* 3).

A first layer of criticism we find in Sinclair's book is that of 'the carceral', or 'the penetentiary', which traditionally derives from accounts that capture the experience of imprisonment, but which Sinclair appropriates to think about the structure of feeling of contemporary London. Some of the themes that Sinclair's work thinks about are captured by *City of Quartz* (1990), Mike Davis's portrayal of Los Angeles as a Fortress City of gated communities and ghettos, a world observed by proliferating CCTV cameras and security guards, resulting in the voluntary incarceration of the rich (in Beverley Hills and San Marino) based on fear of the involuntarily ghettoised underclass Other. Davis stresses that the militarisation of architectural signatures and the observation of the city by means of CCTV generates the restriction of human movement and a tight regulation of social behaviour. The 'mall-as-panopticon-prison', the guarded patrols, the 'endless police data gathering and centralization of communications' are expressions of a technologised surveillance that spread paranoia and agoraphobia amongst the citizens of a penetentiary LA.[65]

'Every city is a carceral city' states Edward Soja in response to Davis's analysis.[66] Despite his admiration for Davis's prophetic anticipation of the 1992 LA riots against social polarisation, Soja criticises *City of Quartz* because Davis's blaming of abstract forces such as neo-liberalism and neo-capitalism leads to 'the dwindling "residual hope" for significant reform [that] can all too easily lead to despondency and withdrawal, or to an inactive waiting for a cleansing apocalypse. In either case, the attention is diverted away from the new opportunities of progressive change built into the fortressed and reterritorialized geographies of the postmetropolis.'[67] Soja is partly right in his criticism but he does misread Davis, whose references to films such as *Robocop* (1987) and *Dragnet* (1987) point to a partly fictional voice, and a blurring of disciplinary boundaries. The subtitle of his book, *Excavating the Future in Los Angeles*, hints at Davis's awareness that (science) fiction is implicated in our vision of the urban environment. Davis understands that imagining disaster, apocalypse or utopia contributes to and changes our historical self-consciousness, and in the process reconstructs the master narrative of the political and individual unconscious.[68] Davis is also useful for his invocation of Jeremy Bentham's infamous Panopticon prison, which becomes symbolic of late twentieth-century strategies of managing public space. The implications are radical, as, in the inventor's sinister words, the Panopticon is

> a method of becoming master of everything which might happen to a certain number of men, to dispose of everything around them so as to produce on them the desired impression, to make certain of their actions, of their connections, and of all circumstances of their lives, so that nothing could escape, nor could oppose the desired effect, it cannot be doubted that a method of this kind would be a very powerful and very useful instrument which governments might apply to various objects of the utmost importance.[69]

Both Davis's and Soja's work also builds on Michel Foucault's seminal analysis of the prison, *Discipline and Punish* (1975). Foucault describes the historical evolution of modern societies into a disciplinary, homogenised network that is under permanent observation, whereby the prisons embedded within the city have a preventative function. Dickens's *Little Dorrit* (1855–7) expresses the idea that the prison system turns the whole of London into a collective prison:

> Black, all night, since the gate had clashed upon Little Dorrit, its iron stripes were turned by the early-glowing sun into stripes of gold. Far aslant across the city, over its jumbled roofs, and through its open tracery of its church towers, struck the long bright rays, bars of the prison of this lower world.[70]

Dickens shows that prisons are not peripheral places on the edge of the city, but that they are integrated into the social fabric because the same strategies of power operate in both loci, and the mechanisms of discipline that control the prisoner also control the citizen. Dickens gives us literary images that visualise how, in Foucault's words, 'the carceral circles widen and the form of the prison slowly diminishes and finally disappears altogether'.[71] Foucault adumbrates the process that Sinclair traces in *London Orbital*, where the Millennium Dome, as an architectural expression of New Labour's political power, ripples out towards the edge to connect with the celebration of Thatcher's power: the M25. Sinclair ends the book with Will Self's vision of the Dome spreading itself to envelop London as an 'invisible membrane' (*LO* 551).

As London is unceasingly being watched by more than 150,000 cameras, perception and observation are central to Sinclair's project.[72] In *Lights Out for the Territory* Sinclair already observed that 'Surveillance abuses the past while fragmenting the present. The subject is split, divided from itself' (*LOFT* 106). The London that emerges in the twenty-first century is 'a Foucault wasteland' (*LO* 169) with the metropolis rationalised into a 'ring-fenced ghetto, city of surveillance, privately policed estate' (*LO* 86). The walk itself forms counter-surveillance, both in content and form: the book maps and criticises changes at the end of the 1990s. The walk takes the shape of an eye – symbolically an act of counter-surveillance, yet the walk also enacts imprisonment by becoming the observed within a London-wide panopticon, with the Dome at its centre as central prison tower.

The great intertext that Sinclair's text cleverly avoids mentioning is Cervantes's *Don Quixote* (1605), yet there are many striking parallels between both projects, and Sinclair's entire body of work. Whereas the mad knight from Cervantes's novel fights windmills, Sinclair takes on the Millennium Dome and the infinite river of macadam, the M25; whereas Quixote is joined by his rustic companion Sancho Panza, Sinclair takes a sundry collection of walkers on the road (from his old friend Renchi and partner-in-crime Chris Petit to Bill Drummond and Rachel Lichtenstein). More strikingly, Quixote is a sun-stricken schizophrenic unable to separate the fictions he and others recount from 'the real': '"I knavery well who I am," answered Don Quixote, "and what is more, I know, that I may not only be the person I have named, but also the twelve peers of France [...] since my achievements will out-rival not only the famous exploits which made any of them singly illustrious, but all their mighty deeds accumulated together."'[73] *Don Quixote*'s inversion of rationality and madness is an important trope for Sinclair, whilst Cervantes's plays with the novel form are also a great inspiration for Sinclair's own daring challenges to the novel form, and to the reader. Milan Kundera's essay on Cervantes provides an illuminating insight here: 'To take, with Cervantes, the world as ambiguity, to be obliged to face not a single absolute truth but a welter of contradictory truths [...] to have as one's only certainty the *wisdom of uncertainty*, requires no less courage.'[74]

Sinclair's analysis of the carceral connects the penitentiary logic of new material spaces to the imprisoning features of current public discourses. Sinclair explicitly connects the discourse of Thatcher's and Blair's New Labour governments as a political continuum, and also counters it through its appropriation and inversion, revealing its inherent emptiness, its pseudo-fascistic rhetoric, while also revealing its 'common sense' logic as madness. In *London Orbital*, he accuses New Labour of supporting '[b]latant white space-ism: architects ignore the implications of where their buildings will be sited. Nothing exists beyond the frame of the idealised sketch' (*LO* 58). Another specific example of this exposure occurs in *London Orbital*, where Sinclair discusses how in the New Labour era rhetoric is used to sell the Lea Valley:

> *Best Value.* Someone somewhere, well away from the action, decided that this banal phrase, implying the opposite, was sexy. Best Value, with the smack of Councillor Roberts's cornershop in Grantham, the abiding myth of Thatcherism, was dusted down and used in every public relations puff of the New Labour era. Best Value. Best buy. Making the best of it. Look on the bright side.
>
> The spin doctors, post-literate and self-deceiving, had no use for subtlety. Best Value. They hammered the tag into their inelegant, overdesigned freebies. These glossy publications, sweetheart deals between government and private developers, political correctness in all its strident banality, existed to sell the lie. Best Value. (*LO* 38)

The repetition of the phrase 'Best Value' works like a mantra that lulls potential buyers into a soporific state, exposing the subtle, fascistic indoctrination that underlies contemporary consumer society. The phrase 'political correctness' points not only to the way in which freedom of speech is curbed by the influence of the (American) New Left, but also to the corrective measures that underlie the disciplinary, carceral society. This language is undercut by Sinclair's irony, destroying the homogenising, depersonalising and amnesiac impulses. Sinclair's mocking of marketing techniques, political and architectural rhetoric is used to expose the mystagogues of modernity who hijack the language of the rational philosopher by mixing the voice of reason and the voice of oracle.

The project is both poetic and, perhaps, if we stick to Sinclair's earlier definition of the term, prophetic; the very form of the book is an attempt to counter the radical changes observed. Sinclair walks counter-clockwise, an attempt to undo events in time, as it were, yet the circular movement itself transgresses materiality: the walk inscribes into the landscape an imaginary circle, a utopian symbol of eternity and infinity that cancels out the power of materiality, reminding us of the power of the imagination, the non-material. Sinclair's temporal project finds another counterpart in the Greenwich meridian line, which the New Labour government and property developers are keen to exploit because it symbolically situates London and Britain, in temporal terms, at the beginning of the world. Everywhere Sinclair walks, he finds previously ignored stones 'erected as markers for a permitted longitude pathway. The copywriters of the Lea Valley Park are keen 'to develop a strategy through which Vision can be made a Reality' (*LO* 126). The point Sinclair makes is that the meridian line, an abstraction, arbitrarily placed in London, is a fiction appropriated by the government and property developers that brand, to turn an Idea into a banal material expression disguised as Ideal through a manipulation, or fictionalisation, of representative space.

A third distinct strand within Sinclair's criticism of New Labour's remapping and rewriting of London's peripheral spaces is the bourgeoisification of space through redevelopment, gentrification and conversion of existing structures. Anna Minton spoke in her whistleblowing report on Great Britain's proliferation of gated communities, *Balanced Communities* (2002), of the 'apocalyptic consequences'.[75] She subsequently explored the security issues in more detail in her book *Ground Control* (2009), which also shows an alarming gap between perceived reality and actuality. In Sinclair's work, one example is the creation and rebranding of 'Enfield Island Village' in north London's Enfield:

> The developers, Fairview, take a relaxed view of the past. 'New' is a flexible term. ENFIELD ISLAND VILLAGE, AN EXCITING NEW VILLAGE COMMUNITY. A captured fort. A workers' colony for commuters who no longer have to live on site. The village isn't new, the community isn't new, the island isn't new. What's new is the tariff, the mortgage, the terms of the social contract. What's new is that industrial debris is suddenly 'stylish'. The Fairview panoramic drawing, removed from its hoarding, could illustrate a treatise on prison reform: a central tower and a never-ending length of yellow brick with mean window slits. (*LO* 68–9)

There are numerous examples of this scattered throughout Sinclair's text, from the conversion of mental hospitals in Epsom, Abotts Langley and Dartford to the Lea Valley developments, Whitely Village and the conversion of military infrastructure such as Royal Gunpowder Mills at Waltham, now rebaptised, rather oxymoronically, 'Paradise Park' (*LO* 127). Lefebvre has some illuminating thoughts on this particular phase of the bourgeois spatial shift. He notes that in the late eighteenth and nineteenth century the change of dominance from the aristocracy to the burgeoning bourgeoisie can be read everywhere in the European land- and cityscapes in the traces of violence against upper-class spatial structures. This bourgeoisification has continued during the twentieth century, and has resulted in both a rewriting of previous spatial structures and the erection of new ones, including the gated community. Lefebvre notes that this shift creates a specific type of space, and the gated community is one spatial form that triumphs:

> Abstract space, the space of the bourgeoisie and of capitalism, bound up as it is with exchange (of goods and commodities, as of written and spoken words, etc.) depends on consensus more than any space before it. [...] within this space violence does not always remain latent or hidden. One of its contradictions is that between the appearance of security and the constant threat, and indeed the occasional eruption, of violence. (*PS* 57)

Lefebvre starts out by noting that physical space inscribes the subject with invisible behavioural rules: space determines how we walk and talk, as it were, and it determines how we can use space, individually and collectively: a park or square invites us to congregate and engage in social activities (walk the dog, play football, picnic, etc). Our 'practice' or use of that space also makes us aware of its limits, the limits of our power: in practice, we are unable to modify or open up space by psychically destroying gates and walls, and we are also inscribed with social laws (self-censorship) that prevent us from doing so. In the case of bourgeois space, the need for consensus invites as many possible restrictions in order to keep everybody happy, and in place. The perfect example of this is the gated community's wilful embrace of space-as-obstacle: rather than openness and mixed land use – the characteristics of the city and London in particular – spatial limits are deliberately chosen and imposed upon the citizen by himself. Lefebvre also notes that it is this willed self-imposition of spatial boundaries that precisely evokes violence and aggression: these pockets of violence are unconscious ways of negating the objectality of their self-chosen enclosure.

J. G. Ballard's fiction traces this process, and what Sinclair's *London Orbital* adds is a keen emphasis on the ways in which it is discourse – both the discourse *of* space but, equally important, the discourse *in* space – that aims to condition our experience of space by manipulating it at the level of representation. The book warns against the fictionalisation of the city in various ways, and how this process actively forgets and suppresses social realities, as well as a cultural heritage that is not wanted by those in power. *London Orbital* ends with Sinclair imagining his project has brought about the Millennium Dome's failure. The Dome is a complete, abject failure: by 'November, the deserted and unloved site was haemorrhaging an estimated £240,000 per month' (*LO* 550). On Millennium Eve, Sinclair spies the Dome from a distance, knowing that his walk has brought about the required centripetal movement that has, perhaps temporarily, countered London's fragmentation and dispersal. His task is accomplished, and we have a glimpse of a London restored in the way that Blake had hoped for London as a New Jerusalem: 'And it could also be the millennial city, of that time when the moral and self-righteous law should be overthrown, and the Multitude return to Unity.'[76]

5

'In Preordained Patterns': Peter Ackroyd and the Voices of London

London is becoming less London: Ackroydopolis

The final chapter of Peter Ackroyd's *London: The Biography* (2000), entitled 'Resurgam', provides us with an illuminating account of one of the symbols of Thatcherism, the regenerated Isle of Dogs, at the beginning of the new millennium:

> If you were to walk across the Isle of Dogs, where the Canary Wharf tower itself is be found, past the enamel panels and the jet mist granite, past the silver cladding and the curved glass walls, you might come across other realities. Here and there still stand late Victorian pubs, marking the corners of otherwise shattered roads. There are council blocks from the 1930s, and council-house estates from the 1970s. Occasionally a row of nineteenth-century terraced houses will emerge like an apparition. The Isle of Dogs represents, in other words, the pattern of London. Certain of the new developments are themselves decked out as if they were Victorian warehouses, or Georgian terraces, or twentieth-century suburban dwellings, thus intensifying the sense of heterogeneity and contrast. This, too, is part of London. This is why it has been said that there are in reality hundreds of Londons all mingled. (*LB* 777)

This passage contrasts greatly to the account of Canary Wharf we get in Sinclair's work. Whereas Sinclair's derisive account stresses architectural monotony and spiritual vacuity in the gentrified Docklands, Ackroyd sees diversity and multiplicity representative of London's unique aesthetic. Whereas Sinclair sees a simulacral architecture that overwhelmingly creates a present that suppresses the unwanted past, Ackroyd sees a harmonious balance between, and continuity of, the past and present, which is representative of what he calls 'the pattern of London'. Where Sinclair sees filthy lucre, greed and an oppressed and displaced under-class, Ackroyd sees social diversity. Where Sinclair argues that Canary Wharf is radically different from the original, organic figure ground of London, Ackroyd is able to connect and see congruence between the city and this mini-Manhattan, to the extent that we might even hear an echo of Thatcher's speech inaugurating Canary Wharf: 'the most thoughtful and wonderful touch that the whole thing is aligned so that, if other buildings don't come in the way, you still have a view of St Paul's, and that environmentally appeals to many of us'.[1]

One of the potential problems with Ackroyd's analysis, one might argue, is that his utopian vision does not present us with the lived experience of the Isle of Dogs and its inhabitants; he acts as a distanced observer interested in the Idea of the place rather than the reality of the Isle of Dogs' (original) inhabitants. Ackroyd mentions the Victorian pubs and the council-house estates but does not talk to its people. The best account of such a direct encounter is to be found in Patrick Wright's classic *A Journey through Ruins: The Last Days of London* (1991), in which Wright records his visit to Dave and Daisy Woodward who have lived in council housing on the Isle of Dogs since before the Second World War. The Woodwards are surprisingly sympathetic to the Docklands develop-ment, preferring the office people in suits to arrogant dock workers in overalls: 'To begin with, they remind me that before London Docklands Development Corporation, there was nothing going on at all. There was no work and everything seemed to be deteriorating.'[2]

Sinclair's vision is primarily concerned with darkness, yet Ackroyd also stresses light: he detects that the rejuvenation of the inner city has spread outward, introducing 'the general brightness of London' (*LB* 777): 'London has opened up; there seems to be more space and more air. It has grown in lightness. In the City towers are clad in silver-blue reflective glass, so that the difference between the sky and the building is effaced' (*LB* 777). Ackroyd reminds us of a line from William Wordsworth's uto-pian poem 'Composed upon Westminster Bridge, 1802' (1807), which depicts London as an urban pastoral dream 'open unto the fields, and to the sky', but by emphasising that the city has changed from a closed system to a more open, fragmented system, Ackroyd is deliberately situ-ating himself as a high postmodernist who embraces the recent changes in the city as a positive, transformative force.

In his classic book on postmodern culture, *The Condition of Postmodernity* (1989), David Harvey observes in Jonathan Raban's classic

London novel *The Soft City* (1974), an 'encyclopaedia' or 'emporium of styles' in which 'all sense of hierarchy or even homogeneity of values [are] in the course of dissolution'.[3] This process of London's opening up to different architectural and spatial traditions has major consequences for the identity of the city and its inhabitants. One might consider this a dilution of some kind of intrinsic 'Londonness', but for others, including Ackroyd, opening the city up towards a new destiny entails new freedoms and new possibilities. Architect Rem Koolhaas has some illuminating thoughts on the effects of globalisation on the urban identity in relationship to recent changes in West European capitals:

> Identity is like a mousetrap in which more and more mice have to share the original bait, and which, on closer inspection, may have been empty for centuries. The stronger identity, the more it imprisons, the more it resists expansion, interpretation, renewal, contradiction. Identity becomes like a lighthouse – fixed, overdetermined: it can change its position or the pattern it emits only at the cost of destabilizing navigation. Paris can only become more Parisian – it is already on its way to becoming hyper-Paris, a polished caricature. There are exceptions: London – its only identity is a lack of clear identity – is perpetually becoming less London, more open, less static.[4]

Over the past few decades, Paris has become an Ideal, simulacral image of its nineteenth-century self, and its creative representations, as in the film *Amélie* (Jean-Pierre Jeunet, 2001), have greatly contributed to shaping our imaginative perception of the city of light and romance. This also means that the image of Paris has become static and stale, and represses other, darker versions of the city, such as the *banlieux* in the film *La Haine* (Matthieu Kasovitz, 1995). In contrast, Koolhaas notes, London is a living city, a dynamic material structure, constantly in flux; and this characteristic will allow its inhabitants to live twenty-first-century lives in a city both ancient and modern. Less is, indeed, more. Whereas for Koolhaas London is becoming 'less London', for Ackroyd the metropolis is becoming just another version of itself, and therefore, 'more London'. In his London Weekend Television lecture, 'London Luminaries and Cockney Visionaries', delivered in 1993, Ackroyd stated that '[s]ometimes it even seems to me that the city itself creates the conditions of its own growth, that it somehow plays an active part in its own development like some complex organism slowly discovering its form.'[5]

Ackroyd has a complex vision of London as a historical process. At the start of the passage from Ackroyd's London biography, he refers to the idea that the residue of material structures allow us to re-enter these historical periods. This reminds us of Sinclair's idea that London 'holds the memory of what it was' and that 'it is possible to walk back into the previous, as an event' (*WCST* 63). Yet the passage ends by giving us a different idea. Ackroyd sees 'hundreds of Londons all mingled', which seems to say architecture is able to evoke earlier Londons as complete worlds. It seems that Ackroyd literally sees different *versions* of previously existing Londons present within the same space. To understand how this might work, we could invoke a passage from Freud's *Civilization and its Discontents* (1907), which tries to debunk the common analogy between the working of the human mind and the development of a city in history. Freud notes:

> Now let us, by a flight of the imagination, suppose that Rome is not a human habitation but a psychical entity with a similar long and copious past – an entity [...] in which nothing that has come into existence will have passed away and all the earlier phases of development continue to exist alongside the latest one. [...] There is clearly no point in spinning out phantasy any further, for it leads to things that are unimaginable and even absurd. If we want to represent historical sequence in spatial terms we can only do it in juxtaposition in space: the same space cannot have two different contents. [...] The city is thus an *a priori* unsuited for a comparison of this sort with a mental organism.[6]

Freud stresses that the city is an unsuitable metaphor for understanding the form of the human mind and the development of memory because the two develop differently: the city can only be viewed in historical terms, which is not the case for the consciousness of man. Yet the passage does lead to an interesting idea about the representation of the city itself: whereas for Freud imagining versions of Rome alongside one another is 'unimaginable and even absurd', writers such as Maureen Duffy, Iain Sinclair and Peter Ackroyd have been exploring the imaginative possibilities of precisely this process in their work. They all use the idea of the palimpsest – a surface of vellum or parchment used for writing on more than once – as a guiding principle because it shows that imaginative writing *is* able to contain many different versions of the city within the same space.

There are direct political implications to this use of the palimpsest: medieval parchment was expensive so it became a contested site that addresses the relationship between economics and writing, between money and language as two systems with different values. The palimpsest forms an imagined clash, then, between the material culture and Idealism. Simultaneously, the writing that was erased stood for ideologies that are suppressed by official powers: power over knowledge via a control, and manipulation, of writing is central to the idea of the palimpsest, which therefore became a central trope within postmodern thought. The first part of this chapter looks at the various ways in which early critics have situated Ackroyd's novels within postmodern theoretical frameworks, paying tribute to, but also showing the limits of, these early interpretations.

The Ackroyd scholar Barry Lewis, who belongs to a second wave of critics who situate the author's work beyond the earlier postmodern models of criticism in the 1980s and 1990s, engages us in a provocative thought experiment which turns Freud's impossible fantasy on its head:

> it is perhaps helpful to reverse the metaphor of the city-as-human and to consider this English writer as if he were a city. He has his landmarks, his suburbs, and his neglected boroughs. As with London, he is very difficult to grasp. This is partly because [...] he 'had made a profession out of evasion, camp denials and sudden changes of perspective'. It is also because his writing sprawls, like the metropolitan space itself. [...] The darkness and disorder of Ackroyd and London – and Ackroyd's London – can only be captured in glimpses and echoes.[7]

Lewis is not talking about the author, but about the sprawling body of work that his engagement with London has produced over the past three decades. This chapter aims to do exactly that: rather than attempting to produce a survey of the author's proliferating *oeuvre*, or Lewis's Ackroydopolis, it practises 'the art of selection'[8] by reading the writer's voluminous works through a single slim work of fiction published around the time of Ackroyd's biography, *The Plato Papers* (1999), a less mystical and more directly political novella than Ackroyd's earlier Gothic works. By taking a 'de-occulted' view of Ackroyd's work and foregrounding the satirical dimensions of this novel, it becomes clear that Ackroyd is attempting to restore a revolutionary, visionary tradition of London writing that revaluates the spoken voice in writing.

A space out of which a few words emerge: Peter Ackroyd, modernism and postmodernism

A first wave of Ackroyd criticism is influenced by the persuasive yet sweeping theses of Jean Baudrillard's *Simulacra and Simulations* (1985) and Brian McHale's *Postmodernist Fiction* (1987). McHale posited that 'the dominant of postmodernist fiction is *ontological'* which led some critics to argue that Ackroyd's works are preoccupied with the negotiation of different ontological realms in terms of one another.[9] These early critics of Ackroyd's work include Susana Onega, Richard Todd, Alison Lee and John Peck and, more recently, Jeremy Gibson and Julian Wolfreys.[10] In his analysis of *Hawksmoor* (1986), Todd speaks of 'the alternative universe of *Hawksmoor'* and of 'Ackroyd's alternative world', indicating that the novel creates seemingly impossible fusions between separate, but very real realms of existence.[11] These critics' subscription to McHale's post-cognitive processes bypasses the idea that Ackroyd's London as a literary site stages a metaphorical and symbolic confrontation between different ethnic and cultural worlds in which language features as a connection between worlds, not a division. Ackroyd's texts stress the epistemological and phenomenological basis of our perception of the world as the foremost means of sense-making: the space of literature is an epistemological space that we make with our eyes and mind.

In order to understand the confusion that Ackroyd's texts create it is necessary to look at his methodology. Ackroyd's pastiches – *The Great Fire of London* (1982), *The Last Testament of Oscar Wilde* (1983), *Hawksmoor* (1986), *Chatterton* (1987) – and historical novels such as *The House of Doctor Dee* (1993) are written by means of a painstaking immersion in historical research and literary fiction in order to imitate the voices and styles of earlier authors (Dickens, Wilde, etc.). As Ackroyd's 'Oscar Wilde' states in his fictional diary: 'In that moment of transition, when I was myself and someone else, of my own time and in another's, the secrets of the universe would stand revealed.'[12] Ackroyd's earlier fiction, then, is a mystical attempt to dislodge the human mind and body trapped in space and time: the author's conditioning by the socio-historical and cultural present can only be transcended temporarily, by acts of historical retrieval supplemented by the creative imagination.

This seemingly esoteric method is carried through in his non-fiction: in his biography of Dickens, Ackroyd holds fictional conversations with the author whose life he is chronicling. Therefore, Susana Onega argues that Ackroyd's

> attempt to recreate a concrete historical period in concrete terms is only a pretext for a much more interesting and disturbing aim, which is to enter the tunnel of time in order to recover the other, suppressed, half of Western civilisation and history: the mythical esoteric, Gnostic and cabalistic elements which have been progressively repressed and muffled since the Middle Ages by the mainstream of rationalism.[13]

Figure 12 Thames Tunnel, Rotherhithe

Yet Ackroyd has himself denied that his methodology is esoteric, or mystical. This is underscored by a specific passage in his LWT lecture:

> In [...] *The House of Doctor Dee*, I have tried to invoke my own vision of the continuing city – that is why some of it is set in the sixteenth century – but I knew, as I was writing these passages, that the speech, the behaviour and beliefs of sixteenth century Londoners were exactly as I described them. I do not believe this to be an act of mediumship or divination – except in the sense that one is divining the historical patterns of London speech or London writing that lie just below the surface of our contemporary language.[14]

Here, Ackroyd explicitly distances himself from any association with mediumship, and the conviction that rings in his phrase 'I knew [...] that the speech, the behaviour and beliefs were exactly as I described them' suggests that we should look towards language, story and mythologies as a form of memory that allows us to retrieve the city in its earlier manifestations.

In the historiographic metafiction *The Great Fire of London*, Ackroyd reworks *Little Dorrit* (1855–7), setting up a formal structure that juxtaposes historical fragments with a contemporary story about filmmaker Spencer Spender, who wants to make a film of Dickens's novel. Rowan Phillips, a homosexual, Canadian teacher of English literature and potential screenplay author of *Little Dorrit*, is forced to give up his quest for Dickens's London: 'I can't really see any proper way of bringing Dickens to life [...] To think you could just take Dickens and bundle him into the twentieth century. We don't live in the same world. We don't even live in the same city.'[15] The point is that Peter Ackroyd, as his Dickens biography evidences, *is* able to evoke Dickens's city and its people by excavating the forgotten and repressed past from the tool that connects us to, and creates continuity with, the past: language.

This becomes evident in *Hawksmoor*, which, drawing elaborately on the occult theory around the Hawksmoor churches and obelisks constructed by Sinclair in *Lud Heat*, explores how unofficial history filters through into the contemporary. Two narrative strands are interconnected. First there is the story of the architect Nicolas Dyer – a thinly veiled version of Nicolas Hawksmoor, who is constructing seven churches in the first decades of the eighteenth century. The churches' geographical pattern and their aesthetic are informed by occult principles with a view to rearranging the energies of the city. Each of the churches is consecrated by sacrificing a male virgin at the site. In the second strand, set in contemporary London, the detective Hawksmoor is investigating a series of murders that seem to be taking place at the Dyer churches, in order to find out that he has become the victim of a historical echo that turns him into both murderer and, in the end, victim.

The intricate temporal construction of the novel, which Alex Murray explores via the idea of echolalia, is also a comment upon the structure of London itself. Dyer pits himself directly against Sir Christopher Wren, the influential architect reshaping the City after the Great Fire of 1666:

> And yet in the way of that Philosophie much cried up in London and elsewhere, there are those like Sir Chris. who speak only of what is Rational and what is Demonstrated, of Propriety and Plainness. [...] The Mysteries must become easy and familiar, it is said, and it has now reached such a Pitch that there are those who wish to bring their matheticall Calculations into Morality, *viz.* the Quantity of Publick Good produced by any agent is compound Ratio of his Benevolence and Abilities, and such like Excrement. They build edifices which they call *Systems* by laying their foundacions in the Air and, when they think they are come on solid Ground, the Buildings disappear and the Architects tumble down from the Clouds. Men that are fixed upon *matter, experiment, secondary causes* and the like have forgot there is such a thing in the World which they cannot see nor or touch nor measure: it is the Praecipice into which they will surely fall.[16]

Wren represents the tyranny of rationalism and anticipates Enlightenment thinking with its belief in the possibility of understanding the world through observation and interpretation of quantifiable data. His plan to literally straighten out London's figure ground after the Great Fire should be situated historically. William Harvey's discovery of the blood's circulation, published in *De motu cordis* (1628), became a dominant model in urban planning from the early eighteenth century onward: Hausmann's Paris and L'Enfant's Washington were 'a vindication of Enlightenment beliefs in the power to create a healthy environment in a highly organized, comprehensive urban design'.[17] Dyer argues against this fallacious anthropomorphic model, which established a direct relationship between the organisation of the material world, and the ethical potential of the city. By taking an Idealist position, he reminds us of the inexplicable mysteries and contradictions of life, with its spiritual and religious dimensions, of the darkness beneath the light. Yet the reference to architects tumbling from the clouds is a reference to their Babylonian ambitions, and also points out the problem, but also the creative and productive force, of language which these militant rationalists forget. Dyer, the architect of the material city, and Ackroyd, architect of the city of words, remind us that our understanding of the world is first and foremost created in and by language. It is at the level of language that we may be able to find the hidden patterns of force within an organism such as London, or England, which the rationalists' 'systems' obscure, and which Ackroyd's texts are trying to retrieve and elucidate. It is the act of writing fiction which, for Ackroyd, has an explanatory or revelatory function in making visible those patterns.

This postmodern city-as-text in Ackroyd's historiographic novels of the 1980s and 1990s is represented as the locus that makes visible a loss of collective memory, as well as an analysis of its processes. Ackroyd attempts to reassemble the layers of traces, residues and narratives of the already-written or built-in opposition to forces which produces a London without memory, or, perhaps, with a memory and history shaped rhetorically by external forces, such as the Thatcher government or the tabloid press. Yet rather than Sinclair's foregrounding of the self in the creation of the city-as-text, Ackroyd depicts the textualised spaces of the city as a repository for a unique sensibility, a structure of feeling and aesthetic specific to London which comes *before* the subject. It is a structure of feeling which can be pinpointed, and dug up through immersion in literary texts and cultural objects, before which the self must be emptied.

There are various shaping influences to Ackroyd's ideas about this process of emptying of the self. Ackroyd is first of all a poet, and not a novelist, and he therefore comes from a tradition rooted in oral communication rather than in writing. Sir Philip Sidney's classic *The Defence of Poesy* (1695) makes a distinction between two different kinds of poet: the *vates*, prophet-poet, and the *poiein*, who is the maker-poet. Whereas Sinclair's foregrounding of the self as site that produces work would align him with the latter, Ackroyd seems to be inclined to cancel out the self. In *The House of Doctor Dee* the narrator invokes the book of Daniel to emphasise 'a theory that the first human being was androgynous',[18] which Ackroyd develops into the idea that the self is a *tabula rasa*: 'I really don't believe that there's anything there, just a space out of which a few words emerge from time to time' (*DD* 81). As we have seen, Duffy's and Sinclair's texts do not accept this posing as a prophet, by showing that the self is a space that is conditioned by power structures that permeate society, which therefore have political implications. One dismissive reviewer of Ackroyd's collection of poetry, *The Diversions of Purley* (1987), published around the time of the first wave of Ackroyd criticism, mockingly called him and Ian McMillan 'The Empty Telephone Boys':

> They represent the triviality that is almost inescapable when poetry becomes introverted, concerned only with itself and language. [...] The vital point which is being overlooked is that, given the impossibility of closing the gap between word and experience, none the less the most interesting things happen when poetry tries with all its might to close it, when they force the language near to breaking-point or sing it into trance in effort to make us see the object or feel the emotion.[19]

This supports the consensus that Ackroyd divorces, as Joyce does in his hypermodernist text *Finnegans Wake* (1939), the world of words from the world of matter, for which he is chastised. Ackroyd's origins as a poet are an important influence upon his conception of the role of the writer, and T. S. Eliot, whose biography Ackroyd wrote (in 1984), is particularly important in moulding Ackroyd's ideas. Eliot's classic essay 'Tradition and the Individual Talent' (1919), which famously makes a claim for the impersonal theory of poetry, gives us an important clue as to the ways in which the poet can function as an empty vessel that verbalises ideas by earlier writers: 'The poet's mind is in fact a receptacle for seizing and storing up numberless feelings, phrases, images, which remain there until all the particles which can unite to form a new compound are present together.'[20] Rather than categorizing Ackroyd as a postmodernist, it would seem more apt to call him a late modernist who aligns himself with repressed intellectual traditions.

Indeed, in his LWT lecture, Ackroyd creates and aligns himself with what he has called 'a tradition of 'London Luminaries and Cockney Visionaries'.[21] He includes within this tradition Blake, More, Dickens, Chaucer, Turner and the performance artist Dan Leno as the most important London voices because of their quest for understanding London. In the lecture, Ackroyd states:

> All of them were preoccupied with light and darkness, in a city that is built in the shadows of money and power; all of them were entranced by the scenic and the spectacular, in a city that is continually filled

with the energetic display of people and institutions. They understood the energy of London, they understood its variety, and they
also understood its darkness.[22]

Ackroyd too creates dark, underground, alchemical Londons that are
used as a weapon, directly, against the rationality associated with the
Enlightenment project, and, indirectly, against Thatcherism and, as
we will see, the New Labour government. Ackroyd's goal is to illuminate and protect 'the variable nature of the city' (*PP* 92), and to avoid
interference in London's evolution 'in preordained patterns' (*PP* 89).
Ackroyd's work sets out to investigate 'the pattern of London', by which
he means that 'the city itself creates the conditions of its own growth,
that it somehow plays an active part in its own development like some
complex organism slowly discovering its form'.[23]

Here we are all one with the city: *The Plato Papers'* hermeneutic puzzle

The Plato Papers is an interesting work within Ackroyd's wider *oeuvre*
because it 'theorises' in fiction how the multiplicity and aesthetic offered
by London can be safeguarded through an engagement with living
speech as a political act. Todd notes that Ackroyd's alignment with the
Gothic mode of writing should be viewed as an indirect reaction to the
ways in which the Thatcherite programme of privatisation and decentralisation expresses itself in the London landscape. At first sight a seemingly light-hearted and playful work, *The Plato Papers* is a novel that
connects, however, with Sinclair's later works such as *Lights Out* and
London Orbital because it is more overtly political about the city's transformation than Ackroyd's dark Gothic novels and historical pastiches
of the 1980s and 1990s.[24] It is driven by the desire for the retrieval of
meaningful urban spaces and relationships wherein the destruction of a
sense of place in the contemporary city is challenged by the shoring up
of powerful London voices, which are derived from the revolutionary,
story-telling traditions of Chaucer, Blake and Dickens.

The Plato Papers is set in the London of the year AD 3705, where the
inquisitive orator Plato lectures on the history of their city. After the
world as we know it has expired, fallen into darkness and subsequently
reborn in light, the London of Ideas becomes a place where the minds
of all Londoners are united into one divine consciousness. An anonymous narrator collects the orations of 'Plato', whose speculations on the
Age of Mouldwarp (AD 1500–AD 2300) result in comical yet insightful

Figure 13   Invisibility and inverse problems, Beckton Alps

misinterpretations that criticise contemporary British society. Plato then journeys back to the London of the late twentieth century by entering a vast, labyrinthine cavern. Upon his return, he is punished for telling his fellow citizens of his findings, which are deemed lies: his subversive musings on the past lead to a divorce from the body politic and his subsequent self-imposed banishment from London. By looking at the present from the vantage point of the future, the novel develops the conceit that contemporary London exists as a form of Plato's cave, where the inhabitants – us – are under the impression that their world is the 'real' one, whilst it actually exists as a kind of underworld to the true city.

Plato's descent from his world into ours is an allegorical one, and the novel centres on a strategic deployment of linguistic defamiliarisation. An important part of *The Plato Papers* is made up of a dictionary of ancient Mouldwarp words and concepts, consisting of a wide variety of entries, from 'biographer' and 'brainstorm' to 'half time' and 'pedestrian'. Plato's hilarious, Johnsonian undertaking 'explains' the meaning of Mouldwarp's lexicon by substituting, confusing or literalizing them, to comic effect: 'dead end' is 'a place where corpses are taken' (*PP* 13), 'logic' is 'a wooden object, as in log table' (*PP* 9) and some 'writers were considered sacred, as in Pope and Priestly' (*PP* 26). Ackroyd's text uses the comic effect of Plato's misinterpretations to satirise the contemporary era.

Plato's disconnection of the words from their original context and their subsequent literalisation allows Ackroyd to elaborate a deliberately fallacious and self-consciously personal interpretation of words we associate with 'our' fallen world. We are given a hermeneutic puzzle that exploits dramatic irony on our behalf and at Plato's expense: we are placed in a position of knowledge, an ironical process that inverts linguistic authority paradoxically: we, Ackroyd's readers, have more control over the language which Plato is trying to decipher, yet we are in no position to inform him, which reduces our power. Plato, or the relationship between us and Plato, resembles modern man, linguistically isolated from others, and attempting to reconstruct a meaningful relationship with his fellow man through the ruins of language. This makes *The Plato Papers*, beyond its comedy, a deeply serious and profound meditation on social relationship at the turn of the millennium.

These literalisations show, through an inversion of the conventional signification, and of the relationship between object and metaphor, the tyranny of language. The text thus becomes an investigation of both the freedom and dangers of both the city as a system of signs, and of language itself, as a prison. Beyond Ackroyd's game-playing, then, lies a frustration with the limitations of traditional signification and causality, which the novel exploits linguistically by turning this dislocation against itself. Paradoxically, for Ackroyd, language is the only means for achieving some degree of freedom, for Platonic transcendence, yet our accessibility is dependent upon our ability to exert our interpretative skills intelligently and creatively. Ackroyd's novel points out the fragility of knowledge itself, and warns us against becoming blind to the possibilities offered by language.

This tragicomic erosion of London at the level of language is also dramatised by the text through the incorporation of another significant, yet dramatically different representation of the city, namely, the description of Harry Beck's London Underground map, originally drawn up in 1935:

> *underground*: the title of a painting of great beauty. It is before you now. Notice how the blue and red lines of light reach out in wonderful curves and ovals, while a great yellow circle completes the design. It is a masterpiece of formal fluency and, although the people of Mouldwarp are considered to be devoid of spiritual genius, there are some who believe this to be their sacred symbol of harmony. It is true that certain spirit names have been deciphered – angel, temple, white city, gospel oak and the legendary seven sisters – but the central purpose of the painting is still disputed. (*PP* 26)

This passage offers itself as a meditation on the problem of representing London. One irony is that Beck's map is not a map but a circuit diagram, an abstract pictorial representation demonstrating the form and workings of the Underground system that bears only an indirect resemblance to the geographical reality. In this context, the diagram functions as a criticism of the contemporary reductive vision of the world's heterogeneity under modes of thinking produced under the Enlightenment. Rod Mengham states that Beck's map forces us 'to think of rationalized space and time, as places where the unexpected is not meant to happen. The Tube map with its symmetries, its rows of diagonals, its repetition of angles, is an excessive rationalisation of something that in reality is much more irregular.'[25] Beck's über-rational diagram is a version of London at its most resistant to being moulded by the human mind, and as a 'sacred symbol of harmony' the most devious, false icon: what is unsettling is the deceptive gap between reality and representation with which it confronts us. However, although the map misrepresents London above ground, it is merely one possible representation, affirming the impossibility of representing London's heterogeneity: 'The air was tainted with the inhuman smell of numbers and machines, but the city itself was in a state of perpetual change' (*PP* 90).

Simultaneously, this passage reminds the reader that Beck's map, rather than presenting a mental map of how the citizen might experience the city, forms the residue of an imaginary London. The Underground diagram portrays London not as the organic form associated with the idealised City of God, but as a rationalised and rationalising machine that negates or suppresses the messiness of urban life, the London of Ideas.

In 'Poem On The Underground' (2009), Michael Donaghy also appropriates Beck's Underground diagram by offering a 3D design that restores the earlier complexity of ancient London maps, which offered a more imaginative approach. The new diagram's inventor inscribes the diagram with significant and trivial events, such as a security alert, a person under a train and a vomiting temp: not only does this new map connect seemingly unconnected people's lives in space, but the 'lines along the third dimension indicate / connections through time: here, the King's Cross fire / leads to wartime bivouacs on station platforms / and further still, to children singing on a sunlit hill'.[26] One might also think of Simon Patterson's famous lithograph 'The Great Bear' (1992), which reimagines Beck's map by renaming the tube stations after distinct groups of famous people: Engineers, Explorers, Film Actors, Saints,

Artists, etc. This randomness has a comic effect, and creates an alternate ordering system of knowledge, and demonstrates how, ultimately, we are all connected. The point about both these works is that their emphasis on the abstracted visualisation emphasises the gap between the raw, messy experience of human life and the totalising systems that erase the human aspect from the imagined city.

The diagram also suggests that the seductive, comforting power of Beck's sublime misrepresentation imposes itself upon Londoners' experience, so that it becomes an integral part of the way London is perceived and understood. The diagram thus becomes a symbol of the way in which the city's structure, as an expression of the flows of power, forms an all-consuming force that *produces* and shapes, dialogically, London, and Londoners: 'The citizens were often bewildered; they lived within fantasies and ambitions which the city itself had created, and they felt obliged to act according to the roles allotted to them. They had no understanding of themselves' (*PP* 94). Ackroyd's text seems to avail itself here of Baudrillard's theory of the simulacrum, whereby the system of signs, divorced from their original referents, 'forgets' or covers up the reality to which it used to refer: 'the whole earth seemed to have been reduced and rolled into a ball until it was small enough to fit their theories' (*PP* 3–4). The latter sentence is a reference to Blake's poem *The Mental Traveller* (1863), which contains a reference to what he claims is a delusional post-Copernican and Newtonian conception of the earth: 'The Guests are scattered thro' the land, / For the Eye altering alters all; / The Senses roll themselves in fear / And the flat Earth becomes a Ball.'[27]

In this context, we are not given the simulacrum reimagined as a postmodern concept by Baudrillard, but a Platonic one. Throughout his *oeuvre*, Ackroyd's Londoners, as Richard Todd notes, have been portrayed as locked in Plato's cave: 'Ackroyd's present-day Londoners remain physically inert, unanimated: they eat simple austere meals, often in unlit rooms that may at times be alive with whispering and shadows, and their encounters with the numinous occur in dreams and visions, with what is often a minimum of physical exertion.'[28] Ackroyd's novel posits that the body of living language contained by the city and its inhabitants offers the possibility of 'remembering' in a Platonic sense. This occurs, for instance, by means of intertextual strategies, by linguistic defamiliarisation and by pointing to the linguistic origin of place: the names of tube stations mentioned above refer to a historical, and sometimes mythical reality, which is present in Londoners' language.

I heard words which the citizens could not hear: Ackroyd, Plato and speech

Scholarship on Ackroyd has thus far focused mostly on Ackroyd's writing, and his writing of the city. Linda Hutcheon, for instance, made *Hawksmoor* one of the textbook examples of her more humanist brand of postmodernist fiction that explored contradictory forms of writing: 'Their sequentially ordered sections are equally disrupted by a particularly dense network of interconnections and intertexts, and each enacts or performs, as well as theorizes, the paradoxes of continuity and disconnection, of totalizing interpretation and impossibility of final meaning.'[29] Another particularly striking example of the foregrounding of the importance of writing in Ackroyd's work can be found in Julian Wolfreys's and Jeremy Gibson's *Peter Ackroyd: The Ludic and Labyrinthine Text* (2000):

> The act of writing the city, and the city's performative projection onto the condition of the subject, effectively dismantles any neat distinction between the word and the world, writing and reality. This is not to suggest that the world, or what we call 'reality' does not exist. Rather, the point is, that Ackroyd's writing, and, specifically, his engagement with the urban space, unfolds the interwoven and essentially textual condition of the world and our perception and comprehension of it.[30]

Gibson and Wolfreys frame Ackroyd's linguistic free play within Derridean terms, so that the work is read as a playful, yet meaningless enterprise. Gibson and Wolfreys note Ackroyd does this 'for no other purpose than the ludic possibility presented in teasing the identity of historical moments'.[31] The result of Wolfreys's and Gibson's relativism is reductive as it diminishes the political and historical dimension of Ackroyd's work; in fact, their foregrounding of Ackroyd's purported interest in purposelessness takes away the possibility of attributing any value or meaning to the works beyond the author's cleverly-clever free play. The texts, ultimately, mean nothing.

Although sometimes in danger of echoing Gibson's and Wolfreys's post-structuralist jargon by speaking of the 'ineffable nature' of the city, Alex Murray has voiced concern over this theoretical approach precisely for that reason: 'London becomes yet another unstable referent, with its history, geography and culture all indefinite and amorphous concepts that Ackroyd works tirelessly to dislocate. Yet the tradition of the London visionary has always been one that is site-specific, of engaged critique of the urban environment through the medium of the imagination.'[32] Murray offers an insightful historicised reading of Ackroyd's early work as a critique of culture and politics in the 1980s and 1990s, and in particular of 'Thatcher's decision to cloak the present in the language of the past [which] served to obscure the present, contributing to the obfuscating ideology of her premiership'.[33] Below I will second Murray's criticism of Wolfreys's and Gibson's rather reductive and relativist reading of Ackroyd's work, first by stressing the political nature of *The Plato Papers*, and, second, by focusing on an aspect that Wolfreys and Gibson gloss over, namely Ackroyd's interest in London *voices*, which they are unable to place within their Derridean framework. Ackroyd's work, in its search for a London voice, privileges living speech as it is retrieved in writing.

The Plato Papers overtly politicises the implications of such linguistic instability, which is intertwined with the evolution of the capitalist modes of production. The idea of race as a means of ordering the world, with racism as a result, is satirised in the following excerpt: 'I have already informed you that in this epoch the earth was divided and dispersed into "races", generally considered to have risen for climatic rather than spiritual reasons' (*PP* 78–9). Heterosexuality as the perceived sexual norm is dismantled in the following passage:

> It has often been noted that the people of Mouldwarp were preoccupied with sexual activity at the expense of all other principles of life; there is even some evidence to suggest that they identified themselves in terms of their sexual orientation. No. There is no cause for embarrassment. Our purpose is to understand, not to lay blame. (*PP* 60–1)

This unpacking of social categories is intertwined with the contemporary subject's blindness to the dangerous erosion of language in the Mouldwarp era. This is explicated by the meaning of '*word processor*: in the old machine culture words were seen as commodities, or items in a line of production. They became a form of manufacture and were, therefore, increasingly standardised; they took on mechanical rather than living proportions, so they could be widely distributed over the world' (*PP* 26). Ackroyd's irony implicitly suggests an intimate connection between the industrial era writing, which is not merely regarded as a system for representation, but as a means of exploitation and repression within the capitalist system.

The Plato Papers forms an important 'hinge' within Ackroyd's *oeuvre* because it not only criticises writing, but the novella also 'theorises' in fiction the importance of living speech in a world dominated by the written sign. By moving from the sprawling novels that imitate London's materiality in his early work to the novella form, he manages to represent the lightness of the 'London of Ideas', whilst the sparseness of the prose established a renewed focus on the important of language. And it is no accident that Ackroyd has chosen 'Plato' as his protagonist: just as in Iris Murdoch's *Acastos: Two Platonic Dialogues* (1986), which also involves an appropriation of the ancient philosopher to meditate on contemporary concerns, Ackroyd reinvents him for a meditation on his own set of concerns. Barry Lewis alerts us to an important intervention by Ackroyd:

> Ackroyd's Plato differs from the Greek Plato in one significant respect: he is an orator. The latter was hostile to oratory because he believed that rhetoric could be a dangerous force, moving people by a power of persuasion divorced from fundamental knowledge of the truth. Socrates prefers dialogue and dialectic, a more inter-active form of teaching that emphasizes the patient exercise of reason. Notwithstanding this, the Plato of *The Plato Papers* is a rhetorician.[34]

Lewis notes that making Plato a rhetorician is convenient because it allows Ackroyd to summarise the history of this future world, yet more is at stake here. The reconfiguration of Plato as a philosopher *for* rather than *against* speech turns the philosopher from a puritan into an impetuous, self-deceiving philosopher who constantly bungles his persuasive explanation, which signposts Ackroyd's interest in retrieving *speech* as an important mode of mindfully engaging with the world.

Mikhail Bakhtin is much more sympathetic than Derrida to Plato's and Socrates's concern for living speech as a means to carry living memory. Bakhtin, in a sense *avant la lettre*, will not have Derrida's deconstruction of speech as writing, as the spoken sign too emerges from dialogic interaction. This is made clear in the following passage, in which Bakhtin speaks about the Socratic dialogue:

> Characteristic, even canonic, for the genre is the spoken dialogue framed by the dialogized story. Characteristic also the proximity of its language to popular spoken language, as near as was possible for classical Greece; these dialogues in fact opened the path to the Attic prose, and are connected with the essential renovation of the

literary-prose language – and with the shift in languages in general. Characteristically this genre is at the same time a rather complex mixture of styles and dialects (we have before us therefore a multi-styled genre, as is the authentic novel).[35]

The Plato Papers is in many ways a dramatisation of Bakhtin's dialogism, as Ackroyd's recuperation of the London voice occurs in such a multi-styled and emphatically heteroglossic text.

As we saw earlier in Ackroyd's defence against the accusation of his employing mediumistic techniques, his texts are divining the historical patterns of London speech or London writing that lie just below the surface of our contemporary language. This *modus operandi* can be clarified by reading Ackroyd's work in terms of Bakhtin's ideas about the heteroglossic nature of language. In his essay 'Discourse in the Novel' (1935) Bakhtin disputes the idea that a unitary or monologic language can exist: language is stratified not only into linguistic dialects in the strict sense of the word but also into languages that are socio-ideological: languages of social groups, 'professional' and 'generic' languages of generations and so forth. As a result of this, the novelist's discourse is characterised by a voice that is internally dialogised:

> For the novelist working in prose, the object is always entangled in someone else's discourse about it, it is already present with qualifications, an object of dispute that is conceptualized and evaluated variously, inseparable from the heteroglot social apperception of it. The novelist speaks of this 'already qualified world' in a language that is heteroglot and internally dialogized.[36]

For Ackroyd, London's multiplicity appears to be the expression of such heteroglossia. Thus Ackroyd's text opens up an imaginative space that comically restructures our thinking about the contemporary city: rather than envisioning the urban environment as a purely written discourse, it is a heterogeneous composite of speech and writing that can be accessed via language. This is underscored by the following quotation, in which Plato discovers a multiplicity of times in Mouldwarp London:

> Their time was everywhere. It forced them to go forward. When I saw them walking in great lines, it was time itself that was moving. But it was not uniform [...] There were certain areas where it moved quickly, and others where it went forward reluctantly or fitfully – and there were places where it no longer moved at all. There were narrow streets in the city where I could still hear the voices of those who had

passed through many years before. Then I made another wonderful discovery. There were some citizens of Mouldwarp who seemed to live in a different time. There were ragged people who wandered with dogs; they were not on the same journey as those whom they passed on the crowded thoroughfares. There were children who chanted songs from an earlier age and there were old people who already had the look of eternity upon their faces [...] The ancient forms of speech and prayer were still in existence, but barely able to stir beneath the burden of this reality. So I heard words which the citizens could not hear, and observed moments of recognition or glances of longing which they never saw. (*PP* 91–2)

In this passage, Ackroyd dramatises the dense stratification of a-chronological times that Plato's defamiliarised perspective of Mouldwarpians' living speech offers. Ackroyd is historicising our lives by representing them as trajectories with specific evolutions rather than as static, a-historical entities frozen in time. *The Plato Papers* explicates, more so than Ackroyd's previous novels, the idea that the experience of time is determined by the temporal and site-specific conditioning of the subject. Thus, 'the fabric of the old [mythical] reality had dissolved or, rather, it had become interwoven with so many others that it could only rarely be glimpsed' (*PP* 53).

The title itself points to the heteroglossic nature of Ackroyd's novella: *The Plato Papers* is made up almost entirely out of verbal communications on several narrative levels: from the Platonic dialogues between Sparkler and Madrigal, and Sidonia, Plato and his soul, the orations of Plato, to the orally related verdict on Plato's corrupting lies and fables. Ackroyd's novella attempts to combine the traditions of these differing perspectives: the textual world forms a prism through which several perceptions are merged. In *The Plato Papers*, we are not only given Plato's point of view, but we also shift to his followers (some doubtful, some admiring), and the collective body politic. This multi-perspectival focalisation of London makes a unity of representation impossible, and undesirable:

the city continued to spread, encroaching upon new ground. It was continually going forward, forever seeking some harmonious outline without ever finding it. I tell you this: Mouldwarp London has no boundaries. It had no beginning and no end. That is why its citizens always seemed so restless [...] It is possible that they continued at their fevered pace in belief that if the pattern was interrupted they, as well as the city itself, might be destroyed. (*PP* 91)

The text's proposition that the city grows 'in preordained patterns' (*PP* 89) that should be safeguarded roots the text within the liberal humanist tradition, and supports its belief in organicism.

The construction of the text itself, however, points also to a questioning of Ackroyd's city as body metaphor. The dislocation of conventional signification, for instance, undercuts any claim towards realism. And although *The Plato Papers* is a novella that appears to promote the organic metaphor, its dialogic nature points us to a more complex representation. This thought is played out most poignantly in an important misinterpretation in the novel, namely the mix-up of Charles Dickens and Charles Darwin. Plato has found *On the Origin of Species by Means of Natural Selection* by Charles D—; but seven 'pages have been removed, and the author's name partially defaced' (*PP* 5). Plato assumes the author to be the novelist Charles Dickens, giving him the opportunity to expose Darwin's theory of evolution as a fiction. This mocks the nineteenth-century obsession with archaeological excavations as comfortable images for the linear development of the city in history, and underscores Ackroyd's belief that there is no linear progression towards perfection: 'the petrified shapes found in rock or ice were created to mock or mimic their organic counterparts' (*PP* 8). A simplistic organicism offers only a falsification of history's complexity, but it functions merely as a model that embodies the ideal of harmony.

If read in the context of Bakhtin's work, it becomes clear that a potential organicism can be recovered at the level of 'London' as a collection of written and spoken languages captured by the act of writing fiction. It is the London novelist's language that is 'organic' because of its ongoing dialogue in the midst of heteroglossia. Bakhtin explains that 'novelistic images seem to be grafted organically on to their own double-voiced language, pre-formed, as it were, within it, in the innards of the distinctive multi-speechedness organic to that language'.[37] This is dramatised in *The Plato Papers* by Plato's voluntary exile from the city: when the citizens of future London deliver their verdict, they speak in one voice – '*Here we are all one city. We are the limbs of the city. We are a common body*' (*PP* 117). It is this unity of voice and unitary language which is mocked and rejected by Ackroyd's text because its monologic dimension stifles the possibility of representing the heterogeneous nature of the modern world.

The strategies of defamiliarisation in *The Plato Papers* thus attempt to restore the reader's fallen sensory perception, which will allow him or her to see the city anew, and to reconceive London's plurality. *The Plato Papers* contains a whole host of references to places being reduced purely to their names: 'go to the white chapel' (*PP* 4), 'he is by the clerk's well' (*PP* 10) are indeed taken out of their contemporary context to emphasise that in the rush of contemporary life Londoners have forgotten the etymology of the place names that connect them in history. When Plato descends into Mouldwarp London, Ackroyd's criticism of the a-historical consciousness becomes clear: 'They were continually building and rebuilding their city. They took pleasure in destruction, I believe, because it allowed them a kind of forgetfulness' (*PP* 91).

The heterogeneous nature of London's space thus lies not so much in its material diversity, but in the heteroglossic nature of the British and London languages that mould our perception of the city. *The Plato Papers* works against the teleological drive and rhythms of capitalism: although the novel voices the idea that London evolves organically, it becomes clear that it is in the dialogic interaction between London, its spoken languages and its representations in fiction that the city and its citizens evolve in their own, idiosyncratic manner. This is what makes the London author important in his or her voicing of the city: its fictions and mythologies influence the city's destiny.

The role of the reader is increasingly important, then: the act of reading becomes a process of transforming writing back into living speech. In the final chapter of *The House of Doctor Dee*, Matthew Palmer has a vision in which he meets Dee, who is singing lines from T. S. Eliot's *The Waste Land*. Palmer then addresses Dee, but his words, it seems, are also directed as an exhortation of the reader:

> Oh you, who tried to find the light within all things, help me to create another bridge across two shores. And so join with me, in celebration. Come closer, come towards me so that we may become one. Then will London be redeemed, now and forever, and all those with whom we dwell – living or dead – will become the mystical city universal. (*DD* 277)

1 Brickwork, Thames Tunnel, Rotherhithe

6. View from Dove's Roof Terrace, Ambrose

3   View from the Trellick Tower, North Kensington

4 Thames Tunnel, Rotherhithe

5   Staircase, The Monument

7 River Lea at the Walthamstow Marshes

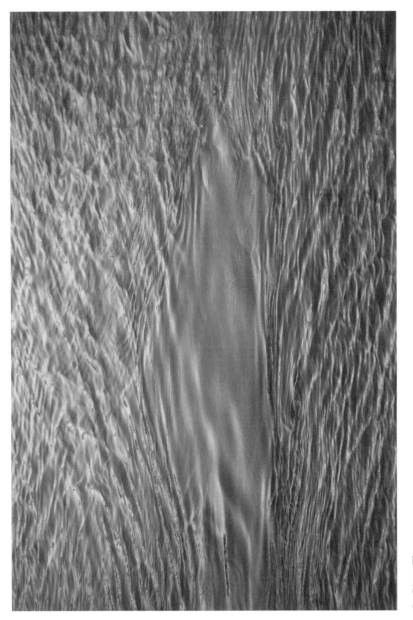

9 River Thames

6
'Beyond the Responsibility of Place': Ian McEwan's Londons

Ian McEwan's moral imagination of the city

In an early Ian McEwan story, 'Psychopolis' (1978), a young British classical musician spends some time in Los Angeles, 'a city at the end of cities [...] a vast, fragmented city without a centre, without citizens, a city that exists only in the mind'.[1] LA is experienced as an abstraction, an Idea rather than as a material reality you can touch and feel; the city becomes a metaphor for the a-historical, desensitised postmodern condition in which placelessness produces a potentially dangerous moral relativity. 'Los Angeles, California, the whole of the United States seemed to me a very fine and frail crust on the limitless, subterranean world of my own boredom.'[2] This points to, but also subtly challenges, Stephen Dedalus's concentrically ordered conception of identity in *A Portrait*, which is also a model for Maureen Duffy. Whereas in Joyce's Eurocentric vision the individual is still subordinate to the nation, in postmodern North America postmodern urbanity causes all levels of identity to become a projection of the self onto the outside world.

For Joyce, America was literally unintelligible – Dedalus is unable to 'learn the names of places in America. Still they were all different places that had those different names' – suggesting that America represents a fundamental break in the nature of the modern experience.[3] In McEwan's work, however, we see a more ambivalent stance to this modernist retrenchment to classic European cultural legacies. After his final performance, the narrator is '[o]verwhelmed by nostalgia for a country I had not yet left'.[4] This sentiment anticipates Jean Baudrillard's paradoxical idea about melancholy for the present in his hyperbolic tour de force *America* (1986). Baudrillard demonstrates how the simulacral aspects of the United States have established a new, dominant model of 'the real' that undermines the original world from which it emerged. McEwan sets part of the story in Venice Beach, Los Angeles, because it ironically invokes the original Venice, a dying city symbolising Europe's waning cultural power. Before returning to London, the musician rejects his classical cultural values and embraces the manifold freedoms offered by America: 'I could be anywhere, I could have saved myself the effort and fare. I wished in fact I was nowhere, beyond the responsibility of place.'[5]

In McEwan's work London plays a key role as the place where troubled, post-imperial Britain reinvents itself as a key node in and force behind a globalised world under the economic and cultural dominance of America. His early stories capture Britain's post-imperial decline by portraying London as a dark city of poverty, crime, sexual perversity and exploitation. *The Child in Time* (1987) creates a dystopian, futuristic wasteland at the heart of a Thatcherised nation. We see a post-Major, scandal-riddled London emerge in *Enduring Love* (1997) and the novella *Amsterdam* (1998), and *Saturday* (2005) voices McEwan's vision of post-9/11 London as the embodiment of Western culture and civilisation under threat from terrorism. This chapter traces the trajectory of McEwan's evolving representations of London whilst drawing attention to the remarkable consistency in his depiction of London as a site of moral contestation.

McEwan's texts are obsessed with testing of ethics, responsibility and agency in a rapidly changing post-war context. Important within McEwan's moral imagination of the city is the struggle between the traditional necessity of the citizen's rootedness in a specific material environment that inscribes the self with shared moral, social and cultural codes, and the fading of clear boundaries in the post-war period that creates social dislocation and cultural uprootedness.

In contrast to post-metropolitan Los Angeles, the ancient European city functions as a unifying site of economic, political and military power and its material boundaries have functioned as geographical and social demarcation lines.[6] The material perimeter that keeps a people together also implies a shared, unitary framework of imagined codes. Robert Lopez states that this moat and/or wall 'need not be materially erected so long as it is morally present, to keep the citizens together, sheltered from the cold, wide world, conscious of belonging to a unique team, proud of being different from the open country and germane to one another'.[7] This material and imaginary division of space reminds one of the mythical founding of Rome by the brothers Romulus and Remus on 21 April 753 BC. Roman mythology has it that the brothers fought over the location of the city, and when Romulus won, Remus defiantly jumped over the trench that indicated the city's boundaries. Remus was slain by his brother, indicating that the city can only work if physical and moral boundaries are respected.

McEwan rewrites Rome's founding myth in his children's novel *The Daydreamer* (1994) in which a boy shares a bedroom with his younger sister, and, in order to prevent fighting, 'they kept the peace by drawing an imaginary line right across their bedroom'.[8] McEwan's work is interested in the respecting or transgressing of boundaries also because they are intertwined with ideas about democracy. The enclosure of ancient Athens enabled the formation of the classical model of democracy: the city-state, or *polis*, depended on clear lines of identity demarcation between insiders (citizens) and outsiders (slaves, barbarians, etc.). The citizenry formed a sovereign body, the Assembly, made up of 6,000 citizens ensuring that in the imagination the city and its citizens were conflated with one another, and with this came, at least theoretically, an irreducible collective civic duty and a deep sense of moral responsibility whereby the individual could not distinguish himself from a social totality, of *demos*.

McEwan's work traces the unravelling connection between 'the private' and 'the public' spheres in the postmodern West, and asks what the ethical consequences are. One prominent influence on McEwan's ideas, as Dominic Head has pointed out, is Iris Murdoch, whose seminal essay 'Against Dryness' (1961) voices concerns about the role of the Welfare State in the post-war period. Whilst establishing a social safety net that makes everyone responsible for one another, it also severs a direct link between citizens because all social relations are mediated by a state. This has a detrimental impact on the potential to realise oneself as a free agent, whilst the ideal of genuine community is undermined as well.[9] McEwan's work brings these ideas into a contemporary context in which the isolation of the self is intensified by increased intervention by the state, and by new technologies and an intrusive media landscape. 'The city is a place that multiplies the "accidents" of human contact', Lewis Mumford states, and McEwan makes the consequences of modern life visible by introducing random accidents, such as the abduction of a child, a hot air balloon adrift or a car crash, at work in the modern world, and the city in particular.[10] The metropolis provides interference that is necessary to dramatise human relationships present beneath the apparent social disconnection whilst the violent eruptions of contingency also lead to a violation of agreed social norms and moral values, leaving us with unsettling and irresolvable ambivalences.

They shone no light on it: Ian McEwan's Darkest London

McEwan's early work voices the post-imperial identity crisis that England was going through in the 1970s. When, in the aforementioned 'Psychopolis', an American friend asks whether England is in a state of total collapse, the narrator discloses the following:

> I said yes and spoke at length without believing what I was saying. The only experience I had of total collapse was a friend who killed himself. At first he only wanted to punish himself. He ate a little ground glass washed down with grapefruit juice. Then when the pains began he ran to the tube station, bought the cheapest ticket and threw himself under a train. The brand new Victoria line. What would that be like on a national scale?[11]

The black irony of committing suicide by jumping under the 'brand new Victoria line' – the name reminding painfully of Britain's imperial heyday – forms a strong yet darkly comic warning against escapist fantasies about returning to Britain's past. McEwan is sceptical about apocalyptic narratives scripted by mass media, and tells us to mind the gap between the imagined nation and lived experience of the individual.

As I have noted elsewhere, McEwan's early short stories portray an archetypal version of what Raymond Williams called 'Darkest London', a 'city of darkness, of oppression, of crime and squalor, or reduced humanity'.[12] London is a place whose darkness is generated by the oppression of the city's underclass, and in response they invoke the mythical dimensions of poetry and literature to protest against their plight. McEwan also engages with the factual, journalistic representation of London in the work of Thackeray and Fielding, which allows a historical reading. McEwan's interest in 'darkness' is not only a metaphor for the British crisis, but it is also a direct reaction to the oil crisis of 1973, which plunged Britain literally into darkness due to a shortage of electricity.[13] The early works deliberately attempt to shock and transgress social and moral boundaries because, after the relaxing of censorship laws meant a reinforced questioning of the boundaries acceptable in the 1960s, the 1970s saw a legal backlash against offensive and obscene material, sparking a war on pornography.

These issues are central in the early London stories, which focus on death and decay, moral decline and sexual perversion. In 'Disguises' (1975) children are abused by an underground network of paedophiles in an Islington home. Much of the action of 'Homemade' (1975), the story in which a young man rapes his sister to lose his much resented virginity, is set in and around north London's Finsbury Park. In 'Pornography' the sleazy protagonist, O'Byrne ('Oh burn'), knowingly spreads the clap around the city by simultaneously sleeping with two nurses (Lucy and Pauline) who work at the same hospital, whilst covering shifts in a Soho porn shop for his brother, Harold. The duo's language conflates economic and sexual terms, as the structure of the following sentence suggests: '"Those American mags," said Harold as he emptied the till of £15 and a handful of silver, "are *good*."'[14] Money literally lies at the centre of the O'Byrnes' world and discourse, turning conventional morality upside down. That the brothers exchange corruption for silver suggests this is a secular world in which language as a vehicle for meaningful communication has itself become corrupted.

The pernicious influence that causes this corruption is America, and the heart of the pornography industry, Los Angeles, in particular. Harold wants to go 'All American' by stocking the imported 'House of Florence' brand of pornography – another ironical inversion of an ancient European city – which is housed in 'a disused church in a narrow terrace street on the Brixton side of Norbury'.[15] The Old World and its religious, moral conditioning are exorcised by American newness. As punishment for his duplicity O'Byrne is castrated by the two nurses, but, as Jack Slay has suggested, the emasculation figures in a complex, contradictory struggle of sexual desire. In a realistic reading, the castration of O'Byrne signifies the protagonist's Dickensian comeuppance, but for O'Byrne, his unmanning provides the ultimate orgasm.[16] Reality and 'perverse' fantasy merge into a seamless narrative climax that translates emasculation into orgasm.

This attempt to cleanse perversion through a purifying act of violence only leads to more corruption, and suggests that the modern city experience introduces interference which creates moral ambiguities that are difficult, even impossible to resolve. The complexity of the urban environment distorts perception so that any clear distinction between innocence and experience is cancelled out. Slay suggests that McEwan's London is ambiguous: '[i]n McEwan's fiction the city is often portrayed as encroaching and dehumanizing; it is, in all senses, an evil entity', that the city 'taints all human contact' and that it frequently 'acts as a destructive force'.[17] Yet, McEwan's fiction also 'shows that the impersonality of the city can be overcome; occasionally, human emotions not only survive but endure'.[18] McEwan takes this ambivalence into dystopian territory in 'Two Fragments: Saturday and Sunday, March 199–' (1978), which projects dark, present-day London into a dystopian future in which the city is plagued by mass unemployment and poverty, without transport, anarchy and war which has reduced the city to rubble. The protagonist, the 29-year-old Ministry worker, Henry, lives with his daughter, Marie, in a south London flat. London's 'sky was thick and angry' and the 'Thames was lower than he had ever seen it. Some said one day the river would dry up and giant bridges would uselessly span the fresh meadows.'[19] On his way to work, as usual, fights break out whilst people collect rain-water. Henry and Marie encounter a street spectacle worthy of West Smithfield's Bartholomew Fair: a gigantic man in a toga and his daughter, naked except for a piece of sacking and reputed to be without blood, stage a gruesome yet compelling performance. After the man takes money from the audience, the sideshow proceeds with the girl pushing 'the tip of the sword half an inch into her belly' and a 'small coin of crimson, brilliant in the sunlight, spread outwards round the shaft of the sword'.[20] McEwan's London is a filicidal spectacle in which, as the comparison between blood and money suggests, the human body is commodified and consumed by the city, yet the description also evokes an incestuous connotation which reinforces the city's corrupting force.

London is strewn with waste: 'Human refuse littered the plain. Vegetables, rotten and trodden down, cardboard boxes flattened into beds, the remains of fires and the carcasses of roasted dogs and cats, rusted tin, vomit, worn tires, animal excrement.'[21] Near the Ministry, 'the air above the fountain was grey with flies. Men and boys came there daily to squat on the wide concrete rim and defecate.'[22] McEwan gets his scatology of London via a text that was an obsession for him as a young writer, *The Waste Land*, and points to the city as a place of capitalist production that produces excess and decadence. Yet, not only may waste provide the fertility for a culture to flourish, but, as Maud Ellmann reminds us, it shows us 'what a culture casts away in order to determine what is not itself, and thus to establish its own limits'.[23] The function of McEwan's emphasis on waste is, then, to establish where cultural and moral borders lie. The focus on physical filth forms an exteriorisation of moral regression, and nowhere does this become clearer than in London, its 'landscape dehumanised and utterly comprehensible'.[24]

When Henry walks along 'avenues of rusted, broken down cars',[25] he stops in Soho to warm himself by a fire and is approached by a Chinaman, who asks him to move a cupboard into his family's Chinatown home:

> The Chinaman walked several feet ahead and was barely visible. We crossed Shaftesbury Avenue into Gerrard Street and here I slowed to a shuffle and stretched my hands in front of my face. A few

upper-storey windows gleamed dully, they gave a sense of direction of the street but they shone no light on it.[26]

We get the sense it is no ordinary darkness that obscures Soho, but a metropolis where culture, technology, civilisation, literacy and law have vanished, leaving behind a dim underworld where society and human thought have been reduced to the basest levels. McEwan's interest in darkness warns against the decline of Western civilisation, culture and humanism, a loss of morals and values established over many centuries. It also cautions against the destruction of an even more precious 'commodity', namely, love as a force that offers a potential redemption of mankind itself.

There was a general feeling of crisis and excitement: Father London in *The Child in Time* (1987)

This formative period was important because it gave a definite shape to McEwan's engagement with the political left, as his overt alignment with feminism and his activities for the Campaign for Nuclear Disarmament (CND) evidenced. In the early eighties, his anti-Thatcherite position was expressed most overtly by his screenplay *The Ploughman's Lunch* (1983), which presents a satirical view of Thatcher's Britain as an unredeemable narcissistic and egotistical society.[27] In the mid-eighties, McEwan developed the post-apocalyptic, dystopian world of 'Two Fragments' and the satire of *The Ploughman's Lunch* into a more rounded and direct attack on the Thatcher government in *The Child in Time* (1987). The novel is set in a Britain projected ten years into the future, suggesting that we are in a third or possibly fourth term of Thatcherism – 'a conscious projection of the straight leftist view'.[28] As the title suggests, time and temporal experience are at the heart of the novel, but the protagonist, Stephen Lewis, also states, 'space and time [are] not separable categories but aspects of one another', and the text brings us into the heart of Britain's politics at London's Whitehall.[29]

The novel narrates the story of the successful children's author, Lewis, who is now working on a government sub-committee on Reading and Writing. Two years before, under his watch, his three-year-old daughter was kidnapped in a south London supermarket. After his wife Julie, a quantum physicist, leaves him to retreat to 'her monastery in the Chilterns' (*CT* 52) because the memory of the disappeared child stands 'between them' (*CT* 65), Lewis is in a state of mental paralysis that threatens to infantilise him.

Lewis has gained his government position through his friend Charles Darke, a publisher turned politician reminiscent of Maureen Duffy's ideologically anchorless Guzzle in *Londoners*:

> Darke had no political convictions, only managerial skill and great ambition. He could join any party. A friend of Julie's from New York was taking the matter seriously and insisting that the choice lay between the emphasis on the collectivity of experience or its uniqueness. Darke spread his hands and said that he could argue for both. (*CT* 37–8)

Darke decides to make his career on the right because it 'was in power and likely to remain so' (*CT* 38). Unashamedly self-promoting and shrewdly opportunistic, he exploits his television appearances, pulls cheap psychological tricks that appeal to the electorate's emotions but makes himself sound 'reasonable and concerned while advocating self-reliance for the poor and incentives for the rich' (*CT* 38). By making Lewis inert and Darke a devilishly attractive character in the tradition of Shakespeare's Iago and Milton's Satan, McEwan tests and shifts the readers' sympathies, making the point that society as a whole is seduced into adapting to this new breed of managerial politics which concentrates on form and appearance rather than content.

This juxtaposition of Lewis and Darke is part of a series of apparent oppositions that contrasts innocence to experience; the country to the city; art to science; childhood to maturity; femininity to masculinity; and innocence to knowledge and experience. These binary oppositions owe much to the Cold War tensions (during the Olympic Games the Russian and American teams are '[e]xchanging insults with a scatological intensity' (*CT* 35)) which loom in the background. More importantly, these binaries are the result of a simplification of the political vision of society: 'Now governmental responsibilities had been defined in simpler, purer terms: to keep order, and to defend the State against its enemies' (*CT* 28). The result is an England divided up into two social spheres of haves and have-nots, a projection of the climate that Thatcher created, and itself a curious hybrid between tabloid truth and dystopian vision.[30] Alan Massie notes that *The Child in Time* 'offers McEwan's view of Thatcher's England, a country teeming with licensed beggars, in which control is exercised in the name of freedom, and where poverty and squalor are to be found everywhere in the midst of affluence. The picture owes as much to science fiction, especially in the cinema, as it does to observation or imagination, but it is powerful enough, even at second-hand.'[31]

London is foregrounded as the place where the state consciously causes these social divisions by inscribing its politico-economic power into the public realm. The Whitehall sub-committee of which Lewis is a member directly controls the process of reading and writing the world around us, and in this future world it decides to take knowledge away from its citizens: 'The idea that the more educated the population the more readily could its problems be solved had faded quietly' (*CT* 28). Here too we find numerous dialectics, some of which are the remnants of McEwan's earlier darkest London. There is a 'hypermarket with a crowded ten-acre car-park' (*CT* 51) and police lose interest in solving Lewis's daughter's disappearance because '[r]iots in a northern suburb, they said, were stretching their resources' (*CT* 23). McEwan exploits pathetic fallacy by making the weather a signifier of the collective crisis of division: what starts as a 'freakishly good summer' turns into 'a prolonged heatwave' (*CT* 37), that leads to an apocalyptic drought:

> Restrictions on water use had reduced the front gardens of suburban West London to dust. The interminable privets were crackling brown. The only flowers Stephen saw on the long walk from the tube station [...] were surreptitious geraniums. The little squares of lawn were baked earth from which even the dried grass had flaked away. One wag had planted a row of cacti. Stronger representations of pastoral were to be found in those gardens which had been cemented over and painted green. (*CT* 85)

This attack on the spiritually exhausted middle classes created and nurtured by Thatcherism gives us an image recycled from *The Waste Land*, which suggests that authentic experience is lost: 'representations of pastoral' and the garden 'painted green' suggest a world in which everything is mediated and constructed. When the rain finally comes, it is 'delivered by gales which stripped most trees bare in less than a week [...] and there was a general feeling of crisis and excitement, at least on television' (*CT* 123).

Dominic Head notes that McEwan is able 'to eschew the pitfalls he associates with "political writing"' as 'a focused critique of Thatcher's Britain [...] but it is also a moving depiction of love, loss and reconciliation centred on the profoundly painful topic of an abducted child'.[32] Indeed, McEwan's novel exposes the paradoxical nature of the social problems that Thatcherism has brought about, but in particular how Lewis's realisation of them results in inaction, and regression. When Lewis is confronted with beggars licensed by the government, he feels his usual ambivalence. To give money ensured the success of the Government programme. Not to give involved some determined facing away from private distress. The art of bad government was to sever the line between public policy and intimate feeling, the instinct for what was right. These days he left the matter to chance. If he had small change in his pockets he gave it. If not he gave nothing. (*CT* 8–9)

Critics have focused on these beggars as an adumbration of *Big Issue*-sellers, yet the passage is actually about the corrosive effects of government intervention on the ability of individuals to connect meaningfully. Thatcher's denial of society inspires unintended collusion whereby the individual is unable to connect directly to others without somehow being mediated by the state.

The trajectory of *The Child in Time* aims to resolve these paradoxes by means of a highly contrived reversal of fortune at the close of the novel. At the outset, Lewis's traumatised consciousness continuously slips back towards daydreams of the pre-modern times. When during one Whitehall meeting his boss, Lord Parmenter, speaks he is reminded of his history teacher's lessons on Charlemagne's court and medieval papacy, and he imagines London's transformation:

> Through the windows he saw not an enclosed car-park and baking limousines but [...] a rose garden, playing fields, a speckled grey balustrade, then rough, uncultivated land which fell away to oaks and beeches, and beyond them the great stretch of foreshore and the blue tidal river, a mile from bank to bank. This was a lost time and a lost landscape. (*CT* 12)

We become curious spectators sinking away into the Thames mud, which is sucking us back into geological history and archaeological deep time. Yet, rather than a ghostly, Gothicised prehistoric morass that hides dark secrets about the nation's past, which we get in Seamus Heaney's work, we find ourselves in a place in harmony with its natural surroundings. The archaeological impetus, which we also find in a novel such as Graham Swift's *Waterland* (1983), is an imagined, romanticised pre-modern England. Another key idea here is given to us by the word 'enclosed', which invokes an image of the womb which is repeated in various forms throughout the novel, suggesting that the dialectics are gendered. The traditional representation of the country as feminine, redemptive and innocent, and the city as masculine and corrupt, is one of the points Adam Mars-Jones picks up on in his polemic, *Venus Envy* (1990). Mars-Jones translates his critique of the novel's potentially misogynist politics into an accusation of McEwan's collusion with Thatcherite discourse:

> *The Child in Time* is consistent in its conflating fatherhood and humanity. It's ironic that McEwan, hardly a Thatcherite, should use the tactic, familiar from governmental rhetoric of recent years, of defining a universal experience in slyly narrow terms, though in this case the substitution is of 'father' for 'man' rather than, say, 'active citizen' for 'citizen'.[33]

Mars-Jones rightly points out McEwan's gendering of social relations, which has the potential to collapse back into traditional patterns, yet it is also a view that is narrow and constricted, and shaped by his own gendered political agenda.

McEwan's representation of the country and the city is through his use of 'envelopment' and 'enclosure', and it points both to the Freudian ideal and imagined wholeness of the subject, identified elsewhere by Claire Colebrook, but especially in relationship to the desire for a controlled space, the chaotic modern world beyond the self.[34] One (false) strategy that McEwan offers is an escape into infantile dreams of imagined wholeness. While Lewis lies in bed, depressed by guilt about, and grief over, his daughter's disappearance, he imagines an escape that absolves him from responsibility:

> He could see the bedroom, the Edwardian apartment block [...] the mess of South London, the hazy curvature of the earth [...] He was rising still higher, faster. At least, he thought, from up here where the air was thin and the city below was taking on geometric design, his feelings would not show, he could retain some composure. (*CT* 22)

Lewis's fantasy of reducing the materiality of the city to an abstraction and abdicating social responsibility in fact enacts a regressive process of infantilisation that is slowly threatening to take him over altogether. It is the artistic process of writing the novel-as-city as a means of creating an ordered, even perfect arranged system of fictional knowledge that imitates the rhythms and patterns of the modern city, which is able avoid this regression.

However, the fact that Charles Darke is experiencing a similar regressive process in the countryside is already a sign that the binary oppositions are false. After being elected as an MP and becoming a Minister, Darke abandons his political career for life as a recluse in the Suffolk countryside, where he regresses back into a childhood state. Indeed, a more complex strategy which McEwan urges us to consider is the more difficult one of 'the forking paths' (*CT* 63), which suggests we need to fully acknowledge and immerse ourselves in the terminal paradoxes and contradictions of modernity.

The novel plays off the idea of the violent, male metropolis that fragments the consciousness against the supposedly feminine countryside that offers the possibility of being at one with Mother Nature. In the country Lewis also wakes 'to the unusual din of birdsong' (*CT* 120–1), and just as Lewis regresses towards infancy in his south London apartment, in the Chilterns '[a]ll sense of progress [...] disappeared [...] The lack of hurry, the disappearance of any real sense of destination, suited him' (*CT* 52). McEwan's point is that the distinction between the country and the city in the modern age is a false one because they are inscribed by the same power and laws.

Lewis is an ex-father whose problem is not the assertion of his masculinity but it is his maturity and its responsibilities that have become impossibly painful. Whereas Darke represents a descent into a right-wing fantasy about the green and pleasant England mythology, in Lewis we find a succession that cancels out his regression. The place where this reinvention occurs is London, a city that forces us to embrace the contradictions of modernity. *The Child in Time* is important to McEwan because for the first time in his writing, light triumphs over darkness. McEwan's novel forms a turning point in a certain mythologisation of the condition of Britain as suffering from decline and disharmony. It also means a major turn in McEwan's earlier vision of London as a place associated with an overbearing masculinity that produces violence, darkness and spiritual barrenness. The novel enacts an imagined change in the destiny of London by creating a new fertility myth that deliberately counters spiritual exhaustion and apocalyptic end-time thinking prevalent at the time. *The Child in Time* thus functions as an important hinge within McEwan's wider *oeuvre* because the novel shifts from an obsession with creating a Darkest London to a city viewed though a modern and modernist lens that leaves the possibility for knowledge to triumph over regressive forces. McEwan's redirection of his dark London anticipates a staunch belief in the continuation of humanist civilisation, which *Saturday*[35] explores in a new century.

'It's a future no one can read': the city, civilisation and the limits of interpretation in *Saturday*

Saturday (2005) narrates twenty-four hours in the life of the neurosurgeon Henry Perowne, whose attempt to enjoy his day off work is thwarted when his intended itinerary through the city is thrown off course when his car collides with that of the underworld figure, Baxter.[36] McEwan aims to represent the tensions and anxieties in the world after the terrorist attacks of 9/11 by setting the novel on a highly specific day – 15 February 2003 – when a million British people took to the streets of the capital to protest against Tony Blair and New Labour's decision to go to war in Iraq. Even more so than *The Child in Time*, this novel avoids political writing by foregrounding its own ambivalence and uncertainties about the condition of the world, whilst pitting the novel as an alternative House of Commons, a debating chamber where the state of things can be discussed. The capital city occupies a central representative position as well: in an interview McEwan also disclosed that *Saturday* is a deliberate attempt to correct his earlier Darkest London: 'Inseparable from the idea of having a novel right in the present was to do London again, or to do London properly.'[37] Although London as embodiment of culture and civilisation triumphs over the forces of darkness, McEwan leaves us with an uncanny sense of ambivalence about the state of the world at the start of the twenty-first century.

As antidote to this anarchy and disorder, *Saturday* uses the classic literary trope of the window as a framing device when Perowne gets up at 3 a.m. and looks out of his bedroom window onto the square in Fitzrovia. We hear echoes of one of the key intertexts of Matthew Arnold's 'Dover Beach' (1867), which impels the narrator's loved one to 'Come to the window, sweet is the night air!', and another intertext, Elizabeth Bowen's *The Heat of the Day* (1949).[38] The setting of the novel also points us to the work of Virginia Woolf, who occupied a house near to Perowne's residence, whilst some of the territory Perowne circumnavigates overlaps with that of *Mrs Dalloway* (1925), a relationship I have traced elsewhere.[39] In Chapter 6 of *A Room of One's Own* (1929), a text that shaped McEwan's engagement with feminism, Woolf looks 'out of the window and [to] see what London was doing on the morning of the twenty-sixth of October 1928'.[40] It is the morning after a particularly moving Shakespeare performance, and Woolf notes an errand-boy, a woman walking a dog, 'there were drifters rattling sticks upon area railings' and 'then a very distinguished gentleman [...] paused to avoid collision with a bustling lady'.[41] Woolf observes that these individuals have not been affected by the Shakespeare performance, and she muses on the effect that the metropolis has on its inhabitants: 'The fascination of the London street is that no two people are ever alike; each seemed bound by some private affair of his own.'[42]

Saturday echoes this point of view when Perowne observes various Londoners in the square below him. He sees 'figures in dark coats'

(*S* 12); a teenage couple on drugs (*S* 64–5), and 'two figures on a bench' (*S* 197). McEwan also emphasises these Londoners' 'separate, self-absorbed' qualities, but there is an even more intense, distancing effect to the clinical descriptions of the neurosurgeon: 'In the lifeless cold, they pass through the night, hot little biological engines [...] with their invisible glow of consciousness – these engines devise their own tracks' (*S* 13). The machine metaphor, linked to consciousness, is important because it connects Perowne with the modernist legacy that runs so strongly through this novel. It also gives us an insight into Perowne's way of viewing the world around him: the neurosurgeon has a rational, curative vision which tricks him into attributing authority to himself: he 'not only watches them, but watches over them, supervising their progress with the remote possessiveness of a god' (*S* 13). This double vantage point, which determines the points of view within the novel, is ours as well: we travel with Perowne inside his consciousness whilst the third-person narrator reminds us we are looking inside his mind. What the novel exposes is that the presence of many ruptures and fissures – between the local and national versus global, the private and the public, culture and science – causes potentially irrecoverable tensions and paradoxes.

Saturday is obsessed with thinking about observation, surveillance, interpretation, and stages many different forms of reading which scrutinise contemporary ethics and politics. London's materiality is constantly and obsessively observed by Perowne, whose is also 'a habitual observer of his own moods' (*S* 5): the perfection of the Fitzrovian square on which Perowne lives (*S* 4–5); 'the orderly grid of medical streets west of Portland Place' (*S* 123); the 'Westway, rearing on concrete piles' (*S* 154); West London's 'streets of frowning' (*S* 158); the discussion of the Post Office Tower, which Perowne likens to a 'machine' and which John Grammaticus despises for its lack of 'human scale' (*S* 197). Perowne is used to reading 'signs' (*S* 12) in the hospital environment, the anti-war protesters' placards (*S* 72), and makes several remarks about reading and visual interpretation, from 'a trick of vision' (*S* 16) to his uncertainty about the war in Iraq. Seeing, reading and interpreting signs are at the foreground of the novel, as are the complications that twenty-first-century London poses.

Perowne is set up as a descendant of the *über*-rational observer of materiality, the detective Sherlock Holmes, who has 'brought detection as near an exact science as it will ever be brought in this world'.[43] Whereas Holmes's 'whole train of thought did not occupy a second', the narration of Perowne's thought processes is, however, curiously inflated.[44] When confronted with Baxter, Perowne's diagnosis of Huntington's disease takes up several pages; other examples include the episode of the burning airplane (*S* 13–19); the diagnosis of Baxter (*S* 91–9); the squash game (*S* 100–17); his analysis of his mother's dementia (*S* 160–7); and Baxter's invasion of his home all take place in a second but the events take many pages to narrate (*S* 205–33). By introducing a rupture between lived experience and its narration, *Saturday* demonstrates how our experience of the contemporary at the beginning of the twenty-first century has become increasingly complex, whilst sense-making processes are increasingly difficult. This dislocated temporality is central to the urban experience: by imposing the constraints of the twenty-four-hour period on the construction of the novel, McEwan makes an explicit connection between both the human body's and the city's circadian rhythms whilst suggesting that this temporal pattern is out of joint. Just as Perowne awakes in a euphoric state of mind, the life of the city is thrown into a state of great anxiety after the attacks on America on 9/11 have made London itself a target, as the opening scene, in which Perowne sees a burning airplane in the skies over London, suggests. Perowne's disturbed body clock suggests then an unconscious response to the troubled times at the beginning of the twenty-first century.

Perowne is not quite Sherlock, as he is unable to experience the world beyond its physical limits, preventing him from connecting with the body politic directly: he lacks creativity and imagination, which his son (the musician Theo) and daughter (the poet Daisy) have in abundance. The gap between London's materiality and Perowne's perceived city is constantly foregrounded: 'doesn't have the lyric gift to see beyond it – he's a realist, and can never escape' (*S* 168). Perowne's lack of control over his reading and interpretation of signs finds its first interpretative challenge in the burning airplane episode at the start of the novel. Perowne is first uncertain about what he exactly sees (a meteor? a comet?), but even after he is convinced it is a burning airplane, there remains a sense of representative difficulty: 'The leading edge of the fire is a flattened white sphere which trails away in a cone of yellow and red, less like a meteor or comet than an artist's lurid impression of one' (*S* 15). Again, the impossibility of accessing the world directly is foregrounded by McEwan: the machines of modernity, from the motor car to mass media, all intervene in the process of making direct contact. The mode of observation captured by the temporal inflation of its narration seems to be an attempt to regain some kind of control over lived experience. The novel's blowing up of events also captures and criticises a new mode of vision introduced by the proliferation of surveillance and security. This produces paranoid ways of watching, and triggers an uncertainty into a heavily distorted, modern experience. Rather than being an omniscient panoptical observer on a Foucauldian scale, Perowne is set up as a limited being whose blindness and inability to make decisions is ours as well.

David James has noted that McEwan exploits a 'perspectival restriction [...] to satirize Perowne's imperious way of viewing the world beyond his terrace, while at the same time synthesizing issues of observation and understanding with a style that modulates from reportage to subjectivism'.[45] Yet two violent incidents in the novel propel him towards a moment of insight when he 'feels himself turning into a giant wheel, like the Eye on the south bank of the Thames, just about to arrive at the highest point – he's poised on a hinge of perception, before the drop, and he can see ahead calmly' (*S* 272). The London Eye functions as a metaphor for the contemporary obsession with surveillance, and its effect upon the self. The encounters with Baxter, and his clashes with his children over Iraq, teach him to acknowledge his own interpretative limits. At the end of the novel he notes: 'It's a future no one can read' (*S* 145). Paradoxically, Perowne's affirmation of interpretative subjectivity and limitedness *is* an insight.

The interpretative limits of Perowne are not simply the result of his conditioning by the mass media, but his crisis is the result of an intensification of perpetual change and an obsession with targets that has emerged under New Labour. Perowne has internalised the New Labour doctrine of achieving targets – 'all targets met' (*S* 143) he notes – but it is the paperwork on Friday – the backlog of referrals, and responses to referrals, abstracts for two conferences, letters to colleagues and editors, an unfinished peer review and contributions to management initiatives – that bring him down. He is also annoyed by the constant changes to the structure of the Trust, and yet more revisions to teaching practices imposed by the government: 'There's to be a new look – there's always a new look – at the hospital's Emergency Plan' (*S* 11).

This is partly a description of a busy professional life inhibited by bureaucracy, but the emphasis on perpetual change in the systemic operations of the health service is also an indictment of policies introduced specifically by New Labour. The limitations of contemporary vision and the partiality of experience that inhibit our understanding of the world are also the product of a particular kind of politics that master the infantilised citizen by subjecting him or her to constant contextual changes. *Saturday* explores the corrosive impact of New Labour's teleology of neurosis and its unrelenting drive for goals upon the human experience: Perowne's need for frames expresses a desire for control over the world, which the control society disallows.

This general climate of limited uncertainty and anxiety is given a concrete socio-political context by Perowne's two related encounters with Tony Blair. In the first one Perowne sees the face of Tony Blair on a number of television screens in a shop window:

> What's showing on every device is the Prime Minister giving a studio interview. The close-up of a mouth, until the lips fill half the screen. He has suggested in the past that if we knew as much as he did, we too would want to go to war. Perhaps in this slow zoom the director is consciously responding to a calculation a watching population is bound to make: is this politician telling the truth. But can anyone really know the sign, the tell of an honest man? (*S* 141–2)

This encounter is mediated, and fits well into the novel's criticism of the role of the mass media in adding to our difficulty of understanding the world's contemporary complexity. This encounter reminds Perowne of his real-life encounter with Blair at the opening party of the Tate Modern on the south bank of the Thames in May 2000, where there still is a spirit of optimism and change in the post-New Labour victory: 'The conversion was bold and brilliant' and there is 'a general euphoria untainted by cynicism' (*S* 142). When Perowne is introduced to Blair, the description starts off with admiration: 'The gaze was intelligent and intense, and unexpectedly youthful. So much had yet to happen' (*S* 143). However, the episode soon turns into a criticism of Blair, who mistakes Perowne for a painter. The neurosurgeon tries to point out the mistake, in vain.

> 'You're making a mistake,' Perowne said, and on that word there passed through the Prime Minister's features for the briefest instant a look of sudden alarm, of fleeting self-doubt. No one else saw his expression freeze and his eyes bulge minimally. A hairline fracture appeared in the assurance of his power. Then he continued as before, no doubt making the rapid calculation that given all the people pushing in around them trying to listen, there could be no turning back. Not without a derisive press tomorrow. [...]
>
> Watching from his car the multiple images cutting between interviewer and guest, Perowne wonders if such moments [...] are increasingly part of the Prime Minister's days, or nights. There might not be a

second US resolution. The next weapons inspectors' report could also be inconclusive. [...] Or, as one former inspector keeps insisting, there might no longer be any weapons of mass destruction at all. (*S* 144–5)

McEwan is creating a complex temporal construct that narratologically connects the past and future into the present moment, stressing the relation between Blair's flawed interpretation and his mistaken interpretation of the evidence for weapons of mass destruction that formed the basis for the Iraq war as *bellum justum* – 'just war'. There is no direct causal link between the two events, but McEwan's decision to set his novel on a day when the war was still uncertain has a curious effect: the protesters are protesting against a war that is going to happen. By placing the reader in a position with retrospective knowledge, McEwan essentially operates a form of dramatic irony, which agains stresses the uncertainty of interpretation. The inevitability of war that Perowne asserts is validated by the war, but, paradoxically, the reader is also aware that Blair's mistake and Perowne's flawed interpretation argue that the future is less easy to predict.

McEwan's text is keen to connect the pending war in Iraq to previous wars, as the following description of a Regency façade – part of the Fitzrovian square – suggests:

That particular façade is a reconstruction, a pastiche – wartime Fitzrovia took some hits from the Luftwaffe – and right behind it is the Post Office Tower, municipal and seedy by day, but at night, half-concealed and decently illuminated a valiant memorial to more optimistic days. (*S* 4)

This reference to the Second World War stresses the continuity of war and destruction in which London will play a role: 'There are people around the planet, well-connected and organised, who would like to kill him and his family and friends to make a point. The scale of death contemplated is no longer an issue; there'll be more deaths on a similar scale, probably in this city' (*S* 81). This anxiety makes it possible to categorise *Saturday* as a particular kind of war literature, which engages with war indirectly by tracing its impact upon the citizens and capital city haunted by the decision to go to war. One may think of T. S. Eliot's *The Waste Land*, Rebecca West's *The Return of the Soldier* (1918), Ford Maddox Ford's *Parade's End* (1924–8), Woolf's *Mrs Dalloway*, and Elizabeth Bowen's *The Heat of the Day* (1949), which are all works that address the topic and effects of war obliquely by capturing the peculiar

Figure 14   Shrapnel Wound (2), St Clement Danes, The Strand

climate and the effects it has on personal lives, and not the actual war scenes and violence on the front.

Whereas London was a direct target in the Second World War, McEwan demonstrates the connection between London as a centre of power and the Iraq war via an analogy in which the public square plays a key role:

> People often drift into the square to act out their dramas. Clearly, a street won't do. On another scale, Perowne considers [...] this could be the attraction of the Iraqi desert – the flat and supposedly empty landscape approximating a strategist's map on which fury of industrial proportions can be let loose. A desert, it is said, is a military planner's dream. A city square is the private equivalent [...] The square's public aspect grants privacy to these intimate dramas. Couples come to talk or cry quietly on the benches. Emerging from small rooms in council flats or terraced houses, and from cramped side streets, into a wider view of generous sky and a tall stand of plane trees on the green, of space and growth, people remember their essential needs and how they're not being met. (*S* 60–1)

The analogy between 'a desert' and 'the perfect square' (*S* 5) suggests the connection between Western civilisation as embodied by a key symbol, the capital city, and another cradle of civilisation, Iraq. The theatre of war and the city as stage are similar because these spaces are produced with the same objectives in mind: the inscription of the private self within the public space and establishing imaginary connections with fellow citizens.

The mind of ancient Rome: Ian McEwan's restoration of mythical vision

Saturday also aims to retrieve mythical vision, and a mythical city, both of which have been lost in the clinical and mediatised perception that is now a general condition within society at the beginning of the twenty-first century. *Saturday* represents the problem of contemporary man's inability to access a historical self-consciousness, and to regain mythical vision. Literature may retrieve both by giving us a sense of the embeddedness of the past in the present by making intertextual connections. The poem that Daisy reads out after Baxter's invasion of the Perowne house, Arnold's 'Dover Beach', occupies a central connection here. Arnold's poem starts off as a meditation on and celebration of Britain, but soon a pessimistic note is introduced in a reference to Sophocles, who heard in the ebb and flow of the Aegean Sea an eternal 'human misery'.[46] The poem ends with the narrator's desperate appeal to his lover: 'And we are here as on darkling plain / Swept with confusing alarms of struggle and flight, / Where ignorant armies clash by night.'[47] The final lines refer to Thucydides's description of night battle in his *The History of the Peloponnesian War* (see chapter 44), during which a Greek army attempted to invade Sicily at night, causing them to kill many of their own in the confusion of darkness.[48] Although critics accused McEwan of smug arrogance, and even Head, McEwan's most subtle critic, noted that '*Saturday* is aligned with "universal values" rooted in the principles of capitalist democracy', there is an ideological undercurrent within the novel that challenges the grounds of the war.[49] Arnold was connecting these concerns about war to wars in his own time – the revolutions of 1848 on the European continent and the 1949 siege of Rome by the French, and McEwan also connects the Iraq war – and Tony Blair's wilful blindness and historical self-consciousness in the run up to the invasion – to a mythical vision that might have prevented him from taking his decision to go to war. *Saturday* recovers mythical vision by uncovering beneath the material surface of contemporary London connections to ancient civilisations.

McEwan's choice of the epigraph from Saul Bellow's *Herzog* (1964) is similarly important. A major influence on Martin Amis and McEwan,

Bellow was a champion of public thinkers in a materialistic country often averse to intellectualism; and Bellow was also preoccupied with meditating on the possibility of the persistence of civilisation, especially in the light of the Second World War and its atrocities. Perowne gets his euphoria, and the exclamation points, from Arnold's voice in *Culture and Anarchy* (1869), yet equally it is Herzog that provides the protagonist with his interest in the problems thrown up by the machine age based on scientific and technological developments: 'There, thought Herzog, like those machines in the lofts he heard yesterday in the taxi, stopped by traffic in the garment district, plunged and thundered with endless – infinite! – hungry, electrical power, stitching fabric with inexhaustible energy.'[50]

Rather than choosing the stream-of-consciousness technique that the radical experimentalists of European high modernism use to portray the self as closed, *Saturday* makes use of Bellow's mode of narration, namely restrictive third-person narration combined with stream of consciousness. Herzog is dependent on the novel's narrator, while simultaneously the narrator is dependent on Herzog's consciousness, without which it could not exist. Bellow makes this contract of mutual dependence between the character and narrator clear by breaking it, when Herzog takes the narration over, and slips into the first-person confessional mode, and back again, within one single sentence:

> Thus I want you to see how I, Moses E. Herzog, am changing. I ask you to witness the miracle of this altered heart – how, hearing the sounds of slum clearance in the next block and watching the white dust of plaster in the serene air of metamorphic New York, he communicated with the mighty of this world, or speaks words of understanding and prophesy, having arranged at the same time a comfortable and entertaining evening – food, music, wine, conversation and sexual intercourse. Transcendence or no transcendence. All work and no games is bad medicine.[51]

Here we see all the central elements of *Saturday* assembled: the social gathering, the importance of music, the significance of food and drink, but also the emphasis on the necessity of sexuality and the private life to counterbalance a successful professional life. Herzog sees his own desire for transformation reflected in the ever-changing cityscape of New York, whilst in McEwan's novel the possibility of change is less clear.

Bellow's novel is also important because it provides a hinge moment within twentieth-century fiction that leads us back to Joyce's recovering of mythical vision. Both Herzog's Homeric journey across America and the continent, as well as the type of narration, form a conscious rewriting of *Ulysses* for the post-war period. Writing after the Holocaust, Bellow's Herzog attempts to revalidate rationality after dehumanising, unspeakable events. Whilst driving through New York: 'He wrote, *Reason exists! Reason* [...] he then heard the soft dense rumbling of falling masonry, the splintering of wood and glass.'[52] This is a direct reference to the second chapter of *Ulysses* in which Stephen teaches Roman history and, while discussing the battle of Asculum, thinks: 'I hear the ruin of all space, shattered glass and toppling masonry, and time one livid final flame.'[53] The perpetual process of making and destruction, both present in the nature of the city and of war is equalised into a continuum by the literary imagination. Perowne becomes aware of this during the episode with the burning airplane, which exposes the effect of that history's cyclicity as a hell of repetition: 'He no longer thinks of waking Rosalind. Why wake her into this nightmare? In fact, the spectacle has the familiarity of a recurrent dream' (*S* 15). These thoughts unwittingly refer to Stephen Dedalus's thoughts in *Ulysses*: '"History," Stephen said, "is a nightmare from which I am trying to awake"',[54] by which he conveyed the idea that ingrained patterns of heroic thought and nationalistic sentiments constantly led to new, futile wars, which also reiterates Arnold's pessimism.

The point is that at the background of our quotidian lives there is always the disturbing, universal and eternal rumble and suffering of war, which connects us throughout space and time. Whereas anxieties close Perowne's mind in the earlier parts of the novel, it is his violent encounter with Baxter which opens up Perowne's consciousness to making historical, and more importantly, mythical connections. Lying in his bed, in the early hours, he thinks of a tour of Nero's palace, the Domus Aurea, during a conference:

> Perowne, knowing nothing about Roman antiquity, was disappointed that the site appeared to be underground [...] The palace lay undiscovered for five hundred years under rubble until the early Renaissance. For the past twenty years it had been closed for restoration, and its partial opening had been part of Rome's millennial celebration. [...] Raphael and Michelangelo had themselves lowered on ropes; marvelling, they copied the designs and paintings their smoking torches revealed. [...] Through his translator, Signor Veltroni offered an image he thought might appeal to his guests; the artists had drilled through this skull of brick to discover the mind of ancient Rome. (*S* 242–3)

The passage stresses how, throughout the ages, knowledge is carried across to others. And although it appears that Perowne knows nothing about Roman antiquity, at the end of the novel Roman classical civilisation and values are retrieved via a personal connection, Daisy's unborn child: 'This baby's life is taking shape – a year in Paris with its enraptured parents, and then to London where its father has been offered a good position in an important dig – a Roman villa to the east of the City. [...] He feels his body, the size of a continent [...] he's a king, he's vast, accommodating, immune' (*S* 269). The ordeal with Baxter has opened him to the mythical dimension of the contemporary experience: Perowne is no longer only able to perceive the present and history, and to experience London only as a material present, but he is able to look backward and connect to the city's mythical origins. One is reminded of T. S. Eliot's claim in 'Tradition and the Individual Talent' (1919): 'He must be aware that the mind of Europe – the mind of his own country – a mind which he learns in time to be much more important than his own private mind – is a mind which changes, and that this change is a development which abandons nothing *en route*, which does not super-annuate either Shakespeare, or Homer.'[55]

In *Saturday* McEwan transforms himself into a writer of urban spaces who draws on a wide variety of traditions, visions and experiences that counter the stereotype of modernism as a pure criticism of a progressive world-view. Simultaneously McEwan makes a confident case for the novel as an imaginary site where democratic debates about the state of the world can be held. With the progression of McEwan's engagement of London, it is the factual representation of London that is increasingly dominant, at the expense of the Darkest London mythology. *Saturday* also argues that due to the pressures of America-led globalisation, London is no longer able to represent the nation's consciousness. The failure of the protest march shows the limits of modern democracy within the nation-state and Britain's subjection to geopolitical forces that it no longer controls. London features centrally as a metaphor for a history of light and learning and as signifier of the continuity of a civilisation whose values are under threat. In *Solar* (2010) this vision of the city is affirmed, when the Nobel Prize winning scientist Michael Beard is circling over the city as they await their descent:

And now here it came again, for the sixth time, the colossal disk of London itself, turning like an intricately slotted space station in majestic self-sufficiency. As unplanned as a giant termite nest, as a rain forest, and a thing of beauty, gathering itself to great human intensity at the centre, along the rediscovered river between Westminster and Tower Bridge, dense with confident, playful architecture, new toys. Briefly, he thought he saw the plane's shadow flitting like a free spirit across St James's and over the rooftops, but this was impossible at such a height. He knew about light.[56]

Ian McEwan does also, and his version of London as a city that embodies the continuation of civilisation's achievements is one which defiantly beats against the currents of pessimism and apocalypticism that run so strongly in the contemporary London novel. Yet, the novel does not resolve anything, but leaves us with a profound sense of uncertainty about the future, and with a sense that the future and fate of our culture and civilisation, at the beginning of the twenty-first century, are increasingly less easy to understand and predict.

7

'In a Prose so Diagonal and Mood-Warped': Martin Amis's Scatological London

'This was no cockneyland of barrowboys and winkles'

Most contemporary London novels cover parts of the city not directly associated with its traditional twin centres of gravity – Westminster and the City – and Martin Amis's novels are no exception.[1] Yet, there is a moment in the third instalment of Amis's London triptych, *The Information* (1995),[2] when the protagonist, a commercially unsuccessful but *über*-literary author, visits his agent, which brings us to one of London's two centres of power:

> Richard Tull, with his own consignment of strictly local concerns, stood forty storeys above the city. He had an authentically frightening hangover and he was in the offices of Gal Aplanalp. Not just above the city, but above the City, within hearing range of Bow Bells, perhaps [...] This was no cockneyland of barrowboys and winkles. Large-scale construction work was taking place all around him: jump-suits, hardhats, trenches, cranes, breeze-blocks in skip-sized packages. A hot-blue magnesium light shone upward through the morning haze. Richard thought of the back yard his study overlooked, where builders were always fucking around, year in year out. To him builders meant destruction. Bum-crack cowboys, knee-deep in pointlessness and slime, and raising nothing but hell. (*I* 125–6)

This image nicely captures the nature of London as an ever-changing city, a place of continuous metamorphosis, as well as depicting the frantic remaking of the face of contemporary Britain's capital. The passage foregrounds London as a material structure; the city is *the* symbolic

167

place where capital generated by the privileged few is invested in physical labour that turns money into matter.

The text, written by Amis at mid-career, makes no bones about its subscription to the idea that at the basis of London and Britain lies the economy. At the start of the 1980s, a brave new world of increasingly globalised economics clashes with Tull's 'strictly local concerns'. The invisible flows of global capital ignore and threaten to overrun the neighbouring territory, the East End, and the mythologies to which 'Bow Bells', 'cockneyland', 'barrowboys' and 'winkles' allude.

Although these changes may be particularly visible in London's economic centre, Tull's reference to the building activity in his private world shows that it is a process that affects all of London. The image, then, is a particularly poignant reflection of the intensely rapid changes that the city, and, by extension, Britain, undergo during Long Thatcherism. The suggested construction mania captures an attitude of a Britain reborn as a node in the global economy, which is lost on the idealist Tull, who does not understand the nature and power of money, nor the social dimension of labour. Tull experiences this remaking of London not as a form of newness but as a form of regression. Although his use of 'pointlessness' appears to mock capitalism as a ceaseless process of production and consumption, he is simply projecting his personal anxieties onto the outside world. Tull's use of 'slime' counters the vertical movement upward by looking downward; in Tull's experience, we are descending back into geological history and archaeological deep time. The passage becomes a subtle comment on, and reworking of, ideas about evolutionary regression, a typically nineteenth-century concern as expressed, for instance, in Dickens's *Our Mutual Friend* (1865), which parodied Social Darwinism by presenting images of evolutionary regression rather than progress.[3] London becomes a prehistoric morass.

Amis also returns us to a London locus that is associated with a towering chronicler of the modern urban experience, T. S. Eliot, who worked as a banker in the City, which features in his hyper-canonical London poem, *The Waste Land*, as a Dantean hell. In Amis's work urban modernity is experienced as a secular hell which is ever faster replacing the pastoral ideal. The hell under construction here, however, is no biblical hell, but a postmodern, vertical city constructed out of glass and steel, arrogantly aspiring to the sky. This is also a criticism of (post-)Thatcherite Britain: the 'hot-blue magnesium light' reminds us of Amis's reference to 'the phosphorescent prosperity [...] of Thatcher's England'.[4]

Most controversially, perhaps, Amis's situating of Tull's agent in the City places the business of literature right at the heart of London, at the centre of Britain's economy, destroying the idea that art and culture are, or can be, in opposition to the financial world. Amis is brutally honest about the new cultural and literary climate that has arisen under Thatcher. Writers and the publishing industry are just another part of an economy whose sole aim is to generate capital, and turn money into matter.[5]

'A vocabulary more refined than your emotions': voice, the city and the moral imagination

Martin Amis's London novels could best be described as a generous dispatch of hate mail addressed to West London and Camden, not the City.[6] Amis's capital city is determined by his mood and the mood is deeply moral and pessimistic. *Money* (1984)[7] depicts London as an imprisoned creature that suffers under man's exploitation, and on the brink of death: 'Blasted, totalled, broken-winded, shot-faced London, doing time under sodden skies' (*M* 159). In the 1980s, the sick city is in a very bad way: 'In summer, London is an old man with bad breath. If you listen, you can hear the sob of weariness catching his lungs. Unlovely London. Even the name holds heavy stress' (*M* 85). In *London Fields* (1989), the London of 1999 is described as a 'Somnopolis. It reeked of it [sleep], and of insomniac worry and disquiet, and thwarted escape' (*LF* 2). London is a city of senile sleepers dreaming up a city of the Un-Dead: when in *The Information* Tull sits drinking a Zombie beside a London canal, we are given an equally dark image of the city: 'There was the street, as midnight neared, after the rain, glossy, with a *noir*ish wet-downed look. And there was the canal, sickly-hued even in the dark, turbid, caustic, like a Chinese medicine of ferocious efficacy' (*I* 149).

In Amis's novels London functions as a machine for moral policing and mapping of millennial anxieties, and his monstrous city presents us with socio-economic and moral decline. In a collection of essays and reviews, *The War against Cliché* (2001), the author singles out cultural democratisation and economic globalisation as culprits because they generate an 'equality of sentiments' and '[e]motional egalitarianism'.[8] The author has also spoken of the moronic inferno – 'a metaphor for human infamy: mass, gross, ever-distracting human infamy'.[9] Within this vision, London's corruptive powers generate a form of consciousness determined by what Peter Childs describes as the loss of 'an ahistorical, prelapsarian time of innocence'.[10] In an interview, Amis states:

The sexualisation and the obscenification of everyday life have been going on for a long time but it's accelerating now. We are being

conditioned to see sexuality everywhere. And that kind of conditioning works. There is a loss of innocence. Since Homer there has been
this argument that the great men have gone, that society is getting
worse. It's a slight fantasy, but the first human words ever were discovered written in shit in some cave wall: 'Children no longer respect
their parents.' [...] As you get older, the more days you live, you get
further away from your childhood soul. And that is happening on
the macro-scale as well. There's a feeling that the planet is not eternal
and everlasting in a way that would not have occurred to you three
hundred years ago. Now the planet has all sorts of contingencies
locked into its future.[11]

Statements like these make Amis one of contemporary fiction's fore-
most mythologisers of loss, and his imagined London is, like that of
J. G. Ballard, Iain Sinclair's *Downriver* and Ian McEwan's *The Child in
Time*, 'unapologetically apocalyptic'.[12] Sinclair even makes a joke about
Amis's hateful representation of Hackney in *London Fields*: 'London
Fields would have to go down on its knees to look Martin Amis in the
eye' (*LOFT* 37).

Simultaneously Amis is attracted to the modern city, the foremost
place where the spirit of the contemporary can be found whilst offering
the locus where morality, or a lack and loss thereof, can be identified and
challenged. Jim Dixon, the protagonist of Kingsley Amis's first novel,
Lucky Jim (1954), laments: '[w]hy hadn't he himself had parents whose
money so far exceeded their sense as to install their son in London?
The very thought of it was torment.'[13] For Martin Amis London is the
imagined place of liberation from parental restraints, and *Yellow Dog*'s
protagonist, Xan Meo, has no difficulty choosing when he is on route
to a pub named 'Hollywood': Meo has a 'choice between the garden
and the city. He chose the city.'[14] In Amis's contradictory attitude to
London we may be able to discern one of the terminal paradoxes of
postmodernity: Amis loves to hate in order to understand his own, and
our, contradictions. Patricia Waugh observes that Amis's attack on contemporary culture is confusing because he condemns both 'the moral
laxity and complacency of liberal culture as much as the heartlessness
of commercial enterprise'.[15]

Amis is particularly adept, like Xan Meo, at groping 'his way into
the thick detail of the city' (*YD* 139) in order to explore Great Britain's
post-imperial decline, and its reinvention as a potent force within a
new international economic order. According to Richard Todd, his
representation of London differs from that of Ackroyd, Sinclair and

Figure 15 View from the Cromwell Tower, Barbican

Carter because they 'have aligned the city by reinventing it as a Gothic construct, whereas Amis deals with it direct'.[16] Todd acknowledges that Amis's version of London lies relatively close to a historically retrievable reality, a thought that is reiterated by Nicolas Tredell who notes, for instance, that '*Money* is partly a realistic novel, catching the surfaces and styles of a period when the pace and texture of reality itself seems to alter dramatically.'[17] Tredell also notes that the novel is an intertextual and metafictional work, which influences our understanding of the city, but perhaps even more important is Amis's brilliant exploitation of language in the creation of his cityscapes. Todd also notes that 'the figurative language [...] is pressed into service [...] to present cityscapes and urban visions that invert the "normal" or mimetic worlds of London and Manhattan'.[18] Amis's London is indeed a heavily distorted textual and intertextual construct driven by fierce linguistic ingenuity that transforms the city into a structure that only obliquely relates to the rationally ordered representation of the city of the *A-Z*. As Tull states in *The Information*, 'if you could speak of landscape, or of *locus*, or of anywhere at all, in a prose so diagonal and mood-warped' (*I* 170).

Classical Amis scholarship concerns itself with the exploration of Amis's verbosity, with form and local texture in relationship to the often provocative, even offensive, thematics developed by the plotting. Todd captures this problem well: 'The doubt is whether the verbal virtuosity expressed in a self-conscious yet faultless ear for varieties of dialogue right across the social spectrum, the acute observation and the almost casual throwaway intelligence of the narration, have really been exercising themselves on a subject-matter worthy of those gifts.'[19] This chapter reads Amis's London fiction as an exploration of his nuclear anxieties, hatred of pornography and the consumer society, the decline of language, but also his own contradictory relationship with money and the moral conflict of his disgust. By opposing the scatological thematics and the comic force of his plotting to the vitality of Amis's local texture, which is characterised by an unrivalled linguistic energy, we will discover a more complex set of arguments.

Simultaneously, Amis's literary resourcefulness creates pockets of linguistic resistance that allow the author to counter the moral decline of the modern city by acting out, verbally, the dislocation of London as a system of signs. This localised textual resistance could be termed Amis's 'entropoetics' – a poetics of decline redeemed by linguistic ingenuity whose aesthetic interference within the wider texture restores the mythology of loss. In an illuminating passage from Amis's debut novel, *The Rachel Papers* (1973), Amis articulates his awareness of this tension between his linguistic inventiveness and his sometimes morally dubious outbursts through his alter ego, twenty-year-old Oxford man Charles Highway:

> One of the troubles with being over-articulate, with having a vocabulary more refined than your emotions, is that every turn in the conversation, every switch of posture, opens up an estate of verbal avenues with a myriad side-turnings and cul-de-sacs – and there are no signposts but your own sincerity and good taste, and I've never had much of either. All I know is that I can go down any one of them and be welcomed as a returning lord.[20]

Highway also offers us an illuminating analogy between the novel and the city. Amis foregrounds the narrators' voice both *in* and *as* a textual space, and invites us to consider his novels as cities just like London, but constructing an imaginative metropolis.[21] Simultaneously, the tracing of intertextual connections from Dante and Dickens to T. S. Eliot and Saul Bellow – which Amis, thinking in monetary terms, considers a form of 'debt' – excavates within Amis's voice a city of words with a complex, secular vision that tests out the ambiguities and contradictions of life in the late twentieth and early twenty-first century.

'This is London, there are no fields': a tour of Amis's urban pastoral

One might consider Amis's mythology of loss as an investigation of contemporary experience by looking at ways in which his interest in London is written within the English tradition of pastoral literature. It is a utopian mode which conventionally concerns the idealised uncomplicated lives of shepherds, who embody a tranquil and uncorrupted existence, and the genre displays a great nostalgia for the lost past associated with a condition of love and peace, without corruption, strife, war and greed. Sir Walter Raleigh, Michael Drayton, John Milton, William Browne, Spenser, Dryden, Pope, Shelley and Arnold have all contributed to this tradition, which evolved over the centuries as a popular mode, and it ran strongly in the work of the Romantics in particular.

Wordsworth's poetry diametrically opposes country to the city, establishing a dialectical relationship that Amis exploits also for his investigation of the contemporary urban experience. In *The Rachel Papers*, for instance, the struggle is conveyed in the names of titular Rachel's competing lovers: Highway versus DeForest. However, Amis's texts contain buried within them suggestions that these changes are perpetual and continuous: 'decline' is perpetual, and thus, not decline, but continuity. In *The Country and the City* (1973), Raymond Williams shows that the organic society is a myth that is used to mourn the mechanisation of modern life in industrial society and under capitalism.[22] Amis's mythology of loss is based on an idealised model of how society should function.

In the nineteenth century literary protest against the mechanised exploitation and destruction of nature appeared in Dickens's work and in utopian-socialist novels such as William Morris's *News from Nowhere* (1890) and Richard Jeffries's *After London: Wild England* (1885). The apocalyptic image of London as a giant in the work of these fin-de-siècle writers refers back to Blake's sleeping Albion: 'The giant was punished for some crime by being buried to the chest in the earth; fire incessantly consumed his head and played about it, yet it was not destroyed.'[23] Blake's poem *Earth's Answer* (1794) personifies Earth as a fallen woman and points to the presence of crippling moral constraints that would potentially liberate through the unfettered release of sexual desire. Amis's mythology of loss uses water as an anthropomorphic fallacy by turning it into a sadomasochistic means of punishment with biblical wrath: 'It was lashing down, just like they said, whipstroke after whipstroke, in climbing anger [...] the rain that fell on London now gave off smoke for reasons of its own' (*LF* 270–1). Whereas the biblical tempest at the end of Iain Sinclair's *Downriver* shows that water is, metaphorically at least, still able to cleanse contemporary corruption, in Amis's work water has itself become tainted by London's compression of sin and corruption: 'The rain is terrible. It wouldn't look so bad in a jungle or somewhere, coming down like this, but in a northern city, suspended from soiled clouds. It's all so desperate when you try to wash something unclean in unclean water' (*LF* 205). Amis's work therefore proposes that no redemption is possible in a world in which the entire atmosphere is contaminated with fallen elements.

Generically, Amis's London novels can thus be read, in oxymoronic terms, as an 'urban pastoral', in which he deliberately brings the original ideas of the pastoral into the city to force a clash that provides knowledge about the state of contemporary consciousness.[24] When William Wordsworth spent three and a half months in London, in 1791, the result was his famous ode to London, 'Composed on Westminster Bridge' (1802), and also Book Seven of *The Prelude*, an often neglected piece of London writing the importance of which lies in its phenomenological exploration of the city as theatre. Wordsworth juxtaposes a blind Beggar, as an archetypal figure of London's underclass, to the spectacle of Bartholomew Fair – 'a phantasma / Monstrous in color, motion, shape, sight, sound!'[25] Amis is also interested in the traumatic sensory stimulation provided by the urban environment as a productive, even revelatory force.

However, whereas Wordsworth was still able to see the sublime in the urban environment, Amis's postmodern city seems a place devoid of the ability to produce epiphany; the 'urban pastoral' appears to be exhausted by centuries of violence and corruption. A passage from *The Information*, in which Richard Tull takes his son Marco for a stroll through 'Dogshit Park' (*I* 137), is illuminating:

> Hand in hand they did their tour of the urban pastoral – the sward beneath the heavenly luminary – its human figures brightly half-clad at rest and play. Walking here he felt the pluralism and the petty pro-miscuity and, for now, the freedom from group hostility. If they were here, these hostilities, then Richard didn't smell their hormones; he was white and middle-class and Labour and he was growing old. It sometimes seemed that he had spent his whole life avoiding getting beaten up (teds, mods, rockers, skinheads, punks, blacks) but his land was gangland no longer: violence would come, if it came, from the individual, from left field, denuded of motive. The urban pastoral was all left field. (*I* 138)

Amis's version of pastoral is determined by the idea that the develop-ment of the city has introduced a high degree of contingency into the lived experience which undermines predictability and causality. In Tull this sparks general distrust of his fellow man, which also destroys the ideal of the community spirit associated with rural life, and conveyed by Wordsworth as a world 'beyond / The reach of common indica-tion'.[26] Amis's advocacy of a sense of community is underscored in the story 'God's Dice' (1987), where the disillusioned narrator juxtaposes his days spent in West London and thinks back to his time in New York in the 1980s:

> Now, in 1985, it is hard for me to believe that a city is anything more or other than the sum of its streets, as I sit here with the Upper West Side blatting at my window and fingering my heart. Sometimes in my dreams of New York danger I stare down over the city – and its looks half made, half wrecked, one half [...] of something larger torn in two, frayed, twangy, moist with rain or solder. And you mean to tell me, I say to myself, that this is supposed to be a *community*?[27]

This dating is important because it ties the loss of the social collective in with the Reagan–Thatcher ideology that emphasised the importance of the individual over the collective. Indeed, in his representation of London, Amis's text seems to agree with Thatcher's claim that there is no such thing as society: the heterogeneity and diversity of the city *appear* as a form of social disconnection and fragmentation without a central set of values to imaginarily bind the inhabitants together.[28] Thus, in its reaction against Thatcherite politics and the manner in which they express themselves directly in a representation of the London landscape as a narrated space that has lost coherence:

> London is full of short stories walking around hand in hand. In the shuffle of the streets you see countless odd pairings, all colours, all ages, all sexes, queens and knaves, jacks and tens, in clubs and diamonds, swords and coins, walking round, hand in hand. You see a dull-faced young woman, stodged out on booze or glands, taking the leaning weight of her elderly companion, a man with misangled legs like broken dividers. No relation. You see a punk girl of seventeen, who would resemble a mad parrot with or without her two black eyes, on the arm of the milkman not quite old enough to be her father. Where's the connection? You see a big-shouldered forty-year-old blonde, rowdily flanked by two Lithuanian bumboys in tanktop T-shirts. Now where do they fit in? London is full of short stories, epics, farces, sitcoms, sagas, soap and squibs, walking round hand in hand. (*M* 257)

Amis's text seems to suggest that the modern city is a place that alienates man not only from himself, but also from his fellow man, a criticism that is in line with modernist writers such as T. S. Eliot and E. M. Forster, but paradoxically he places these seemingly disconnected Londoners within the same narrative space, an act that recovers their connection. Zadie Smith parodies Amis's pessimistic rhetoric in *White Teeth*, suggesting that London functions as a laboratory that mixes together not just narratives, but languages. One of the ideas foregrounded by Amis's text is that the post-war context produces interfering factors within this. First the experience of a constant nuclear threat injects our perception with an anxiety and death drive that undermine our ability to find a transcendent moment that could possibly restore some kind of social harmony. The apocalyptic atmosphere that manifests itself in Amis's representation of London is determined by his nuclear anxieties in a Cold War context. This is suggested by the character Nicola Six, who remembers London being visualised as a target for a nuclear attack when she was young: 'On television at the age of four she saw the warnings, and the circles of concentric devastation, with London like a bull's-eye in the centre of the board' (*LF* 16). Second, there is a dominance of American culture in the broadest sense of the word that drastically changes social forms of living within Europe. Amis therefore juxtaposes London, as a material and mental expression of the Old World, against the young, vibrant energy of American cities such as New York, Chicago and Los Angeles, whose influence now comes to dominate the ancient city infected by traffic jams, increasingly small living spaces, and fast food culture: 'London has jet-lag. London has culture-shock. It's doing everything the wrong way round at the wrong time' (*M* 150).

This American influence is, as we already saw in McEwan's work, embraced by these writers. Both Amis and McEwan are particularly interested in Saul Bellow's exploration of the connection of post-war society and the legacy of the Holocaust, which weighs down morally on the contemporary West. Bellow's influence on both writers lies in his representation of the city as a specific moral structure, and in its metaphor for and measurement of the changing social and cultural dynamics in the twentieth century. What Amis gets from Bellow stylistically has been described by James Wood as 'his streaming syntax and parenthetical interruptions; his glamorous plurals, adjectival massing, often in triplicate his compounds [...] and the redundant, apparently urgent, use of the word "human"'.[29] Yet Amis's work brings Bellow's humanism into the twenty-first century by depicting cities – after the terrorist attacks of 9/11 – in which our 'species consciousness' reintroduces a paradoxical humanism that redeems the new religious and cultural conflicts.

In his representation of the city, Amis's exploitation of the pastoral tradition also introduces a generic problem: the pastoral is first and foremost associated with poetry, and not the novel form, so Amis's harnessing of this tradition into a form associated with the city creates itself a distorting effect that results in a divorce of form from content. Whereas at the level of the local language we see a manifestation of Amis's lamentation for a lost, idyllic past associated with the countryside in brief outbursts of vitriolic gripes, it is the wider plot structure which trashes that apocalyptic, millenarian discourse. In *Money*, for instance, it is the protagonist John Self, the embodiment of unending selfishness and greed, lust and addiction (to sex, fast food, pornography) without any emotional commitment, who is the object of Amis's satire. The novel tells the story of Self, born upstairs in a Pimlico pub, The Shakespeare, and now a partner in a London advertising agency, who flies back and forth between

London and New York to get his film (the title is sometimes *Good Money*, sometimes *Bad Money*) made: 'I am a thing made up of a time lag, culture shock, zone shift' (*M* 264). Self has a flat in West London, on the Portobello Road – 'Its spirit is broken, and so is mine' (*M* 63). Oxford Street, signifier of the booming consumer culture, is a 'bus-torn slum' (*M* 78), and 'a third-generation Italian restaurant' is replaced by a 'Burger Den' because the 'place didn't have what it took: market forces' (*M* 70–1). Self's girlfriend, Selina Street, expresses the logic of 1980s consumerism in a clever statement that obviates any retort: '"Fucking and shopping [are] the only things that girls should be allowed to do much of. Don't you think?"' (*M* 343). Set around the time of the marriage of Charles and Diana in 1981, the novel shows the city plagued by riots: 'There are street celebrations, street rumbles. London is covered in barricades and bunting. The talk is all of royalty and riots' (*M* 231). The pessimistic vision of London is analogous to the description of Self's flat's windows: 'spectral, polluted, nicotine-sodden' (*M* 64).

Again, whilst the local texture confronts us with extremely pessimistic statements, it is the wider trajectory of the novel that undercuts these fantasies of regression. Self is plagued by paranoia and schizophrenia, and his conscience also unconsciously haunts him: 'At night I hear homeless voices out over the flat rooftops. There are sounds of cramped murmuring' (*M* 263). And after his car, a 'Fiasco', is confiscated after drunk driving, Self is forced to break his isolation and to reconnect with the city and its people: 'I walk more in the streets now. Unemployment is a problem' (*M* 269). Ultimately, his plans for the films go belly up, and he finds himself in financial problems so deep that he decides to kill himself. The attempted suicide fails, and at Christmas time 1981 – an overt reworking of Dickens's *A Christmas Carol* (1843) – we find John Self transformed: although he is *'still a high-risk zone […] still inner city'* (*M* 384), the former misanthropist will start a job minding a Hyde Park ice-cream van in the spring, and he has learned a lesson in humility. On the Underground a lady, thinking he is a homeless man, puts 10 pence in his flat-cap: *'Here – I drink, I sing, I babble with my missing tooth. The people hurry from the underground, very mortal, the young half healthy, the old half shrewd – quarter beautiful, quarter wise. Humans, I honour you'* (*M* 394).

This divorce of form and content is even more critical in *London Fields*. The plot is more complex, with a Dickensian sprawl and digression but also much subjective narration and retelling, and postmodern metafictional game-playing. It essentially narrates the story of a failed novelist, Samson Young, who stays in the successful playwright Mark Asprey's flat in Hackney, looking out over the park London Fields.

Young bumps into his story in real life: Nicola Six, a male sex fantasy, is nearing her 35th birthday and wants to plot her own murder – an idea which Amis gets from Muriel Spark's *The Driver's Seat* (1973), for which she selects two opposite characters, the lowlife and darts fanatic Keith Talent and the upper-middle-class City financier Guy Clinch. Much of the action is set in West London, however: in Nicola's Notting Hill flat, Keith's tiny council flat on Golborne Road (Trellick Tower, 'Keith's dark tower looming like a calipered leg dropped from heaven' (*LF* 229)), Guy's expensive mansion in Lansdowne Crescent and a pub called The Black Cross, on the Portobello Road.

Besides being known as the host environment of Spanish immigrants, Notting Hill is a location that traditionally served as the locus for Samuel Selvon's *The Lonely Londoners* (1956), about Afro-Caribbean settlers in West London. Colin MacInnes's evocation of a West Indian community in West London, *City of Spades* (1957), was written a year before the five nights of the Notting Hill Riots (August 1958), which sparked the annual Notting Hill carnival as a reaction. Amis's London is a city inherently violent and chaotic, with carnivalesque riots historically representing its normal state of mind: 'If you ask me, there's a riot here every night. There always has been and there always will be. At eleven o'clock, London is a storm, a rave, a knees-up, a free-for-all' (*LF* 89). Yet Amis's depiction of West London is also shaped by the work of Muriel Spark: not only does *The Driver's Seat* provide the idea for the plot of *London Fields*, but Spark's ghost story 'The Portobello Road' (1956) is a more direct intertext. This story presents Notting Hill's street market as the place where money, desire and language intertwine: 'I hear the tinkling tills, I hear the jangle of loose change and tongues and children wanting to hold and to have.'[30] It is also the location where the three characters Skinny, Kathleen and George encounter the ghost of the narrator, Needle.

The title of the novel itself refers not so much to the Hackney park as to Young's paradisiacal place that represents lost childhood innocence, and, more generally, to the lost dwelling place of shepherds. There is no Eden left in Amis's London, and in the novel we find a brutal world that has lost its innocence and its ability to love and experience human emotions: 'this is London; and there are no fields. Only fields of operation and observation, only fields of electromagnetic attraction and repulsion, only fields of hatred and coercion. / Only force fields' (*LF* 134). This London is the opposite of Eden. In Amis's textual world, the city is a loveless machine for generating, manipulating and exploiting desire; Nicola Six acts out the sex fantasies of both Keith, who is given a slutty version, and Guy, who desires a virginal Nicola. This London is what Philip Tew has called 'an economic system modelled by sexual and competitive urges', which can be read as a criticism of postmodern forms of living driven by money, greed and egoistic fulfilment of one's wants.[31] Deleuze and Guattari speak of 'zones of intensities, fields of potentials', and their anti-organic model of the world and mankind as one immense machinery of wants and desires that need to be fulfilled seems rather apt.[32]

In this respect, *London Fields* is an indirect indictment of Thatcherism. Nicola Six can be read as an analogy for the complex interplay of Thatcherism's confidence game and a suicide. When Six walks down the Golborne Road and is attracting attention from just about everyone '[s]he faced them strongly; she knew she looked enough like the government. She felt no fear. Walking naked up these steps (she told herself), with her bare feet on the wet stone, Nicola would have felt no fear' (*LF* 265). Although Brian Finney notes that 'Amis was opposed to what Thatcher stood for', his fictional narratives' relationship to her Britain is more complex and ambiguous than that makes it seem.[33] In a review of Hugo Young's *The Iron Lady* (1990) for *Elle* magazine, Amis states:

> Mrs Thatcher is the only interesting thing about British power politics; and the only interesting thing about Mrs Thatcher is that she isn't a man. Tricked out with the same achievements, the same style and 'vision', a Marvyn or a Marmaduke Thatcher would be as dull as rain, as dull as London traffic, as dull as the phosphorescent prosperity, the boutique squalor of Thatcher's England (or its southeasterly quadrant).[34]

Yet it is the plot of *London Fields* which redeems this local observation: although Nicola is murdered, and thus gets her desire fulfilled, there is a tiny glimmer of hope in the fact that her murderer, Young, has asked Guy to take care of the traumatised and abused child Kim Talent. Young's suicide also adds to some kind of redemption for the city: his death cleanses his sin, that is, the plotting of the novel itself, while he leaves behind his 'confession' in the form of the novel and his suicide notes. Although there is the sense that Young is himself manipulated, and a construct made up by Mark Asprey and, beyond that, Martin Amis, there also is, for the reader, a genuine sense of comeuppance that restores the order of things. It is not only Dickens whose legacy we feel here but, perhaps more importantly, Dostoevsky's ambiguous reading of St Petersburg as both an underworld and as a heavenly city. London, like Dostoevsky's city, is a place of shifting morality and religious engagement where redemption from sins can be found in the social fabric of human relationships.

'An aggregate of shapes, figures and light': postmodern money and head trauma

Amis sees London, the centre of the British economy, as a dynamo that generates money and corruption in equal measure:

> I have strong moral views, and they are very much directed at things like money and acquisition. I think Money is the central deformity in life, as Saul Bellow says, it's one of the evils that has cheerfully survived identification as an evil. Money doesn't mind if we say it's evil, it goes from strength to strength. It's a fiction, an addiction, and a tacit conspiracy that we have all agreed to go along with. My hatred for it does look as though I'm underwriting a certain asceticism, but it isn't really that way: I don't offer any alternatives to what I deplore.[35]

Amis occupies the typical position of the satirist; and his misanthropy is certainly worthy of the proficient satirist with a stoked-up imagination. Yet Amis's fiction suggests that in the post-war period the increasing complexity and the changing nature of capital causes a crisis in signification. *Other People* (1981)[36] proposes that '[m]oney had recently done something unforgiveable' (*OP* 57); and in *Money* John Self states that '[m]oney [...] is uncontrollable' resulting in 'a gap between things' (*M* 154). These statements indirectly point to the effects of the decoupling of the dollar from the gold standard in 1973, which accelerated the increasingly ephemeral nature of the capitalist system determined by the influence of the stock exchange. As a result of this free-floating capital, a detachment of the signifier from the signified, and the destruction of fixed values, takes place, which manifests in social and cultural schizophrenia that has an impact upon three distinct but interrelated levels, namely a mental and moral dislocation, a simulacral experience of the world, and a decline of language – the psychological violence of which manifests itself in head trauma.

First, we gain a sense of mental dislocation produced by the contemporary urban experience in *Other People*, which tells the story of a young girl, Mary Lamb, who wanders off into London suffering from amnesia. Amis enacts a radically creative dislocation of the conventional signifier–signified system, resulting in an experiment in techniques of defamiliarisation influenced by Craig Raine and Christopher Reid's Martian School of Poetry: 'Not yet stretched by time, her perceptions are without seriality: they are multiform, instantaneous and random, like the present itself [...] She can compare a veil of smoke sliding out of a doorway with a particular flourish of the blanket as she strips her bed' (*OP* 53). London is experienced as a linguistic system where the instability of the sign–signifier system is apprehended, in Mengham's words, 'like another Fall: a decline into anarchy and linguistic isolation'.[37] The absence of chronological time and a clear-cut distinction between language and world establishes a two-dimensional visual experience whereby episodic repetition and language are superimposed on to her conception of the city. When Mary is driven downriver alongside the Thames by detective Prince, she experiences the river as if it is the same stretch over and over again, but metamorphosing. The stretch between Waterloo Bridge and Tower Bridge is 'stretched and taut, as if being tugged at from either end. It shone like scratched armour' (*OP* 204). When arriving at the Isle of Dogs, however, the river squirms back to life: 'Whoever had been holding it tight had let go again. The water writhed now, lunar and millennial beneath the turbid mist [...] There were no people [...] and the rat-like threadbare dogs owned the land' (*OP* 204).

The sacrifice of Hide at the end of the novel runs parallel to the death of the stable sign–signifier system, pointing to a dehistoricised world that produces schizophrenia and an experience of the city as 'an aggregate of shapes, figures and light' (*OP* 53). The postmodern experience of the urban environment is also as a space with a positive potential, however: Amis uses the city's phantasmagoric characteristics to decondition the reader's expectations, forcing a reconnection through cognitive 'play', however dark and violent this play is. Both the city and literature have a role to play in the restoration of our sensibility and disconnection because the alienation and sensory distortion they produce demands we reconnect to the world in new, meaningful ways.

Amis's London is, according to Nicolas Tredell, 'marked by intimidation, violence, division and alienation', and this violence should be taken literally but also figuratively.[38] Amis's exploration of socio-cultural amnesia as trauma is continued in *Yellow Dog* (2003), during the opening of which Meo goes on a fateful stroll from his Camden home to the pub ('Hollywood') where he will receive a head injury. The result is a vignette about the experience of modern London life; a phenomenological investigation into the ways in which we read the urban environment as a sign-system. The street names that indicate Meo's whereabouts

('Xan Meo walked down St George's Avenue ...' (*YD* 5)) are interspersed with contemplations of his garden flat; the way advertising seduces; fashion; and his one-night stand with a continuity girl. Amis gives the reader an image of Meo's consciousness-as-city, contrasting to the X-ray that, a few hours later, visualises his head trauma. By mapping its intricate working in language, Amis points to the importance of the human mind in shaping our perception of the world around us, and emphasises the violently distorting effects that the urban environment can have.[39]

The text not only produces a mental map of Meo, but also creates a catalogue of London life and a satirical, semi-realist cartography of contemporary Camden:

> The rink of Britannia Junction: Parkway and Camden Lock and Camden High Street, the dozen black frames of the traffic lights, the slum of cars. Certain sights had to be got out of the way: that heap – no, that stack – of dogshit; that avalanche of vomit; that drunk on the pavement with the face like a baboon's rear; that old chancer who had clearly been incredibly beaten up in the last five or six hours – and, just as incredibly, the eyes that lurked among the knucklestamps and bootprints harboured no grievance, sought no redress ... (*YD* 6)

This chain of visual impressions of Camden is released *in language*, and this stacking of snapshots renders a palimpsest of filth and violence; in the scatological economy of the text Camden Town embodies urban degeneration. Yet, Amis introduces ambiguity by ironising the narrator: the 'stack' of dogshit and 'avalanche of vomit' are deliberate and grotesque exaggerations that point to the narrator's self-awareness about his misanthropic observations; a moralistic point of view that is projected on to the world by Meo's consciousness.[40] The reader uncovers a dynamic relationship between the raw material rendered by the heterogeneity that London provides and its projection in language; a relationship in which the city's sensory overload stimulates the use of the English language's richness and creativity.

London is used by Amis as a phenomenological laboratory where human perception of the urban world is tested out in refined textual bodies. This is dramatised by a repetition of the same walk *after* Meo has lost his memory, which signifies another Fall:

> So, the rink of Parkway and Camden Lock and Camden High Street, the black gallows of traffic lights. At this time of day you saw guys in

suits heading home with a briefcase in one hand and, in the other, a plastic bag containing provisions for one. Will this be me, myself? he thought. It wasn't only women: he was looking at the men differently too, weighing them, grading them – fearing them. On the phone, with Pearl, he had felt as breakable as a lightbulb [...] (*YD* 141)

London as a container of memory and history is now replaced by an amnesiac city that has to be rediscovered creatively by naming it in language in order to make sense of this simplistically perceived environment. The vagueness of the descriptions ('guys in suits') is mirrored by the return to Meo's primitive state ('provisions'). Curiously, however, this piece of social observation is built on memory: the now less eloquent narrator is forced to take over from Meo almost completely. Amis's texts show that in our capacity to describe and name the outside world lies the power to master the world, but also that the process of one's identification is mediated by the subject's direct relationship to the surrounding space in relation to language.

Second, *London Fields* exploits the disconnection of the conventional signifier–signified relationships by producing a simulacral London. The following description of Marmaduke's replica toys demonstrates an increasingly unstable 'real':

Toys were symbols – of real things. That toy monkey stood for a real monkey, that toy train for a real train, and so on: in miniature. But there seemed to be a disturbing literalism abroad in Marmaduke's nursery. That toy baby elephant [...] pink and gauzy and five feet high [...] was about the size of a baby elephant. And the same sort of thing could be said for Marmaduke's howitzers and grenade launchers and cartridge belts [and] a pucklike boobytrap which could take out three or four toy tanks at a time, was certainly far larger that the actual contrivance now fielded by Nato. (*LF* 220)

This passage shows how Amis ties the usurpation of the representative of the real to his mythology of loss. The passage stresses the relationship between the violence of the narratives dormant in the toys and the destroyed proportion of their referential aspect. Brian Finney observes that Keith even 'more than John Self in *Money* [...] is the typical product of what Baudrillard has called the age of simulation'.[41] An inversion takes place whereby models of the world dominate representations of the world, producing 'the self-liquidation of values itself. Money is caught in the grand cancellation of the sign of the economy.'[42]

In *London Fields*, the world is a society of the spectacle connected via mass media such as television and tabloid newspapers that mould the working-class consciousness. Young narrates how the discourses of such media determine Keith's outlook on and experience of life: 'When Keith goes to a football match, that misery of stringer's clichés *is what he actually sees*' (*LF* 98). Amis's comical inversions demonstrate the dangers when volatility is introduced into the stability of such systems, which have a tendency to disrupt the stability of social categories and introduce interference into communication.[43]

This is related to a third effect, a decline of language. In a way similar to the work of Dickens, Conrad and T. S. Eliot, Amis's texts display careful attention to the way in which the capitalist system of exchange is related to linguistic capital. *London Fields* and *Yellow Dog* are obsessed with the way in which the social spectrum is debased through the dissemination of immoral images and language, and the corruption of language itself. In *Money*, John Self notices a cloud with a peculiar shape: 'Up in the distance basked a hollow pink cloud, a rosy cusp fastened by tendrils at either end, like a vertical eye, a vertical mouth. In its core lay a creaturely essence, meticulous, feminine ...' (*M* 249). This discussion is an echo of Hamlet's dialogue with Polonius: 'Do you see yonder cloud that's almost in shape of a camel?'[44] Whereas in *Hamlet* the problem of interpretation points out the problem of knowledge and perception, in *Money* this echo becomes an indictment of a lack of imagination and an inability to verbalise truth and beauty on the part of Self, whose porn-conditioned mind goes automatically for the banal response: 'And that cloud up there certainly looked like a pussy to me' (*M* 249). In *London Fields*, the ubiquitous permeation of the word 'fuck' is denounced by its exhaustingly offensive repetition throughout the novel. Keith Talent's lack of education and manipulation by the tabloids have eroded, or stalled, his education towards becoming an independent thinking individual: 'In his head, ideas wanted to be named, but remained nameless' (*LF* 295). Here, Amis is working within the dystopian tradition of George Orwell and Anthony Burgess by stressing the importance of education for the creation of healthy, independently thinking citizens; but above all the importance of language: a healthy society can only exist if its citizens are able to conceive its entire landscape in language.[45]

For Amis, the Good and Just are directly connected to a mythic and religious system of language and imagery that has become lost over the ages. *The Information* argues against the coarsening of language and the proliferation of coprolalia, and the way in which the dissemination of pornography corrupts the entire social sphere: 'When he [Darko] came

to London [...] the very air of Oxford Circus was rank with pornography' (*I* 256). *Yellow Dog* shows the negative mutation of English under
the influence of new technologies such as email and text-messaging,
resulting in a 'Yellow Tongue' (*YD* 266). The novel traces the relationship between fashion brands with names such as FCUK (real) and
TUNC (fictional) and the offensive naming of cocktails and alcopops
('Shithead' and 'Dickhead' (*YD* 11)). Similarly, text-messaging abbre-
viates not only the English language, but the moral codes conveyed
in it too, as k8 (Kate), the chatroom girlfriend of tabloid journalist
Clint Smoker, states cryptically: 'i'm very happy to per4m oral 6 any
time [...] as 4 cunnilingus, th@t's strictly verbo10' (*YD* 160). Amis's
play with form highlights how the deformation of language disguises
the pornographic content. Amis's appropriation and manipulation
shows that his criticism offers a low parody of such new productions
of reality, demonstrating that these new modes of representation
are appropriate only for a human consciousness which is mindlessly
engaged with the world. Simultaneously, the witty and international
joke of k8's use of the German 'verboten' upsets Amis's presumed
criticism on a thematic level. The German reference is international
and belongs to the literary voice of the clever narrator, which allows
us to read the local texture against the surface themes of degeneration.
It is literature that has a redeeming role to play, then, as it forges linguistic and historical links with the past by poetic originality as well as
intertextual links.

Amis's scatological economy of postmodern London

This decline of language and human behaviour is illuminated by Amis's
investigation of the relationship between money and excrement. In
Moorcock's *King of the City*, Dennis Dover humorously mocks the 'tiny
goozer' Amis as 'Felix Martin', 'the famous farting novelist', which suggests rightly that Amis's work is littered with coprophilia and references to
excrement. In *London Fields*, Samson Young is shat upon by a pigeon, triggering the following meditation: 'It had this effect on me: despair. I swore
and stumbled around, bedraggled, helpless, the diet of a London pigeon
being something that really doesn't bear thinking about. I mean, what
the digestive system of a London pigeon considers as *waste*' (*LF* 116).[46]
In *Yellow Dog*, the protagonist Xan Meo's visit to 'the savage pubs of
Camden High Street and Kentish Town Road' (*YD* 143) yields the following unsavoury test of manhood: 'Having just consumed a very great
deal of dun-coloured tapwater, Xan's immediate objective was to find

out whether he was man enough to piss his own shit off the back of the porcelain bowl. He wasn't quite man enough to do that, but then this was very butch shit: mutton vindaloo, pork kebab, cajun pizza [sic], jalapeñas relleñas' (*YD* 144). In *The Information*, much of the action is centred on Dogshit Park where the 'sloping green was mud, churned and studded, beige and dun, half soil, half shit' (*I* 135). Another example from *Yellow Dog* is Andrews's mentioning that '[a] man fights ... with his arsehole. Power comes ... in the form of anger, up through the arsehole' (*YD* 303).

Amis's interest in the scatological tradition goes back to the Middle Ages, and especially Rabelais's *Gargantua and Pantagruel* and Chaucer's *The Canterbury Tales* (1478), which are riddled with low comedy and references to excrement. In 'The Miller's Tale', the dandy Absolom is in love with Alison, and, unable to see in the dark, 'gives her a savory kiss on the ass', but he later gets his revenge by sticking a hot poker up the behind of Alison's new lover, Nicolas. This tradition of satirists, from Richard Brinsley Sheridan and Jonathan Swift to Samuel Beckett, also exploited the power of excrement. Amis derives this interest in the power of scatology from Dickens's and T. S. Eliot's portrayal of London as a place where the capitalist system's unceasing processes of production and consumption result in the overproduction of waste in both a literal and metaphorical sense. In *Our Mutual Friend*, Dickens criticises the uneven distribution of wealth, showing by means of parody how urban dwellers 'live off the land', with the wealthy dust contractor, John Harmon, and Lizzie and her father recovering bodies from the Thames. Dickens's *Little Dorrit* (1855–7) connects the Victorian obsession with economics with psychological diseases, while the world turns to its morally and artistically dead ends.

London Fields contains a passage that meditates on Dickens's awareness of the city's accumulation of money as a corrupting force and its metaphorical expression in excrement. In *The Information*, Richard Tull 'kept thinking he smelled of shit' (*I* 236), and when Clinch, who represents 'the scurfy smell of old money' (*LF* 51), brings Nicola Six money, he notes:

It always struck him, the fact that money stank, like the reminder of an insidious weakness in himself. Of course, the poets and novelists had always patiently insisted as much. Look at Chaucer's cock. Look at Dickens (Dickens was the perfect panning-bowl for myth); the old man up to his armpits in Thames sewage, searching for treasure; the symbolic names of Murdstone and Merdle, the financier. But all that was myth and symbol, a way of saying that money could somehow be thought of as smelly, of being scatological. It was frightfully literal-minded of money, he thought, to be actually stinking up the place like this. *Pecunia non olet* was dead wrong. *Pecunia olet.* Christ, heaven stops the nose at it. (*LF* 251)

Like Dickens, Amis translates the city as embodiment of the accumulation of wealth into waste, yet whereas in Dickens the relationship between money and excrement is metaphorical, in Amis's postmodern city the relationship becomes inverted: Guy literalises the idea that money stinks. Amis's London scatology stands in a distinctly modern tradition, which starts with T. S. Eliot. *The Waste Land* also makes similar scatological connections between the city, money and excrement. The text repeats the word 'brown' (61, 175, 208) and the Thames sweats 'Oil and tar' (267), pointing to the sinful industrial production of waste. Similarly, T. S. Eliot's text mentions that the Thames 'bears no empty bottles, sandwich papers. / Silk handkerchiefs, cardboard boxes, cigarette ends / Or other testimony of summer nights' (177–9), evoking excremental images. In *The Poetics of Impersonality*, Maud Ellmann states that such images 'signify the culture's decadence, as well as bodily decrepitude. The self is implicated in the degradation of the race, because the filth without insinuates defilement within.'[47] At the same time, this waste symbolically defines the body and culture, placing a boundary on what it assumes it is, and what it is not.[48]

Freud relates the capitalist system to 'soil': the first thing that man produces is excrement, unconsciously resulting in the human mind's link between labour (working the land) and production in terms of shit: 'Wherever archaic modes of thought have predominated or persist, in ancient civilizations, in myth, in fairy tales and superstitions, in unconscious thinking, in dreams and neuroses – money is brought into the most intimate relationship with dirt.'[49] Freud also states that wealth and waste are equated with one another via an inverse relationship, yet the human consciousness creates an imagined relationship between faeces and gold.[50]

Amis's textual London is an assemblage of the satirical tradition's use of coprophilic images and the entropic tradition of Dickens and T. S. Eliot, which evokes a specific tradition that cautions against the decline of morality and the devaluing of language. Amis's criticism is also anti-Thatcherite because it situates literature too as wholly part of the postmodern market economy that implies a spiritual death. The echoes of Eliot's work are clear in the following passage, when Young finishes a session of sex with 'Necropolitan Nicola' (*LF* 467) they go out walking

> in the dripping alleys, the dark chambers of the elaborately suffering city. We're the dead. Amazing we can do this. More amazing that we want to. Hand in hand and arm in arm we totter, through communal fantasy and sorrow, through London fields. We're the dead. Above, the sky has a pink tinge to it, the cunning opposite of health, like something bad, something high. As if through a screen of stage smoke you can just make out God's morse or shorthand, the stars arranged in triangles, and saying therefore and because, therefore and because. We're the dead. (*LF* 391)[51]

This passage echoes the images and mimics the rhythms of *The Hollow Men* (1925) in particular, which describes London as a city of the dead: 'It is like this / in death's other kingdom / Walking alone / At the hour when we are trembling with tenderness / Lips that would kiss / Form prayers to broken stone.'[52]

If we place Amis's novels in the context of contemporary culture as excremental it becomes clear that Amis's texts express the excesses of late capitalist consumer culture.[53] In *The Consumer Society* (1980), Jean Baudrillard states:

> Everything is finally digested and reduced to the same homogeneous fecal matter (this occurs, of course, precisely under the sign of the disappearance of 'liquid' currency, the still too visible symbol of the real excretion of real life, and of the economic and social contradictions that previously haunted it). All that is past (passed): a controlled, lubricated, and consumed excretion is henceforth transferred into things, everywhere diffused in the indistinguishability of things and of social relations.[54]

In *London Fields*, Nicola Six's penchant for anal sex must be read as a different, but related metaphor that equates labour with economic power. Todd traces the analogy between Amis's bodily obsession to his narrative economy: 'her interest in anal sex as a metaphor both for the repeated stress on the dead-end street location of her apartment and for the dead end into which Samson's narration of the story that awaits his telling finally leads him'.[55] *Yellow Dog* continues this with an exploration of the capital of the global porn industry's obsession with anal sex: '"Pussies are bullshit!" One director said, "With anal, the actress's personality comes out"' (*YD* 269). London, mirrored in and contaminated by 'Fucktown' (Hollywood, Los Angeles), is rewritten as *anus mundi*: Amis's excremental obsession stands for the fleeting, goalless economy of hedonism, and for the spiritual corruption in greedy exchange for money.

Amis's novels are, in the end, an attempt to transform consumption into a refined literary form; in other words, to alchemically turn excrement into gold by means of the creative imagination. Amis's London presents a scatological economy in which the written city functions as an ambivalent site that mediates and transforms local, national and transnational power relationships in writing. Despite the darkness and pessimism, Amis's textual Londons have restorative powers; the economy of Amis's voice holds the city's disintegration together by creating lexical pockets of order. The texts celebrate the powers of the creative imagination, showing that man has the power to destroy *and* create. Ultimately it is in the space of the commanding literary author's voice that a community can reimagine itself, and where the radical contingency of urban life can be kept at bay by reordering the chaos of contemporary experience, so that temporary moments of the sublime can be perceived:

> Outside, the rain stopped falling. Over gardens and the mansion-block rooftops, over the window boxes and TV aerials, over Nicola's skylight and Keith's dark tower [...] the air gave a chastened sigh. For a few seconds every protuberance of sill and eave steadily shed water like drooling teeth. There followed a chemical murmur from both street and soil as the ground added up the final millimetres of what it was being asked to absorb. Then a sodden hum of silence. (*LF* 229)

8
'Through a Confusion of Languages': Mastering London with Salman Rushdie and Hanif Kureishi

'Immigrant energies rushed hungrily into the culture vacuum'

During the Thatcher era and its aftermath, London writing has yielded dark, often apocalyptic visions of a city in decline, though sometimes we encounter a cautious optimism about the possibility of London's survival. The novels of Maureen Duffy and Michael Moorcock represent staunch humanist values that are intimately connected to the fictional and fictionalised archaeology of a London thrashed by government policies of decentralisation and privatisation, while remaining open to the powers of commerce for the city's rewriting. J. G. Ballard, Iain Sinclair, Martin Amis have produced deeply pessimistic projections of London, whilst Ian McEwan 'corrects' his early, dark vision of London by presenting us with a city as pinnacle of Western culture and civilisation that continuous to offer fragile happiness. The Gothic London of Peter Ackroyd is tempered by a tone of optimism and an acknowledgement of the need for rejuvenation and change. What their Londons share is a sense of crisis, which is countered by shoring up London's founding mythologies and its literary history against the city's decline and fragmentation.

These London novelists are joined by a group of immigrant writers whose work is characterised by its non-West European cultural heritage. This new group of London writers includes Salman Rushdie, Hanif Kureishi, Timothy Mo, Zadie Smith and Monica Ali, and more recently, Andrea Levy. Their work represents a trajectory within Britain's recent literary history that sees an imagined England in decline move towards a rebirth in vibrant, exciting writing. This reinvention of Britain was triggered partially by the economic and cultural globalisation occasioned by the worldwide financial upturn in the early 1980s. This process also produced an internationalisation of the British literary imagination, and of the country's consciousness more generally. New images and discourses came to dominate literature, such as the rootless nomad who forced a rejection of the singular national tradition in favour of a fluid, hybrid and transnational identity.

We could start by examining how autochthonous Londoners experience the effects of these changes by looking at a description in Iain Sinclair's *Radon Daughters* (1994). In this novel, Todd Sileen feels he is increasingly displaced within his 'own' territory of Wapping, in East London, whilst a new population is manifesting itself with alarming confidence:

> He was delighted to retreat into a territory that had erased all traces of its previous identity, a territory that matriculated in obscurity. [...] He advanced like a cold front, a cloud charged with iron filings. He bullocked through the flocks of chattering Bengali sweatshop girls. A sharp hit of toxic scent to counter the synapse-destroying diesel fumes, wet newspaper, tandoori, cured leather. Released onto the streets, deliriously made-up, crackling and crinkling in sculpted black jackets over thin bright robes, they rattled their bangles in defensive magic. Tiny wooden heels tapped enquiringly over badly fitted paving stones. Their voices were speedy and gay.
>
> A wedge of Mecca souvenirs – spiritual shortcuts, gimcrack Paradise games, windows raffish with beads and compasses – was rapidly spreading over the washed-out fantasies of pinkeye architects. The game was up. Immigrant energies rushed hungrily into the culture vacuum.[1]

At first glance this description, laden with irony and vitriol, appears potentially xenophobic: the sweatshop girls are treated as prisoners and the commodification of their religion is a metaphysical sham. There is also a lovingness about Sinclair's descriptions of the young women, whose vibrant, new energy he captures. Yet we clearly also see an anger, frustration and anxiety, here, about the narrator's inability to move into the Bengalis' lives and culture: Sileen 'bullocked', suggesting that he associates himself with an animal whose aggression contrasts starkly to the new colourful and graceful culture. The narrator's dark and despondent voice is diametrically opposed to the light chatter of the girls, and suggests a knowingness and self-dramatisation that undermines Sileen rather than the immigrants. Sinclair captures the apparent impenetrability of these new cultures for a particular generation of Londoners who feel displaced in 'their' city. Sileen is only able to experience this new world as a collection of surfaces and objects with an unfathomable meaning, and the passage poses some serious questions about the nature and very possibility of the multicultural society.

This chapter and the next are an attempt to do exactly what Sileen is unable to do, namely, to investigate these new lives, cultures and Londons by looking at the work of Rushdie, Kureishi, Smith and Ali. At the heart of these debates lies an investigation of a complex concept, the multicultural society. Rushdie, like Sinclair, also poses serious questions about the way in which the idea of the multicultural society is offered to us in the rhetoric of public officials. In 'The New Empire within Britain' (1991), written after a decade of Thatcherism, Rushdie states:

> A language reveals the attitudes of the people who use and shape it. And a whole declension of patronizing terminology can be found in the language in which inter-racial relations have been described in Britain. At first, we were told, the goal was 'integration'. Now this word rapidly came to mean 'assimilation': a black man could only become integrated when he started behaving like a white one. [...] And now there's a new word: 'multiculturalism'. [...] Multiculturalism is the latest token gesture towards Britain's blacks, and it ought to be exposed, like 'integration' and 'racial harmony', for the sham it is.[2]

Rushdie's furious analysis of the lexeme 'multiculturalism' exposes it as a rhetorical construct, part of a process of economic and cultural globalisation in the 1980s, which expects a gradual but total assimilation of immigrants who are expected to unconditionally embrace Western culture and values. Rushdie raises one of the questions that *The Making of London* addresses in these final chapters; how contemporary fiction and the London novel in particular have been able to shape our perception of the debate about multiculturalism, which has become an increasingly problematic concept after the terrorist attacks on America and London in 2001 and 2005 respectively. London is important to immigrant writers because, as the former centre of imperial power, the city provides them the imaginative tools for answering these questions whilst offering the possibility for redirecting political and literary authority.

In order to mediate their experience of contemporary London, all these writers use the immigrant's double perspective – they stand both inside and outside the dominant culture – to operate a complex representational system. In *Imaginary Homelands* (1991) Rushdie writes that 'stereoscopic vision is perhaps what we can offer in place of "whole sight"',[3] and in *The Location of Culture* (1994) Homi Bhabha speaks of 'the migrant's double vision as being the truest eye'.[4] This double vision is consciously harnessed to master London, a city which, traditionally, is a site that generates various dialectical tensions, between materialism and idealism, between the self and the Other, et cetera. Michel de Certeau identifies a double bind in the relationship between colonisation and the power of the human voice: 'the writing's effort to master the "voice" that it cannot be but without which it nevertheless cannot exist, on the one hand, and the illegible return of voices cutting across statements and moving like strangers through the house of language, like imagination' (*PEL* 158). It is precisely because of this paradoxical doubling that immigrant writers are better equipped to both understand such processes and to adapt to London's crisis and decline. The trap this sets up, however, is that their vision is in danger of glossing over the more problematic sides of 'assimilation' and a new cultural homogeneity, which Kureishi's and Ali's work warn against in particular.

The assertion of narrative authority at the heart of literary London occurs on several levels. The dismantling of literary authority also takes place in often playful appropriation that mocks and subverts the philosophical pillars and literary canon of the West. In *The Buddha of Suburbia* (1990), Kureishi also 'corrects' some colonial texts, such as Kipling's *The Jungle Book*, by staging them as farce. *The Satanic Verses* (1988) starts with a witty rewriting of Milton's *Paradise Lost* (1667). In Zadie Smith's *White Teeth*, the relationship between London and its 'mongrel' languages creates new utopian spaces where the multicultural society is tested out. Ali's *Brick Lane* stresses the importance of speech in transmitting culturally-specific history, while showing that it is the acquisition of the host language that offers the opportunity for inscription of the migrant self in modernity.

These writers also seize literary authority by dismantling and rewriting the masters' language as a force that inscribes the subject with political and cultural power and codes. Rushdie's almost aggressive engagement with the English language is key to this process. In his introduction to *Mirrorwork* (1997), an overview of fifty years of Indian writing, Rushdie suggests that the English language has provided the space for colonial authors to remake language from within: rather than 'being a post-colonial anomaly, the bastard child of Empire [...] English has become an Indian language'.[5] The implication of this appropriation and subversion is that the representation of London changes also because of the violent process of exchange: the immigrant author is reborn in a new language, whilst that language is simultaneously reinvented. These writers exploit the tensions between oral and written speech to appropriate the city in new, imaginative ways. A striking similarity between *The Satanic Verses*, *The Buddha of Suburbia*, *White Teeth* and *Brick Lane* is that these novels stage London as a narrative battleground where stories collectively form a site of contestation. Rushdie, Kureishi, Smith and Ali foreground the relationship between language and the city, yet the ways in which they do this vary greatly. Rushdie's text dramatises the textual nature of the city by literalising the city and spelling out London as 'Ellowen Deeowen', whilst the narrative is driven by a multitude of different voices. In *The Satanic Verses* the controversial 'legends' about the prophet Mahound start out as oral interpolations, but, in the case of Islamic Koranic stories, they are subsequently 'written'. In order to understand these processes, we must first explore their interest in living speech as a powerful tool for the immigrant's various reinventions.

The place from which one speaks is outside the scriptural enterprise

Twentieth-century philosophy has been dominated by concerns about the problems regarding the status of the sign in written language. For instance, in his writing on the history of the prison system in *Discipline and Punish* (1975), Foucault makes clear that it is writing which serves as a repressive instrument: laws, decrees and registration take place in writing, which, as a device that regulates society becomes omnipresent to the extent that it determines the mental horizon of the subject completely. The centrality of language and discursive practices in our understanding of the world, and the construction of the subject, comes to dominate Foucault's investigations, which show how discourse, especially written language, 'makes' the modern mind and body of man. Drawing on the consequences of Foucault's idea that with writing, language becomes an autonomous discourse that produces the subject, Derrida states that all language in the contemporary is written language. In *Of Grammatology* (1967), Derrida declares himself a proponent of writing, rather than oral culture. Derrida argues, controversially, that '*There is nothing outside of the text* because there is no linguistic sign before writing. Without that exteriority, the very idea of the sign falls into decay.'[6] Derrida thus steps beyond the conventional Aristotelian and Saussurean conception of writing primarily as the representation of speech: 'It is not a simple analogy: writing, the letter, the sensible inscription, has always been considered by Western tradition as the body and the matter external to the spirit, to breath, to speech, and to the logos.'[7]

The Russian Formalist critic Mikhail Bakhtin provides an important, conflicting context here, because his work is obsessed with voice and speech, the heteroglossic nature of which generates a multitude of intended and non-intended meanings. Bakhtin associates orally transmitted knowledge with democratic representation; the living utterance has the potential to subvert the official culture of (historical) writing, whose hegemony for immigrant writers in particular is associated with oppression by their former colonial 'masters'. Whereas Derrida's texts are less comfortable with the indeterminacy in their illusory creation of being, Bakhtin's work forms a celebration of living speech as a carnivalesque means of (temporarily) escaping the official orders of power. This is illuminated by Homi Bhabha, who, although influenced by Derrida, is also attracted to the power of living speech for political reasons:

> Bakhtin's displacement of the author as agent results from his acknowledgement of the 'complex, multiplanar' structure of the speech genre that exists in that kinetic tension in-between two forces of contingency. The spatial boundaries of the object of utterance are contiguous in the assimilation of the other's speech; but the allusion to another's utterance produces a dialogical turn, a moment of indeterminacy in the act of 'addressivity' [...] that gives rise within the chain of speech communion to 'unmediated responsive reactions and dialogic reverberations'.[8]

Whereas Bakhtin and Bhabha advocate speech, Derrida prefers writing as a mode of meaningful communication, a position mocked also by De Certeau in *The Practice of Everyday Life* (1984), when he states that 'the new god writes, but he does not speak; he is an author, but he is not grasped corporeally in an interlocution' (*PEL* 157). De Certeau argues that after the decline of religion as a structuring model of life man prefers writing because it is tied into the comforts of the bourgeoisie: 'In a laissez-faire economy where isolated and competitive activities are supposed to contribute to a general rationality, the work of writing gives birth to both the product and its author' (*PEL* 157). Writing is tied closely to the modern systems of power, so that the voices of the industrial work places are steadily replaced by a scientific and technical discursive dominance, which in its creation of a silent strategy of history produces solitude and inertia in its subject. The result is a displaced, alien enunciation in which man becomes the subject of power and knowledge while also reducing nature (and man's connection to the universe) 'to the status of an inexhaustible fund against the background of which its products appear and from which they are wrested' (*PEL* 157).

De Certeau also suggests that such processes entail the loss of cultural history, because the form and content of oral language as a system distinct from writing contain their own, often subversive version of cultural history. In order to reclaim or reinterpret a received, repressive history, culture must necessarily be received by situating speech as the basis for the scriptural. De Certeau states that 'cultural memory (acquired through listening, through oral tradition) alone makes possible and gradually enriches the strategies of semantic questioning whose expectations the deciphering of written text refines, clarifies, or corrects' (*PEL* 168). A retrieval of the whole subject may therefore be recuperated in oral communication, which remains present as an independent site *alongside* the scriptural enterprise: '*The place from which one speaks is outside the scriptural enterprise*' (*PEL* 158). This communicative displacement causes both speech and writing to be dislodged from their position and to engage in a dialogic interaction.

Bhabha points to the historical importance of rumour for the colonial and postcolonial subject:

> The indeterminacy of rumour constitutes its importance as a social discourse. Its intersubjective, communal adhesiveness lies in its enunciative aspect. Its performative power of circulation results in the contagious spreading [...] The iterative action of rumour, its *circulation* and *contagion*, link it with panic – as one of the *affects* of insurgency. Rumour and panic are, in moments of social crisis, double sites of enunciation that weave their stories around the disjunctive 'present' or the 'not-there' of discourse [...] The indeterminate circulation of meaning as rumour or conspiracy, with its perverse, psychic affects of panic, constitutes the intersubjective realm of revolt and resistance.[9]

In relation to Bhabha's analysis of the working of speech, two key features of speech – circulation and contagion – are particularly important, but they also generate a problem for the emphasis previously placed upon the analogy between language and capital as different, yet related modes of representation. We have not yet taken into account how speech figures in such an economy: as Bhabha notes, the spoken word lies outside official circulation of signs because living speech is not composed of 'material' signs. Therefore speech is much less easily recuperable as a sellable sign than writing is: rather than being locked into a gold standard or other sources of fixed value, the spoken word forms a democratic platform of representation that easily mutates, as Bhabha notes.

It must be stressed that not only immigrant writers exploit this characteristic. Throughout this book we have seen writers harness living speech against the constraints of the written word, from Duffy's, Moorcock's and Amis's foregrounding of London's pubs to Sinclair's and Ackroyd's retrieval of lost London voices. We also saw that Sinclair exploits complex contradictions between speech and writing in his work. Yet the immigrant writers in particular are more comfortable at mastering both the city and literature by foregrounding their voices as powerful, correcting tools within the public realm. London, a metropolitan space where global capitalism rearranges socio-economic flows, is a locus particularly amenable to linguistic infections that mutate particularly on a verbal level. As Michael Hardt and Antonio Negri argue in *Empire* (2000), the 'age of globalization is the age of universal contagion'.[10] The dissemination of information and the physical and mental contact during late capitalism entails the return of such anxieties in full force, symbolised by the rapidly changing demography of London.

'He had the city in his pocket', A to Z: Salman Rushdie's Babylondon

Salman Rushdie is one of the towering figures of late twentieth- and early twenty-first-century literature, and *The Satanic Verses* is a seminal high postmodernist London novel. Rushdie's engagement with the city has been overlooked, however, because of the controversy surrounding the *fatwa* pronounced by Ayatollah Khomeini against Rushdie in 1989. In an interview, Rushdie overtly acknowledges his novel's attempt to master London:

> There's a kind of literary gripe at the moment [...] which is that there aren't any writers who are able to write about contemporary England or contemporary London. That seems to me to ignore an awful lot of writers who are doing exactly that, Martin Amis, for example. One of the things that has really irritated me about everything that's happened around *The Satanic Verses* is that nobody points out that it's a novel about London and that by far the largest chunk of *The Satanic Verses* is an attempt to describe this thing that it calls a city visible

but unseen [...] I've always been interested in writing about London, if only because I've lived here for a very long time.[11]

The Satanic Verses is a cacophonic, complex novel made up of several narrative strands, but at its heart lies Farishta's questioning of his Muslim faith after, in the opening pages of the novel, he miraculously survives a terrorist attack. Farishta's friend and rival, the voice-over artist Saladin Chamcha, also survives the terrorist attack on their flight to London, and metamorphoses into a Beelzebub-like demon. In London, Chamcha falls in love with, and marries, the personification of Englishness, Pamela Lovelace, whilst Farishta is driven towards the British capital in order to pursue his love for the daughter of two Polish émigrés, Alleluia Cone.

Rushdie's text opposes two different versions of London, generated by the difference in vision of the doubles Farishta and Chamcha: 'Where Chamcha saw attractively faded grandeur, Gibreel saw a wreck, a Crusoe-city, marooned on the island of its past, and trying, with the help of Man-Friday underclass, to keep up appearances' (*SV* 439). Rushdie's text dramatises the way in which the subject's perception and experience of the city is related to the subject's psychological make-up. Whereas Farishta is a formerly successful, revered movie star who projects his low self-esteem upon the city, the less successful Chamcha is seduced by the possibilities the city appears to offer. Farishta and Chamcha's competing voices struggle to conquer London, and in particular London's inner city, a city 'visible but unseen' because the critical situation of its ethnic minorities is kept off the political agenda. The novel's many narrative strands weave themselves around a proliferating series of racist incidents, which Farishta, imagining himself to be the Angel Azraeel, counters by setting the city on fire. This contemporary London narrative is ruptured intermittently by three prophetic visions of the traumatised, schizophrenic Farishta, who is unable to tell dream from reality, fiction from fact. In one of the dreams, the scribe Salman, who resides in the fictional city of Jahilia (a version of Mecca), confides that he has manipulated the prophet Mahound's Koranic verses by inserting apocryphal, 'satanic' rewritings, which caused the proclamation of the *fatwa*.

The Satanic Verses is a novel that sets out to master London by thinking of the city as a rewritable text. The novel's awareness of the impossibility of conceiving a London beyond the textual realm is mockingly indicated in the narrative by 'Proper London', and manifests itself in the novel's emphasis on London as a textual construct: Chamcha imagines hearing 'the noise of some approaching doom, drawing closer, letter by letter, ellowen deeowen, London' (*SV* 136). This lexical London is mirrored by Farishta's attempt to cleanse the corruption that London as Western metropolis embodies. When Farishta travels from the coastal village where he falls to earth to London he thinks: '*London shareef, here I come*. He had the city in his pocket: Geographers' London, the whole dog-eared metropolis, A to Z' (*SV* 156). The text's emphasis on pulling apart the letters of the proper noun 'London' is an indication that Rushdie is attempting to destroy the socio-economic and cultural history that is associated with the name of the former colonial centre. Simultaneously, the act of separating the letters from one another suggests that *The Satanic Verses* symbolically attempts to open up a space linguistically in order to insert the immigrant's plight. Critics such as John McLeod have pointed out Rushdie's textualisation of London, yet the subtlety of this apparently simple linguistic play is cleverer than it seems at first reading: both 'ellowen' and 'deeowen' contain the word 'wen', the nickname of London's sprawl.

The Satanic Verses's textualisation, then, sets up the reader's expectation through apparently simple metaphors, such as rewriting and translation. For instance, the novel rewrites London by inscribing Rushdie's home city, Bombay (now Mumbai), into London's fabric. Bhabha states that '[s]uch is the tropic movement of cultural translation, as Rushdie spectacularly renames London, in its Indo-Pakistani iteration, as "Ellowen Deeowen"'.[12] This translation of the West in terms of the East takes place by transplanting Bombay's Bollywood film industry and its culture of gossip into London. Rushdie's native city is described as a heavily mediated city. When Gibreel disappears you 'could say that he had stepped out of the screen, and, in life, unlike the cinema, people know that you stink' (*SV* 13). Similarly, India's newspapers speculating about Farishta's absence in 'cacophonies' (*SV* 13) and another 'illusion unmade by his absence' (*SV* 14) point to the way in which the megastar, as an embodiment of the Indian capital, invokes his own mythology.

Another way in which Rushdie 'inscribes' London with Indian culture is in his representation of Anahita Sufyan's Shaandaar Café and B&B on Brickhall Street (a linguistic transmogrification of Brick Lane and Southall, two areas associated with cultural tensions and social uprising), which functions as a hybrid, multicultural node in the East End. The café, the name of which points to the novel's attempted bridging of cross-cultural divides, is the social focal point for characters such as Hanif Johnson and Jumpy Joshi, and the subject of a police raid that inflames the ethnic tensions in this unacknowledged part of London. At the culmination of violence, the rundown and neglected (and fictional) borough of Brickhall, is described as follows:

> Low-cost high-rise housing enfolds him. *Nigger eat white man's shit*, suggest the unoriginal walls. The buildings have names: 'Isandhlwana', 'Rorke's Drift'. But a revisionist enterprise is underway, and bear, now, the names 'Mandela' and 'Toussaint l'Ouverture'. – The towers stand up on stilts, and in the concrete formlessness beneath and between them there is the howling of perpetual wind, and the eddying of debris: derelict kitchen units, deflated bicycle tyres, shards of broken doors, doll's legs, vegetable refuse extracted from plastic disposable bags by hungry cats and dogs, fast-food packets, rolling cans, shattered job prospects, abandoned hopes, lost illusions, expended angers, accumulated bitterness, vomited fear, and a rusting bath. He stands motionless while small groups of residents rush past in different directions. Some (not all) are carrying weapons. Clubs, bottles, knives. All of the groups contain white youngsters as well as black. (*SV* 461)

This passage shows how Rushdie's novel creates a dense layering of different narrative levels that are sensitive to how the London writer utters the city; how they write the languages characteristic of the city; the urban language; and, what is written on its walls. The excerpt also makes use of a Joycean list from *Ulysses* (1922) or *Finnegans Wake* (1939) that allows its author to imagine a totalising encyclopaedia of London. It is this tension between the apparent rationality of the list and the disparate elements of which it is actually composed which conveys the general confusion of the era. This confusion also shows that at the heart of the social problems lies social exclusion and class politics, which transcend racial boundaries.

'This abridged metropolis'

Rushdie's strategy is paralleled by the novel's inscription and rewriting of immigrant politics into London's history. The novel rewrites the troubled ethnic history of Brick Lane by transfiguring the Jack the Ripper mythology of the late nineteenth century in a new context that displaces the moral ground of the murders. Rushdie creates a pastiche of the original Jack the Ripper by having a copycat killer – the Granny Ripper – who becomes known for his ritual murders of elderly women. This pastiche sees the return of racially motivated violence in the East End.

John McLeod questions the utopian impulse of this textualisation, however. In *Postcolonial London* (2004) he challenges Homi Bhabha's and Ian Baucom's celebratory reading of the immigrant's inscription of himself and his culture into the fabric of London as a relatively comfortable process: 'Rushdie is much more equivocal about Gibreel's tropicalization of London which may *not* be the translative act so cherished by Bhabha and Baucom.'[13] Indeed, *The Satanic Verses* actually questions and criticises those people who are, fanatically or even militantly, driven by a desire to change, or rewrite, the world. McLeod is correct in this assumption: critics tends to translate the vibrancy and energy of Rushdie's writing into a reading of the novels as naively optimistic about the potential inscription of the immigrant into London as central symbol of the West. I would like to second and supplement McLeod's criticism by problematising his idea on two levels. First, Farishta's inscription is more complex and contradictory than he assumes because he is using the *wrong* type of maps and language, and, second, it is not writing that Rushdie uses to address the immigrants' plight but their *voices*.

Maps provide one key to understanding Farishta's failed conquering of London: 'The atlas in his pocket was his master-plan. He would redeem the city square by square, from Hockley Farm in the north-west corner of the charter area to Chance Wood in the south-east' (*SV* 326). Striking in Farishta's methodology is its totalising impetus. The *modus operandi* of Farishta, whose attempt to tame the city by imposing a systematic, rational system onto it is thwarted, forms a comment on, and ironical reversal of, the way in which the former colonial power both mapped India and imposed a foreign linguistic system on its inhabitants. In *Imagined Communities* (1983), Benedict Anderson describes not only how the development of European maps in the light of print-capitalism became a means of moulding a particular colonial people's psyche into nationhood, but also how that process was used to disconnect native peoples from their genealogical connections with the past. Anderson states that 'European-style maps worked on the basis of a totalizing classification' causing 'sites in a sacred Muslim geography' to become profaned because of their connection with Europe.[14] Whereas Richard Sennett finds that American cities and their citizens are submitted by the rationalist logic imposed upon them by governments and developers, *The Satanic Verses* presents London as a site of continued resistance to such forces, as the following reference to the caryatids of St Pancras New Church makes clear:

> But the city in its corruption refused to submit to the dominion of the cartographers, changing shape at will and without warning, making it impossible for Gibreel to approach his guest in the systematic manner that he would have preferred. Some days he would turn a corner at the end of a grand colonnade built of human flesh and covered

in skin that bled when scratched, and find himself in an uncharted wasteland, at whose distant rim he could see tall familiar buildings, Wren's dome, the high metallic spark-plug of the Telecom Tower, crumbling in the wind like sandcastles. [...] In this pandemonium of mirages he often heard laughter: the city was mocking his impotence, awaiting his surrender, his recognition that what existed here was beyond his powers to comprehend, let alone to change. (*SV* 327)

Rushdie alludes here to a figurative tradition of mapping, which is pitted against Farishta's totalising and rationalising project. London will not bend to Farishta's will: he is using the map produced by the rational, 'imperial' powers which he tries to conquer. He thus creates his own submission to their system, whilst operating a tragicomic misinterpretation of the world around him – a trope which Peter Ackroyd exploits in *The Plato Papers*. This gap between the real and its representation is reinforced by the idea that Farishta's language operates a similarly fallacious enterprise: the A–Z, the alphabet, belongs to the master, and his attempt to convert the oppressor's fallen language takes place within that language. For Rushdie, however, it is precisely this 'fallenness' of the metropolis and our language that allows us to escape the power of the master. It is in the slippage between the real and representation that we find the opportunity for subversion. In an illuminating passage in *Imaginary Homelands*, Rushdie states the following:

Fantasy, or the mingling of fantasy and naturalism, is one way of dealing with these problems. It offers a way of echoing in the form of our work the issues faced by all of us: how to build a new, 'modern', world of out an old legend-haunted civilization, an old culture which we have brought into the heart of a newer one.[15]

Rushdie's lexical London therefore becomes a semantic playing field that celebrates the attempts by its various aspiring authors to rewrite the city *metaphorically*. Rushdie's text also stages a number of simulacra to indicate how the city has become distanced from its former representations. The description of Brick Lane as a street corner in a part of town once known for its artists, radicals and men in search of prostitutes, and now 'given over to advertising personal and minor film producers' (*SV* 322) is merely an adumbration of Rushdie's mocking of the way in which the East End has come to be represented through glorified and 'authentic' images of the Victorian city under Thatcher. In the seventh chapter, 'The Angel Azraeel', Rushdie plays a complex game with the proliferation of false representations of London by incorporating 'the huge re-creation of Dickensian London' (421) at the Shepperton film studio where a musical adaptation of Dickens's *Our Mutual Friend* is adapted for the big screen by producer Sisodia: 'Here London has been altered – no, *condensed* – according to the imperatives of film' (*SV* 422). On this set the upmarket squares north of Oxford Street, which Dickens calls 'Stucconia of the Veneerings', lie shockingly adjacent to Portman Square, whilst various Podsnaps cast shady angles. And 'in this abridged metropolis' (*SV* 422), the dustman's mounds of Boffin Bower, supposedly in the near vicinity of Holloway, loom over Fledgeby's rooms in the Albany, at the heart of the West End. *The Satanic Verses* thus playfully foregrounds the novel's own comic misrepresentation of London while making a claim for the restorative powers of the imagination.

It also shows how the former empire itself feeds off its own past in ever corrupt debasement of its, in this case literary, heritage. The simulacral, Dickensian London of *The Satanic Verses* exposes how mainstream mass media project romanticised, Victorian images of the city for its inhabitants to identify with. Similar criticisms are also made, as we saw in Chapter 2, by Michael Moorcock and Raphael Samuel. Rushdie's text thus criticises the misrepresentation of classic narratives as a way of repressing the post-imperial crisis of London, for which ethnic minorities are punished. This is, once again, an ironic reversal of the techniques used by the former imperial power to dominate the colonies. Anderson explains that at first the coloniser's maps were filled with culturally specific signs and symbols which rooted the colonial consciousness in a particular geographical heritage, with specific artistic and linguistic traditions. However, this cultural specificity was steadily erased:

> In its final form all explanatory glosses could be summarily removed: lines of longitudes and latitude, place names, signs for rivers, seas, and mountains, *neighbours*. Pure sign, no longer compass to the world. In this shape, the map entered an infinitely reproducible series, available for transfer to posters, official seals, letterheads, magazine and textbook covers, table cloths, and hotel walls. Instantly recognizable, everywhere visible, the logo-map penetrated deep into the popular imagination, forming a powerful emblem for the anti-colonial nationalism being born.[16]

To escape the tyranny of the coloniser's writing and mapping, Rushdie's contribution to the reinvention of London occurs by means of his emphasis on speech. Rushdie's text opens with Gibreel Farishta and Saladin Chamcha re-enacting Satan's fall from heaven to hell in Book I of John Milton's *Paradise Lost* (1667) towards British soil from the exploding plane. Here the reader is given an abundance of signs that point to the importance of the human voice. Not only are the opening lines of the novel direct speech from Farishta – '"To be born again," sang Gibreel' (*SV* 3) – but his 'words hang crystalline in the ice white night' (*SV* 3). Besides references to Chamcha's career as a voice-over artist, lecturing, singing, Rushdie's narrator implores his reader to 'Listen' (*SV* 5). Narrative power is therefore derived from Rushdie's ambiguous use of oral speech in text: 'In that metropolis of tongues and whispers not even the sharpest ear heard anything reliable' (*SV* 14).

The emphasis on the human voice is later 'corrected' in the novel when the Islamic Koranic legends, starting out as oral interpolations, are written into the text. A specific example of this occurs in the sixth chapter, 'Return to Jahilia', where Gibreel meets the former scribe of Mahound, 'Salman', fired from his duties for his disagreement with the prophet's positioning of women in the Koran, which is regarded a masculine, bureaucratic text repressing women:

> What finally finished Salman with Mahound: the question of women; and of the Satanic verses. Listen, I'm no gossip, Salman drunkenly confided, but after his wife's death Mahound was no angel

Figure 16   The Temple Church

[...] The point about our Prophet [...] is that he didn't like his women to answer back, he went for mothers and daughters. (*SV* 366)

The drunken scribe continues to confess about his alterations of Mahound's reciting, such as his altering of the word Christian to Jew without the Prophet noticing. The point of the excerpt is that it is oral speech that undercuts the authority of Mohammed's scripture: Salman's gossip is credible because it is put in writing, triggering an ambiguous effect whereby the Koran's historical accuracy is undercut by oral communication: 'When the news got around Jahilia that the whores of The Curtain had each assumed the identity of one of Mahound's wives, the clandestine excitement of the city's males was intense' (*SV* 381).

The power of Rushdie's text lies, then, in its complex renegotiation of the relationship between speech and writing, and it is this tension which is used to cleanse the city's corruption. *The Satanic Verses* redeems the declining part of the city by having Gibreel cleanse inner London ('Camden, Brickhall, Tower Hamlets or Hackney' (*SV* 447)) as a symbolic site of injustice and municipal neglect in a fire of biblical proportions on Christmas Eve. Farishta 'wanders through a confusion of languages [...] Babylondon [...] the city becomes vague, amorphous. It is becoming impossible to describe the world' (*SV* 459). Out of frustration of being unable to describe London in its totality and to find a common language to represent the city and its citizens, he is seduced by Azraeel, the trumpet he is carrying, to set Brickhall, and Shaandaar Café, on fire:

> After the stream of fire has emerged from the mouth of his golden trumpet and consumed the approaching men, wrapping themselves in a cocoon of flame, unmaking them so completely that not even their shoes remain sizzling on the sidewalk, Gibreel understands. [...] He is the Archangel Gibreel, the Angel of Recitation, with the power of revelation in his hands. [...] This is a city that has cleansed itself in flame, purged itself by burning down to the ground. [...] There is Gibreel Farishta, walking in a world of fire. In the High Street he sees houses built of flame, with walls of fire, and flames like gathered curtains hanging at the windows. – And there are men and women with fiery skins strolling, running, milling around him, dressed in coats of fire. The street has become red hot, molten, a river the colour of blood. (*SV* 460–2)

Here, Rushdie refers directly to Enoch Powell's anti-immigrant 'River of Blood' speech, to indicate the renewed racial tensions in the East End, which has a history of attracting violent clashes between different ethnic groups. In 1936, for instance, Cable Street was the stage of a battle between Oswald Mosley's British Union of Fascists and some five hundred anti-fascists.[17] However, Rushdie's apocalypse is also an allegorical reworking of a particular event in London's history, which the author describes in the essay 'An Unimportant Fire' (1984). The essay tells of a Bangladeshi family that died from suffocation when they were unable to escape after their cramped top-floor room in a Camden B&B went up in flames. It is an indictment of Camden Council for not taking any action against such 'disease-infested firetraps'.[18] *The Satanic Verses* fictionalises this complaint to suggest that there is a great divide between society and local government, which is depicted as an impenetrable structure. In his criticism, Rushdie's text is on par with Sinclair's and Ballard's exposure of the increasing disconnection of the (local) government from the social reality of the people it is supposed to represent.

However, the re-enactment of this 'unimportant' fire shows also that Rushdie's text upsets the mystical, esoteric strategies of Ackroyd's and Sinclair's early work. Despite Rushdie's restlessly creative and linguistic transfiguration of London, the writer is first and foremost interested in addressing a contemporary social reality that, although it is certainly shaped by historical narratives and cultural discourses, needs to be made visible before corrections are possible: 'What happened here in Brickhall tonight is a socio-political phenomenon. Let's not fall into the trap of some damn mysticism. We're talking about history: an event in the history of Britain. About the process of change' (*SV* 469).

'Like a house with five thousand rooms': Hanif Kureishi's London

Hanif Kureishi is one of contemporary fiction's most popular and controversial writers, who started his career as a dramatist and screenplay writer before moving into prose fiction relatively late in his career. He was born to a Pakistani father and an English mother, and grew up in suburban Bromley, Kent, a place he vilifies, albeit with humour, in much of his work. The protagonist of his first novel, *The Buddha of Suburbia* (1990), Karim Amir, asks himself why his father had condemned 'his son to a dreary suburb of London of which it was said that when people drowned they saw not their lives but their double-glazing flashing before them'.[19] London features centrally in his work for the screen, which includes the London triptych *My Beautiful Laundrette* (1985), *Sammy and Rosie Get Laid* (1988), and *London Kills Me* (1991). The city continues to play a major role in the lives of the protagonists of his prose fiction, which also engages directly with the age of Thatcher by staging the city as theatre where a struggle between politics and Londoners plays itself out. *The Buddha of Suburbia* depicts the capital city as a place that offers potential transformation, a theme that returns in *The Black Album* (1995) – a riposte to Rushdie's *The Satanic Verses* – where London becomes the hot-bed of radicalised young British Muslims.

The Buddha of Suburbia is set in the seventies, during Britain's darkest post-imperial days, the effects of which on London and Londoners are captured very well. Towards the end of the novel, the protagonist, Karim Amir, sees the cityscape undergoing brutal changes that anticipate the climate under Thatcher: 'I walked around Central London and saw that the town was being ripped apart; the rotten was replaced by the new and the new was ugly. The gift of creating beauty had been lost somewhere. The ugliness was in the people, too. Londoners seemed to hate each other' (*BS* 258). One major issue that Kureishi's work addresses is racism in Britain; in *The Buddha of Suburbia*, one of the minor characters, Changez, becomes the victim of a racist attack by members of the National Front, which 'were happening all the time' (*BS* 225). In *The Black Album*, set in the final days of the Thatcher period, the character Zulma suggests rather naively that the new climate of enterprise is blind to ethnicity. The protagonist, Shahid, argues that 'she was a dupe, explaining what racists the Thatcherites were. She might imagine she was an intelligent, upper-class woman, but to them she'd always be a Paki and liable to be patronized. She appreciated the truth of this, but it was a colonial residue – the new money knew no colour.'[20] These passages expose the naive reading of Thatcherism as solely having an impact upon class, but they also highlight one particular characteristic of Kureishi's engagement with London, namely, his representation of the city which lies very close to historical reality. Indeed, like many authors of the period, Kureishi's writing is obsessed with capturing the spirit of the times, but the realistic, semi-documentary *modus operandi* means his work dates relatively quickly. Kureishi's London, rather than being a living character, forms mainly the backdrop, the décor to Londoners' lives – a self-conscious metaphor for the theatrical aspect of the city that the work explores.

At the heart of Kureishi's thinking about London lies a tension between suburb and the city, between centre and periphery, which he uses as structuring devices for meditating on a variety of issues, including sexuality, class and the private and collective identity in contemporary

Britain. The suburbs serve as a reservoir for everything that is to be despised, and in this sense Kureishi's writing fits into this tradition that views the suburban middle classes in Matthew Taunton's words as 'politically conservative and fiercely hostile to socialism'.[21] In *The Buddha of Suburbia* Karim grows up in Bromley, where the marriage of his parents is breaking down: 'But divorce wasn't something that would occur to them. In the suburbs people rarely dreamed of striking out for happiness. It was all familiarity and endurance: safety and security were the reward of dullness' (*BS* 8). In *The Black Album* Shahid also chooses the city, despite its dangers and potential corruption, to the country. When he walks down a dark housing estate amidst burned rubbish: 'It was filthy, and some thug might easily have sprung out with a knife. But he wasn't apprehensive. Rather the spooky shadows of the city than the thin sunlight of the countryside' (*BA* 13).

Kureishi's binary division is a false one, however. His work is anarchic in its aims at upsetting, or 'deconstructing', stable categories because it evades subscription to or evasion of any fixed political or ideological paradigm, whether they are offered by the New Left or Thatcher. Kureishi's hateful depiction of the suburb as a dreary island of the self-contented bourgeoisie, as well as his division of his novel in two halves – 'In the Suburbs' and 'In the City' – are set up deliberately to tempt the reader into a comfortable, knowing position. In an interview, Kureishi alluded to the idea that his conditioning by suburban values had actually made it very hard for him to transform himself: 'Whether the suburbs are out of me is another matter. I certainly wanted to come to London to be with people I thought were cultured. Culture is rather sneered upon in the suburbs. You're considered to be getting above yourself or it's seen as pretentious or financially not viable. So yeah, I got out.'[22] Kureishi does not provide us with an answer to this question, yet a careful analysis of his fictional narratives suggests indeed that the binary division between city and suburb is deceptive, and deliberately so.

Karim wonders, for instance, whether his father 'really did have anything to offer other people, or if he would turn out to be merely another suburban eccentric' (*BS* 22). This paradoxical tautology – suburbia is geographically removed from the centre yet the behaviour and values of its citizens are a powerful factor in determining social and moral norms and stereotypes – undermines the middle-class rules of propriety that are supposed to operate in suburbia. Simultaneously, many of the bohemian city dwellers Karim befriends are also described as eccentrics, which partly effaces the idea that otherness is geographically determined.

When Karim finally manages to escape from Bromley, he moves to a flat in West Kensington, from which he starts to map his surroundings:

> So this was London at last, and nothing gave me more pleasure than strolling around my new possession all day. London seemed like a house with five thousand rooms, all different; the kick was to work out how they all connected, and eventually to walk through all of them. Towards Hammersmith was the river and its pubs, full of hollering middle-class voices; and there were the secluded gardens which fringed the river along Lower Mall and the shaded stroll along the towpath to Barnes. This part of London seemed like the country to me, with none of the disadvantages, no cows or farmers. (*BS* 126)

For Karim, this part of London provides the perfect transition into his new life as Londoner because the area merges urbanity with features associated with the countryside. Karim's class-consciousness is also strikingly present: he is conditioned to think about, and judge, society in terms of class, which is one sign that he is unable to avoid thinking in perceived social categories. Whereas Kensington is expensive and exclusive, West Kensington is middle class, and associated with numerous celebrities, including Ghandi and Christine Keeler but also IRA bombers: 'West Kensington was an area in between, where people stayed before moving up, or remained because they were stuck' (*BS* 127). This part of London is reminiscent of Bromley itself, as Sukdev Sandhu suggests in *London Calling*: 'A borough ten miles south of London Bridge, and a twenty-minute train journey from Victoria, Bromley has long been seen as quintessentially suburban. Neither truly urban nor rural, it is, for its critics, marooned somewhere in-between, a lingering and painful half-life.'[23] Half-life is an apt description: Kureishi's suburbanites are depicted as spiritual zombies, yet Sandhu's term also point out that suburbia is an in-between space. By drawing on Raymond Williams's work, John Clement Ball suggests indeed that suburbia is a 'hybrid space between nature and community, country and city', a 'spatial in-betweenness'.[24] It is therefore curious that Ball subscribes to the binary division set up by Kureishi, as Karim seems to be at home in unconventional spaces that undermine bourgeois safety and comforts.

The metaphor that Amir uses to understand how London works – the house – provides us with an interesting paradox in Kureishi's thinking about the city and its representations. Sandhu notes that Kureishi's work is interested in a celebratory depiction of spaces other than the comfortable bourgeois home, such as mansions and arty flats 'like Fish's flat, which I was borrowing, an impersonal but comfortable place a bit like a hotel' (*BS* 259):

> Kureishi rejects the idea that having a stable, well-decked-out house is an important signifier of a person's value. Bricks and mortar may supply a degree of rootedness, but they can't guarantee happiness. It may be that the Londoners Kureishi shows opting out of this system are rather privileged. To some extent their degentrification is a lifestyle choice, the traditional messiness that is the luxury of well-connected dropouts and would-be bohos. Still, by depicting – with sympathy and approval – crumbling households, unorthodox communities and designs for living that are contingent and slung together, Kureishi offers a vision of domesticity hateful to both Thatcherite and traditional Asian notions of propriety.[25]

Sandhu's assertion is perceptive, yet there is an equally subtle, paradoxical reading here. Essentially, the metaphor Karim uses to understand the city is itself the product of the middle-class thinking that conditions him: even though the house has five thousand rooms, it is still a house, suggesting that he is unable to escape the shadow cast over him by his upbringing. Thus *The Buddha* should not be read as a Bildungsroman, but as an anti-Bildingsroman, as the recording of a failure to develop into an adult who is able to transcend his rather childish tantrum against suburbia. In this sense *The Buddha* reads more like Kureishi's confession of youthful misperception which the author is correcting. This tension we find in the final paragraph of the novel: 'And so I sat in the centre of this old city that I loved [...] I was surrounded by people I loved, and felt happy and miserable at the same time. I thought of what a mess everything had been, but that it wouldn't always be that way' (*BS* 284). The dogged insistence on keeping the idea of the centre clashes with Kureishi's interest in transgressive experiences that in effect efface the city–suburb opposition.

This tension in Kureishi's conceptualisation of London is also present on another level, namely, in the form the city is given by his texts. One sign that Kureishi's text is severely conflicted in its representation of London is that it is unable to violate the realist rules of representation which it sets up for itself. Whereas Rushdie violently tears apart London by means of linguistic play and mixtures of sign system, Kureishi is in a sense replicating the nineteenth-century city and its realist representations. The *Bildungsroman* is primarily linear in terms of its narration, and the descriptions hardly probe beyond the surface of characters' actions, inviting the reader to infer the psychological development of the characters.

Again, the house metaphor used by Kureishi above is illuminating, as it relates to Kureishi's work in the 1980s as a screenwriter. Another writer who moved into the world of film in the late seventies is Ian McEwan, and his foreword to his adaptation of Timothy Mo's novel *Sour Sweet* (1982) for the big screen gives an illuminating account of the spatial relationship between the novel and screenwriting as different art forms:

> There were times during the writing of this screenplay when I thought of Timothy Mo's *Sour Sweet*, as a splendid mid-nineteenth century mansion with many well-lit, well-appointed, well-heated rooms furnished, in the custom of the period, almost to bursting point. I am the hooligan builder [...] Already I have taken my sledge-hammer to the front door [...] Even as a novelist, I would be suspicious. As the modernizer, the adapter, I have nothing but contempt. [...] By the time I am finished, the house will be a roofless shack. There are rooms, whole staircases to be demolished. There are characters to be evicted [...] When I am through with them, these jokers will have nothing to show but what they say or do, and there won't be much of that.[26]

This demonstrates that the relationship between artistic content and form is historically, and geographically, determined. To put it crudely: the novel emerges in Europe in the early eighteenth century and finds its perfection in the nineteenth-century tradition of the sprawling, naturalistic magnum opuses chronicling the life of an entire family and society. Simultaneously this form shares its development with the rise of the modern city, whose growth is underpinned by industrialisation from the early eighteenth century onwards. Film and television belong primarily to America and the twentieth century, and exhibit that epoch's and country's characteristics: an accelerated and fragmented experience of a shrinking, globalised world with at its heart the atomised, uprooted individual. McEwan compares the genre of the screenplay, mockingly, to 'a roofless shack', as the novel form is, in terms of its 'architexture', and prestige, a superior art form.

Kureishi is less certain about the supposed superiority of particular art forms than McEwan, and does not have a clear preference for one particular form. This makes his understanding of the city different from that of Rushdie, McEwan or Amis, who also believe in the novel as the pre-eminent form of capturing the city. In an interview, Kureishi responded to the question whether he considers himself first and foremost a novelist as follows:

> When I was a young man I thought I'd give it all a go, and see which one I liked best, and then after a time I'd settle down and do any one of these things. But actually, I enjoy working in all forms. I enjoy doing films because I enjoy working with the directors. I like novels because it's so private and you can do anything, and I like writing short stories because you can do them in a week.[27]

This makes it seem that Kureishi is interested in London mainly for the subject matter it provides the artist. Yet, at the level of form, we see in his work a similar voracious, or even a deliberate indecisiveness in choosing a particular genre that expresses a desire – as his repetition of 'enjoy' suggests – to master the city. Karim's drive for possession of the centre – the word that is repeated ad infinitum (cf. *BS* 148) – is a fantasy. Karim finds out that there is no materiality to possess, or occupy, because London does not have a centre, there is no 'inside': the city's sheer size makes everyone an outsider. Paradoxically, London does *function* as an imagined centre, and we should locate Kureishi's

Figure 17   Sir Alfred Gilbert's Eros, Piccadilly Circus

understanding of the city as a process that operates a slippage between the imagined city as a generator of desire and actual, lived experience.

This was the extent of my London: Eros and the City

Roland Barthes has noted that 'the city center is felt as the place of exchange of social activities and [...] erotic activities in the broader sense of the word', and traditionally this has certainly been true of London.[28] One may think of Casanova's London as a hunting ground for satisfying his sexual fantasies, but also Virginia Woolf's *Mrs Dalloway* (1925) and Nell Dunn's *Up the Junction* (1962), which turn the city into maps of desire. In his London biography, Peter Ackroyd has an illuminating passage on the statue of Eros at Piccadilly Circus, first unveiled in 1893:

> The statue of Eros has, after all, commanded a strange power. The city itself is a form of promiscuous desire, with its endless display of other streets and other people affording the opportunity of a thousand encounters and a thousand departures. The very strangeness of London, its multifarious areas remaining unknown even to its inhabitants, includes the possibility of chance and sudden meetings. To be alone or solitary, a characteristic symptom of city life, is to become an adventurer in search of brief companionship; it is also the mark of the predator. The anonymity or impersonality of London life is itself the source of sexual desire, where the appetite can be satisfied without the usual constraints of a smaller society. So the actual vastness of London encourages fantasy and illimitable desire. (*LB* 379)

Ackroyd illuminates some of the erotic aspects of the metropolis: the anonymity it provides allows for illicit encounters; the urban loneliness breeds a desire for human contact; its unknowability creates absences that invite their discovery and fire our imagination; the city is a place that multiplies encounters, and thus human, and potentially sexual, contact. And London in particular has its own curious sexual qualities: its labyrinthine spaces may be experienced as exciting. London's long history of fiction and myths is perhaps another source of arousal: the city and its fictions offer themselves as an imaginary space where the self may be reinvented.

In Sam Selvon's chronicle of Caribbean immigrants arriving in the London of the 1950s, *The Lonely Londoners* (1956), it is indeed loneliness that becomes either a destructive force, or a source that generates sexual energy which transforms the self. An immigrant who is constantly wooing the (white) ladies, Sir Galahad, acknowledges the statue of Eros on Piccadilly Circus as an important node within the city; he describes the square as follows:

> Always, from the first time he went there to see Eros and the lights, that circus have magnet for him, that circus represents life, that circus is the beginning and ending of the world. Every time he go there, he have the same feeling like when he see it first at night, drink coca-cola, any time is guinness time, Bovril and the fireworks, a million flashing lights, gay laughter, the wide doors of the theatres, the huge posters, everready batteries, rich people going into tall hotels, people going to the theatre, people sitting and standing and walking and talking and laughing and buses and cars and Galahad Esquire, in all this, standing in the big city, in London. Oh Lord.[29]

Galahad's rampant desire places sexuality, and the city as a place for sexual conquest, at the centre of the world. Selvon's description of Piccadilly Circus also becomes a social critique that ties sexuality into the spectacle of the city, whilst also pointing out its socio-economic dimensions. The arousing aspects of the city as an overwhelmingly sensory and sensual structure are translated into the commercial aspects of the city, as the references to Coca-Cola, Bovril and Guinness suggest. Indeed, by literally buying into the commercial sign systems Galahad (thinks he) is able to occupy a place in modernity, of which sexual encounters are an affirmative symbol.

Love, physical pleasure and sexuality are some of the central occupations within Kureishi's conception of London. This interest sets his work apart from many other authors of his generation; whereas for many male writers love, carnality and sexuality are the well-trodden *topoi* of the classics, Kureishi renegotiates them as topics that require renewed and often humorous investigation. During the marital breakdown of the Amirs, Karim's father, Haroon – the titular hero – becomes engaged in an affair with Eva, whilst Karim himself becomes the youthful lover of the sexually voracious Jamilia. Karim is simultaneously involved in some sort of sexual relationship with Eva's son, Charlie. After Karim moves to London, he soon learns to become what Ackroyd qualifies as a 'predator' with an unceasing sexual appetite, which he quenches with various people, and his fellow actress, Eleanor, in particular. The description of the difference between, and connection of, sex and love, illuminates the different ways in which the city evokes desire. When

Karim starts a relationship with Eleanor, this is primarily a physical relationship, which he juxtaposes to his idea of love:

> Sex I loved; like drugs, it was play, headiness. I'd grown up with kids who taught me sex was disgusting. It was smells, smut, embarrassment and horse laughs. But love was too powerful for me. Love swam right through the body, into valves, muscles, bloodstream, while sex, the prick, was always outside. I did want then, in a part of myself, to dirty the love I felt, or, somehow, to extract it from my body. (*BS* 188)

Karim foregrounds himself as a psychologically fragmented structure and it is this divided self which generates a multidirectionality of desire; a mobility of lust that drives him towards various sexual partners. The satisfaction of his bodily desires and the eroticism is also generated by the more abstract qualities of the metropolis: 'The city blew the windows of my brain wide open. But being in a place so bright, fast and brilliant made you vertiginous with possibility: it didn't necessarily help you grasp those possibilities' (*BS* 126). The erotic nature of the city, for Kureishi, lies in its foregrounding of contingency: potential is potency, a potent aphrodisiac, which he pits against any rigid social paradigms and middle class *mores* in particular.

Julian Barnes shares Kureishi's interest in love, bodily pleasures and sexuality, and both their first novels are conspicuously similar in their translation of the centre–suburb tension into terms of sexuality. Published a decade before *The Buddha*, Barnes's *Metroland* (1980) chronicles the story of Chris and Toni who grow up in a suburban area to the north-west of London served by the western stretch of the Metropolitan Line – hence the name Metroland – a place associated with the comforts of homeownership, family values and conformity. Like Kureishi, Barnes appears hostile to suburbia, and he aligns himself with the literary and cultural elite, including poets and novelists like the modernists E. M. Forster and T.S. Eliot, Graham Greene and social commentators like C. F. G. Masterman and T. W. H. Crosland. The overt intertexual network of *Metroland* plays up this suburb-bashing tradition, contrasting the confidence of a self-conscious artistic culture against the city to the purported disinterest in culture and the political conservatism of the suburbs.

Metroland presents us with a renegotiation of sexuality in geographical terms. Barnes's rebellious Toni offers a paradoxical, counterintuitive interpretation of sex in the suburbs:

> London, he explained, was the centre of power and industry and money and culture and everything valuable, important and good; it

was therefore, *ex hypothesi*, the centre of sex [...] But in the suburbs, Toni went on [...] you are in a strange intermediate area of sexual twilight. You might think of the suburbs – Metroland, for instance – as being erotically soporific; yet the grand itch animated the most unlikely people. You never were where you were [...] It was here, he maintained, that the really interesting bits of sex took place.[30]

Even the radical, left-wing idealism of Toni allows for his ambivalence to suburban spaces when it comes to sexuality, which is mirrored by the more conservative Chris who also transcends the boundaries of suburban propriety in *Metroland*. This inversion of conventional perceptions of the suburbs, which we also get in Ballard's radical work, is not present in Kureishi's novels. When Haroon leaves with Eva, the new couple move to the city centre to pursue a bohemian lifestyle.

Kureishi's work continuously and persistently fulminates against the sexual aridity of the suburbs, and posits the city as the exclusive site of a genuine understanding of desire and sexuality. John McLeod puts it as follows:

The alleged freedom, multiracial tolerance, cultural novelty, sexual licence and narcotic adventurousness of the city find its musical expression in the bongos of Hyde Park and, significantly, in the music of the Doors. Indeed, in citing their song, 'Light My Fire', [Kureishi] emphasizes London's popular-cultural Promethean possibilities in sexual terms as a form of 'longing'. This also reminds us that some of Kureishi's most important means for expressing the city's subversive agency include sexuality and youth, deemed key elements of that 'inferno of pleasure and madness'.[31]

It is therefore all the more striking that Kureishi seems to have a traditional attitude in his understanding of the relationship between desire and the city.

McLeod's interpretation of the city as the place of desire does misrepresent the subtlety of what Kureishi's novels are doing. McLeod's quotation from the novel suggests that the sexual pleasure and excitement Karim finds in the city is derived from his own experience. Yet the original passage he quotes from comes right at the end of the first part, 'In the Suburbs', and runs in full as follows:

In bed before I went to sleep I fantasized about London and what I'd do there when the city belonged to me. There was a sound that London had. It was, I'm afraid, people in Hyde Park, playing bongos with their hands; there was also the keyboard on the Doors's 'Light My Fire'. There were kids dressed in velvet cloaks who lived free lives; there were bookshops with racks of magazines printed without capital letters or the bourgeois disturbance of full stops; there were shops selling all the records you could desire; there were parties where girls and boys you didn't know took you upstairs and fucked you; there were all the drugs you could use. You see, I didn't ask much of life; this was the extent of my longing. (*BS* 121)

Given the positioning of this passage *before* Karim's move to London, we are to assume that his image of London is constructed pre-emptively through his imagination, in which we find a dense stratification of sources. The projection of London before he sleeps suggests that the metropolis is, to a large degree, an imaginary place interspersed unconsciously with dreams of sexual conquests. Simultaneously the city is constructed through the collective, popular imagination in which (mass) media play a major role. Indeed, the artificial construction of this imagined city is stressed by the retroactive correction of his London fantasy, as 'I'm afraid' suggests. In this sense there is a discrepancy between the young Karim, whose is driven by an almost infantile desire to possess the city completely, and the mature Karim who retrospectively narrates the novel. Kureishi's novel argues that London is partly a projection of one's inner longings, a city of the mind.

What happens in this slippage between the fantasy and 'the real' should therefore be located in an understanding of the non-material force that drives Kureishi's characters: desire. Karim's longing for mastery of the city runs parallel to the attempted discovery of his own potentiality. Karim's profession as an actor gives us a clue to how this process structures his identity; and the stage director Pyke teaches him about the paradoxical nature of acting:

[Y]ou are trying to convince people that you're someone else, that this is not-me. The way to do his, he said: when in character, playing not-me, you have to be yourself. To make your not-self real you have to steal from your authentic self. A false stroke, a wrong note, anything pretended, and to the audience you are as obvious as a Catholic naked in a mosque. The closer you play to yourself the better. Paradox of paradoxes: to be someone else successfully you must be yourself! (*BS* 219–20)

It is Karim's move to the city, and the chance to discard his former self, that offers him the opportunities to enact this paradox. Yet, at the same time, this process of identification runs parallel to the immigrants' structuring of their identity, as Bhabha stresses in his analysis of the psychology of the immigrant Other:

> The emergence of the human subject as socially and physically authenticated depends on the *negation* of an originary narrative fulfilment, or of an imaginary coincidence between individual interest or instinct and the General Will. Such binary, two-part identities function in a kind of narcissistic reflection of the One in the Other, confronted in the language of desire by the psychoanalytic process of identification. For identification, identity is never an a priori, nor a finished product; it is only ever the problematic process of access to an image of totality.[32]

Bhabha's analysis of the immigrant identity is heavily influenced by Lacan, who reconfigures Freudian psychoanalysis rooted in an imagined wholeness of the subject, the ego. Lacan offers the self not as a fragmented structure that is aiming to achieve some kind of wholeness, but he acknowledges that the self remains a continuous process, a fluid construction because the imagined wholeness itself is merely a fantasy. The immigrant's constant tussle between One and Other makes the immigrant therefore suitable to act out, and adapt to, different identities. This conception of identity is affirmed by Sahid in *The Black Album*: 'There was no fixed self; surely our several selves melted and mutated daily? There had to be innumerable ways of being in the world. He would spread himself out, in his work and in love, following his curiosity' (*BA* 228).

The playing out of these particular kinds of narrated identities – and the exploitation of difference – make Kureishi's work particularly suitable for undermining any seemingly stable set of ideologies through its denial of the authority of the centre. Bart Moore-Gilbert states:

> The Left is also acknowledged as having been an important focus in the creation of a 'long front' of different kinds of oppressed constituencies against the dominant order. Even Thatcher's enterprise culture, so enthusiastically embraced by Nassar in *Laundrette*, promised a new (if spurious) kind of community embracing all sectors of society. Kureishi's scepticism about all these formations is based primarily on a conviction that their conception of a 'common culture' is achieved at the cost of denigration of, or blindness to, difference.[33]

Kureishi's work, then, warns against the paradoxically homogenising forces of multiculturalism disguised as oppressive narratives of assimilation and integration by suggesting that love and sexuality are forces generated by the (imagined) city and transcend any reductive political ideologies.

In this sense, Kureishi pits the sexual imagination against any imprisoning paradigm, in which the city functions as an important catalyst. Ball finds that *The Buddha* has an important function within Kureishi's wider oeuvre as it subverts earlier representations of London as a potentially utopian space of cultural diversity:

> *The Buddha of Suburbia* thus qualifies and ironizes the author's previous constructions of London as an enabling space inclusive of peoples and processes that represents 'the world'. However cosmopolitan it may seem, however demographically diverse and detached from Britain, Kureishi's 'London' will at a certain point flatten that world into a spectacle. Though seeming to compress world-space, it cannot substitute for the world since there will always be psychic and geographic gaps that only the real traversing of cultural and physical distance can overcome.[34]

Ball's emphasis on 'real' spaces is rather odd: as we saw, Karim's conception of London is already constructed and in place before his arrival in the city, and the city as an imagined, desired structure always operates a gap between the real and fantasy. Indeed, at the end of *The Black Album* Shahid and his girlfriend Deedee spend time by the sea, and it gives us an image of the protagonist, ultimately, being imprisoned behind the double-glazing he so desperately wanted to smash whilst paradoxically suggesting that it is exactly the frame it provides that we need to see ourselves clearly:

> He looked out of the window; the air seeming to be clearer. It wouldn't be long before they would be walking down to the sea. There was somewhere she fancied for lunch. He didn't have to think about anything. They looked at one another as if to say, what new adventure this? (*BA* 230)

9

'Kyan you imagine dat?': The New London Languages of Zadie Smith and Monica Ali

The new middle ground

Zadie Smith and Monica Ali joined the immigrant voices of Rushdie and Kureishi, engaging with London after New Labour had come to power. The overwhelming critical and popular reception of their first novels, *White Teeth* (2000) and *Brick Lane* (2003) respectively, at the beginning of the new millennium, demonstrates that these writers have had a major impact upon the contemporary British literary imagination, in which the capital city plays a central role. Smith's critically acclaimed, popular, prize-winning novel turned her, almost overnight, into a global literary superstar. Ali also shot to fame though her novel evoked considerable protest from the (male) Brick Lane Bengali population about their representation, which reignited when the novel was turned into a film by Sarah Gavron in 2007.

The work of both authors consciously shifts away from postmodern literature's obsession with the representation of the city-as-text in favour of a more grounded vision that reasserts the city's materiality, a move that is complemented by the modified realism in which both writers work. Whereas Michael Moorcock made a bold claim for the power of fiction to be able to change social reality, the protagonist of *White Teeth*, Irie Jones, is more sceptical of the utopian powers of the literary imagination. She observes 'lives that were stranger than fiction, funnier than fiction, crueller than fiction, and with consequences that fiction can never have'.[1] Whereas in Rushdie's and Kureishi's work we are presented with a delirious, ecstatic image of a London that offers itself up to be conquered, in Smith's and Ali's work we find a more sober approach. Ali in particular embraces a quietude and carefulness in her depiction of Britain's multicultural society at the beginning of the twenty-first century.

The Londons created by Smith and Ali are nonetheless different from one another. Smith's vibrant and energetic novel is the product of her time at Cambridge, 'the regurgitation of the kind of beautiful, antiquated, left-side-of-the-brain liberal arts education', yet it also coincided with, and captured the euphoria of, Tony Blair's and New Labour's victory in 1997, the year Smith graduated.[2] Whether this was a happy accident or not, Smith and her novel went on to become the New Labourite dream model, a representation of how the multicultural society could triumph, at least in the imagination. In fact, it might be said that *White Teeth* offers itself as the new middle ground – a term that Lorna Sage uses to describe the realism of women writers such as Iris Murdoch and Margaret Drabble – that would allow the heterogeneous, diverse communities to be able to live and flourish together.[3] Published after 9/11 and in a new climate of uncertainty, Ali's novel is more cautious about the possible success of the multicultural society. Despite its muted tone, however, the novel is a criticism of the various ways in which New Labour failed to help socially deprived and oppressed groups. Simultaneously, the novel functions as a 'manual' that supports New Labour's model of multicultural Britain by showing the female, Muslim immigrant how she can gain access to the modernity often denied to them by their male-dominated environment.

'Kyan you imagine dat?' Zadie Smith's orthographies of the London immigrant

Zadie Smith descends from a Jamaican mother and an English father, but she is a Londoner born and bred. After spending her early childhood in the north-west London borough of Brent, a multicultural, predominantly working-class area, she soon moved to and was raised in Willesden. From this particular London territory Smith has written three novels: the rapturously received *White Teeth*, the less lauded *The Autograph Man* (2002) and the critically praised transatlantic comic epic and homage to E. M. Forster, *On Beauty* (2005). What is most striking about her debut novel is the energy and exuberance with which she depicts her fictional world, but also the sheer size of the work, and its impressive, complex engagement with history.

Although *White Teeth* offers, according to Dominic Head, 'an end-of-millennium vision that self-consciously promotes a utopian hybridity', the optimism of Smith's novel is actually much more ambiguous.[4]

White Teeth in fact voices an uncertainty about the future of multiculturalism. Set mainly in the seventies and in the run-up to the new millennium, Smith's novel is a complex interweaving of different strands of narrative that speculates on the development and (mal)functioning of multicultural society. The novel chronicles the lives of three generations of families living in the suburb of Willesden Green, and is focalised though the half-white, half-black teenager Irie Jones. She is the daughter of Clare Bowden, a Jamaican immigrant, and Archie Jones, a white Englishman. Archie's best friend is the Pakistani Samad Iqbal, who is married to Alsana and the father of twin sons, Magid and Millat. Samad feels that English life is damaging his ethics, and decides to send Magid to Bangladesh to give him a pure Islamic education – he returns an atheist, very British, and interested in science, whilst his brother turns to Islamic fundamentalism. The third family are the Oxford-educated, Jewish-Catholic Chalfens, with the father Marcus, a genetic scientist working on a highly controversial transgenic FutureMouse©-project, employing Irie and Magid, alienating his own son, Josh.

In order to understand the London we encounter in the novel, it is first necessary to investigate the general rules of representation. The novel begins in 1974, when Archie, after a failed suicide attempt, meets Clara at a party. The narration of this encounter is illuminating because it reveals how Smith moves away from Rushdie's magical realism towards a reassertion of the boundary between the real and the fictional:

> But first a description: Clara Bowden was beautiful in all senses except maybe, by virtue of being black, the classical. Clara Bowden was magnificently tall, black as ebony and crashed sable, with hair plaited in a horseshoe which pointed up when she felt lucky, down when she didn't. At this moment it was up. It is hard to know whether that was significant. (*WT* 23)

We are given a clear set of representational rules. We are back in the realm of realism, where factual description of physical appearances allows the reader to deduce the character's inner world. The plaited hair, for instance, acts as signifier of Clara's mental constitution. At the same time, this traditional realistic device is undercut by both the self-conscious foregrounding of the description *as* a description, and by the narrator's irony. The realism is further challenged in the final line, which stresses the uncertainty of this late twentieth-century world: there are limits to knowing the world and ourselves.

The scene that follows continues to challenge any comfortable idea of what the narrative status of this represented world is. Smith appropriates a cliché from the history of narratology – the Cinderella fairy tale in which a poor, plain girl transforms herself into a mesmerising beauty – and mixes it up with classic Hollywood iconography. When Archie looks at Clare floating down the stairs, the crowd goes silent:

> In real life he had never seen it. But it happened with Clara Bowden. She walked down the stairs in slow motion, surrounded by afterglow and fuzzy lighting. And not only was she the most beautiful thing he had ever seen, she was also the most comforting woman he had ever met. [...] She gave him a wide grin that revealed possibly her one imperfection. A complete lack of teeth in the top of her mouth. (*WT* 24)

The description self-consciously sets up an epiphanic moment worthy of fairy tales and Hollywood cinema: fiction is threatening to overrun reality. Yet, the scene turns into a moment of deflation, which punctures and challenges the representative power of fictional narration. This novel is an attempt to somehow restore realism, and to bring back materiality. Smith is clearly removing herself from Rushdie's euphoric attempt to work at the level of representation, and she constantly foregrounds the gap between the immigrant experience and writing: '"The gulf between books and experience,"' intones the bosom friend of Irie's father Archie, Samad Iqbal, solemnly, '"is a lonely ocean"' (*WT* 240).

The status of writing is questioned even further through a comic, visual device that Smith borrows from Lawrence Sterne's *Tristram Shandy* (1760–7). The text employs *Shandy*'s inquisitive graphic deformations by inserting boxes, questionnaires, a family tree, stories and jokes that break up her narrative. Whereas Sterne's anti-novel represents the traumatic breakdown of linearity, realism and (literary) conventions, Smith is seeking a non-mythical totality while questioning the meaning of (writing within) a fragmented society in which TV and Hollywood render what she in a riposte to an attack by James Wood called 'image-led, speechless times'.[5] The deformations function not only as violent disruptions of the smooth reading process that point to the artificial status of this text's attempt to capture historical truth, but they are highly specific criticisms of contemporary society in which mass media prescribes ideal beauty for women (*WT* 265), and the implicitly racist distribution of scholarships in modern Great Britain (*WT* 250).

The London we are presented with in *White Teeth* also differs vastly from the ones we encountered in the work of Rushdie and Sinclair.

Whereas they are interested in linguistic ingenuity and the subversive potential of myth, Smith's territory is realistic, and more firmly aligned with that of Amis and McEwan. This shift can be accurately pinpointed by looking at Lefebvre's categorisation of the various relationships between writing and the city:

> There is the *utterance of the city*: what happens and takes place in the street, in the squares, in the voids, what is said there. There is the *language* of the city: particularities specific to each city which are expressed as discourses, gestures, clothing, in the words and use of words by the inhabitants. There is *urban language*, which one can consider as language of connotations, a secondary system and derived within the denotative system [...] Finally there is the *writing* of the city: what is inscribed and prescribed on its walls, in the layout of places and their linkages, in brief, the *use of time* in the city by its inhabitants.[6]

Smith's London is distinctive because she moves away from the post-modern representation of the city as text and shifts to an interest in the various languages of the city as described by Lefebvre.

This shift still affects the narrator's, and our, vision of London because the restless narrative breaks up our own perception of the metropolis, and the resulting fragmentation mimics the contemporary experience. In the following excerpt, Clara Bowden moves house from Lambeth to 'a newly acquired, heavily mortgaged, two-storey house in Willesden Green' (*WT* 46), in 1974:

> Travelling in the front passenger seat of the removal van, she'd seen the high road and it had been ugly and poor and familiar [...] but then at the turn of a corner suddenly the road had exploded in green-ery, beautiful oaks, the houses got taller, wider and more detached, she could see parks, she could see libraries. And then abruptly the trees would be gone, reverting back into bus-stops as if by the strike of some midnight bell; a signal which the houses too obeyed, trans-forming themselves into smaller, stairless dwellings that sat *splay* opposite derelict shopping arcades, those peculiar lines of establish-ments that include, without exception,
> one defunct sandwich bar still advertising breakfast
> one locksmith uninterested in marketing frills (KEYS CUT HERE)
> and one permanently shut unisex hair salon, the proud bearer of some unspeakable pun (*Upper Cuts* or *Fringe Benefits* or *Hair Today, Gone Tomorrow*).

It was a lottery driving along like that, looking out, not knowing whether one was about to settle down for life amongst the trees or amidst shit. (*WT* 47)

This passage emphasises both the repetitious nature of London's (commercial) spaces, as the listing suggests, but simultaneously it stresses the heterogeneous, diverse nature of London: high roads *explode* into greenery and stairless dwellings sit *splay* opposite shopping arcades, etc. The experience of reading this passage also suggests that it is the city rather than the spectator, still at the centre, that moves. The play with form, such as the indentation of the list, replicates this spatial discomfort on the page, whilst Smith also emphasises the writing *onto* London. The reference to the lottery suggests that the modern metropolis also foregrounds the contingency within the urban environment, which undercuts the subject's autonomy and agency. Smith's text appears to make the argument that London's multifarious geography and architecture is perfect, then, for the testing out of the problems of multicultural society in the late twentieth century. London's spaces *invoke* the clashing and connection of different social and ethnic groups. Smith's London is therefore at once a violent place whilst, paradoxically, also safe, enclosed space, a laboratory, a thought that is reinforced by the teleological drive of the novel, which brings together several disparate social groups at the end.

Such spatial violence also expresses itself in different forms of Smith's representation of spoken language. *White Teeth* portrays a London where the relationship between the city and its 'mongrel' languages creates new, utopian spaces where the multicultural society is tested out. The novel incorporates a host of different registers, accents and patois, and Smith is particularly adept at representing what could be called the orthographies of London's immigrants. When Clara is pregnant with Irie in 1974, for instance, she says: 'And I arks the doctor what it will look like, half black an' half white an' all dat bizness [...] Dere's even a chance it may be blue-eyed! Kyan you imagine dat?' (*WT* 67). Here we see the orthography of the Jamaican immigrant, Smith's manipulation of signs on the page to represent a particular type of immigrant *speech* in order to undercut the hegemony of received pronunciation.

Smith's exploitation of, or working in, this orthographical tradition goes back to earlier writers such as Sam Selvon and Jean Rhys, both of whom foreground the (Caribbean) immigrant's struggle with the English language by deliberately highlighting the grammatical mistakes and poor vocabulary through semi-phonetic representation of speech on the page. Selvon's *The Lonely Londoners* (1956), the story of disillusioned West Indians living in west London without connecting with the autochthonous Londoners, continually reminds the reader of the narrator's 'poor' command of the host language by mistakes in the tense and case: 'When Moses sit down and pay his fare he take out a white handkerchief and blow his nose.'[7] Jean Rhys's short story 'Let them Call it Jazz' (1960) is narrated by the homeless and alcoholic Caribbean immigrant Selina, who is taken to Holloway prison. She distrusts books: 'One day a nice girl comes around with books and she give me two, but I don't want to read so much. Beside one is about a murder, and the other is about a ghost and I don't think it's all like those books tell you.'[8] This distrust of written language becomes intertwined with the prison space, suggesting that colonial history is carefully orchestrated through discursive strategies. Selina retreats into singing songs such as the Holloway Song, which she picks up from another, anonymous singer. She states: 'One day I hear that song on trumpets and these walls will fall and rest.'[9] Rhys's text implies that the prison song itself becomes an imaginary space where the subject, who belongs nowhere, is able to sustain his or herself.

Yet, rather than a penitentiary space, Smith's London feels like a liberated, heterogeneous space which is matched by and created by a particular kind of Bakhtinian heteroglossia, namely the mixture of languages spoken by the new generation of youngsters growing up in this society: Millat's crew 'of a new breed: *Raggastani*' (*WT* 231) who join other street crews, including Becks, B-boys, Indie kids, wide-boys, ravers, rude-boys, Acidheads, Sharons, Tracies, Kevs, Nation Brothers, Ragas and Pakis. They manifest themselves as a kind of cultural mongrel of the last three categories, speaking 'a strange mix of Jamaican patois, Bengali, Gujarati and English. Their ethos, their manifesto, if it could be called that, was equally a hybrid thing' (*WT* 231).

White Teeth's emphasis on London's new 'breeds' of hybrid, spoken languages comes to permeate the text. This 'mutation' of received pronunciation by that of immigrant language shows how the English language is reinvented from the inside out, but more generally it comes to signify a kind of linguistic equivalent of miscegenation, as the ironic, clever emphasis on 'breed' suggests.

Kris Knauer reads with Smith's utopian ideal, noting that 'Like languages, cultures keep evolving, inscribing themselves on the physicality of the city with each new generation' yet he does not address some of the fundamentally conflicting ideas within the novel, and one might argue that Smith's equation of language and culture is one of the potentially problematic, even naive theses of the novel.[10] This more sceptical approach we find, for instance, in Richard Bradford's dismissal of Smith's satire as 'rather heavy-[handed] (for example, the militant group joined by Millat is called the Keepers of the Eternal and Victorious Islamic Nation: KEVIN)'.[11] Smith is none too subtle, yet in his criticism of her playful thinking about multiculturalism through names and naming Bradford overlooks a wider cultural debate. The novel depicts London as an experimental space where the mixture of genes and languages makes a wider point about the relationship between language and culture. Not only do we find the hybridised names of 'Abdul-Jimmy' and 'Abdul-Colin (*WT* 520) and 'Abdul-Mickey' (*WT* 521), but Smith historicises the contemporary debates about multiculturalism:

> This has been a century of strangers, brown, yellow and white. This has been the century of the great immigrant experiment. It is only this late in the day that you can walk into a playground and see? Find? Isaac Leung by the fish pond, Danny Rahman in the football cage, Quang O'Rourke bouncing a basketball, and Irie Jones humming a tune. Children with first and last names on a direct collision course. Names that secrete within them mass exodus, cramped boats and planes, cold arrivals, medical checks. (*WT* 326)

This passage is a direct parody of the passage from Amis's *Money* about '[on] the streets you see countless odd pairings, all colours, all ages, all sexes' (*M* 257): whereas Amis stresses the radical disconnection of postmodern Londoners occasioned by an a-historical condition, Smith offers the city as a historical construct that forces present debates about immigration to be situated in a long history of Diaspora.

An act of open mutiny: *White Teeth* and history

Smith's text opens up a dialogic space where she is able to question received versions of history. For example, gossip is used to rewrite history in 'the much neglected, 100-year-old, mildewed yarn of Mangal Pande' (*WT* 99), an Indian Sepoy (soldier) for the English in the mid-nineteenth century, who discovers that the grease they use for the bullets in their guns was made of pig fat. The reader is given two versions, one told by Pande's great-grandson Samad Iqbal, who states that Pande makes history by being heroically executed after attacking his lieutenant, starting what the English call the Great Indian Mutiny of 1857, or what Iqbal calls 'the movement'. On the other hand, Archie relies on the writings of the contemporary historian Fitchett, whose version turns the Pande story into a mockery: Pande, a Hindu, 'is half drunk with bhang, and wholly drunk with religious fanaticism' (*WT* 254). Smith's novel subverts this version: 'But when Archie was in school the world seemed far more open to its own fictionalisation. History was a different business then: taught with one eye on narrative, the other on drama, no matter how unlikely or chronologically inaccurate' (*WT* 254). However, Iqbal's story is questioned as well: his version is derived from a book by the obscure Indian historian, A. S. Misra, who makes the tenuous connection between Pande's actions and Indian independence in 1947. Smith's text ultimately implies that Archie's unwitting guess – either Pande's gun was faulty, that he was bullied into fighting his lieutenant, or his speculation that Pande 'just couldn't do it. Maybe he wasn't the type' (*WT* 260) – is correct: Archie and Samad have in a sense re-enacted a similar story, when during the Second World War Archie is unable to kill the Nazi eugenicist, Dr Sick. However, this is not the point: it is the indeterminacy of meaning in both writing and speech that drives home the uncomfortable point that this history is perhaps irretrievable.

White Teeth's indeterminacy forms an ambiguous warning against the possibly fascistic tendencies of narrative fabrication: Micky, the owner of O'Connell's Pool House, warns Samad about his Mangal Pande story: 'You're creating a *repetitive syndrome* that puts all these buggers off their *culinary experience*' (*WT* 185). Smith's text warns of the dangers that arise when particular stories, such as the Pande history, turn into mythology through repetition: Iqbal's oral repetition of this story mythifies his grandfather in order to make himself look good, and is thus just another form of falsification. *White Teeth* explores many forms of repetition: in the text, there is an analogy between Mangal Pande's mutiny, the description of the assassination of Indira Ghandi by her bodyguard as 'an act of open mutiny' (*WT* 197), 'mutinous Millat' (*WT* 218), and the implicit comparison between eugenics programmes of the Nazis and contemporary genetic engineering in the release of both Dr Sick and SuperMouse©.

Smith's questioning of historical truth also renegotiates London's past itself. Where Moorcock and Duffy celebrate London's popular mythologies, Smith is intent on destroying these mythological origins in both form and content. The centre of London, as a Victorian city built on the spoils of empire, comes to be viewed as the production of a particular, falsified national history. When Millat and his fellow KEVIN-members emerge from the Charing Cross tube station, they find Trafalgar Square with the statues

Figure 18   Nelson's Column, Trafalgar Square

of Nelson, Havelock, Napier and George IV all facing Big Ben. Abdul-Colin notes that the English love their false icons, and he continues:

> [W]hat is it about the English that makes them build their statues with their backs to their culture and their eyes on time? [...] Because they look to their future to forget the past [...] They have no faith, the English. They believe in what men make, but what men make crumbles. Look at their empire. This is all they have. Charles II Street and South Africa House and a lot of stupid-looking men on stone horses [...] This is what is left. (*WT* 504–5)

Smith exploits London's most important public square as a site where monuments mould national memory into a particularly heroic, even mythical past. She exploits and exposes what Paul Ricoeur in his analysis of Virginia Woolf's *Mrs Dalloway* (1925) calls the oppressive and repressive power of 'monumental time', whereby monuments produce an unbearable gap between the eternity represented by the monument and the temporal experience of our everyday life as mortals.[12] Smith points out the double political edge of this process. Although for the autochthonous Briton this monumental time may have a mythical grandeur that generates a sense of belonging, for others this may produce a destructive, haunting quality that brings back past humiliations and traumas. As a remembrance of particular events, history and its created heroes are petrified and public space becomes a museum of propaganda for the nationalist cause that thrives by producing a nationalist, enlightened imperial narrative while being blind to the colonial counter-narrative. The passage bites home even more since it is Havelock who sentenced Mangal Pande to death (*WT* 255). Simultaneously, this passage is a meditation on the nature of historical materialism. While the material space of Britain's empire has dissolved, these statues have a proud as well as painful significance: the statues have in vain turned their eyes not towards the past but to the future, as embodiments of a colonial history that is implicitly glorified. Nelson, who sailed the seas and conquered empire in the name of civilising Enlightenment, is mocked. But by employing her modified form of realism, Smith is able to keep London's function as the socio-economic and political centre, which is part of her iconoclastic enterprise.

White Teeth situates peripheral Willesden, in north-west London, in relation to both the historical centre of London and the East End history of ethnic conflict. Willesden is described as a nice area that stands in great contrast to 'Whitechapel, where that madman E-knock someone or another gave a speech that forced him into the basement while kids broke the basement windows with the steel-capped boots. Rivers of blood silly-billy nonsense' (*WT* 62–3). And although Willesden has a 'wrong side' (*WT* 55), the borough is represented by Smith as a suburban utopia, a space of freedom that provides the citizen with enough private space for individual reflection. In a long, lyrical excerpt, Irie walks the streets of Willesden Green to experience a Proustian moment that bleeds into a Joycean epiphany. She ponders the nature of memory, defining the purest memory as the streets of one's childhood, yet again the nostalgia is undercut by humour and a contemporary cultural plurality that seems to offer a utopia:

> [S]he found herself dragged forward by the hair to their denouement, through the high road – *Mali's Kebabs, Mr Cheungs, Raj's, Malkovich Bakeries* – she could reel them off blindfold; and then down under pigeon-shit bridge and that long wide road that drops into Gladstone Park as if it's falling into a green ocean. You could drown in memories like these, but she tried to swim free of them [...] Past tense, future imperfect. (*WT* 459)

Here Willesden becomes a personal memory theatre that comes into being as a result of her movement through place. The idea that Irie can reel off the restaurants' names blindfold reminds one of Joyce's favourite party trick: the naming of all the shops in Dublin's central street.[13] However, it is the disparate origin of the names that reveals the utopian nature of Willesden Green: rather than Rushdie's violent Brickhall where different ethnicities are in conflict with one another, here London's different ethnic groups appear to balance each other out. Thus, Pilar Cuder-Domínguez's assertion that *White Teeth* strikes 'at the very heart of the middle-class, heterosexual, patriarchal values that have persisted to this day in the English identity, [Smith suggests] that the class struggle is as prominent as the racial one' is certainly not wholly true, yet Dominic Head's claim about Smith's naïve subscription to the multicultural society is a slight misrepresentation as well.[14] Bruce King comes closer to understanding the more ambivalent currents within *White Teeth*:

> *White Teeth* was the desired multicultural novel of a new multicultural England, a celebration of London as an international city in which peoples and cultures of the world were cross-pollinating. It did not show, however, a new multicultural homogeneity which was replacing old England. The new generation knew each other from school and lived together, but *White Teeth* was also a story of conflicts, of new

resentments, of new stereotypes, a novel of an England still in turmoil. It was not going to be easy to get beyond race, class, difference.[15]

Smith's text is, as King suggests, more ambiguous in its assessment of multicultural metropolis, as the following quotation indicates:

> Because we often imagine that immigrants are on the move, footloose, able to change course at any moment, able to employ their legendary resourcefulness at every turn [...] and step into their foreign lands as *blank people*, free of any kind of baggage, happy and willing to leave their difference at the docks and take their chances in this new place, merging with the oneness of this greenandpleasantlibertarianlandofthefree [...] weaving their way through Happy Multicultural Land. [...] Because this is the other thing about immigrants [...] they cannot escape their history anymore than you yourself can lose your shadow. (*WT* 465–6)

This passage subverts the idea that Smith's work is a one-sided, optimistic celebration of suburban London as utopian space of multicultural harmony. In the light of this excerpt *White Teeth* contains a darker side where the ethnic and religious tensions manifest themselves.

Smith's text stresses the necessity of narrative as a means to weave the immigrant into the fabric of the host society, and as a means to rewrite established versions of history. Yet the novel is aware of postmodernity's stressing of the unreliability of any narrative – both oral as well as written, which perhaps challenges Moorcock's 'authentic' London voice and Ackroyd's Cockney tradition. By emphasising living speech Smith shows that she masters London on her own terms, and is able invent a new form of narrative authenticity. *White Teeth* connects urban spaces to the human voices it harbours, resulting in a space of linguistic contagion in which the oral communication plays a major role, and this the text foregrounds as a development with potential. *White Teeth* is heteroglossic and heterotopic in nature because it notes how contemporary London enforces transgressions of almost all orders of socio-economic and cultural life, resulting in a sometimes forced and violent communication, dialogue and confrontation.

A kind of translation: reading Monica Ali's *Brick Lane* as enactment of New Labour's model of Britishness

Despite many obvious differences and being published fifteen years apart, Salman Rushdie's *The Satanic Verses* and Monica Ali's *Brick Lane* have much in common. Both novels are set in London's East End, a part of the city with a long and often dark history in providing a home to the Cockney working class and many groups of immigrants. Like Rushdie, whose novel exposes the ways in which the Thatcher regime wilfully ignored the inner city's decline, Ali also unveils what Rushdie calls 'a city visible but unseen'. This revealing of the deliberately ignored is apocalyptic (etymologically 'apocalypsis' means to unveil, to tear away): Rushdie's inner city is redeemed by Gibreel Farishta's setting fire to Brickhall, the symbolic site of municipal neglect. Ali's narrative opens up, however, another world hitherto unnoticed, namely, that of Tower Hamlets' female Muslim population struggling to survive in a cityscape of 'grey towers, the blown-by forgotten strands of sky between them'.[16] *The Satanic Verses* sparked protest marches, book burnings and the fatwa pronounced by Ayatollah Khomeini; *Brick Lane* sparked protests on a smaller scale when it was first published, and, in July 2006, Bangladeshis living in the East End threatened the film production company, Ruby Films, with street blockades and book burnings in order to protest against their alleged misrepresentation.

Critics have looked at the content (the socio-political issues) or at the form (the problems of representation) of *Brick Lane* and the connection between the two. Jane Hiddlestone asserts that 'the work is at once a revealing depiction of a space conventionally shielded from the public gaze, and a somewhat fetishized portrait of a subject already formed by Orientalist myths and stereotypes'.[17] Pilar Cuder-Domínguez notes that the novel 'powerfully transmits the plights of Bangladeshi women in South London [sic] at the turn of the century'.[18] James Wood has looked at the formal aspects, noting that '*Brick Lane* is a great achievement of the subtlest storytelling – the kind that proceeds illuminatingly, in units of characters rather than in wattage of "style".'[19] In a fascinating essay exploring Ali's novel in relation to the English tradition of the novelistic form, Alistair Cormack states that the novel 'is particularly of interest as an examination of the double bind that female migrants face, treated as alien by their host nation and as commodities by the men in their own communities'.[20] David James points out Ali's stylistic gift: 'it is precisely the tempered, unobtrusive style in which she conveys her heroine's thoughts in open space that allows the reader to witness through an intimate lens the consequences of Nazneen's racial self-consciousness'.[21]

Ali's novel not only reflects a specific historical moment of deferred arrival, but its form also mimics a political, economic and ideological moment at which a new British narrative is consciously being formulated. Whereas *The Satanic Verses* is a direct attack on the local authorities and the Thatcher regime, which, by choosing to glorify Victorian values and ignoring the darker fringes of English imperial history turned a blind eye to the inner city's citizens' plight, *Brick Lane* can be read as a response to New Labour's attempts to translate their ideas about Britishness into reality. Rather than a direct indictment of the ignorance of Sylhetis (the ethnic group that comprises the majority of Bangladeshis in the UK), the novel's tracing of the personal journey of a Bangladeshi woman from a suffocating, arranged marriage into independent financial selfhood represents, on the one hand, an attack on the gap between the fallacious idea of the classless society as promoted by politicians in post-war Britain and the reality of what Dominic Head calls 'the installation of a new underclass'; it simultaneously criticises the local and national political system for failing to endorse an emancipatory project for Muslim women.[22]

In *The State of the Novel* (2008), Head writes that *Brick Lane* presents us with 'a model of multiculturalism that might flow from different perceptions of love'.[23] On the one hand, we find Nazneen's arranged marriage to Chanu, and, on the other hand, she finds romantic love in her affair with Karim, a relationship in which she ostensibly has some sort of autonomy. Although Nazneen chooses to stay with Chanu and her family, the importance lies in her ability to choose, which establishes her agency, whilst the novel also shows that 'over the question of romantic love, there is no cultural divide'.[24] This conservative choice, for Head, maps the novel 'onto a longstanding tradition of social mores in the English novel, where the sensible alliance is invariably promoted over the path of reckless desire. This is the genuine multicultural gesture.'[25] Head's analysis is problematic in two ways. First, he seems to interpret Ali's supposed deference to the conservative English tradition as an act of multiculturalism, whereas it really is a form of assimilation. Second, Head misrepresents the novel's conclusion, which ends with Nazneen's and Chanu's separation, not a celebration of marriage. The point that the novel makes is that, in order to truly liberate herself, Nazneen must leave both men and find economic independence, the Woolfian room of one's own, if you like. Indeed, Head's idea that 'the emancipated principal chooses the notional path of oppression' is odd, particularly in the light of the resistance that the novel was given by Bangladeshi men: Nazneen decides against travelling back to Bangladesh with Chanu, forcing a geographical split that also serves as their divorce. Whereas Head's analysis is as though Ali is rewriting Jane Austen for the East End, the novel is actually about a woman who makes a bold step from an ancient ideological system into the modern world.

In order to show how these problems interlock in the gendered and economic context of the novel, I will first reframe some of the questions surrounding mimetic representation by revisiting the novel's exploration of problems of narrative representation. The novel demonstrates how the problematic move into epistolary language, different kinds of translations and the importance of myths in Bangladeshi culture can be read as metaphors for the failure of New Labour to represent certain groups of citizens in the early twenty-first century: the violation of the rules of representation set up in the novel externalise the tension in the narrative of Britishness by pointing out the ways in which New Labour leaves behind large numbers of the population it supposedly represents.

The rules of representation

Brick Lane tells the story of the young Bengali woman Nazneen who, at the age of eighteen, is married off to the middle-aged Chanu and subsequently displaced from a hut in a Bengal village to a bleak, Tower Hamlets low-rise housing estate, Rosemead Block. Unable to speak English, Nazneen is confined to the cramped flat, marooned in a concrete cityscape offering nothing but the view of 'dead grass and broken paving stones' (*BL* 12), an alcoholic woman and drug-dealing Bengali addicts. Whereas Chamcha's and Farishta's rebirths in *The Satanic Verses* are violent, comic and immediate struggles, Nazneen's rebirth is a gradual, seventeen-year-long trajectory, taking place through the slow acquisition of English, which enables her to escape the determinism that is ingrained in her belief in fate. The pompous and foppish Chanu, who has a degree in English Literature from Dhakha University, is employed by the local council and hopes for a promotion (which the reader is painfully aware will never arrive). After the sudden death of her baby son from tonsillitis, the narrative picks up in 2001, when Nazneen and Chanu have two daughters (Shahana and Bibi) and Nazneen starts an affair with Karim, an energetic and idealistic entrepreneur who, as a local amateur politician, organises community meetings and a protest march to put the Bengali community on the mainstream political map. After Chanu returns to Bangladesh, Nazneen remains in London with her daughters, starting a business based on her skills as a seamstress, which enables her to inscribe herself into the space of capitalist modernity.[26]

Ali uses a realist method for delivering this transformation, starting with the title of the novel. Unlike Rushdie's veiling of concrete reality by using the fictional 'Brickhall', the naming of an existing London street roots this story into the material reality of the East End. The novel is also explicit about time, making the connection between the Thatcher decade and the New Labour era: the first part of the novel is set in 'Tower Hamlets, London, 1985' (*BL* 12) and the second half starts in 'Tower Hamlets, February 2001' (*BL* 145). Ali deliberately asks the reader to contemplate the relationship between Thatcher and New Labour, for instance when a neighbour sells his flat, which was bought under Thatcher: '"He did Right to Buy," said Shahana. "Fifteen years ago, paid five thousand pounds in cash"' (*BL* 266). This specific mentioning of time and place gives the novel a clear and raw political thrust: rather than New Labour's rhetoric of change and Tony Blair's promise that there would be 'no forgotten people' in New Labour's Britain, *Brick Lane* shows a painful continuation of similar policies through the lack of genuine interest in this particular section of the British population.[27]

Ali's representation of Nazneen's world is rendered in the language of realism. Take for instance the following example, in which Nazneen, lying in bed, senses her depression about the meaninglessness of her life as a housewife:

> Now, she thought, where's the harm? She rolled over to wrap herself up in the bed covers to float free for a while. Nothing came to her mind. She stared at the ceiling. Remember to pack his hat, she thought [...] Then nothing. The fridge needs cleaning. More toilet roll. She slapped the bed. Write to Hasina. That was better. Wash a few clothes out, before too much piles up. No, no, no. She pulled the covers over her head. Ice e-skating, she said out loud. (*BL* 116)

Such passages are very conventionally mediated mimetic formulations of Nazneen's inner life. The flicking back and forth between the third-person narrator and her consciousness is narrated to reflect Nazneen's ruptured identity and its ultimate wholeness as represented by the same narrating entity: the educated and liberated Nazneen that has developed by the end of the novel is retroactively reconstructing her personal journey to independence. In the process we are given an insight into an entire community, and over a period of time: from her friend Razia (who considers herself British) and the extortive money lender Mrs Islam to the radicalised Muslim men such as Karim and the power-wielding Dr Azad, Ali's narrative manages to show how the Bengali individuals relate to one another in a wide variety of ways, the prerequisite for what Raymond Williams considered the realistic novel.[28] This also makes it possible to argue that the modified realism of Ali represents a crisis in multicultural Britain. In Williams's words, a '[s]ociety is outside the people, though at times, even violently, it breaks in on them'.[29]

In his review of the novel, defender of the realist tradition Wood states that Nazneen's 'knowledge is framed in ignorance [...] such simplicity on Ali's part, such authorial reticence coupled with such authorial sympathy, is a strenuous achievement'.[30] Wood lauds the manner in which Ali manages to defamiliarise the reader's perspective without degrading Nazneen. However, Ali's novel exploits Nazneen's frame of reference in different ways; not only is the protagonist 'ignorant', but she is also conditioned by a particular kind of knowledge and vocabulary, namely, the rural, Bangladeshi context that is transplanted into the metropolitan, 'British' context. The mixing of two different sets of signs becomes a means for the reader to trace Nazneen's progress into modernity: after her arrival in London, Nazneen, not equipped with the vocabulary to name the new environment and its objects, is forced to contextualise the urban and domestic world by means of her rural Bengali frame of reference. For instance, Nazneen's mother is ripening 'like a mango on a tree' (*BL* 7) and the midwife 'is more desiccated than an old coconut' (*BL* 8). In London, the 'sofa and chairs were the colour of dried cow dung, which was a practical colour' (*BL* 15). Chanu 'likes to keep [the television] glowing like a fire in the corner of the room' (*BL* 27). Schoolchildren are described as 'pale as rice and loud as peacocks' (*BL* 44) and Nazneen's friend Razia 'had tamed the machines that stood guard by talking to them softly, like a mahout calms an angry elephant' (*BL* 101). Thus, the result is a kind of narrative 'double vision', whereby the semantic system of Nazneen's old world is superimposed onto Tower Hamlets.

Homi Bhabha's post-colonial theory of the immigrant's double vision has drawn much on the analysis of Rushdie's work, on *The Satanic Verses* in particular. Rushdie's novel makes use of linguistic schizophrenia to explore the problems of cultural hybridity and engages in acts of blasphemy to give voice to alienation. In the famous Club Hot Wax scene, Rushdie juxtaposes two opposing ideas of the immigrant's identity: either man's identity is immutable, fixed or infinitely malleable. Bhabha notes that cultural translation works on both a personal and political, national level: Ali's inscription of the English context with alien imagery 'reveals the interstitial; insists in [sic] the textile superfluity of folds and wrinkles' and becomes the 'unstable element of linkage', the indeterminate temporality of the in-between, that has to be engaged in creating the conditions through which 'newness comes into the world'.[31] If we also take into account that '[c]ultural translation desacralizes the transparent assumptions of cultural supremacy, and in that very act, demands contextual specificity', Nazneen's personal transformation must necessarily be read also as a political and ideological inscription of this multiple Other – female, married off, semi-literate, financially dependent, Muslim – onto the map of mainstream politics.[32]

A related question, here, is that of the status of the immigrant novelist. In his post-war history of the novel in English, Randall Stevenson notes that '[l]ike women writers, immigrant novelists were "insiders and outsiders" at the same time, as Rushdie suggests: part of English society, yet also partly "outside of it, alien and critical," their work often strengthened by the doubling and diversifying of vision this entailed'.[33] Although this appears to leave the question of gender and the problem of multiple Otherness aside, Ali's (like Smith's) comfortable form of narrative, coupled with the narrative journey of self-knowledge, suggests that the immigrant writer has, over the past twenty-five years, arrived and contributed to what Stevenson calls 'the democratization of voice and vision'.[34] In a way, Ali's narrative makes a confident statement about the immigrant writer – including female immigrant writers – presented as forming an integral part of the British literary establishment, indeed of the public realm and consciousness.

Ironically, this does not apply to all British citizens, whose political representation falls short: Ali's novel is trying to have Nazneen inhabit the reality of public space and to supplement the shared standpoint of the Bengali community: the democratic common ground that is, physically and linguistically, shared by all members of the body politic. Not only is there Karim's struggle to form the Bengal Tigers as a (masculine) representative forum, but *Brick Lane* foregrounds the importance of education for Nazneen as a means of breaking out of her imprisoning situation. This pedagogical investigation starts with the role of mythologies within Bangladeshi culture. *Brick Lane* opens with a story about Nazneen's troubled birth in East Pakistan, 1967, a story which grows in mythical status the more it is repeated. The story, which instils in her a passive, submissive attitude towards 'fate', shows how Nazneen formulates herself through this mythological construction of her guiding life principles, which she must unstitch in order to insert herself into public life.

The importance of the public space is evidenced by the disconnection between her geographical and linguistic reality when, early on in the novel (Chapter 3), Nazneen tries to cross an East End street on her own: 'To get to the other side of the street without being hit by a car was like walking out in the monsoon and hoping to dodge the rain drops. A space opened up before her. God is great, said Nazneen under her breath. She ran' (*BL* 43). This passage indicates that she literally has no linguistic horizon to interpret the signs that order everyday life

Figure 19 Counter-surveillance, Brick Lane

in the West. Instead she suffers from semantic tunnel vision, ensuring that the place for symbolic transition becomes an obstruction instead, reinforcing the analogy between Nazneen's physical and linguistic imprisonment. The East End is portrayed as an illegible world: lacking the vocabulary to nominate objects around her, the city is either coated in signifieds derived from an alien frame of reference, or simply left unuttered, which is not to say that she does not comprehend the world around her. Statements such as '[s]he sensed rather than saw' (*BL* 63) indicate that Nazneen possesses a dormant intelligence that is made available to her by the acquisition of the English language.

Ali ironises and dramatically exploits this illegibility of the East End by inserting a comic sequence in which the family go on their first family day trip for twenty years, in London's tourist centre. Sightseeing becomes dramatised in the episode, which diametrically opposes London's centre to the gloomy descriptions of the East End. After Chanu dresses up in the stereotypical guise of a tourist, wearing a baseball cap and money belt and equipping himself with a guidebook, they leave 'the grimy colours of Bethnal Green Road' (*BL* 239) to visit Buckingham Palace and have a picnic in the colourful surrounding of St James's Park. Chanu, reading the Palace through eyes that are conditioned by the English language, views the building as the guidebook wants him to see it, and tells his daughter to '[l]ook at this beautiful building' (*BL* 242). Nazneen is sceptical about her role as tourist because she cannot formulate this role for herself. She resists the prescriptive text of the guidebook, and instead fantasises about the destruction of Buckingham Palace and its replacement with 'something elegant and spirited, with minarets and spires, domes and mosaics, a beautiful garden instead of this bare forecourt. Something like the Taj Mahal' (*BL* 241).

Ali's pseudo-realistic depiction is partly derived from the didactic novel tradition, popular particularly in the eighteenth and nineteenth centuries, and which has strong links with the *Bildungsroman*. One can think of *Jane Eyre* (1847) and also of Charles Dickens's *David Copperfield* (1849–50): by keeping the threshold low, a large, poorly educated audience could be instructed with moral lessons and be persuaded of specific socio-political ideas. Mary Shelley's *Frankenstein* (1818), for instance, traces the progress of Victor Frankenstein's Creature, an alien outsider unseen at the farther margins of society, who is given the opportunity by a poor peasant family (the DeLaceys) to learn English, and educate and humanise himself by reading. Set against the background of the industrial revolution, the destructive, rationalising effects of which the novel criticises, it is a *Bildungsroman* written in a mimetic mode. In this sense, Nazneen is another Modern

Prometheus, who is not created from clay and water nor by electricity, but the articulation of herself in English. The important connecting point between Frankenstein and *Brick Lane* is that the education process occurs outside the official institution: both the Creature and Nazneen are forcedly autodidacts, whose trajectory of self-realisation is not provided for within the socio-economic infrastructure of mainstream society.

A kind of translation

This hiatus in the configuration of the social sphere, which deflates New Labour's rhetoric about better education for everyone through radical reform, prosperity and social mobility that would be provided by the Third Way, is expressed through series of ruptures in the mimetic economy of the novel.[35] An important structuring device is Ali's many-layered mediation on translation of the post-colonial subject in relationship to the language used by that subject to construct an identity. The subversion of the comfortable rules of representation indicate, on the one hand, that Nazneen's growth is far from straightforward, and, on the other, that complex socio-economic forces have a distinct impact on the possibility of individuals' ability to achieve such personal growth.

Both *The Satanic Verses* and *Brick Lane* are meditations on the (im)possibility of metaphorically translating the post-colonial subject into the modern West. However, whereas *The Satanic Verses* depicts the violent rebirths of its protagonists Saladin Chamcha and Gibreel Farishta, *Brick Lane* explores Nazneen's reinvention of herself as gradual change. *Brick Lane* contains a 'warning' against the written words, in the form of the myth of Makku Pagla, a fellow villager with whom Nazneen grows up in a small village in the Mymensigh district, who commits suicide: 'Books had cracked him, and the more cracked he became the more books he read' (*BL* 63). A core aspect of the contemporary debate about Britishness revolves around the importance of mastering the English language. Cormack states that

> In *Brick Lane* English does not appear to be remade, but rather is used intact as a novelistic lingua franca. There is an unavoidable irony in depicting Nazneen's struggle with English entirely within that language. The focalisation becomes a complicated multiple mediation. The narrator reviews the story, as we have seen, from a vantage point after the events have occurred, with an understanding far in advance of Nazneen, but with access to her thoughts. These are rendered in English with a bat squeak of mockery.[36]

Cormack's reference to the importance of English being appropriated and remade comes from Rushdie, who in *Mirrorwork* (1997) writes that:

> Indian writing in English has been called 'twice-born' [...] to suggest its double parentage [...] it seems to me to rest on the false premise that English, having arrived from outside India, is and must remain an alien there. But my own mother-tongue, Urdu, the camp-argot of the country's earlier Muslim conquerors, became a naturalised subcontinental language long ago; and by now that has happened to English, too. English has become an Indian language.[37]

However, the assumption that English is not remade in *Brick Lane* can be problematised as a gendered issue. Rushdie's linguistic doubling does return in a story about an exorcism taking place in the village when Nazneen is still a young girl:

> Ke Katha koyre, dekha deyna
> Ke Katha koyre, dekha deyna
> Node chode, hater kache

> Faster and faster went the chanters and faster flew the words. The white cloths tied around the fakir's waist and arms streamed behind him, making visible his huge energy with which he would fight the evil jinni.

> Ke Katha koyre, dekha deyna
> Who talks, not showing up
> Who talks, no showing up
> Moves about, near at hand

> The servant boy disappeared in a vortex of wheeling limbs.

> I search for him
> In the sky and the earth
> Myself, I do not know
> I search for him. (*BL* 333)

Here, the tripartite structure clearly expresses the trajectory of Nazneen's linguistic transformation, from one language into the other, leaving both intact. Thus, for Ali, the goal of the transformation is different from

Rushdie's masculine strategy of Indian 'conquering' of English: Nazneen is able to escape from her submissive condition by modestly, quietly assimilating into British culture. Whereas Rushdie, writing in the early eighties, was intensely sceptical of multiculturalism and the British identity, *Brick Lane*'s final scene suggests that Britishness and the migrant identity can go together successfully, thus reinforcing New Labour's narrative of the inclusiveness of the contemporary notion of British identity.

However, there are signs that Ali gently subverts this apparently clear-cut rebirth into (re)discovered Britishness. Whereas Amit Chaudhuri's *A Strange and Sublime Address* (1991) 'warns' the reader about the intricate and manifold meaning of the Bengali word 'Amma', Ali leaves this untranslated.[38] Other examples concern Nazneen's mother becoming possessed by an evil 'jinni' and Shahana's pulling of 'Chanu's daaton from the toothbrush mug' (*BL* 331), which remains untranslated ('spirit' and 'toothbrush', respectively). By leaving such culturally specific words intact, Ali defamiliarises her British audience and forces it to undergo Nazneen's semantic amputation.

Another problem related to translation is highlighted by the form of letters written by Nazneen and her sister, Hasina, who remains in Bangladesh. Consider the following example, in which her sister indicates that she is prostituting herself to make ends meet:

> *Sister I have not know what to tell and this is how no letter is coming before. Now I have news. In morning soon as husband go out for work I go away to Dhaka. Our landlady Mrs Kashem is only person who know about it. She say it is not good decision but she help anyway. She say it is better get beaten by own husband than beating by stranger. But those stranger not saying all the time they love me. If they beat they do in all honesty.* (*BL* 46)

Cormack asserts that 'with Hasina's letters we feel the surface of realism being stretched, but not actually breaking' (*BL* 716). This is certainly true: the representation of these translated letters in italics is an indication of a different narrative level. The epistolary interruptions, on the one hand, destroy the smooth reading process by pointing to the act of writing itself (a metatextual device which mocks the comfortable ways in which the reader is sucked into constructing a solid reality) whilst, on the other, paradoxically, the italics indicate the author's awareness of this artificiality, thus restoring the credulity, by way of excuse, as it were.

There is another important problem, however, beyond the italics: Ali's move into the epistolary mode reaches a compromise by occupying a middle ground that can only be described as a kind of translation. Hasina's Bengali is semi-illiterate, which is indicated by the semi-illiterate English, as if the two correspond on a one-to-one basis. This epistolary mode also raises the problem of what Raymond Williams called 'the orthography of the uneducated'.[39] Whereas Zadie Smith exploited this comically, Ali's narrative is more serious. Its presentation of Hasina's incorrect use of language assumes there is a proper, standard way to speak or write. This is for instance reinforced by Nazneen's value judgement about her daughter Shahana, whose 'written Bengali was shocking' (*BL* 147). Looked at from this point of view, it is the orthographic representation of broken Bengali in broken English – a distinctly English middle-class tradition – which destroys the general mimetic tendencies of the text: the rules of representation are ruptured through the authorial intrusion and its implicit reframing of Nazneen in the middle-class, New Labourite culture she enters at the close of the book.

For Williams, who is speaking about Tressell's celebration of the working classes in his novel *The Ragged-Arsed Philanthropists* (1914), this bourgeois tradition is, however, part of a broader narrative strategy:

> For he [Tressell] is saying that it is terrible for people to have to live like this when they are doing useful and good work, and could do more useful and better work in different circumstances. It is terrible to live like this, to be this vulnerable to the whims of others, to be this vulnerable to the accidents of trade and the imbecilities of the system. It is terrible also, however, to be vulnerable not only to propaganda and the self-justifications of others who have an interest in perpetuating ignorance, but to an ignorance that gets built in, inside people themselves; an ignorance that becomes their commonsense. Being a prisoner can come to seem common sense, or can be made to seem human.[40]

Williams's ideas resonate with Nazneen's experience in *Brick Lane*, which shows how Nazneen is suffering under the whims of Chanu and Mrs Islam whilst revealing the 'imbecilities of the system' in New Labour's Britain: the only partially successful move into epistolary language, which assumes a direct translation or effect, indicates a violation of representation. The odd, muddled translations suggest a dislocation in terms of representation in the outside world, to which Nazneen has no access. The implicit irony driving the novel is, then, that the reader is given access to the consciousness of a citizen who remains unrepresented within the collective consciousness. The novel is a cartography of what is forgotten or repressed by mainstream politics, which, in the post-9/11 climate is more focused on arresting the highly visible presence of male, Muslim extremists. The less obvious, and visible, problems in British multicultural society are easily forgotten, resulting in a general climate of asymmetrical multiculturalism driven by a repressive assimilation rather than a more profound dialogic mixture of cultural values.

'After the riot, everything was going to change'

Razia's optimistic closing words of the novel ('"This is England," she said. "You can do whatever you like"' (*BL* 413)) are problematic, and mock Rushdie's cheerfulness. The novel puts forth the idea that the politico-economic and cultural forces that are present in contemporary Britain are inhibiting self-realisation and the formation of an inclusive idea of Britishness: Ali's novel appears to not so much put on an equal footing as to insinuate a strong resemblance between New Labour's Britain and the Muslim world. Ali's novel points to Nazneen's entrapment within the domestic realm, but it simultaneously addresses the ways in which politics are present in contemporary Britain as well. Nazneen understands that public life is regulated by laws: '[t]he sign screwed to the brickwork was in stiff English capitals and the curlicues beneath were Bengali. No dumping. No parking. No ball games' (*BL* 13). Later on in the novel, she notices another sign: 'The notice said: No smoking, no eating, no drinking. All the signs, thought Nazneen, tell you what not to do' (*BL* 51). Tower Hamlets emerges as a place of impossibility, trapping these immigrants within their estates. Both the Muslim fundamentalists and local authorities are hindering the possibility towards development of the self. When Nazneen's lover, Karim, has prepared the protest march and states that Allah is the uniting force behind Muslims around the world, she thinks: 'Oh, Karim, why do you see only what you want to see' (*BL* 349). Live music to support the march is not allowed because it is un-Islamic, as is recorded music: 'That's banned as well' (*BL* 345). A similar link can be found in the extortionist Mrs Islam, whose sons demand taxes on goods they already receive interest on: 'Taxing him, as if they were the government' (*BL* 295).

Brick Lane is thus a discursive quest for liberation from this carceral territory. When Nazneen has built up experience in her new language, she states:

> The windows were fixed with thick metal grilles that had never been opened and notices were screwed to the brickwork that read

in English and Bengali: Vandals will be prosecuted. This was pure rhetoric. The notices were scrawled over in red and black ink. One dangled by a single remaining screw. Someone had written in careful flowing silver spray over the wall Pakis. And someone else, in less beautiful but confident black letters, had added, Rule. (*BL* 194)

Ali uses images to suggest the relationship between the Bengali residents of council estates in Tower Hamlets and their political representatives. The suggested tension between white and Bengali occupants plays itself out outside the public arena: the public notices mirror the Blairite spin, which is overcoded by the writing. Mass media are also singled out, as is Bengali racism: 'The white press had made them up to give Bangladeshis a bad name. The Tower Hamlets Bugle was the worst offender (but all white newspapers were culprits); if you read that rubbish you'd think that our boys were getting as bad as the blacks' (*BL* 323).

Like Rushdie's *The Satanic Verses* and Smith's *White Teeth*, *Brick Lane* culminates in a fictional protest riot, which embodies the frustration of the lack of representation within the mainstream political spectrum. During the climactic ending of the novel, the street is the scene of the 'MARCH AGAINST THE MULLAHS', whereby the white, 'autochthonous' population protests against the changing ethnic demography of the borough after a boy has been stabbed. However, Ali's narrative also undercuts Rushdie's optimism: 'Restaurant owners stood by, nerves flickering across important faces. All the mixed-blood vitality of the street had been drained. Something coursed down the artery [*Brick Lane*], like a bubble in the bloodstream' (*BL* 394). Like the work of Rushdie and Zadie Smith, Ali's text refers to Enoch Powell's Rivers of Blood-speech, yet her engagement with Powell's extreme views is more complex. Ali suggests that the recent demographic changes have caused a kind of ethnic and cultural homogenisation of the territory, suggesting that London's ghettoisation is a much greater obstacle to multiculturalism than in the more optimistic fictions of Rushdie and Smith.

Shortly after the riot, in 'March 2002' (*BL* 402) local councillors flock to the estate and the narrator notes: 'After the riot, everything was going to change' (*BL* 405):

Politicians came and walked around the estate with their hands behind their backs to show that they were not responsible, leaning forward slightly to indicate that they were looking to the future. A councillor in a corduroy jacket and round-necked shirt came to Nazneen's flat and looked at the hallway where the plaster had come off. He had a reporter and a photographer with him. The photographer took a picture of the councillor with his hands against the bricks. (*BL* 406)

When the councillor talks to Nazneen, almost incidentally inscribing her into public space, he asks:

'How many children do you have?'
'Two,' said Nazneen.
The councillor looked disappointed. He went away.
  Television crews came in the afternoon. There was nothing to film, so they filmed each other. They returned after dark and filmed the boys riding round in cars. They found the disused flats where the addicts gathered to socialize with their addictions, and filmed the grotty mattresses and the bits of silver foil. It was a sensation. It was on the local news. (*BL* 406)

The provocative tone, aided by the thrust of the narrative acceleration that mimics media soundbites, is here composed of hopeless cynicism and venomous loathing at the racist stereotyping: there will *not* be any change, at least, not in the way that New Labour's rhetoric projected in 1997. In an analysis of Raymond Williams's idea of socio-cultural change, Sean Matthews notes the 'passive and active meanings in the word: change is at once what happens to us (the Industrial Revolution), but also what we do, in that complex of action, understanding and artic-ulation'.[41] This helps us understand the complexity and importance of Ali's novel, which, rather than frantically emphasising the possibility of change, as is the case in Rushdie's work, traces a slow, drawn-out process of social evolution stressing that the means to vocalise this are an indis-pensable component of the actual manifestation of positive change.

  The gendered position of *Brick Lane* posits that Rushdie's masculine apocalypticism – underpinned by the Marxist notion that only a revo-lution will make the underclass visible – is misguided. Ali foregrounds the problem of multiculturalism first and foremost as an economic problem, as a social and class issue. During a panel discussion on mul-ticultural Britain after the London bomb attacks on 7 July 2005 with Hanif Kureishi, Salman Rushdie and Monica Ali amongst others, Colin MacCabe suggests that the gap between the Muslim community and mainstream British society was locked into the question of economic inequality. The following dialogue ensued:

HK [Hanif Kureishi]: So you are saying that these divisions can be translated into class divisions?

SR [Salman Rushdie]: You see, I don't agree with that. This is old left thinking, which is that economics is primary, and I don't think that's necessarily so.

MA [Monica Ali]: If you look at what is happening in some sections of what I would term the Islamist community, it's hard to think there isn't some kind of link with the economic situation. All the effort that the government put into inspecting mosques – if it put as much into schooling, housing, surely that would have more impact.

Ali's reaction suggests her general understanding is that we need to understand democratic, economic and cultural developments as intricately related to one another.[42]

Brick Lane also warns against mythologising by showing Chanu's fallacious appropriation of Bangladesh's national poet Tagore as 'the true father of [the] nation' (*BL* 147). In order to understand fully their Bengali identity, Chanu forces his daughters, Bibi and Shahana, to learn Tagore's poem 'Golden Bengal' by heart through obsessive repetition: 'In the sixteenth century, Bengal was called the Paradise of Nations. These are our roots. Do they teach these things in the school here? Does Shahana know about the Paradise of Nations? All she knows about is flood and famine. Whole bloody country is just a bloody basket case to her' (*BL* 151). Chanu, who suffers from 'Going Home Syndrome' (*BL* 381) and consistently expresses a desire to return, is not prepared to admit the discrepancy between his Bengali mythology of loss, built on a romanticised version of Bangladeshi identity, and the realities of contemporary Bangladesh revealed to the reader in the letters from Nazneen's sister Hasina. The point is that the hiatus that lies between Chanu's rhetoric ('Chanu, captivated by his own oration' (*BL* 266)) and reality implicitly reflects New Labour's inability to overcode the actuality of life in Tower Hamlets: Chanu's failure to be promoted is an expression of the limited social mobility in New Labour's Britain.

Finally, Nazneen unwraps herself from the reductive mythology about her existence in the world, and accepts that she has agency and self-determination, and can become visible by entering the public space, by reformulating herself in terms of the West, and by creating agency, by exploiting her economic skills in a new national narrative of Britishness characterised by its global dimensions. This is demonstrated through engagement with female writers: next to a reference to Virginia Woolf ('Mr Dalloway', *BL* 22), the description of Nazneen's mother, Rupban, 'who is famous for crying' (*BL* 10) makes us aware that Ali engages with the complex deterministic narratives of Muriel Spark, whose famous

The Prime of Miss Jean Brodie (1961) is a study, in Patricia Waugh's words, 'of psychological myth-making imperatives of power politics and Fascism'.[43] *Brick Lane* propels the reader back to a time before the socio-cultural revolutions of the 1960s. This awareness is also illustrated by a reference made by Shahana, who warns her sister against arranged marriage, to Tennyson's *The Lady of Shalott* (1842): 'And your husband will keep you locked up in a little smelly room and make you weave carpets all day long' (*BL* 329). It is therefore all the more important that Nazneen is able to liberate herself by means of the commercial exploitation of the representation that keeps her imprisoned. The final chapter ends with Chanu now returned to Bangladesh and Nazneen entering a partnership to set up a clothing business, with the two generations of Bangladeshi women going to an ice rink, set up earlier in the novel as the symbolic passage into modernity and the desired public space, showing that Nazneen, whilst not compromising herself ('The crisscross patterns of a thousand surface scars [...] the unchanging nature of what lay beneath' (*BL* 413)), has made the imaginary transition into British culture: 'To get to the ice physically – it hardly seemed to matter. In her mind she was already there' (*BL* 413).

Conclusion: London Undone?

The Great Fires of London

London has become the source and subject of an intense and ferocious imaginative energy since the mid-1970s, when Britain was overcoming post-imperial socio-economic decline and cultural atrophy. Margaret Thatcher's rise to power in 1979 proved to be an incendiary turning point, yet the perpetuation of Thatcherite policies in the New Labour era provoked a continued response in British literature. The result is a body of exceptional work by writers who have unconditionally committed their writing to chronicling the many lives of London. They have also allowed us readers, in Angela Carter's words, to feel and capture the *Zeitgeist*: 'it seems to me that the times *shine through* certain writers, so that we think they see more clearly than we do, whereas in reality they are making *us* see more clearly.'[1] Their writing has persistently voiced concern about the radical changes that the face of London has undergone, whilst expressing their fury at the various forms of injustice witnessed by the city and its inhabitants. Richard Todd notes that '[w]hat is certain is that none of these fictions, all of them in different ways inspired by the Thatcher decade and its aftermath, would have been inspired, promoted, reviewed, sold and read a generation ago, because they could not even have been written.'[2] Their collective aim has been to resist and reverse the increasing fragmentation of the metropolis, and to humanise it, to recover the human scale through literary devices such as metaphor and strategic deployment of intertextuality.

One of the strongest images that remains in the mind after reading these London novels is of the metropolis as 'a world of fire' (*SV* 462). Fire, ancient symbol of life, creation and alchemy, of fiery consumption and destruction, but also of love and desire, presents us with a complex,

Figure 20   Great Fire of London, the Temple Church

ambiguous metaphor. In these London fictions, fire operates as a structuring element that connects Londoners throughout the ages. Iain Sinclair and Peter Ackroyd have, each in their own way, been capturing what the former calls

> the heat of history. In the white Portland stone of the Hawksmoor churches you could see the fossils coming back to life. Alan Moore thinks of fire as a cultural constant – perhaps in the play against a tradition of London fog and dirt. Heat and its contrary, damp, are part of a duality of the city. Inspiration and stupidity. Energy and lethargy.[3]

Within the writing of these authors, this heat starts with the Great Fire of 1666, but it returns in their engagement with the continued effects of the Second World War that left deep traces within the traumatised postwar consciousness. Michael Moorcock's *Mother London*, for instance, does not only investigate the effects of the Blitz but the novel weaves the incomprehensible destruction of human lives during the Holocaust into his representation of London. In *London Fields*, Amis connects the heat of the Holocaust to the modern city as a consumerist hell, which ripples out towards the peripheral London of *Kingdom Come*, dominated by mega shopping malls such as Bluewater and Westfield. In Maureen Duffy's *Capital* we also feel the heat of history, and in *Londoners* we hear an echo of the Blitz in the IRA bomb attack on the pub The Nervern. Indeed, a similar sensorial reawakening lies in the heat of the bomb attacks in Ballard's *Millennium People*, which reminds us of London's history of anarchism and revolt via Ballard's reworking of the attacks on the Greenwich Observatory in Conrad's *The Secret Agent*.

And in the revolt of middle class Londoners against their gated community in *Millennium People* we feel a Mediterranean temperament creep into the traditionally reserved British temperament: we have seen a resurgence of European cultural and aesthetic influence. In the city we find, beyond its squares teeming with people, marinas and mini-harbours that introduce a major change in London's figure ground, at least at the level of represented spaces. Whether London is slowly changing from a city dominated by labour into one in which leisure features more prominently is doubtful. The city may see more people holidaying, but this tourist's vision of London is simply another form of carefully, rationally organised labour for its inhabitants. Only on the surface, London has become a city of play, a ludic city, in which the dominating presence of the London Eye, the Millennium Dome and the Gherkin feature as signifiers that allude to London's rebirth. The city certainly is a healthier place: the Thames is once again a living river and the 'London mists made entirely of respiratory betrayals and the gasps of asthmatics' (*I* 281) have diminished. The city, at least in the way it is represented to us, has become once more a vibrant, youthful-*looking* place, which, if not quite reliving the Swinging Sixties, is experiencing another creative reinvention on a major scale. It has the cosmetic surgery to prove it; its many architectural nose-jobs to liposuction the city undoubtedly make the city appear a lighter and brighter place. In Peter Ackroyd's words 'London has opened up; there seems to be more space and more air. It has grown in lightness. In the City towers are clad in silver-blue reflective glass, so that the difference between the sky and the building is effaced' (*LB* 777). What has partially been lost in this process of reconstruction is what Martin Amis calls London's 'pub aura', its grimy, dark network of spaces where we may temporarily step outside the official world, and be at one with our fellow citizens.

In Ballard's work, we also find an Eastern heat infect the cold rational capital of Britain. The gated community of *Millennium People* is essentially a reworking of Ballard's internment in a Japanese war camp during the Second World War, whilst his rewriting of a text such as *Dracula* in *High-Rise* adumbrates the various ways in which London, after 1980, becomes overtaken by foreign capital; the presence of Russian oligarchs and oil sheiks, and, often less visibly, an underworld of immigrants and asylum seekers, turns London into a foreign country. The economic and cultural forces of globalisation have made Britain and London less insular. Yet, as Sinclair's invasion of the Isle of Doges suggests, the City and Canary Wharf have started to manifest themselves increasingly as miniature city states. One consequence is that London is increasingly less representative of the nation, of a Britain which itself has undergone numerous changes.

It is a similar heat that Salman Rushdie uses to tropicalise London in *The Satanic Verses*, to counter an English constitution and 'moral fuzziness that was meteorologically induced' (*SV* 354). Just like the cries of Londoners observed by the narrator of William Blake's 'London', this heat is generated by a genuine sense of moral outrage, and a desperate outcry of injustice, and it is Gibreel Farishta's trumpet with fire – with the revelatory truth – that attempts to cleanse the city from the sins and corruption it harbours. 'For truth is extreme, it is *so* and not *thus*, it is *him* and not *her*; a partisan matter, not a spectator sport. It is, in brief, *heated*' (*SV* 354).

Yet different fires blaze within these texts as well. In Martin Amis's work, during the Cold War the threat of nuclear annihilation generates an apocalyptic climate in the metropolis, whilst his experiments with the city as a laboratory for the laws of thermodynamics shows that our modern consumerism is slowly burning up the world while leaving in its wake an ever-growing heap of waste. A new kind of heat, namely that of global warming, has generated a new scatological poetics, which is chased by Ian McEwan's *Solar*, for instance. Yet it is J. G. Ballard's exploration of climate change, from his first novel, *The Drowned World* (1962) to the solar cult in *Kingdom Come*, which locates London at the centre of our slow-motion environmental crash: 'In my mind the fires still burned, moving through the streets of Brooklands and the motorway towns, the flames engulfing crescents of modest bungalows, devouring executive estates and community centres, football stadiums and car showrooms, the last bonfire of the consumer gods' (*KC* 280).

There is another kind of fire in these novels, generated by new anxieties in the post-9/11 world, which have re-asserted the symbolic importance of the capital city. The London of Ian McEwan's *Saturday* is the site where the Blitz and the Iraq War resonate with one another, ebbing out to add to the universal rumble of war the background noise of mankind. Ballard's *Millennium People* is also a re-imagining of the attacks on New York's World Trade Center on 11 September, 2001, which set the world on fire, while the simulacral inferno created by the mass media consumes London.

The skies over London are again no longer safe. The airplanes over London, described by Amis as 'the slow-moving crucifixes of the sky' (*OP* 17), suggest that science and technological advances have, at least to a certain degree, supplanted religion, yet after the terrorist attacks on 9/11 religion has pushed itself back to the forefront of discussions about the contemporary. Salman Rushdie's *The Satanic Verses* already adumbrates, in a related image, this troublesome relationship between religions in the increasingly secular West. The novel starts with Gibreel Farishta's and Saladin Chamcha's re-enactment of Satan's expulsion from heaven in *Paradise Lost* (1667) by falling out of the sky after their aeroplane has been blown up by terrorists, pointing out that increased travel has not only created new, modern forms of Diaspora, but that the modern experience is determined by the possibilities additionally offered by space. In McEwan's *Saturday* London's post-9/11 airspaces introduce a new anxiety into our twenty-first-century existence. The entropic heat and Gothic darkness that characterised McEwan's London in the seventies and eighties has disappeared to make way for a post-9/11 London which is overshadowed by religious tensions and a host of global problems that will not be easy to solve. Yet, even in these dark, uncertain times, London is once again a city of Light and learning, the place where such problems are connected to the city as a place of the imagination and the intellect. Ian McEwan's *Solar* contains a passage that captures this new uncertainty whilst placing trust in our ability to find solutions to the complex array of problems that we are facing:

> These days, whenever he came in over a big city he felt the same unease and fascination. The giant concrete wounds dressed with steel, these catheters of ceaseless traffic filing to and from the horizon – the remains of a natural world could only shrink before them. The pressure of numbers, the abundance of inventions, the blind forces of desire and needs looked unstoppable and were generating a heat, a modern kind of heat that had become, by clever shifts, his subject, his profession. The hot breath of civilisation. He felt it, everyone was feeling it, on the neck, in the face. (*So* 109)

Simultaneously, we also find in all these writers' works the heat of love, carnality and sexual desire as a force that drives, and sometimes redeems, the modern world. In Maureen Duffy's novel we find lonely Londoners who crave physical and mental companionship.

Hanif Kureishi's novels are shot through with the arrows of Eros, showing us central London as a sensory and sexual aphrodisiac, whilst Ballard explores new forms of 'perverse' posthuman sexuality in London's peripheral spaces. Martin Amis's work locates London at the centre of the world that is dying at the same rate as its ability to love declines. Once again it is Eros whose powers may contribute to solving some of the problems we are currently facing.

Sinclair's references to heat also speak of the mental energy and sheer creative fury generated by the frantic, obsessive nature with which these writers have written their textual Londons. Together these writers re-created various Londons in words, a memory map to sustain hope in what sometimes seemed a grim place, a new Darkest London. The result is a collaborative palimpsest, which results in a paradox: although their writing protested against some of the radical changes experienced by the city, its imaginative energy has also contributed to the city's reinvention.

'There was no centre': the dispersal of London in fiction

Iain Sinclair suggests, however, that the body of writers who hold the capital together in their collective work has now fallen apart:

> Monica Ali doesn't live in Brick Lane, and in her novel she has cre-ated a model from some place else. Zadie Smith has some grand take on the city, which has multicultural elements in it but which is basically suburbanized. Unlike Moorcock they are not creating a new mythology of the city. That is why the city is falling apart. [...] There will be many books on the place that is not Brick Lane, simply because that street no longer exists. It has lost its mystery.[4]

Whether a period of damp, stupidity and lethargy has actually set in remains to be seen. If there is a downturn in the exciting, energetic London novel of the past decades it can partly be attributed to the wider problems in the publishing industry, which now refuses to pub-lish anything as boldly inventive and radical as Sinclair's *Downriver*, which is one of contemporary fiction's major contributions to keeping alive the novel as an innovative, flexible form that is able to express modernity's terminal paradoxes. Literature itself is an acknowledged integral part of the market economy, a process that is enhanced by the current rapid changes in the publishing industry: no pretence that art and culture stand outside the financial world. As London remains the site where those in power make decisions and where the impact is felt immediately and often brutally, its literature is aware of this relation-ship like no other. The contemporary London novel could be dimin-ished by the very market forces which it challenged, and it has become a victim of what Milan Kundera has called the 'termites of reduction'. Yet it is Angela Carter who recuperates this apparent disintegration of Sinclair's territorial imperative, and who reminds us: 'Mother London, Iain Sinclair says, is splitting into segments: a queasy glamour extin-guished the mad, bad past in Whitechapel, the rest of the places go hang [...] and yet these stories show how impossible it is to pull down an imaginary city.'[5]

What we have certainly seen is a series of major shifts and develop-ments in London's fiction since the early 1980s. The organic metaphor used by Peter Ackroyd in his biography of London, which is based on the traditional principle of organisational unity of the city and closely related to traditional anthropomorphic associations has become increasingly problematic, if not obsolete. Sinclair notes 'Repeated walks, circuits, attempts to navigate – to get to the heart of the labyrinth – proved frustrating. There was no centre' (*LOFT* 107). Whereas Maurice Ash, in *A Guide to the Structure of London* (1972), could still speak of London as a disconnected collection of villages,[6] Will Self thinks of the city as a 'mighty ergot fungus, erupting from the very crust of the earth; a growing, mutating thing, capable of taking on the most fantastic pro-fusion of shapes'.[7] Self's remark is symptomatic of the changing ways in which London authors are remaking contemporary London. The city has undergone a transformation that sees an increasing complexity in its operational processes, and, at the level of its representations in fic-tion, we see a dispersal of London, which Sinclair has himself enacted and countered in *London Orbital*.

Geographically this dispersal of the city has resulted in a clear shift towards the east of the city: Brick Lane in particular has become 'a mythological battleground' (*SV* 283), with works such as Rushdie's *The Satanic Verses*, Ali's *Brick Lane*, Jeremy Gavron's *An Acre of Barren Ground* (2005) and Tarquin Hall's *Salaam Brick Lane* (2005) being just a few of the recent books covering this now overwritten territory. Andrew Gibson states that 'London is at a historical watershed. The mythologies of what English culture has taken to be "the capital" are being trans-formed and in many instances disintegrating. We are obsessed with stories about "historic London" because the London about which the stories are composed is a London that is rapidly being superseded.'[8]

Despite these radical changes in the city's literary representation, the Thames certainly remains a centre of literary activity. Carter's description of the Thames as 'a great, wet wound' points to the violence that has accompanied the process of making London in text.[9] J. G. Ballard finds that the river – 'a rush of ugly water [...] unimpressed by the money terraces of the City of London' (*MP* 180) is now the only real element within a simulated, virtual London. For Iain Sinclair, the Thames is perhaps the only site of proper London continuity: the river '*is* time: breathless, cyclic, unstoppable' (*D* 304) and Peter Ackroyd's *Thames: Sacred River* (2007) forms yet another celebration of the river's history, and, more importantly, its mythological aspects.

This absence of a clear centre, an 'inside', and of a geographically uniting force has a number of related causes. London is increasingly a less urban, and increasingly a suburbanized city. In *The Information*, Glynn Barry notes: 'In the early darkness Holborn was still yellowly illuminated by its shop windows, and abandoned: That was the modern city: worked in, but not lived in' (*I* 429). This de-urbanisation of the London imagination also means that a certain depreciation and rejection of the values and characteristics that we traditionally associate with city life – heterogeneity and multiplicity, concentration and density, specialisation, tension, drive, progress and change – has taken place. The proliferation of gated communities and new developments that introduce a radically different figure ground in London's organic, messy structure create a break in, or, paradoxically, further, what Ackroyd calls 'the pattern of London'.

Yet this is not suburbanisation in its traditional, pre-war manifestations. The work of Hanif Kureishi suggests that postmodern spatiality creates 'in-between spaces' that erase the tradition binary opposition between the city centre and its periphery. Ballard's work pushes this vision of London even further by reading London in terms of the postmetropolis. One result of the de-urbanisation of London is an increased regionality whereby the city, suburb, the country, village, inner city, satellite city become blurred and absorbed into a homogeneous cityregion. Ballard celebrates the city's boundaries as a network structure where the city is in motion and inhabitants immerse themselves in a transient experience. Iain Sinclair's exploration of the M25 in *London Orbital* features within this process as an attempt to counter the fragmentation. What these writers also respond to is the alarming intensification of observation and modes of surveillance within the public sphere, which is having a major impact upon the relationship between the private and public worlds. Writers such as Ballard and Sinclair, but McEwan and Ali also, pose difficult questions about the ownership of the space we share and to which we all have access. Yet they also give us an aesthetic critique of the changes in ways of looking we currently experience. Their literature works against the pornographic gaze (in the case of Sinclair and Amis) and the clinical, curative gaze (in the case of McEwan), but it also uses new modes of looking to reflect a rapidly changing world.

A series of important and interconnected changes are related to recent shifts in literature, which has moved from a high postmodernist obsession with representations of the city-as-text to a more sober representation that stresses the importance of understanding London as a material structure. There is a new desire for 'the real', as David Shields argues in *Reality Hunger* (2010), which sees various moves towards the factual, conservative strand of writing that Moorcock identifies in London novels. We also see a shift away from the dark, Gothic Londons, and the mystical or occult modes in writers such as Ackroyd and Sinclair, which dominated the London novel for a long time. In his introduction to a re-issuing of Iain Sinclair's *Lud Heat* and *Suicide Bridge*, Michael Moorcock complains:

> It could be argued that the Occult has in the nick of time come to the aid of a threatened Orthodoxy. Talismans and omens are eagerly snapped up by a technologically-challenged middle class. Some days, any old bone will do. Little visionary peels are slipped into Professor Lodge's jellies. The modern English novel contains almost as many ghosts and visitations as a Radcliffe three-decker. Spontaneous combustion should soon become an acceptable literary convention.[10]

As the narrator of *Yellow Dog* mentions jocularly: 'The air smelt of cheap ghosts' (*YD* 125). However, if we trust Moorcook, London's ghosts lie dormant, waiting to be awakened by a new generation of writers.

Simultaneously, the apocalypticism and millenarian drive of many writers has dissipated. Sinclair, McEwan and Amis used the dystopia and science fiction tropes as a way of understanding changes in contemporary Britain, yet at the beginning of an already troubled twenty-first century it seems that writers have a desire to understand the limits of the way in which we can know the world around us. During postmodernism London's endless multiplicity and heterogeneity undermined clear distinctions between genres: 'The form [that] has developed shifts between reportage, poetry, biography, archaeology: fiction has been stripped of its privileged status.'[11] Yet one result of this shift to the factual pole is that the novel as a mode of capturing the city may be less potent in the first place.

Indeed, the obsession with London's mythology has now been replaced by an emphasis on the realism of factual history. Although there is a continued focus on the past there is a marked shift from a focus on London's mythological history to a more factual interest in London's historical lives. The increasing dominance of immigrant narratives benefits from an unstitching and rewriting of traditional fictional and mythical narratives, to demythologise perception in general. The diminishing power of this mythical vision might pose a threat to our imagination of the city: myth, as a source and particularly democratic producer of its own peculiar knowledge. However, even in the most factual of London writers – Ian McEwan is a particularly important example – we find mythologies pushing through the surface of fictional narratives, also waiting to be excavated.

The restoration of London voices

One important shift after postmodernism's obsession with the possibility of writing as a way of deconstructing the linguistic underpinnings of social categories is a renewed interest in the voices of London. This emphasis is important because it allows us to read a revolutionary tradition into the map of London, one that sees a restoration of London voices: the privileging of living speech *in text* keeps the city floating free, out of reach from organisation by political powers; contemporary London narratives operate by an elusive mixture of the written and the spoken.

The way in which Michael Moorcock, Maureen Duffy, Iain Sinclair and Peter Ackroyd align their work with previous oral traditions of London is an important means of restoring a sense of the city's identity. Moorcock works in the tradition of writers such as Dickens, Arthur Conan Doyle and Robert Louis Stevenson, and re-creates London as an authentic myth. Maureen Duffy's work excavates London's mythical history, and brings out its alternative voices. Sinclair, in his idiosyncratic way, lets through the elder voices. Ackroyd places himself amongst Cockney Visionaries such as Chaucer, Blake, More, and Dickens, who produced London as a dark, mystical place. These traditions of 'authenticity' produce London by emphasising the spoken voice.

Yet, we also see a diversification of London voices. We have moved from an imagined city that is exclusively white in the work of J. G. Ballard, Michael Moorcock, Iain Sinclair, Ian McEwan and Martin Amis, to a new London imagination that includes, and is even dominated by, writers such as Salman Rushdie, Hanif Kureishi, Zadie Smith, Monica

Ali and Andrea Levy. Rushdie, Smith and Ali are debunking the binary opposition between myth and fiction as a fictional revisioning of the colonial schemata set up under Empire, and they counter the power of writing by foregrounding the city's new voices. They also open up an imaginative space that restructures our thinking about the contemporary city. Rather than envisioning the urban environment as a purely written discourse, it becomes a verbal enterprise caught in text. These writers privilege textualised living speech because the dialogic possibilities of such a mode of writing generate ambiguities that allow the author greater political and poetic liberties. The sheer verbal and imaginative energy and confidence with which these writers have stormed the house of fiction has caused a dislocation that has upset the order of things.

The work of these writers does not celebrate London's state of crisis, but what their representations share is a cheerful optimism about the future of the metropolis, and, above all, the possibilities it offers to inscribe new voices and histories into the urban fabric. They have contributed to London's emergence as a polymorphic presence generated in a dense layering of languages, histories and mythologies. They make it clear, however, that there is no such thing as 'authentic' London. The London voice is not tied to a particular origin or literary genealogy, but it emerges from a constant interaction between the city and its people. Thus, the consequences are not as clear as Gibson represents them. The radical juxtaposition between white, male fictions and postcolonial stories of London is itself a fiction, and although London certainly *looks* different, after 9/11 skin colour might be a deceptive way of classification whereas a true clash might be about the hegemony of the Judaeo-Christian tradition, and the West's secularisation. Rushdie's *The Satanic Verses* and Ali's *Brick Lane* show for instance that the 'colonisation' of the East End by Bengalis is more of a continuation than radical discontinuity. As we have seen, the literature of Rushdie, Smith and Ali is not merely about rewriting history and inscribing the immigrant self into the urban fabric. The work of these authors takes in models that are derived from West European intellectual and literary traditions, so that ultimately our perception of London should not change as radically as the cultural ambulance chasers pretend. The rich diversity of London voices appears to be more a process of supplementing rather than supplanting; of adding rather than erasing. London's finest representations are characterised, ultimately, by their dialogic nature, which allows its inhabitants to sustain life in a city that continues to invite the literary writer to imaginatively make and remake these infinite Londons.

Notes

Introduction

1. J. G. Ballard, 'Introduction', *Crash* (London: Vintage, 1995; first published by Jonathan Cape, 1973), p. 4.
2. Professor Richard Burdett used these words in a lecture delivered at the London School of Economics, 26 April 2004.
3. Michael Hebbert, *London: More by Fortune than Design* (Chichester: John Wiley & Sons, 1998), pp. 5–7. Roy Porter notes that 'Not since the Romans has London possessed a unified government, a government relevant to all its needs. Administration has been fragmented, often deliberately.' Roy Porter, *London: A Social History* (London: Penguin, 2000; first published by Hamish Hamilton, 1994), p. 3.
4. Sue Brownhill, 'Turning the East End into the West End', in *British Urban Policy*, ed. Rob Imrie and Huw Thomas (London: Sage, 1999), p. 48.
5. Richard Todd, *Consuming Fictions* (London: Bloomsbury, 1996), p. 166.
6. In his analysis of Blake's work, Julian Wolfreys also suggests that there is such a thing as a 'real' London: 'Blake's words deconstruct the purely real, purely representable London in order to transform it into a world of words and discourse, with a topography which resists mapping in the conventional sense, and yet which Blake himself maps without fixing it in place.' Julian Wolfreys, *Writing London: The Trace of the Urban Text from Blake to Dickens* (Basingstoke: Macmillan, 1998), p. 38.
7. Ibid., p. 4.
8. Peter Ackroyd, *London: The Biography* (London: Chatto & Windus, 2000), p. 2. Further references in the text are parenthetically abbreviated as *LB*.
9. Aidan Dun, *Vale Royal* (London: Goldmark, 1995), lines 13–15.
10. Quoted in Andreas Knaack, *Constructions of London in Martin Amis's* London Fields. See: www.knaack.textfabrik.net/
11. J. M. Coetzee, *Youth* (London: Secker & Warburg, 2002), p. 63.
12. J. M. Coetzee, 'What is a Classic?', in *Stranger Shores* (London: Secker & Warburg, 2001), pp. 1–2.
13. T. S. Eliot, *The Waste Land* (London: Faber and Faber, 1969), pp. 59–80, lines 60, 207.
14. Ibid., lines, 22, 60.
15. Frank Budgen, *James Joyce and the Making of* Ulysses (Bloomington: Indiana University Press, 1960; originally published by Grayson & Grayson, 1934), p. 68.
16. Maureen Duffy, *Capital* (London: Harvill, 2001; first published by Jonathan Cape, 1975), p. 17. Further references in the text are parenthetically abbreviated as *C*.
17. Steve Inwood notes that 'All this amounts to under four pages of modern text.' See Steve Inwood, *A History of London* (London: Macmillan, 1998), p. 13.
18. Ibid., p. 14.

19. See the First Book of John Milton's *The History of Britain* (1670). Collected in *The Prose Works of John Milton. With a Biographical Introduction by Rufus Wolmot Griswold. In Two Volumes* (Philadelphia: John W. Moore, 1847).

20. Michael Moorcock, 'Lost London Writers', in *London Bone* (London: Scribner, 2001), pp. 239–40.

21. Iain Sinclair, *Lights Out for the Territory* (London: Granta, 1997), pp. 145–6. Further references in the text are parenthetically abbreviated as *LOFT*.

22. Frank Budgen, *James Joyce and the Making of* Ulysses (London: Grayson & Grayson, 1934), p. 69.

23. Iain Sinclair, *White Chappell, Scarlet Tracings* (London: Goldmark, 1987), p. 134. Further references in the text are abbreviated parenthetically as *WCST*.

24. William Cobbett, *Cobbett's Weekly Political Register*, 5 January 1822.

25. Max Byrd, *London Transformed* (New Haven and London: Yale University Press, 1978), p. 4.

26. Ibid., p. 7.

27. See Victor Sage, 'The Poetics of Mimesis: Aristotle, Tragedy and Realism', in *Theatre Theories: From Plato to Virtual Reality*, ed. Anthony Frost (Norwich, UK: Pen & Inc, 2000), pp. 25–42.

28. Victor Sage, 'Dickens and Professor Owen: Portrait of a Friendship', in *Le Portrait* (Paris: University of Paris-Sorbonne, 1999), pp. 87–101, p. 101.

29. Peter Ackroyd states: 'London is established upon commercial and financial speculation, and the pattern of its housing has followed similar imperatives. It has grown largely from speculative building, advancing in succeeding waves of investment and profit-taking while being momentarily stilled in periods of recession.' See Ackroyd, *LB*, p. 139.

30. Michel Foucault, *The Order of Things: An Archaeology of the Human Sciences* (London: Routledge, 2002; first English edn., Tavistock, 1970; originally published as *Les Mots et les Choses* by Editions Gallimard, 1966), p. 185.

31. Ibid., p. 191. On page 192 Foucault also quotes Barbon's *A discourse concerning coining the new money lighter* (1696), which states that money has replaced coins as the measurement of value.

32. Jean-Joseph Goux, *The Coiners of Language*, trans. Jennifer Curtiss Gage (Norman and London: University of Oklahoma Press, 1994; originally published as *Monnayeurs du langage* by Editions Galilée, 1984), p. 91.

33. Rod Mengham, *The Descent of Language* (London: Bloomsbury, 1993), p. 147.

34. Karl Marx and Friedrich Engels, *The Communist Manifesto*, trans. Samuel Moore (London: Penguin, 1985; first published in German in 1848), p. 83.

35. Martin Amis, *London Fields* (London: Jonathan Cape, 1989), p. 175. Further references in the text are parenthetically abbreviated as *LF*.

36. Tony Tanner, *City of Words: American Fiction, 1950–1970* (London: Jonathan Cape, 1971), p. 34.

37. It is rather unfortunate for Tanner to use the word 'labyrinths' at this point, as he is trying to show, exactly not that human existence is labyrinthine, but its representations thereof.

38. Italo Calvino, *Invisible Cities*, trans. William Weaver (London: Vintage, 1973), p. 14.

39. Michel de Certeau, 'Walking the City', in *The Practice of Everyday Life*, trans. Steven Rendall (Berkeley and London: University of California Press, 1984), p. 97. Further references in the text are abbreviated parenthetically as *PEL*.

40. See Algirdas Julian Greimas, 'For a Topological Semiotics', in *The City and the Sign: An Introduction to Urban Semiotics*, ed. M. Gottdiener and A. P. Lagopoulos (New York: Columbia University Press, 1986), pp. 25–59. In 'Continuities and Discontinuities' Lefebvre states that 'It is this difficulty upon which one must now insist, that of conceiving of the city as a semantic system, semiotic or semiological system arising from linguistics, urban language or urban reality considered as a grouping of signs [...] However, it is not enough to examine this without recourse to context. To write on this writing or language, to elaborate on the *metalanguage of the city* is not to know the city and the urban [...] The city cannot therefore be conceived as *a* signifying system, determined and closed as a system.' *Writings on Cities*, trans. and ed. E. Kofman and E. Lebas (Oxford: Blackwell, 1996), p. 108.

41. Salman Rushdie, *The Satanic Verses* (London: Vintage 1998; first published by Viking, 1988), p. 136. Further references in the text are abbreviated parenthetically as *SV*.

42. Raban states: 'London [...] is the language you've always known, the language from which *being* you, *being* me, are inseparable [...] the city goes soft; it awaits an imprint of identity'. Jonathan Raban, *Soft City* (London: Hamish Hamilton, 1974), pp. 1–2.

43. David Mitchell, *Ghostwritten* (London: Sceptre, 1999; first published by Hodder & Stoughton, 1999), pp. 276–7.

1   Maureen Duffy's Londons

1. Nonetheless her writing has exerted a subtle but important influence upon many writers working in the post-war period: Fevvers, the heroine of Carter's *Nights at the Circus* (1984), derives her name from a minor character of Duffy's *The Microcosm*, the ex-actress Feathers.

2. In 1977 Duffy founded the Authors' Licensing and Collecting Society (ALCS), the internationally recognised authority that collects and distributes fees to writers whose works have been copied, broadcast or recorded. Besides this she was Chairman of the Greater London Arts Literature Panel (1979–81), the Authors' Lending and Copyright Society (1982–94), and the British Copyright Council from 1989 (Vice Chairman, 1981–6); Vice Chairman of the Copyright Licensing Agency from 1994; President of the Writers' Guild of Great Britain (1985–8); Co-founder of the Writers' Action Group (1972–9); Vice President of the European Writers Congress from 1992, and Beauty without Cruelty from 1975; Fellow of the Royal Society of Literature, 1985. She also acted as the President of the European Writers' Congress (EWC)/La Fédération des Associations Européenes d'Écrivains.

3. Dickens set up 'the Guild of Literature and Art, Dickens's version of a kind of life insurance scheme for writers and artists' and protecting writers by means of copyright. See Sage, 'Dickens', p. 90.

4. In Duffy's historical work *England*, she identifies and defends two sociological developments that undermine the post-imperial British identity. The first is an influx of immigrants: 'Immigration has always been part of our culture [...] But in the past the migrants have been largely pale-skinned [...] The arrival of Caribbean workers [...] and then Asian entrepreneurs [...] has added a recognizable strand to the population that's still being assimilated.'

The second is the global dissemination of capital, and as a result of both factors, the English sense of the self that has been mythically constructed over centuries 'is now seen to be receding further from our present, we are susceptible to suggestions that seem to threaten its image even further'. See Maureen Duffy, *England: The Making of the Myth from Stonehenge to Albert Square* (London: Fourth Estate, 2001), pp. 241, 242.

5. Paul Magrs, 'Maureen Duffy', in *The Cambridge Guide to Women's Writing in English*, ed. Lorna Sage (Cambridge: Cambridge University Press, 1999), p. 205.

6. Maureen Duffy, *Londoners: An Elegy* (London: Methuen, 1983), p. 97. Further references in the text are parenthetically abbreviated as *L*.

7. Maureen Duffy, *That's How It Was* (London: Virago, 2002; first published by Hutchinson, 1962), p. 22. Further references in the text are parenthetically abbreviated as *THIW*.

8. Ralph Tymms, *Doubles in Literary Psychology* (Cambridge: Bowes & Bowes, 1949), p. 99.

9. Walter Besant, *London* (London: Chatto & Windus, 1892; reprint 1925), pp. 14–15.

10. Christoph Bode, 'Maureen Duffy: A Polyphonic Sub-version of Realism', in *(Sub)Versions of Realism: Recent Women's Fiction in Britain*, ed. Irmgard Maassen and Ann Maria Stuby (Heidelberg: Carl Winter, 1997), pp. 41–54, p. 47.

11. Julian Wolfreys, *Writing London, Volume 2: Materiality, Memory, Spectrality* (Basingstoke: Palgrave Macmillan, 2004), p. 103.

12. Ibid., p. 93.

13. James Joyce, *A Portrait of the Artist as a Young Man* (London: Penguin, 1992; first published in *The Egoist*, 1914–15), p. 12.

14. James Joyce, *Ulysses* (London: Penguin, 1992; first published, Paris: Shakespeare & Co, 1922), p. 30.

15. Duffy, *England*, p. 242.

16. This passage, which alludes to *Ulysses'* 'Oxen in the Sun' chapter, which is set in the maternity ward of a hospital, becomes ironical in Duffy's context; as Joyce's narrator states: 'It is not why therefore we shall wonder if, as the best historians relate, among the Celts [...] the art of medicine shall have been highly honoured.' See Joyce, *Ulysses*, p. 501. Although Joyce's chapter parodies Dickens's sentimentality, Duffy in her turn is criticising Joyce for his male-centred vision in his masterpiece.

17. Lyndie Brimstone, 'Keepers of History: The Novels of Maureen Duffy', in *Lesbian and Gay Writing*, ed. Mark Lilly (Basingstoke: Macmillan, 1990), pp. 23–46, p. 34.

18. One may think of Dickens's representation of the Thames as a primeval swamp in *Our Mutual Friend* (1864–5), Joyce and T. S. Eliot, but also Seamus Heaney and J. G. Ballard, whose *The Drowned World* (1962) is a descent through archaeopsychic time. To demonstrate the counter-example we have the Persephone myth and, for instance, Margaret Atwood's *Surfacing* (1973).

19. Rod Mengham notes: 'The Neanderthals inhabit a universe in which they are open to visual, tactile, and aural stimuli, but which they cannot organize conceptually. Without a language with tenses that determine the differences between past, present and future, and without the means of defining the limits of personal agency, they cannot relate phenomena through time and space. [...] As far as one can tell, the life of a Neanderthal would be radically

discontinuous, a process of being bombarded by fragments of experience not even searching for, let alone finding, a meaningful context.' Mengham, *Descent*, p. 5.

20. Bode, 'Maureen Duffy', p. 41.

21. Richard Lehan, *The City in Literature: An Intellectual and Cultural History* (Berkeley: University of California Press, 1998), p. 110.

22. Peter Ackroyd has shown a renewed interest in the Middle Ages with *The Clerkenwell Tales* (2003) and his biography of Chaucer (2004).

23. Tymms, *Doubles*, p. 105.

24. William Shakespeare, *The Tempest*, V.1.186–7, I.2.404.

25. Claire Colebrook, *Gilles Deleuze* (Oxford: Routledge, 2002), p. 105.

26. The full list is: Brahms (*L* 14); Guliemo Maconi and Thomas Edison (*L* 14); Kurt Weill and Berthold Brecht (*L* 15, 181); Dickens's Marley from *A Christmas Carol* (1843) (*L* 17, 35); Samuel Taylor Coleridge (*L* 17, 132); Ivan Goncharov's *Oblomov* (*L* 17); W. B. Yeats (*L* 21, 98, 153, 211); Dante's Virgil (*L* 23); François Rabelais (*L* 28); Averoes and Avenzoar (*L* 35); Charles d'Orleans (*L* 35); John Donne (*L* 37, 93); Roberts Burns (*L* 37); T. S. Eliot (*L* 37); Edmund Spenser (*L* 37); John Keats (*L* 37); John Clare (*L* 37); Virgil (*L* 38); Horace (*L* 38); Dante (*L* 38); Shakespeare (*L* 38, 83, 103, 132); Dante Gabriel Rossetti (*L* 38); Robert Lowell (*L* 38); Ben Jonson (*L* 41); Dylan Thomas (*L* 51); Matthew Arnold (*L* 58, 86); Handel (*L* 72); Franz Kafka (*L* 85); Graham Greene (*L* 92); Botticelli (*L* 93); Jean-Paul Sartre (*L* 95); George Orwell (*L* 97); Henry James (*L* 105); Arnold Bennett (*L* 121); Somerset Maugham (*L* 129); E. M. Forster (*L* 129); Joe Orton (*L* 139); St Augustine (*L* 139); James Joyce (*L* 141); Aristotle (*L* 142, 145); Plato (*L* 142); Pier Pasolini (*L* 152); John Cleland (*L* 152); Oscar Wilde (*L* 153); Herman Melville (*L* 163); and Stanley Kubrick (*L* 215).

27. Bode, 'Maureen Duffy', p. 50.

28. Wolfreys, *Writing London, Volume 2*, p. 105.

29. Doris Teske, *Die Vertextung der Megapolis: London im Spiel postmoderner Texte* (Trier: Wissenschaftlicher Verlag Trier, 1999, in German), p. 174, my translation.

30. Duffy herself used the word in the poem *Parsiphae*, which opens with the line: 'Cuntsmell on my hands.' See Maureen Duffy, *Evesong* (London: Sappho, 1975).

31. Joyce, *Ulysses*, p. 719.

32. Ibid., p. 240.

33. Deborah Parsons, *Streetwalking the Metropolis: Women, the City and Modernity* (Oxford: Oxford University Press, 2000), pp. 2–3.

34. Juvenal, *The Sixteen Satires*, trans. and intro. Peter Green (Harmondsworth: Penguin, 1979), p. 136.

35. Deborah Parsons has shown the exceptions to the rule in her book *Streetwalking the Metropolis*.

36. Maureen Duffy, *Collected Poems* (London: Hamish Hamilton, 1985), p. 12.

37. Bode, 'Maureen Duffy', p. 49.

38. Virginia Woolf, *A Room of One's Own*, in *The Norton Anthology of English Literature: Volume 2*, ed. M. H. Abrams (New York and London: W. W. Norton, 1993; first published 1929), pp. 1977–8. In a next move, Woolf draws on Coleridge's ideas to translate this psychological duality into terms of literary creation: 'Coleridge perhaps meant this when he said that the great mind

is androgynous. It is when this fusion takes place that the mind is fully fertilised and uses all its faculties. Perhaps a mind that is purely masculine cannot create, any more than a mind that is purely feminine, I thought. [...] Perhaps the androgynous mind is less apt to make these distinctions than the single-sexed mind. He meant, perhaps, that the androgynous mind is resonant and porous; that it transmits emotion without impediment; that it is naturally creative, incandescent and undivided' (p. 1978). Woolf lists Shakespeare, Keats, Sterne, Cowper, Lamb and Coleridge as having androgynous minds, and, understandably, keeps intact the idea that the male and female are different: she needs to defend women *as* women.

39. Inwood, *History of London*, p. 19.
40. Angela Carter, 'Notes for a Theory of Sixties Style', *Nothing Sacred* (London: Virago, 1980; first published in *New Society*, 1967), p. 89.
41. Peter Ackroyd states in *Dressing Up*: 'it would be a mistake to assume that the transvestite shares the male transsexual's aspiration towards complete femininity. He is indisputably and permanently male and he will, unconsciously or surreptitiously, leave clues to his male gender even within the most complete dressing up ... [It] is a bizarre but effective way of displaying the limits of what might otherwise be a perfect illusion.' Peter Ackroyd, *Dressing Up: Transvestism and Drag – The History of an Obsession* (London: Thames & Hudson, 1979), pp. 19–20.

2   Michael Moorcock's Authentic London Myths

1. Michael Moorcock, *Mother London* (London: Scribner, 2000; first published by Secker & Warburg, 1988) and *King of the City* (London: Scribner, 2001; first published by Scribner, 2000). Further references in the text are parenthetically abbreviated as *ML* and *KC*, respectively.
2. Moorcock, 'Lost London Writers', in *London Bone*, pp. 240–1.
3. Inwood, *History of London*, 936.
4. Porter, *London*, pp. 453–4.
5. F. R. Leavis, *The Great Tradition: George Eliot, Henry James, Joseph Conrad* (London: Chatto & Windus, 1948), p. 2.
6. Colin Greenland, *Michael Moorcock: Death is no Obstacle* (Manchester: Savoy, 1992), p. 22.
7. In an article for the *Guardian*, Sinclair notes, however, that Moorcock is included in the latest edition of the *Oxford Companion to English Literature*, edited by Margaret Drabble: 'He's included, quite generously summarised, and not just as a "science fiction writer of the 1960s." But how strange it must feel, to be allowed into the club, while most of your colleagues and former collaborators, the characters around whom so much of your work has been constructed, lead an extra-curricular existence, banished from the official canon.' Iain Sinclair, 'Crowning glory: Michael Moorcock's London', *Guardian*, 23 November 2000. http://www.guardian.co.uk/books/2000/nov/23/london reviewofbooks [accessed 5 July 2008].
8. Michael Moorcock in his 2002 Introduction to Jeff Gardiner's *The Age of Chaos: The Multiverse of Michael Moorcock* (Stockport: The British Fantasy Society, 2002), p. 11.

9. Moorcock, *London Bone*, p. 8.
10. Claude Lévi-Strauss, *The Savage Mind* (London: Weidenfeld & Nicolson, 1966; first published as *La Pensée Sauvage* in 1962), p. 16.
11. David L. Pike, *Subterranean Cities: The World beneath Paris and London, 1800–1945* (Ithaca, NY: Cornell University Press, 2005), pp. 68–9.
12. The subterranean world stands for the alternative, subversive imagination, a narrative convention that is underscored by the post-Situationist poetic terrorist Hakim Bey in *T. A. Z.*, which speaks of troglodytes as 'anarchists forced into hiding after the Entropy Wars [...] the Trogs have kept alive for over 200 years the folk memory of the Autonomous Zone, the myth that someday it will appear again'. See Hakim Bey, *T. A. Z.: The Temporary Autonomous Zone, Ontological Anarchy, Poetic Terrorism* (New York: Autonomedia, 1991; first published 1985), p. 85.
13. Inwood, *History of London*, p. 777.
14. Inwood also notes: 'Tube sheltering was conspicuous, visible of course to every evening or early-morning underground traveller, and it soon became part of the "myth" of the Blitz. In reality London did not become a city of troglodytes. Only one Inner Londoner in eighteen slept in the Tube system on its busiest night, and in mid-November [1940], when a rough census of shelters was conducted, only 4 per cent slept in the Tube, while 9 per cent slept in other public or communal shelters [...] 27 per cent used domestic and brick shelters [...] and 60 per cent stayed in their own beds. In this respect, the "real" Londoner was more stoical than the "mythical" one, and the myth is a myth of timidity.' Ibid., pp. 796–7.
15. Ibid., p. 790.
16. We find similar examples of this theme parkification in Andrew Cowan's *Pig* (London: Michael Joseph, 1994), where in a northern mining town an old steelworks is about to be turned into an entertainment park called *LeisureLand*, which is abandoned by the project developers. In Julian Barnes's *England, England* (London: Jonathan Cape, 1998) the defining characteristics of English life and culture are condensed into a Theme Park on the Isle of Wight. Visitors find the stereotypical architectural signifiers of Englishness, such as Big Ben and Buckingham Palace, but also actors who play mythical characters such as Robin Hood and King Arthur, and literary giants such as Dr Johnson. A Dickens theme park, which cost £62 million to build, 'Dickens World', was opened in 2007 in Chatham Dockyard, Kent.
17. Porter, *London*, p. 468.
18. Raphael Samuel, *Theatres of Memory: Vol. 1 – Past and Present in Contemporary Culture* (London: Verso, 1994), p. 402.
19. Ibid., p. 411.
20. Moorcock pitches independent writers and self-published magazines, which embody the counterculture of the sixties, against the 'official' mass media and the government fabulators. The former offer resistance to the forces of mass media by alternative, underground sources such as the small, independent press that publishes Mummery's books of obscure London narratives, countercultural sixties newspapers such as *International Times* and magazines such as *Oz* and the 1972 magazine *Frendz*. As Moorcock's text refers to a demonstration at the Old Bailey after the latter magazine has been banned in 1968 (*ML* 88–9), Moorcock points directly to London as a place

where official power censors minority voices, a theme that is present in the work of Duffy as well.

21. Sinclair, 'Crowning glory: Michael Moorcock's London', *The Guardian*, 23 November 2000. http://www.guardian.co.uk/books/2000/nov/23/london reviewofbooks [accessed 5 July 2008].

22. Angela Carter, 'Michael Moorcock: *Mother London*', in *Expletives Deleted* (London: Chatto & Windus, 1992), p. 116.

23. See Angela Carter's introduction to Greenland's *Death is no Obstacle*, p. iii.

24. See Anthony Powell, *The Strangers are All Gone* (London: William Heinemann, 1982), p. 7.

25. Mikhail M. Bakhtin, *The Dialogic Imagination*, ed. Michael Holquist, trans. Caryl Emerson and Michael Holquist (Austin: University of Texas Press, 2002; first published 1981), p. 262.

26. Ibid., p. 266.

27. In his essay on Angela Carter's fiction, Robert Eaglestone shows the close affinity between Carter and Moorcock by referring to a remark of Carter in *Shaking a Leg*: 'But even her Englishness is "English in the great tradition of pantomime, of radical dissent and continuous questioning, the other side of imperialism, if you like" as she writes of Michael Moorcock.' See Robert Eaglestone, 'The Fiction of Angela Carter', in *Contemporary British Fiction*, ed. Richard J. Lane, Rod Mengham and Philip Tew (Cambridge: Polity Press, 2003), pp. 195–210, p. 201.

28. Roger Luckhurst, 'The Contemporary London Gothic and the Limits of the "Spectral Turn"', *Textual Practice* 16(3), 2002: 527–46, pp. 528–9.

29. In *King of the City*, sixties media icon Christine Keeler is described as a 'potent myth, but she hadn't sought that potency and couldn't deliver what it was the people had expected' (*KC* 226). Keeler's failure is clarified by President Bill Clinton's intern Monica Lewinsky: 'all she had to offer the world in the end was her notoriety. You can only lift your skirt and show your knickers for so long before people start casting around for a new diversion' (*KC* 226).

30. Brian Baker, 'Maps of the London Underground: Iain Sinclair and Michael Moorcock's Psychogeography of the City', *Literary London Journal*, March 2003, http://www.literarylondon.org/london-journal/march2003/baker.html [accessed 4 October 2006].

31. Kate Fox, *Watching the English: The Hidden Rules of English Behaviour* (London: Hodder & Stoughton, 2004), p. 89.

32. Another brothel forms the centre stage in Moorcock's *The Brothel in Rosenstrasse* (London: New English Library, 1982), where the fictional German city of Mirenburg in 1900 has Europe's most famous brothel, which is described as having 'the ambience of an integrated nation, hermetic, microcosmic. It is easy, once within, to believe the place possessed of an infinity of rooms and passages, all isolated from that other world outside' (p. 32). This representation is potentially problematic, as this place of women's exploitation and commoditisation is misrepresented as a utopian site of universal harmony.

33. Lawrence Phillips, *London Narratives* (New York and London: Continuum, 2006), p. 152.

34. Lévi-Strauss, *Savage Mind*, p. 17.

35. Ibid.
36. In his introduction to Gardiner's book, Moorcock states about his own work: 'I believe I should be able to turn my hand to almost any form at the drop of a hat – *belles letters*, criticism, fiction of various kinds, film scripts, tv work (sic), short stories, novels, reminiscence, music and lyrics, what ever you can do. I think that some ideas are best expressed in semi fiction, some in fiction, some in non-fiction and so on. Genres present their own method. You use the best tool for the job' (Gardiner, *Age of Chaos*, p. 10).
37. The narrator of *London Bone*, Raymond Gold, is a jack of all trades: 'I have bought and sold, been the middleman, an agent, an art representative, a professional mentor, a tour guide, a spiritual bridge-builder. These days I call myself a cultural speculator' (p. 105).
38. Lévi-Strauss, *Savage Mind*, pp. 21–2.
39. See Baker, 'Maps'.
40. See Inwood, *History of London*, p. 788.
41. Claude Lévi-Strauss, *Myth and Meaning* (London and New York: Routledge, 2001; first published in the UK by Kegan Paul, 1978), pp. 29–30.
42. Gardiner, *Age of Chaos*, p. 89.
43. In *A Cure for Cancer* 'the air was jeweled and faceted, glistening and alive with myriad colours, flashing, scintillating, swirling and beautiful' (London: Alison & Busby, 1971), p. 55. Cornelius also states: '"The multiverse. All layers of existence seen at once. Get it?"' (p. 55).
44. From Michael Moorcock's 'Multiverse', on his website http//:www.micha elmoorcock.com [accessed 3 February 2006].
45. Greenland, *Death is no Obstacle*, p. 96.
46. Ibid., p. 104.

3 J. G. Ballard versus London

1. J. G. Ballard, 'Airports', *The Observer*, 14 September 1997. See www.jgballard. com/airports.htm [accessed 15 August 2008].
2. J. G. Ballard, *High-Rise* (London: Triad/Panther, 1977; first published by Jonathan Cape, 1975), p. 9.
3. Harker notes: 'I was not able to light on any map or work giving the exact locality of the Castle Dracula, as there are no maps of this country as yet to compare with our own Ordnance Survey Maps.' Bram Stoker, *Dracula* (London: Penguin, 2003; first published by Archibald Constable, 1897), p. 8. He also writes: 'It seems to me that the further East you go the more unpunctual are the trains. What ought they to be in China?' (p. 8).
4. Ibid., p. 20.
5. See Franco Moretti, '*Dracula* and Capitalism', in *Signs Taken for Wonders: On the Sociology of Literary Forms* (London: Verso, 1988), pp. 83–98, p. 85. Harker states: 'This was the being I was helping transfer to London, where, perhaps for centuries to come, he might, amongst its teeming millions, satiate his lust for blood, and create a new and ever widening circle of semi-demons to batten on the helpless.' Stoker, *Dracula*, p. 60. Van Helsing states: 'And so the circle goes on ever widening.'
6. Lehan, *City in Literature*, p. 96.

7. Iain Sinclair, *Crash: David Cronenberg's Post-Mortem on J. G. Ballard's 'Trajectory of Fate'* (London: British Film Institute, 1999), p. 8.

8. Lehan refers to Richard Wasson's article 'The Politics of *Dracula*', *English Literature in Transition* 9(1), 1966: 24–7.

9. J. G. Ballard, *Super-Cannes* (London: Flamingo, 2000), p. 249.

10. Martin Amis, *The War against Cliché* (London: Jonathan Cape, 2001), p. 108.

11. J. G. Ballard, 'The Voices of Time', in *The Voices of Time* (London: Indigo, 1997; first published as *The Four-Dimensional Nightmare*, London: Victor Gollancz, 1963), p. 10.

12. In an interview Ballard states that 'In the suburbs you find uncentred lives. The normal civic structures are not there. So that people have more freedom to explore their own imaginations, their own obsessions. And the discretionary spending power to do so.' See Sinclair, *Crash*, p. 84.

13. Lewis Mumford, *The City in History: Its Origins, Its Transformations, and Its Prospects* (Harmondsworth: Penguin, 1973; first published by Secker & Warburg, 1961), pp. 552–3.

14. Ibid., p. 559.

15. Edward Carter, *The Future of London* (Harmondsworth: Penguin, 1962), p. 74.

16. Ballard writes: '[it] is now a suburb not of London but of London Airport, and one can see the influence of Heathrow in the office buildings that resemble control towers and huge shopping malls whose floors remind the visitor of a terminal concourse.' J. G. Ballard, 'Shepperton Past and Present', in *A User's Guide to the New Millennium* (London: HarperCollins, 1996), pp. 194.

17. Nick Davis, '"An Unrehearsed Theatre of Technology": Oedipalization and Vision in Ballard's *Crash*', in *Imagining Apocalypse*, ed. David Seed (Basingstoke: Macmillan, 2000), p. 148.

18. J. G. Ballard, *Crash* (London: Vintage, 1995; first published by Jonathan Cape, 1973), p. 47. Further references in the text are parenthetically abbreviated as *Cr*.

19. In a similar fashion, Julian Barnes's *Metroland* underscores this renegotiation of sexuality in terms of place: 'London, he explained, was the centre of power and industry and money and culture and everything valuable, important and good; it was therefore, *ex hypothesi*, the centre of sex [...] But in the suburbs, Toni went on [...] you are in a strange intermediate area of sexual twilight. You might think of the suburbs – Metroland, for instance – as being erotically soporific; yet the grand itch animated the most unlikely people. You never were where you were [...] It was here, he maintained, that the really interesting bits of sex took place.' Julian Barnes, *Metroland* (London: Jonathan Cape, 1980), p. 157.

20. Michel Foucault, Preface to Gilles Deleuze and Félix Guattari, *Anti-Oedipus*, trans. Robert Hurley, Mark Seem, and Helen R. Lane (London and New York: Continuum, 2004; first published by Athlone Press, 1984. Originally published as *L'Anti Oedipe* in 1972 by Les Editions de Minuit, Paris), p. xxii.

21. Gilles Deleuze and Félix Guattari, *A Thousand Plateaus: Capitalism and Schizophrenia*, trans. Brian Massumi (London and New York: Continuum, 2002; first published in Great Britain 1988 by Athone Press. Originally published as *Mille Plateaux*, volume 2 of *Capitalisme et Schizophrénie*, 1980, by Les Editions de Minuit, Paris), p. 18.

22. J. G. Ballard, *Kingdom Come* (London: Fourth Estate, 2006), p. 78. Further references in the text are parenthetically abbreviated as *Kc*.

23. Mumford, *City in History*, pp. 561–72.

24. See Edward W. Soja, *Postmetropolis: Critical Studies of Cities and Regions* (Oxford: Blackwell, 2000), pp. 145–348.

25. Ballard, *User's Guide*, p. 195.

26. Soja, *Postmetropolis*, p. 325.

27. Ballard, 'Introduction' to *Crash*, p. 4.

28. J. G. Ballard, *The Kindness of Women* (London: HarperCollins, 1991), p. 197.

29. Ibid., p. 272.

30. Soja, *Postmetropolis*, p. 352.

31. *Kingdom Come* also confirms a tacit agreement between Iain Sinclair and Ballard in their joint resistance to the Millennium Dome as a signifier of New Labour's power, and as a symbol of how politics are visibly inscribed into the landscape. This Ballard–Sinclair pact started in the late 1990s, with Sinclair's own turn away from the centre of London, which he deemed overwritten, and sparked an increased interest in the work of Ballard, which resulted in a book on Ballard's *Crash* and David Cronenberg's adaptation for the screen, *Crash* (1996). *Kingdom Come* continues the wrath that Sinclair bestowed upon the Dome in *London Orbital* (2000), a book that is both driven by and a homage to Ballard's work. In the film, *London Orbital* (2002), Ballard orders Sinclair: 'I want you to blow up Bluewater.'

32. J. G. Ballard, *Millennium People* (London: HarperCollins, 2003), p. 3. Further references in the text are parenthetically abbreviated as *MP*.

33. Colebrook, *Deleuze*, p. 65.

34. Sinclair in Sebastian Groes and Iain Sinclair, 'An Interview with Iain Sinclair', *Pretext*, Autumn 2005 (Norwich: Pen & Inc), pp. 65–80, p. 74.

35. J. G. Ballard, *The Atrocity Exhibition* (London: HarperPerennial, 2006; first published by Jonathan Cape, 1970), pp. 99–100.

36. *PS* 58–9.

37. David James, *Contemporary British Fiction and the Artistry of Space* (London and New York: Continuum, 2008), p. 92.

38. See Sebastian Groes, 'From Shanghai to Shepperton: Crises of Representation in J. G. Ballard's Londons', in *J. G. Ballard: Contemporary Critical Perspectives*, ed. Jeannette Baxter (London and New York: Continuum, 2009), pp. 78–93.

39. Umberto Eco, in Gottdiener and Lagopoulous, *The City and the Sign*, p. 63.

40. In an interview, Iain Sinclair echoes this assessment: 'in England many cultural venues have something odd about them. Take Tate Britain, which used to be a prison, the Millbank Penitentiary. When you enter the building from the back, you can still actually see some of the cell blocks. Even now you can feel the spirit of imprisonment. Tate Modern has all the qualities of a hospital. There is something Fritz Langian about it.' See Groes and Sinclair, 'Interview', p. 73.

41. Milan Kundera, 'The Depreciated Legacy of Cervantes', in *The Art of the Novel*, trans. Linda Asher (London: Faber and Faber, 1999; first published in French as *L'Art du roman* by Editions Gallimard, 1986), p. 11.

42. See Michael White, 'God will judge me, PM tells Parkinson', *Guardian*, 4 March 2006, http://www.guardian.co.uk/politics/2006/mar/04/labour.uk2 [accessed 3 December 2009].

43. Jeanette Baxter, 'Ballard Interview', *Pretext* 9 (Norwich: Pen & Inc, 2004), p. 31.
44. Quoted in Inwood, *History of London*, p. 602.
45. Arnold states: 'The modern spirit has now almost entirely dissolved those habits [subordination and deference], and the anarchical tendency of our worship of freedom in and for itself, of our superstitious faith [...] in machinery, is becoming very manifest. [...] this and that body of men, all over the country, are beginning to assert and put in practice an Englishman's right to do what one likes; his right to march where he likes [...] All this [...] leads to anarchy.' Matthew Arnold, *Culture and Anarchy* (London: Cambridge University Press, 1963), p. 76.
46. Dominic Head, *Ian McEwan: Contemporary British Novelists* (Manchester: Manchester University Press, 2007), pp. 183–4.
47. Joseph Conrad, *The Secret Agent* (London: Penguin, 1994; first published 1907), pp. 35–7.

4 Iain Sinclair's London

1. Todd, *Consuming Fictions*, p. 176.
2. Rod Mengham, 'Introduction' to *An Introduction to Contemporary Fiction*, ed. Rod Mengham (Cambridge: Polity Press, 1999), p. 3.
3. Peter Barry, *Contemporary British Poetry and the City* (Manchester and New York: Manchester University Press, 2000), pp. 174–5.
4. Robert Bond, 'Wide Boys Always Work: Iain Sinclair and the London Proletarian Novel', *Literary London Journal*, September 2003. http://www.literarylondon.org/london-journal/september2003/bond.html [accessed 4 October 2006].
5. Maurice Merleau-Ponty, *Phenomenology of Perception*, trans. Colin Smith (London: Routledge & Kegan Paul, 1962), p. 17.
6. William Wordsworth, *The Prelude*, Book III, line 63. First published in 1850.
7. Sinclair speaks of having auditory hallucinations during the 1970s, when he was working in Truman's Brewery (Brick Lane), and in the Whitechapel Gallery he heard the words 'Ramsey holds the key'. See Kevin Jackson's book-length interview with Sinclair, *The Verbals* (Tonbridge: Worple Press, 2003), pp. 71–2.
8. Andrew Gibson, 'Altering Images', in Joe Kerr and Andrew Gibson (eds), *London: From Punk to Blair* (London: Reaktion Books, 2003), p. 292.
9. Brian Baker, *Iain Sinclair* (Manchester: Manchester University Press, 2007), p. 86.
10. Iain Sinclair, *Edge of the Orison* (London: Hamish Hamilton, 2006), p. 93.
11. Simon Perril, 'A Cartography of Absence: The Work of Iain Sinclair', *Comparative Criticism*, 19, 1997: 309–39, p. 313.
12. This is a strategy that Alex Murray also argues for in *Recalling London: Literature and History in the Work of Peter Ackroyd and Iain Sinclair* (New York and London: Continuum, 2007), pp. 148–50.
13. Peter Brooker, 'A Novelist in the Era of Higher Capitalism: Iain Sinclair and the Postmodern East End', Conference Paper for the 3Cities Project, 2003, http://www.nottingham.ac.uk/3cities/brooker.htm [accessed 18 July 2005].

14. Ibid.
15. Rachel Potter, 'Culture Vulture: the Testimony of Iain Sinclair's *Downriver*', *Parataxis: Modernism and Modern Writing* 5, Winter 1993–4: 40–8.
16. Robert Sheppard, *Where Treads of Death: Five Books of Iain Sinclair Reviewed* (Liverpool: Ship of Fools, 2004), p. 3.
17. Groes and Sinclair, 'Interview', p. 68.
18. Iain Sinclair, *Lud Heat and Suicide Bridge* (London: Vintage, 1995; *Lud Heat* originally published by Albion Village Press, 1975, and *Suicide Bridge* by Albion Village Press, 1979), p. 14. Further references in the text are abbreviated parenthetically as *LH*.
19. Iain Sinclair, *London Orbital: A Walk around the M25* (London: Penguin, 2003; first published by Granta, 2002), p. 158. Further references in the text are abbreviated parenthetically as *LO*.
20. Groes and Sinclair, 'Interview', p. 67.
21. Iain Sinclair and Dave McKean, *Slow Chocolate Autopsy* (London: Phoenix House, 1997), p. 84.
22. Wolfreys, *Writing London, Volume 2*, p. 205.
23. Perril, 'Cartography', p. 312.
24. Ibid., p. 315.
25. Bond states: 'Now, the question whether or not Sinclair is interested in the process of decipherment and whether it leads to any fixed outcome is firstly undercut by the question of *how* to understand the city, as a text, as a physical structure etc.' Robert Bond, *Iain Sinclair* (London: Salt, 2005), p. 168.
26. Teske, *Vertextung*, p. 145. My translation. Original sentence in German: 'Die Metropole ist eine Sammlung von Texten, die der Buchantiquar Sincalir in ihrer materiellen Form anspricht. Die Stadt ist voll von Buchhandlungen and fliegenden Buchhändlern, einzelne Bucher bewegen sich – ähnlich wie die "Metataphorai" von de Certeau oder Barthes' Graffiti – beinah "selbständig" auf unvorhersagbaren Bahnen durch den städtischen Raum.'
27. See Gottdiener and Lagopoulos's Introduction to *The City and the Sign*, p. 16.
28. Sinclair imagines there exist secret meanings to the composition of eight churches designed by Nicholas Hawksmoor, who after Sir Christopher Wren was the most important builder of churches in London following the Great Fire of 1666. Together these churches 'are only one system of energies, or unit of connection, within the city' (*LH* 17, 20).
29. Sinclair, *LH*, p. 28; bold script in the original.
30. James Webb, *The Occult Establishment: Vol. II. The Age of the Irrational* (Glasgow: Richard Drew Publishing, 1981), p. 10.
31. Michel de Certeau, 'Mystic Speech', in *Heterologies*, trans. Brian Massumi (Manchester: Manchester University Press, 1986), p. 90. First published as 'L'énonciation mystique' in *Recherches de science religieuse*, 64(2), 1976: 198–215.
32. Denise Riley, *The Words of Selves: Identification, Solidarity, Irony* (Stanford: Stanford University Press, 2000), pp. 33–4.
33. Iain Sinclair, *Radon Daughters* (London: Jonathan Cape, 1994), p. 287.
34. Patrick McGrath's narrator of *Spider* states that the act of writing 'feels like being written'. Patrick McGrath, *Spider* (New York: Poseidon, 1990), p. 107.
35. Baker, *Iain Sinclair*, p. 2.

36. Iain Sinclair, *Downriver* (London: Paladin, 1991), p. 352. Further references in the text are abbreviated parenthetically as *D*.

37. Joyce, *Ulysses*, p. 242.

38. Wolfreys, *Writing London, Volume 2*, p. 196.

39. *Downriver* contains an oblique reference to Blake's prophetic blood running down palace walls: 'I ran my palms over the walls. I made them bleed' (*D* 280).

40. Here, Sinclair not only refers the Thatcher regime itself, but the Roman Catholic Church housed in the Papal Palace as well; Blake's 'palace' is Lambeth Palace (the Protestant establishment) and the Palace of Westminster (the home of the secular wing of the government).

41. 'Eisenbahnangst' is German for 'railway fear' and alludes, in the light of German concentration camps and the Holocaust, to fear of railways as a recognised syndrome connected to the Holocaust, a connection which is strengthened by its resonance with *Einbahnstrasse* (1928) by Walter Benjamin, who committed suicide when fleeing from the Nazis.

42. Iain Sinclair's letter to Angela Carter reprinted in her *Expletives Deleted*, pp. 126–7.

43. William Blake, *Jerusalem: The Emanation of the Giant Albion*, ed. David Bindman (London: The William Blake Trust/The Tate Gallery, 1991), Plate 31, pp. 47, 178.

44. Baker, *Iain Sinclair*, p. 86.

45. Photographer Mike Seaborne captured the billboard advertisement that visualised the Canary Wharf skyline as a conflation of Venice and New York. See Kerr and Gibson, *London*, p. 180.

46. Margaret Thatcher, 'Speech inaugurating Canary Wharf', http://www.marga retthatacher.org/document/107834 [accessed 5 July 2007]. Originally delivered on 29 November 1989.

47. Tony Tanner, *Venice Desired* (Cambridge, MA: Harvard University Press, 1992), p. 5.

48. Ibid.

49. Victor Sage, 'Black Venice: Conspiracy and Narrative Masquerade in Schiller, Zschlokke, Lewis and Hoffman', *Gothic Studies*, 8(1), 2006: 52–72 (pp. 52–3).

50. Oscar Newman, *Defensible Space: Crime Prevention through Urban Design* (London: Macmillan, 1972).

51. Alan Clark quoted in Julian Barnes, *Letters from London* (London: Picador, 1995), p. 241.

52. This Bakhtinian reading can also be extended to the Corporation in the fourth section 'Living in Restaurant', where the fictional 'Sinclair' and his fellow documentary maker have been engaged in 'four months of heroic eating' (*D* 91), which points to the grotesque gluttony of the Pantagruellian Thatcher gang.

53. Julia Kristeva, *The Powers of Horror: Essays on Abjection*, trans. Leos S. Roudiez (New York: Columbia University Press, 1982), p. 205.

54. I would like to thank Dr Tim Jarvis for suggesting this connection.

55. Jonathan Swift, 'The Progress of Beauty', in *The Complete Poems*, ed. Pat Rogers (London: Penguin, 1983), pp. 192–5, lines 13–15, 22.

56. Swift, 'The Lady's Dressing Room' *Complete Poems*, pp. 448–52, lines 117–18.

57. Swift, 'A Beautiful Young Nymph Going to Bed', *Complete Poems*, pp. 453–5, lines 10–11, 19–20.
58. Swift, 'Nymph', lines 65–8.
59. Swift, 'Lady's Dressing Room', lines 13, 60.
60. In *Downriver* Todd Sileen 'was gathering about him the works of Joseph Conrad. All of them; every envelope, every (certified) drop of ink' (*D* 35). This symbolic collection of the (literary) body of Conrad is also a reversal of the drive towards fragmentation.
61. Angela Carter calls the Thames 'a wet wound'. See 'Adventures at the End of Time', in the *London Review of Books*, 13(5), 7 March 1991, p. 17.
62. Pike, *Subterranean Cities*, pp. 68–9.
63. In *The Production of Space*, Lefebvre notes: 'The arrogant verticality of skyscrapers [...] introduces a [...] phallocratic element into the visual realm; the purpose of this display, of this need to impress, is to convey an impression of authority to each spectator. Verticality and great height have ever been the spatial expression of potentially violent power' (*PS* 98).
64. Mengham, *Contemporary Fiction*, p. 6.
65. Mike Davis, *City of Quartz: Excavating the Future in Los Angeles* (New York: Vintage, 1992; first published 1990), pp. 224, 254.
66. Edward W. Soja, 'Heterotopologies: A Remembrance of Other Spaces in the Citadel-LA', in *Postmodern Cities and Spaces*, ed. Sophie Watson and Katherine Gibson (Oxford: Blackwell, 1995), p. 29.
67. Ibid., p. 302.
68. See Fredric Jameson, 'Progress Versus Utopia; or, Can We Imagine the Future?' *Science Fiction Studies*, 9, 1982: 147–58.
69. Jeremy Bentham quoted in Peter Hall, *Cities in Civilization: Culture, Innovation, and Urban Order* (London: Weidenfeld & Nicolson, 1998), p. 665.
70. Charles Dickens, *Little Dorrit* (Oxford: Oxford University Press, 1999), pp. 636–7.
71. Michel Foucault, *Discipline and Punish*, trans. Alan Sheridan (London: Penguin 1979; first published as *Surveiller et punir*, Paris: Gallimard, 1975), p. 298.
72. For an analysis of London's CCTV network, see Niran Abbas, 'CCTV: City Watch', in *London*, ed. Kerr and Gibson, pp. 131–8.
73. Miguel de Cervantes, *Don Quixote de la Mancha* (Ware: Wordsworth Classics, 1993), p. 32.
74. Milan Kundera, 'The Depreciated Legacy of Cervantes', in *The Art of the Novel*, trans. Linda Asher (London: Faber, 1999; first published as *L'Art du Roman* by Editions Gallimard, 1986), p. 6.
75. Anna Minton, *Balanced Communities: The UK and the US Compared* (London: RICS, 2002), p. 13.
76. E. P. Thompson, *Witness against the Beast: William Blake and the Moral Law* (Cambridge: Cambridge University Press, 1993), p. 194.

5   Peter Ackroyd and the Voices of London

1. Margaret Thatcher, 'Speech inaugurating Canary Wharf', http://www.margaretthatcher.org/document/107834 [accessed 5 July 2007]. Originally delivered on 29 November 1989.

2. Patrick Wright, *A Journey through Ruins: The Last Days of London* (Oxford: Oxford University Press, 2009; first published by Radius, 1991), pp. 224–33, p. 227.
3. David Harvey, *The Condition of Postmodernity* (Oxford: Basil Blackwell, 1989), p. 3.
4. Rem Koolhaas and Bruce Mau, *S, M. L. XL* (Köln: Taschen, 1997; first published in New York by Monacelli Press, 1995), p. 1248.
5. Peter Ackroyd, 'London Luminaries and Cockney Visionaries', in *The Collection: Journalism, Reviews, Essays, Short Stories, Lectures* (London: Chatto & Windus, 2001), p. 342.
6. Sigmund Freud, *Civilization and its Discontents*, trans. James Strachey (New York: Norton, 1962; first published as *Das Unbehagen in der Kultur* in 1907), pp. 17–18.
7. Barry Lewis, *My Words Echo Thus: Possessing the Past in Peter Ackroyd* (Columbia, SC: University of South Carolina Press, 2007), p. 2.
8. Peter Ackroyd, *The Plato Papers* (London: Chatto & Windus, 1999), n.p. Further references in the text are abbreviated parenthetically as *PP*.
9. Brian McHale, *Postmodernist Fiction* (London: Routledge, 1999; first published by Methuen, 1987), p. 10.
10. See, for instance, Alison Lee, *Realism and Power: Postmodern British Fiction* (London and New York: Routledge, 1990); Susana Onega, *Metafiction and Myth in the Novels of Peter Ackroyd* (Columbia, SC: Camden House, 1998); John Peck, 'The Novels of Peter Ackroyd', *English Studies*, 75(5), 1994: 442–52.
11. Todd, *Consuming Fictions*, p. 172.
12. Peter Ackroyd, *The Last Testament of Oscar Wilde* (London: Hamish Hamilton, 1983), p. 181.
13. Susana Onega, 'British Historiographic Metafiction in the 1980s', in *British Postmodern Fiction*, ed. Theo D'Haen and Hans Bertens (Amsterdam-Atlanta: Rodopi, 1991), p. 57.
14. Ackroyd, 'London Luminaries', p. 350.
15. Peter Ackroyd, *The Great Fire of London* (London: Hamish Hamilton, 1983), p. 159. Further references in the text are abbreviated parenthetically as *GFL*.
16. Peter Ackroyd, *Hawksmoor* (London: Penguin, 1993; first published by Hamish Hamilton, 1985), p. 101. Further references in the text are abbreviated parenthetically as *H*.
17. Richard Sennett, *Flesh and Stone: The Body and City in Western Civilization* (London and Boston: Faber and Faber, 1994), p. 265.
18. Peter Ackroyd, *The House of Doctor Dee* (London: Hamish Hamilton, 1993), p. 81. Further references in the text are abbreviated parenthetically as *DD*.
19. Grevel Lindop, 'The Empty Telephone Boys', *PN Review*, 15(6), 1989: 43–6, p. 45.
20. T. S. Eliot, 'Tradition and the Individual Talent', in *Selected Prose*, ed. John Hayward (London: Penguin, 1953), pp. 21–30, p. 27.
21. Ackroyd, 'London Luminaries'.
22. Ibid., p. 346.
23. Ibid., p. 342.
24. Todd, *Consuming Fictions*, p. 196.
25. Rod Mengham, 'End of the Line', in *London*, ed. Kerr and Gibson, pp. 199–212, p. 199.
26. Peter Donaghy, 'Poem On The Underground', *Collected Poems* (London: Picador, 2009), p. 196.

27. See Blake's *The Mental Traveller* (1863), lines 61–4. In *Milton*, plate 29, Blake similarly states that the earth 'as a Globe rolling thro Voidness [...] is a delusion of Ulro'.
28. Todd, *Consuming Fictions*, p. 170.
29. Linda Hutcheon, *A Poetics of Postmodernism: History, Theory, Fiction* (London and New York: Routledge 1999; first published 1988), pp. 14–15.
30. Jeremy Gibson and Julian Wolfreys, *Peter Ackroyd: The Ludic and Labyrinthine Text* (Basingstoke: Macmillan, 2000), p. 170.
31. Ibid., p. 21.
32. Murray, *Recalling London*, pp. 24, 46.
33. Ibid., p. 42.
34. Lewis, *My Words*, p. 120.
35. Bakhtin, *Dialogic Imagination*, p. 25.
36. Ibid., p. 330.
37. Ibid., pp. 330–1.

6   Ian McEwan's Londons

1. Ian McEwan, 'Psychopolis', in *In Between the Sheets* (London: Vintage, 2006; first published by Jonathan Cape, 1978), p. 110.
2. Ibid., p. 117.
3. Joyce, *Portrait*, p. 12.
4. McEwan, 'Psychopolis', p. 134. See also Jean Baudrillard, *America*, trans. Chris Turner (London and New York: Verso, 1988; first published as *Amérique*, Paris: Bernard Grasset, 1986).
5. McEwan, 'Psychopolis', p. 348.
6. In the earliest hieroglyphics the ideogram representing the city was made up of a cross enclosed in a circle: the two intersecting lines symbolised the crossroads (the place where people meet) whilst the circle represented a wall and/or moat enclosing the city, marking 'the space within which the citizens cohere and the space beyond which they need protection'. See Lehan, *City*, p. 13.
7. Robert Lopez, *The Birth of Europe* (London: Phoenix, 1962), pp. 27–8.
8. Ian McEwan, *The Daydreamer* (London: Vintage, 1995; first published by Jonathan Cape, 1994), p. 24.
9. Murdoch notes: 'We have suffered a general loss of concepts, the loss of a moral and political vocabulary. We no longer use a spread-out substantial picture of the manifold virtues of man and society. We no longer see man against a background of values, of realities, which transcend him. We picture man as a brave naked will surrounded by an easily comprehended empirical world.' Iris Murdoch, 'Against Dryness', in *The Novel Today*, ed. Malcolm Bradbury (Manchester: Manchester University Press, 1977; first published 1961), p. 26.
10. Mumford, *City in History*, p. 354.
11. McEwan, 'Psychopolis', p. 110.
12. See Sebastian Groes, 'Ian McEwan and the Modernist Consciousness of the City in *Saturday*', in *Ian McEwan: Contemporary Critical Perspectives*, ed. Sebastian Groes (New York and London: Continuum, 2009), p. 99. We find archetypal images of dark London in William Blake's poem 'London' (1794),

in which the narrator walks through the city to hear the (out)cries of babies, child labourers, a prostitute and soldier mingle into a universal shout of injustice that 'Runs in blood down Palace walls'. Dickens's *Little Dorrit* (1855–7) meditates on the social and mental prisons that incarcerate citizens in mid-Victorian London, which is described as a 'lower world'. Charles Dickens, *Little Dorrit* (London: Penguin, 1999), p. 298. Joseph Conrad's criticism of British imperialism, *Heart of Darkness* (1904), presents us with 'a mournful gloom, brooding motionless over the biggest, and greatest, town on earth' whilst reminding us that London was also once a colonial outpost. Joseph Conrad, *Heart of Darkness*, ed. Robert Hampson (London: Penguin, 1995), p. 15.

13. See, for instance, Andy Beckett's description of power cuts due to the global oil crisis and strikes by British coal miners in the winter of 1973 in *When the Lights Went Out: Britain in the Seventies* (London: Faber and Faber, 2009), pp. 136–7.
14. Ian McEwan, 'Pornography', in *In Between the Sheets*, p. 3.
15. Ibid., p. 8.
16. Ibid., p. 11. During an earlier sexual encounter with Lucy, it emerges that O'Byrne is turned on when she strangles him and denigrates him by saying: '"Worm ... worm ... you little worm. I'm going to thread on you little worm." [...] "Yes," he whispered', which suggests that O'Byrne's castration is a form of pleasure. See McEwan, 'Pornography', p. 12.
17. Jack Slay, *Ian McEwan* (Boston, MA: Twayne, 1996), pp. 22, 60, 147.
18. Ibid., p. 61.
19. Ian McEwan, 'Two Fragments: Saturday and Sunday, March 199–', in *In Between the Sheets*, pp. 44, 45.
20. Ibid., pp. 44–5.
21. Ibid., p. 39.
22. Ibid., p. 38.
23. Maud Ellmann, *The Poetics of Impersonality* (Brighton: Harvester, 1987), pp. 92–4.
24. McEwan, 'Fragments', p. 52.
25. Ibid., p. 52.
26. Ibid., p. 54.
27. See M. Hunter Hayes and Sebastian Goes, '"Profoundly dislocating and infinite in possibility": Ian McEwan's Screenwriting', in *Ian McEwan: Contemporary Critical Perspectives*, ed. Groes, pp. 26–42.
28. D. J. Taylor, 'Ian McEwan: Standing up for the Sisters', in *A Vain Conceit: British Fiction in the 1980s* (London: Bloomsbury, 1988), p. 59.
29. Ian McEwan, *The Child in Time* (London: Picador, 1988; first published by Jonathan Cape, 1987), p. 44. Further references in the text are abbreviated parenthetically as *CT*.
30. The social division of Thatcher's England is suggested in descriptions such as the following: 'The first lived locally in modernised Victorian terraced houses which they owned. The second lived locally in tower blocks and council estates. Those in the first group tended to buy fresh fruit and vegetables, brown bread, coffee beans, fresh fish from a special counter [...] In the second group were pensioners buying meat for their cats, biscuits for themselves. And there were young mothers, gaunt with fatigue, their mouths set hard around cigarettes, who sometimes cracked at the checkout and gave a child a spanking' (*CT* 15).

31. Allan Massie, *The Novel Today* (Harlow: Longman, 1990), p. 51.
32. Head, *Ian McEwan*, pp. 70, 72.
33. Adam Mars-Jones, *Venus Envy: On the Womb and the Bomb* (London: Chatto & Windus, 1990), p. 22.
34. See Claire Colebrook, 'The Innocent as Anti-Oedipal Critique of Cultural Pornography', in *Ian McEwan: Contemporary Critical Perspectives*, ed. Groes, pp. 43–57.
35. Ian McEwan, *Saturday* (London: Jonathan Cape, 2005). Further references in the text are abbreviated parenthetically as *S*.
36. See Robert McCrumb, 'The Story of His Life', in the *Guardian*, 23 January 2005, http://www.guardian.co.uk/books/2005/jan/23/fiction.ianmcewan [accessed 12 October 2007].
37. Ian McEwan in interview with Melvyn Bragg for the *Southbank Show*, Season 28, Episode 13. First broadcast 20 February 2005 on ITV.
38. Matthew Arnold, *The Poems of Matthew Arnold*, ed. K. Allott (London: Longman, 1965), p. 6. Chapter Two of Bowen's *The Heat of the Day* starts with the protagonist, Stella Bowen, looking out of the window of her apartment, waiting for Harrison.
39. See Groes, 'Ian McEwan and the Modernist Consciousness of the City in *Saturday*'.
40. Virginia Woolf, *A Room of One's Own*, in *The Norton Anthology of English Literature: Volume 2*, ed. M. H. Abrahms (New York and London: W. W. Norton, 1993; first published 1929), p. 1976.
41. Ibid.
42. Ibid.
43. Arthur Conan Doyle, *A Study in Scarlet* (London: Penguin, 1981; first published by Ward Lock, 1887), p. 40.
44. Ibid., p. 25.
45. David James, 'The New Purism', *Textual Practice* 21(4), 2007: 687–714, p. 702.
46. Arnold, *Poems*, 'Dover Beach', l. 18.
47. Ibid., ll. 35–7.
48. See also Head, *Ian McEwan*, p. 190.
49. Dominic Head, *The State of the Novel* (Chichester: John Wiley, 2008), p. 123.
50. Saul Bellow, *Herzog* (Harmondsworth: Penguin, 1965; first published by Weidenfeld & Nicolson, 1964), p. 172.
51. Ibid., p. 173.
52. Ibid., pp. 172–3.
53. Joyce, *Ulysses*, p. 28.
54. Ibid., p. 42.
55. Eliot, *Prose*, p. 25.
56. Ian McEwan, *Solar* (London: Jonathan Cape, 2009), p. 108. Further references in the text are abbreviated parenthetically as *So*.

7 Martin Amis's Scatological London

1. There are a few exceptions, such as Ian McEwan's *The Child in Time* (1987), Alan Hollinghurst's *The Line of Beauty* (2004), which brings us to the heart of Thatcher's Westminster, and Sebastian Faulks's *A Week in December* (2009), which contains scenes set in Westminster and the City.

2. Martin Amis, *The Information* (London: Jonathan Cape, 1995). Further references in the text are abbreviated parenthetically as *I*.
3. See Sage, 'Dickens and Professor Owen'.
4. Martin Amis, 'A PM, a President, and a First Lady', in *The War against Cliché*, p. 19. First published in *Elle*, October 1989.
5. This passage is, amongst others, a fictional engagement with one of the controversial episodes in Amis's life, when he left his agent and partner of his long-time friend Julian Barnes, Pat Kavanagh, of whom Gal Aplanalp is a thinly disguised version. For more details of the controversy see Brian Finney's *Martin Amis* (Abingdon: Routledge, 2008), pp. 24–5.
6. Adam Mars-Jones has described his London trilogy as 'a mighty triptych, love poem to West London from which love is excluded'. See Adam Mars-Jones, 'Looking on the Blight Side', *Times Literary Supplement*, 4799, 24 March 1995, p. 19.
7. Martin Amis, *Money* (London: Jonathan Cape, 1984). Further references in the text are abbreviated parenthetically as *M*.
8. Amis, *The War against Cliché*, p. xiii.
9. Martin Amis, *The Moronic Inferno* (London: Jonathan Cape, 1986), pp. 10–11.
10. Peter Childs, *Contemporary Novelists: British Fiction since 1970* (Basingstoke: Palgrave Macmillan, 2005), p. 47.
11. Sebastian Groes and Martin Amis, 'A Hatred of Reason: Martin Amis in Conversation with Sebastian Groes', *The London Magazine*, ed. Sebastian Barker, June/July 2004, pp. 44–51, p. 49.
12. Carter, *Expletives Deleted*, p. 126.
13. Kingsley Amis, *Lucky Jim* (London: Penguin, 1961; first published by Victor Gollancz, 1954), p. 178.
14. Martin Amis, *Yellow Dog* (London: Jonathan Cape, 2003), p. 6. Further references are abbreviated parenthetically as *YD*.
15. Patricia Waugh, *Harvest of the Sixties* (Oxford and New York: Oxford University Press, 1995), p. 31.
16. Todd, *Consuming Fictions*, p. 196.
17. Nicolas Tredell, '*Money: A Suicide Note*', *The Literary Encyclopedia*, 26 November 2009, http://www.litencyc.com/php\sworks.php?rec+true&UID=574 [accessed 4 March 2010].
18. Richard Todd, 'Looking-glass Worlds in Martin Amis's Early Fiction: Reflectiveness, Mirror Narcissism, and Doubles', in *Martin Amis: Postmodernism and Beyond*, ed. Gavin Keulks (Basingstoke: Palgrave Macmillan), p. 24.
19. Todd, *Consuming Fictions*, p. 189.
20. Martin Amis, *The Rachel Papers* (London: Jonathan Cape, 1973), p. 154.
21. Nicole LaRose hints at this possibility, but she does not actually follow it through: 'If the reader is to gain agency and navigate through the text, he or she is required to identify the information through a reading that relates to an urban orientation.' See Nicole LaRose, 'Reading *The Information* on Martin Amis's London', *Critique: Studies in Contemporary Fiction* 46(2), Winter 2005: 160–76, p. 160.
22. Raymond Williams, *The Country and the City* (London: Chatto & Windus, 1973), pp. 9–12.
23. Richard Jeffries, *After London: Wild England* (Oxford: Oxford University Press, 1980; first published by Cassell and Company, 1885), pp. 206–7.

24. Jim Crace's *Arcadia* is an imaginative account of how a millionaire's 'only *civic* fantasy [is] to display his wealth at last by building a market' in the fictional Covent Garden-like Woodgate. Jim Crace, *Arcadia* (London: Penguin, 1998; first published by Jonathan Cape, 1992), p. 155.

25. William Wordsworth, *The Prelude*, Book Seven, ll. 687–8.

26. Ibid., ll. 635–6.

27. Martin Amis, 'God's Dice', in *Einstein's Monsters* (London: Penguin, 1995), pp. 6–7. Originally published as 'Bujak and the Strong Force' in the *London Review of Books* (1987).

28. In an interview with *Woman's Own* (23 September 1987), Lady Thatcher provocatively proclaimed that 'we have gone through a period when too many children and people have been given to understand, "I have a problem, it is the Government's job to cope with it!" or "I have a problem, I will go and get a grant to cope with it!", "I am homeless, the government must house me!" and so they are casting their problems on society and who is society? There is no such thing! There are individual men and women and there are families and no government can do anything except through people and people look to themselves first. It is our duty to look after ourselves and then also to help look after our neighbour and life is a reciprocal business [...] There is no such thing as society. There is a living tapestry of men and women and people and the beauty of that tapestry and the quality of our lives will depend upon how much each of us is willing to take responsibility for ourselves and each of us is prepared to turn around and help by our own efforts those who are unfortunate.'

29. James Wood, 'England', in *The Oxford Guide to Contemporary Writing*, ed. John Sturrock (Oxford: Oxford University Press, 1996), pp. 113–41, pp. 137–8.

30. Muriel Spark, 'The Portobello Road', in *The Portobello Road and Other Stories* (Helsinki: Eurographica, 1989), p. 58.

31. Philip Tew, *The Contemporary British Novel* (London: Continuum, 2004), p. 94.

32. Deleuze and Guattari, *Anti-Oedipus*, p. 94.

33. Finney, *Martin Amis*, p. 20.

34. Martin Amis, 'A PM, a President, and a First Lady', in *The War against Cliché*, p. 19. First published in *Elle*, October 1989.

35. John Haffenden, *Novelists in Interview* (London and New York: Methuen, 1985), pp. 13–14.

36. Martin Amis, *Other People* (London: Penguin, 1983; first published by Jonathan Cape, 1981). Further references in the text are abbreviated parenthetically as *OP*.

37. Mengham, *Descent of Language*, p. 3.

38. Nicolas Tredell, '*The Information*', *The Literary Encyclopedia*, 6 April 2009, http://www.litencyc.com/php\sworks.php?rec+true&UID=3464 [accessed 27 January 2010].

39. The tragedy of Meo's cerebrovascular disaster can also be viewed in the light of Amis's interest in ageing and degenerative brain diseases. In a review of the Richard Eyre film of Murdoch's life, *Iris* (2001), for the *Guardian*, Amis states of Iris Murdoch's death from Alzheimer's disease: 'Alzheimer's is symmetrical, too, in its way: each new impoverishment is an awareness of loss. [...] Certain

cerebrovascular disasters are called "insults to the brain" [...] the more prodigious the brain, the more studious (and in this case protracted) the insult. Iris's brain was prodigious.' Martin Amis, 'Age Will Win', *Guardian*, 21 December 2001. Collected in *On Modern British Fiction*, ed. Zachary Leader (Oxford and New York: Oxford University Press, 2002), pp. 265–9.

40. When Meo leaves his house, 'he turned briefly to assess it – a customary means of assessing himself, assessing where he was positioned, where he was placed' (*YD* 5).

41. Brian Finney, 'Narrative and Narrated Homicides in Martin Amis's *Other People* and *London Fields*', *Critique: Studies in Contemporary Fiction* 37(1), Fall, 1995: 3–15.

42. Arthur Kroker and David Cook, *The Postmodern Scene: Excremental Culture and Hyper-Aesthetics* (London: Macmillan, 1988), p. iv.

43. See Dominic Head, *The Cambridge Introduction to Modern British Fiction, 1950–2000* (Cambridge: Cambridge University Press, 2002), pp. 212–13 and 242–3.

44. William Shakespeare, *Hamlet*, III.ii.364–7.

45. In *Money*, John Self is reading Orwell's *1984* and *Animal Farm*, but he fails to read the latter novel as an allegory – a literal reading that again affirms the implosion of hierarchies.

46. See also Christopher Reid, 'Academy of the Aleatoric': 'The smutty pigeon on a parapet / pecks for crumbs like a sewing-machine. / It gathers all the greys of London, / murky and mottled, into the bunch of its wings.' In *Arcadia* (Oxford: Oxford University Press, 1979), p. 11.

47. Ellmann, *Poetics of Impersonality*, p. 93.

48. In Saul Bellow's *Mr Sammler's Planet*, Sammler muses: 'A human being, valuing himself for the right reasons, has and restores order, authority. When the internal parts are in order. They must be in order. But what was it to be arrested in the stage of toilet training! [...] Who had raised the diaper flag? Who had made shit a sacrament?' (Harmondsworth: Penguin, 1972; first published by Weidenfeld & Nicolson, 1970), p. 39.

49. Sigmund Freud, *The Standard Edition of the Complete Psychological Works of Sigmund Freud*, trans. James Strachey, Anna Freud, Alix Strachey and Alan Tyson, Vol. 9 (London: Hogarth, 1953–74), p. 174.

50. Ibid., Vol. 12, p. 187.

51. We find a repetition of such passages throughout the novel. Compare this passage for instance with: 'We're out walking. We can do this. *Oh* – what you see in London streets at three o'clock in the morning, with it trickling out the eaves and flues, tousled water, ragged waste. Violence is near an exhaustible. Even death is near. But none of it can touch Nicola and me. It knows better, and stays right out of our way. It can't touch us. It knows this. We're the dead' (*LF* 260).

52. T. S. Eliot, 'The Hollow Men', in *T. S. Eliot: The Complete Poems and Plays* (London: Faber and Faber, 1969), p. 84.

53. Todd, *Consuming Fictions*, p. 164.

54. Jean Baudrillard, *The Consumer Society: Myths and Structures* (London: Sage, 1998), p. 137.

55. Todd, *Consuming Fictions*, p. 195.

8 Mastering London with Salman Rushdie and Hanif Kureishi

1. Sinclair, *Radon Daughters*, p. 18.
2. Salman Rushdie, 'The New Empire within Britain', in *Imaginary Homelands* (London: Granta, 1992; first published 1991), p. 137.
3. Rushdie, *Imaginary Homelands*, p. 19.
4. Homi K. Bhabha, *The Location of Culture* (Abingdon: Routledge, 2004; first published 1994), p. 8.
5. Salman Rushdie, *Mirrorwork: 50 Years of Indian Writing, 1947– 1997* (London: Vintage, 1997), p. x.
6. Jacques Derrida, *Of Grammatology*, trans. Gayatri Chakravorty Spivak (Baltimore and London: Johns Hopkins University Press, 1997 [1974]; first published as *De la Grammatologie* by Les Editions de Minuit, 1967), pp. 14, 158.
7. Ibid., p. 35.
8. Bhabha, *Location of Culture*, p. 270.
9. Ibid., pp. 286–7.
10. Hardt and Negri base their argument on the idea that, as Joseph Conrad implies in *Heart of Darkness* (1904), the colonial projects of the past are centred on a fear of disease and degeneration that the colonies were associated with. What is more, when Céline travels into Africa, he finds not death and disease, but 'an overabundance of life ... [t]he disease of the jungle is that life springs up everywhere, everything grows, without bounds. What horror for the hygienist!' See Michael Hardt and Antonio Negri, *Empire* (Cambridge, MA and London: Harvard University Press, 2000), p. 135.
11. Alastair Niven, 'Salman Rushdie with Alastair Niven', in *Writing Across Worlds: Contemporary Writers Talk*, ed. Susheila Nasta (Abingdon: Routledge, 2004), pp. 131–2.
12. Bhabha, *Location of Culture*, p. 328.
13. John McLeod, *Postcolonial London* (Abingdon: Routledge, 2005; first published 2004), p. 151. McLeod reads against Bhabha's *The Location of Culture* (2004), pp. 169–70, and Ian Baucom's *Out of Place* (Princeton, NJ: Princeton University Press, 1999), p. 212.
14. Benedict Anderson, *Imagined Communities: Reflections on the Origin and Spread of Nationalism* (London and New York: Verso, 2003; first published 1983), pp. 173 and 170–1 respectively.
15. Rushdie, *Imaginary Homelands*, 19.
16. Anderson, *Imagined Communities*, 175.
17. See 'The Battle of Cable Street', in Ed Glinert's *The London Compendium* (London: Penguin, 2003; first published by Allen Lane, 2003), p. 279.
18. Rushdie, *Imaginary Homelands*, p. 142. Camden Council is transfigured in the following description: 'The building occupied by the Brickhall community relations council was a single-story monster in purple brick with bullet-proof windows, a bunker-like creation of the 1960s, when such lines were considered sleek. It was not an easy building to enter; the door had been fitted with an entryphone and opened on to a narrow alley down one side of the building which ended at a second, also security-locked, door. There was also a burglar alarm' (*SV* 464).

19. Hanif Kureishi, *The Buddha of Suburbia* (London: Faber and Faber, 1990), p. 23. Further references in the text are abbreviated parenthetically as *BS*.
20. Hanif Kureishi, *The Black Album* (London: Faber and Faber, 1995), p. 72. Further references in the text are abbreviated parenthetically as *BA*.
21. Matthew Taunton, *Fictions of the City: Class, Culture and Mass Housing in London and Paris* (Basingstoke: Palgrave Macmillan, 2009), p. 86.
22. Robert McCrum, 'I got out of the suburbs, but did they get out of me', *The Observer*, 25 Febraury 2001, http://www.guardian.co.uk/book/2001/feb/25/fiction.hanifkureishi [accessed 7 October 2009].
23. Sukhev Sandhu, *London Calling: How Black and Asian Writers Imagined a City* (London: HarperCollins, 2003), p. 233.
24. John Clement Ball, *Imagining London: Postcolonial Fiction and the Transnational Metropolis* (Toronto: University of Toronto Press, 2004), p. 231.
25. Sandhu, *London Calling*, p. 244.
26. Ian McEwan, *Soursweet* (London: Faber and Faber, 1988), p. v.
27. McCrum, 'I got out of the suburbs'.
28. Roland Barthes, 'Semiology', in *The City and the Sign*, ed. Gottdiener and Lagopoulos, p. 96.
29. Sam Selvon, *The Lonely Londoners* (New York: Longman, 2001; first published by Alan Wingate, 1956), p. 90.
30. Julian Barnes, *Metroland* (London: Picador, 1990; first published by Jonathan Cape, 1980), p. 157.
31. McLeod, *Postcolonial London*, 139.
32. Bhabha, *Location of Culture*, pp. 72–3.
33. Bart Moore-Gilbert, *Hanif Kureishi* (Manchester and New York: Manchester University Press, 2001), p. 202.
34. John Clement Ball, 'The Semi-Detached Metropolis: Hanif Kureishi's London', *Ariel: A Review of International English Literature* 27(4), October, 1996: 1–27, p. 24.

9   The New London Languages of Zadie Smith and Monica Ali

1. Zadie Smith, *White Teeth* (London: Hamish Hamilton, 2000), p. 459. Further references in the text are abbreviated parenthetically as *WT*.
2. Zadie Smith in an interview on the website of her publisher, Random House: http://www.randomhouse.com/boldtype/0700/smith/interview.html [accessed 3 June 2008].
3. See Lorna Sage, *Women in the House of Fiction* (Basingstoke: Macmillan, 1992), pp. 72–113.
4. Head, *Modern British Fiction*, p. 187.
5. Zadie Smith, 'This is How It Feels to Me', *The Guardian*, 13 October, 2001: http://www.guardian.co.uk/books/2001/oct/13/fiction.afghanistan [accessed 17 October 2006].
6. Lefebvre, *Writings on Cities*, p. 115.
7. Selvon, *Lonely Londoners*, p. 23. The poor command is a double-take, as the lyrical section narrated using the stream-of-consciousness technique shows (pp. 101–10).

8. Jean Rhys, 'Let them Call it Jazz', in *Tigers are Better-Looking* (London: André Deutsch, 1968; first published in *The London Magazine*, 1960), pp. 62–3.

9. Ibid., p. 64.

10. Kris Knauer, 'The Root Canals of Zadie Smith: London's Intergenerational Adaptation', in *Zadie Smith: Critical Essays*, ed. Tracey L. Walters (New York: Peter Lang, 2008), p. 175.

11. Richard Bradford, *The Novel Now* (Oxford: Blackwell, 2007), p. 207.

12. See Paul Ricoeur, *Time and Narrative*, volume 2 (Chicago: University of Chicago Press, 1990; first published as *Temps et Récit*, by Editions du Seuil, 1984), pp. 109–10.

13. Jackson Cope, *Joyce's Cities: Archaeologies of the Soul* (Baltimore and London: Johns Hopkins University Press, 1981), p. 34.

14. Pilar Cuder-Domínguez, 'Ethnic Cartographies of London in Bernardine Evaristo and Zadie Smith', *European Journal of English Studies* 8(2), 2004: 173–88, p. 188.

15. Bruce King, *The Oxford English Literary History: The Internationalization of English Literature*, Vol. 13 (Oxford: Oxford University Press, 2005; first published 2004), pp. 289–90.

16. Monica Ali, *Brick Lane* (London: Doubleday, 2003), p. 33. Further references in the text are abbreviated parenthetically as *BL*. I would like to thank Alistair Cormack – with whom I had discussions about realism and the novel form – in developing my thinking about Ali's novel.

17. Jane Hiddleston, 'Shapes and Shadows: (Un)veiling the Immigrant in Monica Ali's *Brick Lane*', *Journal of Commonwealth Literature* 40(1) 2005: 57–72, p. 63.

18. Cuder-Domínguez, 'Ethnic Cartographies', p. 176.

19. James Wood, 'Making it New,' *The New Republic*, 8 and 15 September 2003, p. 31.

20. Alistair Cormack, 'Migration and the Politics of Narrative Form: Realism and the Postcolonial Subject in *Brick Lane*', *Contemporary Literature* 47(4), Winter 2006: 695–721, p. 700.

21. David James, *Contemporary British Fiction and the Artistry of Space* (London and New York: Continuum, 2008), p. 75.

22. Head, *Modern British Fiction*, p. 75.

23. Head, *State of the Novel*, p. 80.

24. Ibid., p. 81.

25. Ibid.

26. The East End tradition of sweatshops goes back before modernity. Even before the nineteenth century, the East End boroughs were generating trade and handling lucrative imports in poorly paid and often dangerous sweatshops. In 1884, the medical journal *The Lancet* reported: 'We visited one tailor's workshop in Hanbury Street. There was only one toilet, which flushed its contents outside the pan and across the yard. In the top room 18 people were working. In the heat of the gas and stoves, surrounded by mounds of dust, breathing an atmosphere of wool particles containing dangerous dyes, it is not surprising that tailors' health breaks down from lung diseases.' In 1906, an exhibition called 'The Sweated Industries' was held at the Queen's Hall in Bayswater as a protest against the conditions. Tailoring was traditionally

an occupation for Jewish immigrants, with over one thousand tailoring workshops in the East End by 1888.

27. In his first big policy speech since his 1997 victory, Tony Blair addressed an audience on a south London housing estate and contended that radical shift in attitudes and values were needed to tackle poverty, fatalism and low expectations: 'I don't want there to be any forgotten people in the Britain that we want to build.' The speech can be heard at the Spoken Words Service of Glasgow Caledonian Service: http://www.spokenword.ac.uk/record_view.php?pbd=gcu-a0a1a6-b

28. In *The Long Revolution* (1961), Williams offers a fourfold classification of the novel (social description, social formula, personal description, personal formula), arguing that the crisis of the novel was brought forth by an abandonment of traditional realism in its creation of a sense of society: 'The realist novel needs, obviously, a genuine community: a community of persons linked not merely by one kind of relationship – work or friendship or family – but many interlocking kinds. It is obviously difficult, in the twentieth century, to find a community of this sort' (Raymond Williams, *The Long Revolution* (London: Chatto & Windus, 1961, p. 312)). *Brick Lane* would fit into the 'personal formula' category: 'Here, as in the novel of social formula, a particular pattern is abstracted from the sum of experience, and not now societies, but human individuals, are created from that pattern. This has been the method of powerful and on its own terms valid fiction, but it seems to me to be rapidly creating a new mode, the fiction of special pleading. We can say of novels in this class that they take one person seriously, but then ordinarily very serious indeed' (p. 310).

29. Ibid., p. 309. In *Brick Lane*, the domestic narrative shows how the realism is challenged by Nazneen: 'Life made its pattern around and beneath and through her. Nazneen cleaned and cooked and washed. She made breakfast for Chanu and looked on as he ate, collected his pens and put them in his briefcase, watched him from the window as he stepped like a band leader across the courtyard to the bus stop on the far side of the estate. Then she ate standing up at the sink and washed the dishes. [...] In the afternoons she cooked and ate as she cooked so that Chanu began to wonder why she hardly touched her dinner, and she shrugged in a way that suggested that food was of no concern to her' (*BL* 31).

30. Wood, 'Making it New', p. 29.

31. Bhabha, *Location of Culture*, p. 326.

32. Ibid., p. 327.

33. Randall Stevenson, *The Oxford English Literary History: The Last of England?*, vol. 12 (Oxford: Oxford University Press, 2005; first published 2004), p. 501.

34. Ibid., p. 522.

35. See Colin McCaig, 'New Labour and Education, Education, Education', in *New Labour in Government*, ed. Steve Ludlam and Martin J. Smith (London: Macmillan, 2001), pp. 184–201.

36. Cormack, 'Migration', pp. 710–11.

37. Rushdie in his introduction to *Mirrorwork*, pp. x–xi.

38. Chaudhuri states: 'All in all, a Bengali family is a tangled web, an echoing cave, of names and appellations, too complicated to explain individually.' Amit Chaudhuri, *A Strange and Sublime Address* (London: Heinemann, 1991), p. ii.

39. In *Writing in Society* (1983), Raymond Williams states of the representation of the working-class English in Tressell's *The Ragged-Arsed Philanthropist*: 'He uses all the devices of what I call the orthography of the uneducated: all that torturing of the already tortured nature of the English spelling, to indicate someone's pronunciation is not standard, not educated. This always lead to the most extraordinary contortions, since if you believe that English sounds are represented by English spelling, so that there is a standard from which some "dialect" divergence can be identified by a spelling divergence in which it is really different in a novel for somebody to say "I love you"' spelled I LOVE YOU and to say "I love you"' spelled I LUV YER. But different in what sense? We are asked to take the first seriously, or at least to wait and see how it works out. The second is marked for a different response. What sort of emotion is that? "I luv yer". Probably very vulgar and inadequate. You are represented as feeling or thinking through your spelling, although of course you're not spelling anyway; the writer is spelling, you're just talking in the language of your own place.' Raymond Williams, *Writing in Society* (London: Verso, 1991; first published 1983), p. 255.
40. Ibid., p. 256.
41. Sean Matthews, 'Change and Theory in Raymond Williams's Structure of Feeling,' *Pretexts: Literary and Cultural Studies* 10(2), 2001: 175–94, p. 181.
42. See Colin MacCabe, 'Multiculturalism after 7/7: A CQ Seminar', *Critical Quarterly*, 48(2), 2006: 1–44, p. 10.
43. Waugh, *Harvest of the Sixties*, p. 121.

Conclusion: London Undone?

1. Angela Carter, 'Introduction', *Expletives Deleted*, pp. 3–4.
2. Todd, *Consuming Fictions*, p. 197.
3. Groes and Sinclair, 'Interview', p.76.
4. Ibid., pp. 75–6.
5. Carter, 'Sinclair', p. 126.
6. Maurice Ash, *A Guide to the Structure of London* (Bath: Adams and Dart, 1972), p. 1.
7. Will Self, *My Idea of Fun: A Cautionary Tale* (London: Penguin, 1994 [1993]), p. 304.
8. Andrew Gibson, 'Altering Images', in *From Punk to Blair*, ed. Kerr and Gibson, p. 293.
9. Carter, *'Downriver'*, p. 120.
10. Sinclair, *Lud Heat*, p. 4.
11. Groes and Sinclair, 'Interview', p. 75.

Select Bibliography

Ackroyd, Peter, *The Collection: Journalism, Reviews, Essays, Short Stories, Lectures* (London: Chatto & Windus, 2001).

—— *Dressing Up: Transvestism and Drag – The History of an Obsession* (London: Thames & Hudson, 1979).

—— *The Great Fire of London* (London: Hamish Hamilton, 1983).

—— *Hawksmoor* (London: Penguin, 1993; first published by Hamish Hamilton, 1985).

—— *The House of Doctor Dee* (London: Hamish Hamilton, 1993).

—— *London: The Biography* (London: Chatto & Windus, 2000).

—— *The Plato Papers* (London: Chatto & Windus, 1999).

Adams, Anna, *Thames: An Anthology of River Poems* (London: Enitharmon, 1999).

Ali, Monica, *Brick Lane* (London: Doubleday, 2003).

—— *In the Kitchen* (London: Scribner, 2009).

Amis, Kingsley, *Lucky Jim* (London: Penguin, 1961; first published by Victor Gollancz, 1954).

Amis, Martin, 'God's Dice', in *Einstein's Monsters* (London: Penguin, 1995; first published as 'Bujak and the Strong Force' in the *London Review of Books* (1987), pp. 25–48.

—— *Experience* (London: Jonathan Cape, 2000).

—— *Heavy Water* (London: Jonathan Cape, 1998).

—— *The Information* (London: Jonathan Cape, 1995).

—— *London Fields* (London: Jonathan Cape, 1989).

—— *Money* (London: Jonathan Cape, 1984).

—— *The Moronic Inferno* (London: Jonathan Cape, 1986).

—— *The Rachel Papers* (London; Jonathan Cape, 1973).

—— *The War against Cliché* (London: Jonathan Cape, 2001).

—— *Yellow Dog* (London; Jonathan Cape, 2003).

Anderson, Benedict, *Imagined Communities: Reflections on the Origin and Spread of Nationalism* (London and New York: Verso, 2003; first published 1983).

Arnold, Dana, *Re-presenting the Metropolis* (Aldershot: Ashgate, 2000).

Arnold, Matthew, *The Poems of Matthew Arnold*, ed. K. Allott (London: Longman, 1965).

Ash, Maurice, *A Guide to the Structure of London* (Bath: Adams & Dart, 1972).

Ashcroft, Bill, 'The Rhizome of Post-colonial Discourse', in *Literature and the Contemporary Fictions and Theories of the Present*, ed. Roger Luckhurst and Peter Marks (Harlow: Longman, 1999), pp. 111–25.

Augé, Marc, *Non-Places: Introduction to an Anthropology of Supermodernity*, trans. John Howe (London and New York: Verso, 1995; first published as *Non-lieux* by Editions du Seuil in 1992).

Bachelard, Gaston, *The Poetics of Space*, trans. Maria Jolas (Boston: Beacon Press, 1969; first published as *La poétique de l'espace* by Presses Universitaires de France, 1958).

Baker, Brian, 'Maps of the London Underground: Iain Sinclair and Michael Moorcock's Psychogeography of the City', *Literary London Journal*, March 2003; http://www.literarylondon.org/london-journal/march2003/baker.html [accessed 4 October 2006].

—— *Iain Sinclair* (Manchester: Manchester University Press, 2007).

Bakhtin, M. M., *The Dialogic Imagination: Four Essays*, ed. Michael Holquist, trans. Caryl Emerson and Michael Holquist (Austin: University of Texas Press, 2002; first published 1981).

Ball, John Clement, 'The Semi-Detached Metropolis: Hanif Kureishi's London', *Ariel: A Review of International English Literature* 27(4), October 1996: 1–27.

—— *Imagining London: Postcolonial Fiction and the Transnational Metropolis* (Toronto: University of Toronto Press, 2004).

Ballard, J. G., 'Airports', *The Observer*, 14 September 1997: www.jgballard.com/airports.htm [accessed 15 August 2008].

—— *Cocaine Nights* (London: Flamingo, 1996).

—— *Concrete Island* (London: Jonathan Cape, 1974).

—— *Crash* (London: Vintage, 1995; first published by Jonathan Cape, 1973).

—— *High-Rise* (London: Triad/Panther, 1977; first published by Jonathan Cape, 1975).

—— *Kingdom Come* (London: Fourth Estate, 2006).

—— *Millennium People* (London: HarperCollins, 2003).

—— *Super-Cannes* (London: Flamingo, 2000).

—— *The Unlimited Dream Company* (London: Jonathan Cape, 1979).

—— *A User's Guide to the Millennium* (London: HarperCollins, 1996).

Balshaw, Marian and Kennedy, Liam (eds), *Urban Space and Representation* (London: Pluto, 2000).

Barker, Paul, 'Tired of London', *Prospect Magazine*, December 2002, pp. 18–21.

Barry, Peter, *Contemporary British Poetry and the City* (Manchester: Manchester University Press, 2000).

Barthes, Roland, *Empire of Signs*, trans. Richard Howard (London: Jonathan Cape, 1983; first published in French as *L'Empire des Signes*, 1970).

Baudelaire, Charles, *The Painter of Modern Life*, trans. Jonathan Mayne (London: Phaidon, 1964).

Baudrillard, Jean, *America*, trans. Chris Turner (London and New York: Verso, 1986; 1999; first published as *L'Amérique* by Bernard Grasset in Paris, 1986).

—— *The Consumer Society: Myths and Structures* (London: Sage, 1998).

—— *Simulacra and Simulations*, trans. Sheila Faria Glaser (Ann Arbor: University of Michigan Press, 1994; originally published as *Simulacres et Simulation* by Gallilée in 1985).

Baxter, J., *J. G. Ballard: Contemporary Critical Perspectives*, ed. Jeannette Baxter (London and New York: Continuum, 2009).

—— *J. G. Ballard's Surrealist Imagination: Spectacular Authorship* (Aldershot: Ashgate, 2009).

Beckett, Andy, *When the Lights Went Out: Britain in the Seventies* (London: Faber and Faber, 2009).

Bellow, Saul, *Herzog* (Harmondsworth: Penguin, 1965; first published by Weidenfeld & Nicolson, 1964).

Besant, Walter, *London* (London: Chatto & Windus, 1892; reprint 1925).

Best, Anna (ed.), *Occasional Sights: A London Guidebook of Missed Opportunities and Things that Aren't Always There* (London: The Photographers' Gallery, 2003).

Bey, Hakim, *T. A. Z.: The Temporary Autonomous Zone, Ontological Anarchy and Poetic Terrorism* (New York: Autonomedia, 1991; first published 1985).

Bhabha, Homi K., *The Location of Culture* (Abingdon: Routledge, 2004; first published 1994).

Bidwell, Bruce and Linda Heffer, *The Joycean Way: A Topographic Guide to 'Dubliners' and 'A Portrait of the Artist as a Young Man'* (Dublin: Wolfhound, 1981).

Blaut, J. M., *The Colonizer's Model of the World: Geographical Diffusionism and Eurocentric History* (New York and London: Guildford Press, 1993).

Bode, Christoph, 'Maureen Duffy: A Polyphonic Sub-version of Realism', in *(Sub)Versions of Realism: Recent Women's Fiction in Britain*, ed. Irmgard Maassen and Ann Maria Stuby (Heidelberg: Carl Winter, 1997), pp. 41–54.

Bond, Robert, *Iain Sinclair* (London: Salt, 2005).

——— 'Wide Boys Always Work: Iain Sinclair and the London Proletarian Novel', *Literary London Journal*, September 2003: http://www.literarylondon.org/london-journal/september2003/bond.html [accessed 4 October 2006].

Borden, Iain, Joe Kerr, Jane Rendall with Alicia Pivaro (eds), *The Unknown City: Contesting Architecture and Social Space: A Strangely Familiar Project* (Cambridge, MA and London: MIT Press, 2001).

Boyer, Christine M., *The City of Collective Memory: Its Historical Imagery and Architectural Entertainments* (Cambidge, MA: MIT Press, 1996).

Bradford, Richard, *The Novel Now* (Oxford: Blackwell, 2007).

Brimstone, Lyndie, '"Keepers of History": The Novels of Maureen Duffy', in *Lesbian and Gay Writing*, ed. Mark Lilly (Basingstoke: Macmillan, 1990), pp. 23–46.

Brooker, Peter, 'A Novelist in the Era of Higher Capitalism: Ian Sinclair and the Postmodern East End', Conference Paper for the 3Cities Project: http://www.nottingham.ac.uk/3cities/brooker.htm [accessed 18 July 2005].

Brownhill, Sue, 'Turning the East End into the West End', in *British Urban Policy*, ed. Rob Imrie and Huw Thomas (London: Sage, 1999), pp. 43–63.

Budgen, Frank, *James Joyce and the Making of* Ulysses (Bloomington: Indiana University Press, 1960; originally published by Grayson & Grayson, 1934).

Byrd, Max, *London Transformed* (London: Macmillan, 1978).

Calder, Angus, *The Myth of the Blitz* (London: Jonathan Cape, 1991).

Campbell, John, *Margaret Thatcher: Grocer's Daughter to Iron Lady* (London: Vintage, 2009).

Carter, Angela, *Expletives Deleted* (London: Chatto & Windus, 1992).

——— *Nothing Sacred* (London: Virago, 1980).

Certeau, Michel de, 'Mystic Speech', in *Heterologies*, trans. Brian Massumi (Manchester: Manchester University Press, 1986; first published as 'L'énonciation mystique' in *Recherches de science religieuse*, 64(2), 1976), pp. 198–215.

——— *The Practice of Everyday Life*, trans. Steven Rendall (Berkeley and London: University of California Press, 1984).

Chaudhuri, Amit, *A Strange and Sublime Address* (London: Heinemann, 1991).

Childs, Peter, *Contemporary Novelists: British Fiction since 1970* (Basingstoke: Palgrave Macmillan, 2005).

——— (ed.), *The Fiction of Ian McEwan: A Reader's Guide to Essential Criticism* (Basingstoke: Palgrave Macmillan, 2006).

Colebrook, Claire, *Gilles Deleuze* (Oxford: Routledge, 2002).

Cope, Jackson, *Joyce's Cities: Archaeologies of the Soul* (Baltimore and London: Johns Hopkins University Press, 1981).

Cormack, Alistair, 'Migration and the Politics of Narrative Form: Realism and the Postcolonial Subject in *Brick Lane*', *Contemporary Literature* 47(4), Winter 2006: 695–721.

Crace, Jim, *Arcadia* (London: Penguin, 1998; first published by Jonathan Cape, 1992).

Deleuze, Gilles, *Negotiations* (New York: Columbia University Press, 1995).

Deleuze, Gilles and Félix Guattari, *Anti-Oedipus*, trans. Robert Hurley, Mark Seem and Helen R. Lane (London and New York: Continuum, 2004; first published in English by Athlone Press, 1984; originally published as *L'Anti Oedipe* by Les Editions de Minuit, Paris, 1972).

——— *A Thousand Plateaus: Capitalism and Schizophrenia*, trans. Brian Massumi (London and New York: Continuum, 2002; first published in Great Britain by Athlone Press, 1988; originally published as *Mille Plateaux*, volume 2 of *Capitalisme et Schizophrénie* by Les Editions de Minuit, Paris, 1980).

Derrida, Jacques, 'Of an Apocalyptic Tone Recently Adopted in Philosophy', trans. John P. Leavey, Jr., *Semeia* (1982): 63–97.

——— *Of Grammatology*, trans. Gayatri Chakravorty Spivak (Baltimore: Johns Hopkins University Press, 1997 [1974]; first published as *De la Grammatologie* by Les Editions de Minuit, 1967).

——— 'Voice ii', *Boundary 2*, 12(2), 1984: 76–93.

——— *Writing and Difference*, trans. Alan Bass (London: Routledge, 1991).

Donald, James, 'Metropolis: The City as Text', in *Social and Cultural Forms of Modernity*, ed. Robert Bocock and Kenneth Thompson (Cambridge: Cambridge University Press, 1992), pp. 417–61.

Dudgen, Piers, *Dickens' London: An Imaginative Vision* (London: Headline, 1994).

Duffy, Maureen, *Capital* (London: Harvill, 2001; first published by Jonathan Cape, 1975).

——— *England: The Making of the Myth from Stonehenge to Albert Square* (London: Fourth Estate, 2001).

——— *Londoners: An Elegy* (London: Methuen, 1983).

——— *That's How It Was* (London: Virago, 1983; first published by Hutchinson, 1962).

Dun, Aidan, *Vale Royal* (London: Goldmark, 1995).

Eco, Umberto, 'Interpretation and History', in *Interpretation and Overinterpretation*, ed. Stefan Collini (New York and Cambridge: Cambridge University Press, 1992).

Eliot, T. S., *T. S. Eliot: The Complete Poems and Plays* (London: Faber and Faber, 1969).

Ellin, Nan, *Postmodern Urbanism* (New York: Princeton Architectural Press, 1996).

Ellmann, Maud, *The Poetics of Impersonality* (Brighton: Harvester, 1987).

Feldman, David and Gareth Stedman Jones (eds), *Metropolis London: Histories and Representations since 1800* (London: Routledge, 1989).

Finney, Brian, 'Narrative and Narrated Homicides in Martin Amis's *Other People* and *London Fields*', *Critique: Studies in Contemporary Fiction* 37(1), Fall 1995: 3–15.

——— 'Peter Ackroyd, Postmodernist Play and *Chatterton*', *Twentieth Century Literature* 38(2), 1992: 240–61.

Forty, Adrian, 'Masculine, Feminine or Neuter' in *Desiring Practices: Architecture, Gender and the Interdisciplinary*, ed. Katerina Rüedi, Sarah Wigglesworth and Duncan McCorquodale (London: Black Dog, 1996), pp. 140–55.

Foucault, Michel, *Discipline and Punish*, trans. Alan Sheridan (London: Penguin, 1979; first published as *Surveiller et punir*, Paris: Gallimard, 1975).

—— *The Order of Things: An Archaeology of the Human Sciences* (London: Routledge, 2002; orig. English edn., Tavistock, 1970; originally published as *Les Mots et les Choses* by Editions Gallimard, 1966).

—— 'Of Other Spaces', *Diacritics*, Spring 1986: 22–7 (originally published as 'Des Espaces Autres' in *Architecture-Mouvement-Continuité*, October 1984).

Fox, Kate, *Watching the English: The Hidden Rules of English Behaviour* (London: Hodder & Stoughton, 2004).

Frosch, Thomas R., *The Awakening of Albion* (Ithaca and London: Cornell University Press, 1974).

Freud, Sigmund, *Civilization and its Discontents*, trans. James Strachey (New York: Norton, 1962; first published as *Das Unbehagen in der Kultur* in 1907).

Gardiner, Jeff, *The Age of Chaos: The Multiverse of Michael Moorcock* (Stockport: The British Fantasy Society, 2002).

Gasiorek, A. (2005). *J. G. Ballard* (Manchester: Manchester University Press).

Gibson, Jeremy and Julian Wolfreys, *Peter Ackroyd: The Ludic and Labyrinthine Text* (Basingstoke: Macmillan, 2000).

Glinert, Ed, *The London Compendium* (London: Penguin, 2003; first published by Allen Lane, 2003).

Gottdiener, M. and Alexandros P. Lagopoulos (eds), *The City and the Sign: An Introduction to Urban Semiotics* (New York: Columbia University Press, 1986).

Goux, Jean-Joseph, *The Coiners of Language*, trans. Jennifer Curtiss Gage (Norman and London: University of Oklahoma Press, 1994; originally published as *Monnayeurs du langage* by Editions Galilée, 1984).

Greenland, Colin, *Michael Moorcock: Death is no Obstacle* (Manchester: Savoy, 1992).

Groes, Sebastian, 'Ian McEwan and the Modernist Consciousness of the City in *Saturday*', in *Ian McEwan: Contemporary Critical Perspectives*, ed. Sebastian Groes (London and New York: Continuum, 2009), pp. 99–114.

—— 'A Kind of Translation: Reading Monica Ali's *Brick Lane* as Enactment of New Labour's Model of Britishness', *American, British and Canadian Studies* 8, June 2007: 120–38.

—— 'From Shanghai to Shepperton: Crises of Representation in J. G. Ballard's Londons', in *J. G. Ballard: Contemporary Critical Perspectives*, ed. Jeannette Baxter (London and New York: Continuum, 2009), pp. 78–93.

—— '"A Thousand Eyes Round About and Within": London as a Carceral City in the Work of Iain Sinclair', in *City Visions: The Work of Iain Sinclair*, ed. Robert Bond and Jenny Bavidge (Newcastle: Cambridge Scholars Press, 2007), pp. 174–86.

—— and Martin Amis, 'A Hatred of Reason: Martin Amis in Conversation with Sebastian Groes', in *The London Magazine*, ed. Sebastian Barker, June/July 2004, pp. 44–51.

—— and Iain Sinclair, 'An Interview with Iain Sinclair', *Pretext*, Autumn 2005 (Norwich: Pen & Inc): 65–80.

Hall, Peter, *Cities in Civilization: Culture, Innovation, and Urban Order* (London: Weidenfeld & Nicolson, 1998).

—— *Cities of Tomorrow* (Oxford: Blackwell, 1998).

—— *London Voices, London Lives* (Bristol: Policy Press, 2007).

Hardt, Michael and Antonio Negri, *Empire* (Cambridge, MA and London: Harvard University Press, 2000).

—— *Multitude* (London: Hamish Hamilton, 2005; first published in the USA by Penguin Group (USA), 2004).

Harvey, David, 'Between Space and Time: Reflections on the Geographical Imagination', *Annals of the Association of Geographers* 80, 1990: 418–34.

—— *The Condition of Postmodernity* (Oxford: Blackwell, 1989).

—— *Spaces of Capital: Towards a Critical Geography* (Edinburgh: Edinburgh University Press, 2001).

—— *Spaces of Hope* (Edinburgh: Edinburgh University Press, 2000).

Hayles, N. Katherine, *Chaos Bound: Orderly Disorder in Contemporary Literature and Science* (Ithaca and London: Cornell University Press, 1990).

Head, Dominic, *The Cambridge Introduction to Modern British Fiction, 1950–2000* (Cambridge: Cambridge University Press, 2002).

—— *Ian McEwan: Contemporary British Novelists* (Manchester: Manchester University Press, 2007).

—— *The State of the Novel* (Chichester: John Wiley, 2008).

Hebbert, Michael, *London: More by Fortune than Design* (Chichester: John Wiley, 1998).

Held, David, *Models of Democracy* (Cambridge: Polity Press, 1996).

Hetherington, Keith, *The Badlands of Modernity: Heterotopia and Social Ordering* (London and New York: Routledge, 1997).

Hiddleston, Jane, 'Shapes and Shadows: (Un)veiling the Immigrant in Monica Ali's *Brick Lane*', *Journal of Commonwealth Literature* 40(1), 2005: 57–72.

Hutcheon, Linda, *Irony's Edge: The Theory and Politics of Irony* (London: Routledge, 1995; first published 1994).

—— *A Poetics of Postmodernism: History, Theory, Fiction* (London and New York: Routledge, 1999; first published 1988).

Inwood, Steve, *A History of London* (London: Macmillan, 1998).

Irigaray, Luce, *This Sex Which Is Not One*, trans. Catherine Parker (Ithaca: Cornell University Press, 1985).

Jackson, Peter, *Maps of Meaning: An Introduction to Cultural Geography* (London: Routledge, 1989).

James, David, *Contemporary British Fiction and the Artistry of Space* (London and New York: Continuum, 2008).

—— 'The New Purism', *Textual Practice* 21(4), 2007: 687–714.

Jameson, Fredric, *Postmodernism, or the Cultural Logic of Late Capitalism* (London: Verso, 1991).

—— 'Progress Versus Utopia; or, Can We Imagine the Future?' *Science Fiction Studies* 9, 1982: 147–58.

Jeffries, Richard, *After London: Wild England* (Oxford: Oxford University Press, 1980; first published by Cassell and Company, 1885).

Jenkins, Simon, *Landlords to London: The Story of a Capital and its Growth* (London: Constable, 1975).

—— *Thatcher and Sons* (London: Penguin, 2007; first published by Allan Lane, 2006).

Joyce, James, *A Portrait of the Artist as a Young Man* (London: Penguin, 1992; first published in *The Egoist*, 1914–15).

—— *Ulysses* (London: Penguin, 1992; first published in France by Shakespeare & Co, 1922).

Kermode, Frank, *The Sense of an Ending* (London, Oxford and New York: Oxford University Press, 1965).

Kerr, Joe and Andrew Gibson (eds), *London: From Punk to Blair* (London: Reaktion Books, 2003).

King, Bruce, *The Oxford English Literary History: The Internationalization of English Literature*, Vol. 13 (Oxford: Oxford University Press, 2005; first published 2004).

Knaack, Andreas, *Constructions of London in Martin Amis's* London Fields. Available at: www.knaack.textfabrik.net/ [accessed 5 July 2007].

Knauer, Kris, 'The Root Canals of Zadie Smith: London's Intergenerational Adaptation', in *Zadie Smith: Critical Essays*, ed. Tracey L. Walters (New York: Peter Lang, 2008), pp. 171–86.

Kunstler, James Howard, *The City in Mind* (New York: Free Press, 2001).

Kristeva, Julia, 'La Femme, ce n'est jamais ça', *Tel Quel* 59, Autumn, p. 20.

—— *The Powers of Horror: Essays on Abjection*, trans. Leos S. Roudiez (New York: Columbia University Press, 1982).

Kroker, Arthur and David Cook, *The Postmodern Scene: Excremental Culture and Hyper-Aesthetics* (London: Macmillan, 1988).

Kureishi, Hanif, *The Black Album* (London: Faber and Faber, 1995).

—— *The Buddha of Suburbia* (London: Faber and Faber, 1990).

Lane, Richard, Rod Mengham and Philip Tew (eds), *Contemporary British Fiction* (Cambridge: Polity Press, 2003).

LaRose, Nicole, 'Reading *The Information* on Martin Amis's London', *Critique: Studies in Contemporary Fiction* 46(2), Winter 2005: 160–76.

Lee, Alison, *Realism and Power: Postmodern British Fiction* (London and New York: Routledge, 1990).

Lefebvre, Henri, *The Production of Space*, trans. Donald Nicholson-Smith (Oxford: Blackwell, 1991; first published as *Production de l'espace* in 1974).

—— *Writings on Cities*, trans. and ed. Elenore Kofman and Elizabeth Lebas (Oxford: Blackwell, 1996).

Lehan, Richard, *The City in Literature: An Intellectual and Cultural History* (Berkeley: University of California Press, 1998).

Lévi-Strauss, Claude, *Myth and Meaning* (London and New York: Routledge, 2001; first published in the UK by Kegan Paul, 1978).

—— *The Savage Mind* (London: Weidenfeld & Nicolson, 1966; originally published as *La Pensée Sauvage* in 1962).

Levin, Thomas Y., Ursula Frohne and Peter Weibel (eds), *CNTR[SPACE]: Rhetorics of Surveillance from Bentham to Big Brother* (Cambridge, MA: MIT Press, 2002).

Lewis, Barry, *My Words Echo Thus: Possessing the Past in Peter Ackroyd* (Columbia, SC: University of South Carolina Press, 2007).

Luckhurst, Roger, *'The Angle Between Two Walls': The Fiction of J. G. Ballard* (Liverpool: Liverpool University Press, 1997).

—— 'The Contemporary London Gothic and the Limits of the "Spectral Turn"', *Textual Practice* 16(3), 2002: 527–46.

—— *Science Fiction* (Cambridge and Malden, MA: Polity Press: 2005).

Lynch, Kevin, *The Image of the City* (Cambridge, MA: MIT Press, 1960).

MacCabe, Colin, 'Multiculturalism after 7/7: A CQ Seminar', *Critical Quarterly* 48(2), 2006: 1–44.

Machen, Arthur, *The London Adventure* (London: Martin Secker, 1924).

Magrs, Paul, 'Maureen Duffy', in *The Cambridge Guide to Women's Writing in English*, ed. Lorna Sage (Cambridge: Cambridge University Press, 1999), pp. 205–6.

Manguel, Alberto, *City of Words* (London: Continuum, 2008).

Mars-Jones, Adam, *Venus Envy: On the Womb and the Bomb* (London: Chatto & Windus, 1990).

Marx, Karl and Friedrich Engels, *The Communist Manifesto*, trans. Samuel Moore (London: Penguin, 1985; first published in German in 1848).

Massie, Alan, *The Novel Today* (Harlow: Longman, 1990).

McEwan, Ian, *The Child in Time* (London: Picador, 1988; first published by Jonathan Cape, 1987).

—— *The Daydreamer* (London: Vintage, 1995; first published by Jonathan Cape, 1994).

—— *First Love, Last Rites* (London: Vintage, 2006; first published by Jonathan Cape, 1975).

—— *In Between the Sheets* (London: Vintage, 2006; first published by Jonathan Cape, 1978).

—— *The Ploughman's Lunch* (London: Methuen, 1985).

—— *Saturday* (London: Jonathan Cape, 2005).

—— *Solar* (London: Jonathan Cape, 2009).

McHale, Brian, *Postmodernist Fiction* (London and New York: Routledge, 1999).

McLeod, John, *Postcolonial London* (Abingdon: Routledge, 2005; first published 2004).

Mengham, Rod, *Charles Dickens* (Horndon: Northcote House, 2001).

—— *The Descent of Language* (London: Bloomsbury, 1993).

—— (ed.), *An Introduction to Contemporary Fiction* (Cambridge: Polity Press, 1999).

Menke, Richard, 'Narrative Reversals and the Thermodynamics of History in Martin Amis's *Time's Arrow*', *MFS: Modern Fiction Studies* 44, 1998: 959–77.

Merleau-Ponty, Maurice, *Phenomenology of Perception*, trans. Colin Smith (London: Routledge & Kegan Paul, 1962).

Milton, John, *The History of Britain* (1670). Collected in *The Prose Works of John Milton. With a Biographical Introduction by Rufus Wolmot Griswold. In Two Volumes* (Philadelphia: John W. Moore, 1847).

Minton, Anna, *Balanced Communities: The UK and the US Compared* (London: RICS, 2002).

—— *Ground Control: Fear and Happiness in the Twenty-First-Century City* (London: Penguin, 2009).

Moorcock, Michael, *King of the City* (London: Scribner, 2001 [2000]).

—— *London Bone* (London: Scribner, 2001).

—— *Mother London* (London: Scribner, 2000; first published by Secker & Warburg, 1988).

Moore-Gilbert, Bart, *Hanif Kureishi* (Manchester and New York: Manchester University Press, 2001).

Moretti, Franco, '*Dracula* and Capitalism', in *Signs Taken for Wonders: On the Sociology of Literary Forms* (London: Verso, 1988), pp. 83–98.

Morris, William, *News from Nowhere, or an epoch of rest: being some chapters from a Utopian Romance*, ed. Krishan Kumar (Cambridge: Cambridge University Press, 1995).

Mumford, Lewis, *The City in History: Its Origins, Its Transformations, and Its Prospects* (Harmondsworth: Penguin, 1973; first published by Secker & Warburg, 1961).

Murakami, Haruki, *Underground: The Tokyo Gas Attack and the Japanese Psyche*, trans. Alfred Birnbaum and Philip Gabriel (London: Harvill, 2000; first published as *Andaguraundo* (1997) and *Yakusoku sareta basho de* (1998)).

Murray, Alex, *Recalling London: Literature and History in the Work of Peter Ackroyd and Iain Sinclair* (London and New York: Continuum, 2007).

Nasta, Susheila (ed.), *Writing Across Worlds: Contemporary Writers Talk* (Abingdon: Routledge, 2004).

Newman, Oscar, *Defensible Space: Crime Prevention through Urban Design* (London: Macmillan, 1972).

Niven, Alastair, 'Salman Rushdie with Alastair Niven', in *Writing Across Worlds: Contemporary Writers Talk*, ed. Susheila Nasta (Abingdon: Routledge, 2004), pp. 125–35.

O'Hagan, Andrew, 'A City of Prose', *London Review of Books* 27(15), August 2005, p. 39.

Onega, Susana, 'Interview with Peter Ackroyd', *Twentieth Century Literature* 42(2), 1996: 208–21.

Onega, Susana and John A Stotesbury (eds), *London in Literature: Visionary Mappings of the Metropolis* (Heidelberg: Carl Winter, 2002).

Parsons, Deborah L., *Streetwalking the Metropolis: Women, the City and Modernity* (Oxford: Oxford University Press, 2000).

Peck, John, 'The Novels of Peter Ackroyd', *English Studies* 75(5), 1994: 442–52.

Perril, Simon, 'A Cartography of Absence: The Work of Iain Sinclair', *Comparative Criticism* 19, 1997: 309–39.

Phillips, Lawrence, *London Narratives: Postwar Fiction and the City* (London and New York: Continuum, 2006).

—— (ed.), *The Swarming Streets: Twentieth-Century Literary Representations of London* (Amsterdam-New York: Rodopi, 2004).

Phillips, Mike, *London Crossings* (New York and London: Continuum, 2001).

Pike, David L., *Subterranean Cities: The World beneath Paris and London, 1800–1945* (Ithaca, NY: Cornell University Press, 2005).

Porter, Roy, *London: A Social History* (London: Penguin, 2000; first published by Hamish Hamilton, 1994).

Potter, Rachel, 'Culture Vulture: The Testimony of Iain Sinclair's *Downriver*', *Parataxis: Modernism and Modern Writing* 5, Winter 1993–4: 40–8.

Powell, Anthony, *The Strangers are All Gone* (London: William Heinemann, 1982).

Powell, Enoch, 'Rivers of Blood'-speech', in *The Telegraph*, 6 November 2007. Available at: http://www.telegraph.co.uk/comment/3643826/Enoch-Powells-Rivers-of-Blood-speech.html [accessed 3 June 2008].

Preston, Peter and Paul Simpson-Houseley (eds), *Writing the City: Eden, Babylon and the New Jerusalem* (London and New York: Routledge, 1994).

Pringle, David, *Earth is an Alien Planet* (San Bernardino: Borgo, 1979).

Raban, Jonathan, *Soft City* (London: Hamish Hamilton, 1974).

Rennison, Nick, *Waterstone's Guide to London Writing* (London: Waterstone's, 1998).

Reynolds, Mary T., 'The City in Vico, Dante, and Joyce', in *Vico and Joyce*, ed. Donald Phillip Verene (Albany: State University of New York Press, 1987), pp. 111–22.

Rhys, Jean, 'Let them Call it Jazz', in *Tigers are Better-Looking* (London: André Deutsch, 1968; first published in *The London Magazine*, 1960).

Ricoeur, Paul, *Time and Narrative*, volume 2 (Chicago: University of Chicago Press, 1990; first published as *Temps et Récit* by Editions du Seuil, 1984).

Riley, Denise, *The Words of Selves: Identification, Solidarity, Irony* (Stanford: Stanford University Press, 2000).

Rushdie, Salman, *Imaginary Homelands* (London: Granta/Penguin, 1991).

—— *Mirrorwork: 50 Years of Indian Writing, 1947–1997* (London: Vintage, 1997).

—— *The Satanic Verses* (London: Vintage, 1998; first published by Viking, 1988).

Sadler, Simon, *The Situationist City* (Cambridge, MA: MIT Press, 1998).

Sage, Victor, 'Black Venice: Conspiracy and Narrative Masquerade in Schiller, Zschlokke, Lewis and Hoffman', *Gothic Studies* 8(1), 2006: 52–72.

—— 'Dickens and Professor Owen: Portrait of a Friendship', in *Le Portrait* (Paris: University of Paris-Sorbonne, 1999), pp. 87–101.

—— 'The Poetics of Mimesis: Aristotle, Tragedy and Realism', in *Theatre Theories: From Plato to Virtual Reality*, ed. Anthony Frost (Norwich, UK: Pen and Inc, 2000), pp. 25–42.

Samuel, Raphael, *Island Stories: Theatres of Memory II* (London and New York: Verso, 1998).

—— *Theatres of Memory: Vol. 1 – Past and Present in Contemporary Culture* (London: Verso, 1994).

Sandhu, Sukhev, *London Calling: How Black and Asian Writers Imagined a City* (London: HarperCollins, 2003).

Selvon, Sam, *The Lonely Londoners* (New York: Longman, 2001; first published by Alan Wingate, 1956).

Sennett, Richard, *Flesh and Stone: The Body and City in Western Civilization* (London and Boston: Faber and Faber, 1994).

Sheppard, Robert, *Where Treads of Death: Five Books of Iain Sinclair Reviewed* (Liverpool: Ship of Fools, 2004).

Short, John Rennie, *The Urban Order* (Oxford: Blackwell, 1996).

Short, John Rennie and Yeong-Hyun Kim, *Globalization and the City* (New York: Longman, 1999).

Simmel, Georg, 'The Metropolis and Mental Life', in *The Sociology of Georg Simmel*, ed. and trans. Kurt H. Wolfe (New York: Free Press), pp. 409–24.

Sinclair, Iain, *Crash: David Cronenberg's Post-Mortem on J.G. Ballard's 'Trajectory of Fate'* (London: British Film Institute, 1999).

—— 'Crowning Glory: Michael Moorcock's London', *Guardian*, 23 November 2000. Available at: http://www.guardian.co.uk/books/2000/nov/23/london reviewofbooks [accessed 5 July 2008].

—— 'Customising Biography', *London Review of Books* 18(4), 1996: 16–18.

—— *Downriver* (London: Paladin, 1991).

—— *Edge of the Orison* (London: Hamish Hamilton, 2006).

—— *Lights Out for the Territory* (London: Granta, 1997).

—— *London Orbital: A Walk around the M25* (London: Penguin, 2003; first published by Granta, 2002).

—— 'A London View', in *Granta 65: London: The Lives of the City*, ed. Ian Jack (London: Granta, 1999).

—— *Lud Heat and Suicide Bridge* (London: Vintage, 1995; *Lud Heat* originally published by Albion Village Press in 1975, and *Suicide Bridge* by Albion Village Press in 1979).

—— *Radon Daughters* (London: Jonathan Cape, 1994).

—— *White Chappell, Scarlet Tracings* (London: Goldmark 1987).

—— and Marc Atkins, *Liquid City* (London: Reaktion, 1999).

—— and Rachel Lichtenstein, *Rodinsky's Room* (London: Granta, 1999).

—— and Dave McKean, *Slow Chocolate Autopsy* (London: Phoenix House, 1997).

Sinfield, Alan, *Literature, Politics and Culture in Postwar Britain* (London: Athlone, 1997).

Slay, Jack, *Ian McEwan* (Boston, MA: Twayne, 1996).

Smith, Zadie, *The Autograph Man* (London: Hamish Hamilton, 2002).

—— *On Beauty* (London: Hamish Hamilton, 2005).

—— *White Teeth* (London: Hamish Hamilton, 2000).

Soja, Edward, 'Heterotopologies: A Remembrance of Other Spaces in the Citadel-LA', in *Postmodern Cities and Spaces*, ed. Sophie Watson and Katherine Gibson (Oxford: Blackwell, 1995), pp. 6–39.

—— *Postmetropolis: Critical Studies of Cities and Regions* (Oxford: Blackwell, 2000).

Spark, Muriel, 'The Portobello Road', in *The Portobello Road and Other Stories* (Helsinki: Eurographica, 1989).

Stern, J. P., *On Realism* (London and Boston: Routledge & Kegan Paul, 1973).

Stevenson, Randall, *The Oxford English Literary History: The Last of England?* Vol. 12 (Oxford: Oxford University Press, 2005; first published 2004).

Stoker, Bram, *Dracula* (London: Penguin, 2003; first published by Archibald Constable, 1897).

Swift, Jonathan, *The Complete Poems*, ed. Pat Rogers (London: Penguin, 1983).

Taylor, D. J., *A Vain Conceit: British Fiction in the 1980s* (London: Bloomsbury, 1989).

Tanner, Tony, *City of Words: American Fiction, 1950–1970* (London: Jonathan Cape, 1971).

—— *Venice Desired* (Cambridge, MA: Harvard University Press, 1992).

Taunton, Matthew, *Fictions of the City: Class, Culture and Mass Housing in London and Paris* (Basingstoke: Palgrave Macmillan, 2009).

Teske, Doris, *Die Vertextung der Megalopolis: London im Spiel postmoderner Tetxte* (Trier: Wissenschaftlicher Verlag Trier, 1999 [In German]).

Tester, Keith (ed.), *The Flâneur* (London: Routledge, 1994).

Tew, Philip, *The Contemporary British Novel* (London: Continuum, 2004).

—— *Zadie Smith* (London: Palgrave Macmillan, 2009).

Tew, Philip and Rod Mengham (eds.), *British Fiction Today* (London and New York: Continuum, 2006).

Thatcher, Margaret, 'Speech inaugurating Canary Wharf'. Available at: http://www.margaretthatacher.org/document/107834 [accessed 5 July 2007]. Originally delivered on 29 November 1989.

Thomas, Susie, *Hanif Kureishi* (Basingstoke: Palgrave Macmillan, 2005).

Thompson, E. P., *The Making of the English Working Class* (London: Gollancz, 1963).

—— *Witness against the Beast: William Blake and the Moral Law* (Cambridge: Cambridge University Press, 1993).

Todd, Richard, *Consuming Fictions* (London: Bloomsbury, 1996).
———— 'Looking-glass Worlds in Martin Amis's Early Fiction: Reflectivenes, Mirror Narcissism, and Doubles', in *Martin Amis: Postmodernism and Beyond*, ed. Gavin Keulks (Basingstoke: Palgrave Macmillan), pp. 22–35.
Tschumi, Bernard, *Architecture and Disjunction* (Cambridge, MA: MIT Press, 1994).
Tymms, Ralph, *Doubles in Literary Psychology* (Cambridge: Bowes & Bowes, 1949).
Vidler, Anthony, *The Architectural Uncanny: Essays in the Modern Unhomely* (Cambridge, MA and London: MIT Press, 1992).
Vinen, Richard, *Thatcher's Britain* (London: Simon & Schuster, 2009).
Walters, Tracey L. (ed.), *Zadie Smith: Critical Essays* (New York: Peter Lang, 2008).
Watson, Sophie and Katherine Gibson (eds.), *Postmodern Cities and Spaces* (Oxford: Blackwell, 1995).
Waugh, Patricia, *Harvest of the Sixties* (Oxford and New York: Oxford University Press, 1995).
Webb, James, *The Occult Establishment: Vol. II. The Age of the Irrational* (Glasgow: Richard Drew Publishing, 1981).
Weber, Max, *The City*, trans. and ed. Don Martindale and Gertrud Neuwirth (New York: Free Press, 1958; first published in German in 1921).
Westwood, Sallie and John Williams (eds), *Imagining Cities: Scripts, Signs, Memories* (London: Routledge, 1997).
White, Jerry, *London in the Twentieth Century: A City and its People* (London: Viking, 2001).
Wick Sizemore, Christina, *A Female Vision of the City: London in the Novels of Five British Women* (Knoxville: University of Tennessee Press, 1989).
Williams, Raymond, *The Country and the City* (London: Chatto & Windus, 1973).
———— *The Long Revolution* (London: Chatto & Windus, 1961).
———— *Writing in Society* (London: Verso, 1991; first published 1983).
Wolfreys, Julian, *Writing London: The Trace of the Urban Text from Blake to Dickens* (Basingstoke: Macmillan, 1998).
———— *Writing London, Volume 2: Materiality, Memory, Spectrality* (Basingstoke: Palgrave Macmillan, 2004).
———— *Writing London, Volume 3: Inventions of the City* (Basingstoke: Palgrave Macmillan, 2007).
Wood, James, 'England' in *The Oxford Guide to Contemporary Writing*, ed. John Sturrock (Oxford: Oxford University Press, 1996), pp. 113–41.
———— 'Making it New', *The New Republic*, 8 and 15 September 2003, pp. 29–31.
Woolf, Virginia, *A Room of One's Own*, in *The Norton Anthology of English Literature: Volume 2*, ed. M. H. Abrams (New York and London: W. W. Norton, 1993), pp. 1926–86 (first published 1929).
Wright, Patrick, *A Journey through Ruins: The Last Days of London* (Oxford: Oxford University Press, 2009; first published by Radius, 1991).
———— *On Living in an Old Country: The National Past in Contemporary Britain* (London: Verso, 1985).

Index